MANDIE

and the SECRET TUNNEL
and *Other Stories*

MANDIE MYSTERIES

Mandie and...

———

Mandie: Her College Days
New Horizons

MANDIE

and the SECRET TUNNEL

and *Other Stories*

Lois Gladys Leppard

BethanyHouse
Minneapolis, Minnesota

Published by Bethany House Publishers
11400 Hampshire Avenue South
Bloomington, Minnesota 55438

Bethany House Publishers is a division of
Baker Publishing Group, Grand Rapids, Michigan.

Printed in the United States of America by
Bethany Press International, Bloomington, MN.

ISBN   9-780-7403-2230-3

The Library of Congress has cataloged a previous edition as follows:

Leppard, Lois Gladys.
  The Mandie collection / Lois Gladys Leppard.
      v. [1–   ]   cm.
  Summary: A collection of tales featuring Mandie, an orphan, and her friends as they solve mysteries together in turn-of-the-century North Carolina.
    ISBN-13: 978-0-7642-0446-3 (pbk.)
    1. Children's stories, American. [1. Family life—North Carolina—Fiction. 2. Orphans—Fiction. 3. Christian life—Fiction. 4. North Carolina—History—20th century—Fiction. 5. Mystery and detective stories.] I. Title.
    PZ7.L556May   2007
    [Fic]—dc22

                                                                    2007023752

ABOUT THE AUTHOR

LOIS GLADYS LEPPARD worked in Federal Intelligence for thirteen years in various countries around the world before she settled in South Carolina.

The stories of her own mother's childhood as an orphan in western North Carolina are the basis for many of the incidents incorporated in this series.

Visit her Web site: *www.Mandie.com.*

MANDIE'S TRAVELS

MANDIE
AND THE
SECRET TUNNEL

For My Mother,
Bessie A. Wilson Leppard,
and
In Memory of Her Sister,
Lillie Margaret Ann Wilson Frady, Orphans of North Carolina
Who Outgrew the Sufferings of Childhood

CONTENTS

"The Lord is my shepherd,
I shall not want—"
(Psalm 23:1)

CHAPTER ONE

MANDIE

"Don't get so close, Amanda. You might fall in." Her mother grasped the back of her long, dark skirt.

Mandie tried to pull free. Her tear-filled blue eyes sought a glimpse of her father through the homemade wooden coffin resting by the open grave.

"I want to go with you, Daddy!" she was mumbling to herself. "Take me with you, Daddy!" she tugged at her long, blonde braid in her grief.

Even in her sadness she was afraid of being scolded by her stern mother. She dared not cry out in anguish. Her voice trembled as she whispered, "How can I live without you, Daddy? You were the only one who ever loved me. I can't bear it alone!"

Preacher DeHart's deep voice echoed throughout the hills. "We all know Jim Shaw was a good man. He drew his last breath talking to God. We trust his soul is at peace."

His voice grew louder and more emphatic. "But, friends and loved ones, I am here to remind you of one thing! When the time comes for you to face your Maker, you will be damned to hellfire and brimstone if you have lived a sinful life!"

Mandie trembled as she heard the words.

"You will incur the wrath of God and your soul will burn in hell forevermore," he continued. "Above all, let us remember the Ten Commandments and keep them holy, live by them and walk the straight and narrow path in preparation for the hereafter. Otherwise, I admonish you, your soul will burn in hell! Your soul will be used to feed the fires of the devil! When you have sinned and come short of the glory of God, He will forsake you. He will punish you!"

The child was overcome by fear and grief as the final words were said for her father and the coffin was lowered into the ground. The clods of mountain woods dirt hit the casket with a thud. She gasped for breath and, falling on her knees beside the grave, she appealed to God, "What have I done to cause you to take my daddy away, dear God? You know I can't live without my daddy, God. I love him so much, dear God!"

The crowd standing nearby silently wiped away tears. The earth was smoothed into a mound and a rough marker was pounded into the soil with an axe. It read, "James Alexander Shaw; Born April 3, 1863; Died April 13, 1900." Such a small remembrance for such a big-hearted man. Jim Shaw had no enemies. Everyone had been his friend.

It was April, but it was still cold in the Nantahala Mountains of North Carolina. Mandie, trembling with cold and emotion, couldn't stop shaking enough to rise from her knees, so her mother grabbed her arm and pulled her up and away from her father's grave. Her legs would hardly carry her.

Through her blinding tears she caught a glimpse of Uncle Ned standing at the edge of the woods. Uncle Ned, the old Cherokee Indian, came often to the Shaws' neighborhood selling hand-woven baskets. He and Mandie's father had been good friends. He had loved her father, too. She suddenly jerked free from her mother, running to the tall Indian for comfort. Uncle Ned stooped to catch her in his arms, his necklace of shells softly brushing against her face.

"Uncle Ned, God doesn't love me anymore! He took my daddy away from me!" she cried.

"My papoose! Father—good man. Not gone far—only to happy hunting ground." His pronunciation was good, but his grammar was poor. He stroked her blonde hair as she buried her wet face against his deerskin jacket.

"Amanda, come now. We're goin' home. Right now!" The plump woman shouted to the girl. "Come, git in the wagon!"

"Uncle Ned, please come to see me. I love you." Mandie quickly kissed his redskinned cheek and turned to obey her mother.

The old Indian held her hand. "I make promise—your father. I look out for you. I keep promise." He smiled and released her hand.

Her heartbeat quickened as she heard his words. There would be someone to watch over her. But Uncle Ned could never overrule her mother; she had always bossed her father around. But then, Uncle Ned had his whole tribe behind him! He would indeed keep his word to her father.

Etta Shaw snatched the girl's hand and slapped her face. "Hesh up! Git in the wagon! This minute!" She gave the girl a shove and called instructions to her sister.

Mandie's sister, Irene, all but lifted her up as she forced the girl to climb into the waiting wagon, the same one that had brought her father's casket to the cemetery. All the other mourners had already turned down the long hill ahead of them.

"Now set down and shet up!" Irene was two years older, and eleven-year-old Mandie was afraid of her rough ways. She knew she couldn't resist. She gave one last pitiful look at Uncle Ned, who stood witnessing the scene with his keen black eyes, and fixed her gaze ahead.

She would go home now, but she would come back as soon as she got the chance. Her eyes stayed on the mound of earth until they were down the side of the mountain and the row of trees blocked her view.

Sitting in the back of the wagon with her sister, Mandie suddenly realized that her mother had not shed a tear. Neither had her sister. She turned to look at her mother. Etta Shaw was busily talking and laughing with Zach as they bumped on down the rough road. She didn't love my daddy, she was thinking. She acts like she's glad he's gone. How could she laugh as though she had already forgotten he ever existed?

Her thoughts turned back to the happy times with her father. He was always laughing, always ready to take her side in any disagreement with her mother and Irene. She could see his smiling face, his red curly hair, his blue eyes twinkling with some little secret between them. He had always been there to comfort his dear Mandie through the trials and tribulations of her eleven years, and then suddenly he was gone. God had taken him away.

Mandie was beginning to realize the way things really were. She could never remember being loved by her mother. Young as she was, she knew Irene was her mother's favorite. As far back as she could recall, Irene had always been given the new dresses which were later shortened to fit her, even though the dresses were made with rows of tucks around the skirts that could have been let out as Irene grew. She had never had a brand new dress in her life. The old, dark blue frock she was wearing had been made for Irene and, although it was almost threadbare, it had been hemmed yesterday for her to wear to her father's funeral. Mandie tugged at the faded fabric wishing she could be rid of the dress.

"Why don't they hurry up and get home?" she cried to herself. Her mother and Zach were leisurely riding along, talking too low for Mandie to understand what they were saying, with an occasional loud laugh from her mother. Irene kept herself busy snatching at the bushes as the wagon brushed past them on the narrow dirt road.

At last they got down to Charley Gap and their log cabin came into sight. It was huddled in the trees at the bottom of the slope. The hill to the north behind it gave protection against the cold mountain winds in the winter. The clearing around the house was already full of wagons and buggies and horses. People were standing around talking under the chestnut trees. Zach drove their wagon straight to the barn.

Mandie knew she would never be able to escape her mother that day. She would have to help wait on all these people who had come to eat and drink as soon as her father had been laid out in the front room on Friday. Today being Sunday, the whole congregation had come after the church services, which had included the last rites for her father. She knew none of them had been home yet to eat and that meant work for her. She had never been near a death before and she couldn't understand why they all acted like it was a party. Why don't they all go home and leave me alone? she wondered. I want to be by myself and think.

The chickens clucked and scattered as her mother jumped down from the wagon. "Let's git to the kitchen and see about the vittles."

She waited to see that Mandie was coming along behind her. Mandie scooped up her fluffy white kitten, who had come to greet her, and ran toward the house.

"See you in a little while, Zach. Gotta git this crowd fed. Better come on up and git something to eat yourself," Etta called back.

"Be along in a minute, Etta." Zach spit tobacco juice as he replied and began unharnessing Molly.

Irene jumped down from the wagon as a tall, gangly boy came up. She put on her best smile and smoothed her skirts as she tossed her dark hair.

"Hello, Nimrod," she giggled. "Wanta take a walk up to the springhouse 'fore Ma puts me to work?"

"Shore, Irene," the boy answered eagerly. "Druther slip off any day than work. Let's go git a long, cool drink of that sprang water."

The two hurried off behind the cabin before Etta missed Irene.

As Mandie walked through the crowd in the front room, she saw old Mrs. Shope take a dip of snuff, stick her sweetgum toothbrush in her toothless mouth, and then remark, "Poor child. He was all she had. Things is goin' to be rough now for all of 'em."

Mrs. DeWeese shook her gray head. "No, not so long as that thar Zach Hughes is around." She smiled a knowing grin.

Mandie fled through the door into the kitchen, not wanting to hear anymore, and, above all, not wanting to speak to any of these people. They were mostly her mother's kinfolk and friends. This was her mother's part of the country. Her father had always told her his people lived a long way off, but he had never said where.

The big, round oak table was loaded with food the people had brought, but it held no enticement to her nervous stomach. The warmth from the wood cookstove felt good to her. The heat thawed her somewhat and she wanted to talk.

"Mama," she began, unsure of herself, "where did my daddy come from?"

Etta Shaw stopped to look at her and she set down the plates from the cupboard. "What do you mean, where did he come from?"

"Well, you always said he was raised in a city somewhere—"

"That's right," Etta interrupted. "He was book read. That's all'n you need to know. Now git all the knives and forks out, and the glasses. We'll be needin' all of 'em. And run git that first piece of ham hanging on the right side in the smokehouse."

Mandie gave a sigh and obeyed. She longed for the day to end.

CHAPTER TWO

MANDIE LEAVES HOME

The full moon was coming up between the hills of Charley Gap as Mandie sat on the doorstep, wrapped in the quilt from her bed.

All the people had finally left and she, her mother, and Irene had gone to bed. She had listened, as she lay there on her cornshuck mattress, to be sure they were asleep, and then cuddling Snowball, her kitten, she had climbed down the ladder from the attic room where she slept with her sister. She couldn't go to sleep.

She was thinking of her past and wondering about her future without her father. She was remembering Preacher DeHart's words about God, "He will punish you!" What had she done wrong? Why was she being punished?

A soft whistle that sounded like a bird came from the nearby trees. She rose quickly as she saw Uncle Ned coming toward her, his soft moccasins soundless.

She ran to meet him, dragging the quilt and dropping Snowball. "Oh, Uncle Ned! I'm so glad you came!"

"I come find story why Jim Shaw go to happy hunting ground."

The old man put his arm around the child as they sat down on a nearby log.

"He had a bad cold, Uncle Ned, a real bad cold, and it just got worse."

"Cold?" The old Indian did not understand.

"Yes. Mama said it was new—ah—new moanie. He—he told me—he told me he was going to Heaven—that he would wait for me there." She broke into sobs.

"Don't make tears, Papoose. He wait. He always keeps promise." Uncle Ned wiped her eyes with the comer of the quilt. "When he go?"

"Today is Sunday. It was day before yesterday, Friday. Oh, why did he leave me? Why couldn't I go with him?"

"You little papoose now. Must be big squaw first. Big God, He say when you come. We do what He say. Remember? Jim Shaw, he tell us about Big God. Cherokee believe him. Jim Shaw one of our people."

She turned quickly to look at him. "My father, one of your people? But my father was a white man—red hair, blue eyes—and you are an Indian!"

"Yes. And his father look same. Your daddy never want tell you his Mama Indian squaw. Him one of our people. Him—"

Mandie interrupted excitedly, "My grandmother was an Indian? Are you really my Uncle Ned?"

"Jim Shaw—one brother. He never come see. Jim Shaw take me for brother."

"Is my grandmother still living?"

"No, she go to happy hunting ground when Jim Shaw little brave."

"What about my grandfather? Is he living?"

"I do not know. Jim Shaw never tell me when he come to see Cherokee."

"My daddy used to come to see you? Where do you live, Uncle Ned?"

"Over the hills. That way." He pointed toward one of the hills above the cabin. "Follow Nantahala River."

"Could I come to see you sometime?"

"No, bear get Papoose. Wolf, panther wait for Papoose to come."

"But they don't get you."

"I shoot with arrow." He patted the sling over his shoulder holding his huge witch hazel bow and his arrows with turkey feathers. "I kill."

"I've never been anywhere except to school and to church. The schoolhouse is just down the road apiece, and we go in the wagon to church at Maple Springs. And all the Sunday school teacher ever says is 'Honor thy mother and thy father,' and all that stuff. I never can remember the rest of it. Uncle Ned, do you think God really means for us to honor our mother?"

"Big Book say that?"

"Yes, that's what it says, the Bible."

"Then you do what it say. Jim Shaw say, we don't do what Big Book say, we don't get see Big God."

"But my mother—" she hesitated.

"I know. I see. I hear. She bad squaw."

The girl smiled at his description. "Even if she is bad, do I still have to honor her?"

"Book say that?"

"The Bible doesn't say whether your mother has to be good or bad. It just says honor thy mother."

"Then close ears, eyes. Honor mother." Uncle Ned stood up. "Papoose go sleep now. I come again soon. Go now."

Mandie scrambled to her feet and picked up Snowball, who was rubbing around her feet. She would go back to bed, but now she would have other things to think about. She was part Cherokee Indian! Why had her father never told her? If she could get enough courage, she would ask her mother about it.

Back in her bed, with Snowball curled up by her side, she finally fell asleep. Her mother woke her, yelling from downstairs. It was morning, but Mandie felt as though she had just closed her eyes.

"Git up, Amanda. Work to be done. Amanda, you hear me?"

"Yes, Mama." She sat up. Irene was still asleep. She reached over and shook her sister. "Irene, Mama is up."

"Leave me alone. I'm not ready to git up yet." Irene pulled the cover over her head.

Mandie quickly dressed in the early morning chill, remembering cold mornings when she was small and her father had held her in his lap by the fireplace downstairs while he put on her shoes and stockings.

Then she remembered her conversation with Uncle Ned. Maybe she could catch her mother in the right mood if she hurried and she could ask some questions about what Uncle Ned had told her. But when she reached the last rung of the ladder, her mother was waiting for her with the milk bucket.

"Go milk Susie while I start breakfast. Git a move on," Etta Shaw scolded.

Without a word, Mandie took the bucket, set Snowball down as she went outside and raced with the kitten to the barn. She didn't mind Susie at all. Susie was her friend. She always stood still and made mooing sounds while Mandie milked her, but when her mother tried it, Susie kicked up a fuss and would turn the bucket over if she got a chance. She would also use her tail to slap Etta Shaw in the face. Only Jim and Mandie were able to handle her and now that her father was gone, she could see the job falling entirely upon her.

"Good morning, Susie." She rubbed the cow's head. "You gonna give me a good bucketful of milk this morning? If you don't, Mama will scold me and I want to get her in a good mood so I can find out some things." She drew up the little three-legged stool. Susie looked back at her and began her mooing, and the bucket was soon full to the brim.

"Thank you, Susie. Now I'll let the bars down so you can get outside and get your breakfast. Please don't go too far away, because I know I'll have to come and get you tonight." The cow moved out into the pasture. She set the milk bucket down and followed. It was such a beautiful spring morning. Her eyes roamed over the fields, seeing her father as she remembered him and she fell to her knees on the soft, green grass.

"Dear God, please take good care of my daddy," she implored. "And, dear God, I still love you even if you don't love me anymore."

She hurried back to the house, certain that her mother would be pleased to see so much milk, but she only took the bucket and set it on the sideboard.

"Git a move on, Amanda. School today, as usual." Going to the ladder, she called, "Irene, git up. Breakfast is ready. School today."

Mandie sat down to her grits and biscuits with honey without another word. She kept staring at her father's empty place at the table. She could see it was no time to talk to her mother.

Irene joined her and then they prepared their lunch in baskets their father had bought from Uncle Ned. They put in sausage and biscuits, and buttermilk in tightly closed jars which would be warm by the time recess came at school. They took their sunbonnets down from the pegs by the door, tied them on, and together they began their mile-long walk down the road to the one-room schoolhouse. Even Irene was glad to get away from her mother to enjoy the company of her classmates.

There were only sixteen pupils in the school and one teacher, Mr. Tallant. They were divided into four groups of four, one group in each corner of the big schoolroom. Mr. Tallant would go from group to group giving assignments, listening to reading and recitation of arithmetic. He was not a strict schoolmaster and as long as a student made good grades he pretended not to notice the passing of notes during the time they were reading to themselves.

Mandie frequently received notes written in poetry from Joe Woodard, whose father was the only doctor in the vicinity. Joe had been her best friend from the day she had begun school, young, shy, and bewildered. Joe was two years older, an experienced hand in the schoolroom, and he immediately took Mandie under his protection. Irene was jealous and made life miserable for the boy.

Joe passed a folded note to Mandie with the explanation that he had had to return home with his mother after her father's funeral because his father, the doctor, had to make some urgent sick calls. Even though he lived a good two miles from the Shaws, he showed up there quite often. Etta Shaw tried her best to get him interested in Irene, but Joe had eyes only for Mandie. His note told her that he had permission to walk home with her, and his father would pick him up on his way home.

The two strolled along the road, ignoring Irene who tagged by the side. Joe carried Mandie's books and she tried to listen to his attempt to cheer her up, but her thoughts kept reverting to the fact that her father would not be home when she got there. Her father usually finished the many chores around the farm by the time school was over each day and almost always lately he would be splitting logs at the chopping block for the fence he planned to put around the property. She knew this would take quite a while because the farm had one hundred and twenty acres. The pile had steadily grown and he had begun hauling the rails around the boundary line a few days before he became ill.

"I'm sure glad to feel the weather getting warmer," Joe remarked, throwing back his thin shoulders and taking a deep breath. "When hot weather comes I always feel better, for some reason."

"I never thought about it," Mandie remarked. "Yeh, I suppose I like hot weather better, too, even though there are spiders and bugs and snakes crawling around."

"I ain't afraid of them things. I'm bigger than they are," Irene put in.

"You might be bigger, but you'd still better not fool around with snakes," Joe told her.

"That's why Daddy planted the gourds, to keep the snakes away from the house," Mandie added.

"Yeh, I know," Joe said. "Here comes Snowball. It's a miracle to me how that kitten knows when you're coming home."

"He's smart. He always knows." Mandie stopped to pick up the kitten. "He knows when it's time to go to bed, too. He waits for me at the ladder every night."

As they walked into the yard, Etta Shaw saw them coming and was waiting to give out the chores.

"Change your dress, Mandie. The yard needs sweeping after all that mob of wagons and people here yesterday," and turning to Irene, she said, "You can churn the milk, Irene."

Mandie hurried upstairs and changed into her old faded dress and came back down to find Joe waiting with the broom in his hand.

"I'll help," he told her. "You pick up the trash, papers, and things around and I'll do the sweeping. We'll get it done in no time."

"Thanks, Joe," Mandie said.

The rough handmade broom always made blisters on her hands and then when she had to wash dishes her hands would feel like they were on fire.

She ran about collecting papers, moving rocks out of the way that had been used to prop wagon wheels. Joe swept furiously and they were soon finished.

Etta Shaw came to the front door with the water bucket. She took the gourd dipper out of the pail and handed it to Mandie. "Fetch me some water. And then take this bucket of slop down to the hog walla." She indicated another bucket sitting in the doorway.

So, between Mandie and Joe they brought the water from the spring and then went to feed the pigs. By that time, Dr. Woodard was pulling up in his buggy.

"And how are you today, Mandie?" the doctor greeted the girl.

"Fine, Dr. Woodard." She smiled shyly at the old man.

"Come in, Dr. Woodard," Etta yelled from the doorway. "You younguns come in, too. We'll have a piece of that pound cake Mrs. Shope brought yesterday."

"I only want a glass of sweetmilk," Mandie told her. She didn't want anything that would remind her of yesterday.

"Well, Etta, what are you going to do now?" Dr. Woodard asked, as they all sat at the round table in the kitchen.

"Marry the first man that'll have me, Doc. That's the only thing I can do. I'm poor as Job's turkey, you know." She smiled as she tossed her head.

Mandie's heart thumped loudly. *Marry—another man—soon as my father is gone,* she was thinking.

"Well, I suppose so. You could never make it on your own here with two girls and no man around. I certainly wish I could have saved Jim, Etta. He was a fine man. He'll be hard to replace."

Mandie jumped up and ran out the back door. Joe came closely on her heels. She had tears in her eyes and didn't want Joe to see. He followed her as she raced up the mountain road to the cemetery where her father was buried and fell on her knees beside his grave, weeping uncontrollably.

"Mandie!" was all Joe said as he caught up with her, but she understood.

Finally she rose and wiped her tears on her apron. Joe held her small white hand.

"Just wait, Mandie. One day you and I will grow up and I will see that you are taken care of."

"That's a long time, Joe. Things may get worse."

"But I'll be around to help in the meantime," he assured her.

Joe came to the Shaw house more frequently after that and went with Mandie to put wild flowers on her father's grave. It was always a silent affair, neither speaking until they were back down the rough road.

Only one month after Jim Shaw had been laid to rest, Etta Shaw and Zach Hughes went into town together and came back to say they were married, and he moved into their house.

Mandie had seen him around a lot. He belonged to the same church and he was always offering to bring supplies from the store for them, or take them somewhere. He had never paid much attention to Mandie, but evidently he had been doing a lot of thinking and she was shocked when she was told what was planned for her.

They were sitting around the supper table on Friday night, two weeks after the wedding, when it happened.

"Well, Amanda," began Etta, clearing her throat. "We're afixin' to send you to live with the Brysons over yonder at Almond Station. They have a new baby and need some help."

"Mama!" was all she could say.

"Now, no argument! It ain't but two hoots and a holler away. We can't make a livin' here as 'tis and you'll just be one less mouth to feed. They'll give you a better home than we got here and plenty to eat," Etta told her.

"But, Mama—"

"Now, Amanda," Zach Hughes cut in. "We have already made the arrangements. They'll be here atter you tomarra morning so git your thangs together tonight."

Mandie, knowing she was beaten, fled from the table and went outside to sit in the dark under the chestnut trees. Snowball followed her and spread himself out across her feet.

She wished with ail her might that Uncle Ned would come to see her. He had promised to watch over her and he had shown up at least once a week since her father had died. But he had already been there on Wednesday night and she didn't have much hope.

"Please, God, help me!" she pleaded, her face turned toward the moonlit sky. "Even if you don't love me anymore, won't you please help me?"

"Papoose need help. Me help." She couldn't believe her eyes when Uncle Ned stepped out from behind the tree in front of her and came forward. "Me help Papoose."

"Uncle Ned, how did you know? I didn't expect you again this week."

The old man sat down on the uncovered roots of the tree. "I know things. I hear things. I walk, no sound. I watch Papoose. Sit. Pow-wow. Tell trouble."

She sat down next to the old man and put her head against his deerskin jacket. She repeated what her mother and Zach had just told her.

"I know. I listen to talk. So, I come back." He put an arm around the child.

"But what can I do, Uncle Ned?"

"Papoose must go. Uncle Ned watch over her at new house. I promise Jim Shaw. I keep promise."

"I wish you were really my uncle." She smiled wistfully at the old Indian. "Then I could go live with you. You said I'm part Cherokee. Couldn't I just go home with you, Uncle Ned, please?"

"No, Papoose must get book learning. Jim Shaw say, you must go to school. When Papoose big squaw, then Papoose live with Cherokees."

"Amanda! Amanda!" Etta was calling from the back door. "Where're you at? Git back in this house and rid up these dishes!"

The old man quickly rose. "I go now. I watch Papoose new house. Better squaw not see me. I come again—full moon." He kissed the top of her head and silently disappeared into the darkness.

"Amanda!" Etta still yelled for her.

She walked slowly back to the house, the house where she had so many memories of her father, the house her father had built, now taken over by another man. She would leave because she would be forced to go, but she would come back someday. She would return to her father's house.

Before the first streak of light was in the sky the next morning, Mandie quietly rose, dressed, and hurried up the mountainside to her father's grave. Snowball bounced along before her.

She hurried, stumbling over the rough rocks, because she knew her mother would be looking for her. The weather was warmer now, but it was still chilly early in the morning. She held up her long skirt to keep it from getting wet in the early morning dew, and then seeing Indian Paintbrush blooming along the way, she quickly let go of her skirt and picked a handful of the bright flowers and ran on. Out of breath, she dropped on her knees by her father's grave and made a hole with a stick to plant the tiny bunch of flowers.

She sat back and folded her hands under her chin as she looked toward the sky. "Dear God, what time I am afraid I will put my trust in thee. I don't know what I did to cause you to take my daddy. I don't understand it, but I still love you."

Rising, she fought back the tears and ran back down the dirt road. She saw Mr. and Mrs. Bryson arriving in their buggy as she hastily ran in the back door and was confronted by her mother.

"Where've you been? Why, your skirt's all wet." Etta bent to touch the fabric. "I hear the Brysons now, so you'd better git your grits there in a hurry if you want any breakfast."

Etta went on into the front room where Mandie could hear her greeting the visitors. She slid into a chair and spooned out grits into her plate. She ate quickly, without saying a word to Snowball, as she fed him beneath the table. It was all she could do to keep from choking on the food. She was so fearful of what lay ahead for her. She had never spent a night away from home in her life and now she was being sent away to live with strangers.

Etta stuck her head through the doorway, "Git a move on, Amanda. They're in a hurry."

She jumped up, snatched Snowball up in her arms, and turned to face her mother defiantly. "I'm taking Snowball with me!"

"Well, take him. Be one less cat around here. Now come in here and meet the people you're goin' to live with."

Etta pushed her forward into the front room. A very fat young woman, evidently dressed in her Sunday-go-to-meeting clothes, sat near the door and a short, thin man stood nearby talking to Zach.

"My, my, she's an awful little thing," the woman exclaimed. "Is she big enough to be any good around the house?" The man silently turned to listen and look.

"Course she is. She's eleven year old atter all. Be twelve next week," Etta told the woman. "Just the age for you to train her the way you want."

Etta gave the girl another shove. "Now git your things, Amanda."

Mandie climbed the ladder and blindly crammed her few belongings into the flour sack her mother had given her. She picked up Snowball and went back downstairs. The Brysons were in a big hurry to get going.

Etta attempted to put an arm around the child. "Now you be a good girl. And remember we still love you."

Amanda tore loose, fighting the tears and the hatred she felt at that moment and ran into the yard, the Brysons following. She did not look back as they rode off until she knew her mother would be gone from the yard. Then she wiped her eyes and took one long, last look at her father's house.

CHAPTER THREE

THE SECRET JOURNEY

Sarah Bryson was the same age as Mandie, and at first Mandie thought she had found a friend. But soon she learned that Sarah was doing things she shouldn't and blaming them on Mandie, telling lies and getting her into trouble. And the Brysons always believed their daughter. Mandie was punished with a hickory switch on her legs, which she had never experienced in her life. Her father had never allowed it. Mandie was desperately afraid of the Brysons and no matter what she did, she could not please them with anything.

The new baby was an adorable little boy named Andrew and Mandie loved him immediately. But he was not her only duty. She had to help hoe corn and bring in the cows. And with a sinking heart, she learned she would not be allowed to attend school. Furthermore, she had to stay home and watch Andrew while the Brysons went to church on Sunday!

Preacher DeHart came to preach on the first and third Sundays every month at the Brysons' church. The other Sundays he was at Maple Springs, the church Mandie belonged to back home. When he learned that the girl was living with the Brysons and was not allowed to come to church he came to see her.

"Remember the Sabbath Day to keep it holy, Amanda, even though you have to tend to the baby and can't go to church," he told her, as they sat in the Brysons' kitchen on Sunday afternoon after dinner. "You mustn't do anything to sin on the Lord's Day."

Mandie, always frightened by the big man's loud words, meekly said nothing, but, "Yes, sir, yes, sir."

She had known the preacher all her young life and she believed the bad things he said would happen to her if she did not live the right kind of life.

Her birthday came and went and no one even mentioned it. She wished the days by until the full moon when Uncle Ned had promised to visit her.

She sat in the swing under a tree in the backyard that night waiting for him, and when he made his stealthy appearance, she ran to him crying, pouring out her troubles.

"Don't cry, Papoose," he comforted her. "Cherokee think. I keep watch over Papoose. Cherokee think what to do."

The old Indian returned each week, but had not been able to come up with any solution to her problems. However, after Mandie had been living there for a few weeks, she happened to overhear a conversation which gave her some hope.

She was singing to the baby as she tried to rock him to sleep in his cradle in the room she shared with him. Mr. and Mrs. Bryson were in the next room and did not know the door was open.

"What are we going to do with that girl? She just can't do nothing right. We're gonna hafta git shed of her," Mrs. Bryson was speaking shrilly.

"Looks like Jim Shaw's brother over in Franklin would take care of her," Mr. Bryson replied.

"You know there's been hard feelings between Jim and John Shaw ever since Jim married—"

"That don't make no difference," Mr. Bryson interrupted. "This girl is the old man's niece and he ought to be responsible for her. He's got the money to support her."

"Well, I'm sure he knew Jim died and he never went near them." Mrs. Bryson changed the subject. "I think we orta git Dr. Woodard to look Andrew over. He's been lookin' mighty peaked lately."

"Seems all right to me, but I'll send word tomorrow if you want," her husband promised.

Mandie had stopped rocking the cradle when she heard the name and location of her father's brother. She would find him herself. And of all things—they were going to have Dr. Woodard come to see Andrew! That meant she could get a message to Joe. Maybe things weren't so hopeless after all. She didn't want to lose touch with Joe. He was her only connection with her father's house. Joe would be seeing her sister at school and would know what was going on.

Andrew had finally dropped off to sleep. She picked up an old catalogue lying nearby and tore off a corner of a page that didn't have much printing. She quickly found a pencil in her bag of personal belongings and wrote a message. "Going to Franklin to live with Daddy's brother, John. Terrible place here."

Dr. Woodard came two days later and Mandie was overjoyed to see the old man as he pulled up in his buggy.

"And how are you, Amanda? Joe hasn't been over to your ma's lately, but he says your sister is mean as ever." He laughed as he tweaked her long, blonde braid. "You all right?"

"I'm fine, Dr. Woodard," she said, watching for the Brysons as she followed the doctor into the house. "Please give this to Joe for me," she whispered, pulling the folded piece of paper out of her apron pocket and giving it to him. "Please don't tell anyone."

Dr. Woodard winked at her and put the paper in his vest pocket. "Be glad to, Amanda. Now I have to see the baby."

It was full moon that night and the old Indian showed up after suppertime. Mandie had rocked Andrew to sleep and was sitting in the yard when he appeared out of the trees. She got up and ran to him.

They sat down on the tree stump near the big black washpot hanging on its fork, with the two washtubs on a nearby bench shielding them from view.

"I have news, Uncle Ned," Mandie told him. "I overheard Mr. and Mrs Bryson talking about me. They said my Uncle John lives in Franklin. I have no idea which way that is. I need Cherokee help to get there, because I am going to live with him."

A big smile broke across the old man's face. "I glad. I am. Papoose go to uncle. No more trouble. Cherokee help. Find way. Bring food." He was almost as excited as the girl.

"When, Uncle Ned? I need to go as soon as possible. These people here don't like me and I'm afraid they might send me somewhere else."

"Next moon, I come back. I go now. Find way. Make plans with Cherokee. Must hurry." He rose.

"Thank you, Uncle Ned. Thank all of your people, or I should say, my people. They are my people, too, if they were my daddy's people."

"Yes, you Cherokee papoose. You go live with real uncle. Go to book school," he told her.

She wiped a tear of joy from her eyes, as he silently stole away into the darkness. "Thank you, dear God, thank you," she whispered as she looked up at the sky full of twinkling stars.

Doctor Woodard returned two days later to check on Andrew and he brought an answer to Mandie's message to Joe.

"I'm getting to be a regular mailman," he laughed, as he tucked a small piece of paper into Mandie's apron pocket when she followed him out to his buggy. She gave his big hand a quick squeeze and ran away to the outhouse where she could read the note in privacy.

"My father takes me to Franklin with him sometimes. Happy that you are going there. I will see you on my next visit there with my father—soon, I hope, Joe."

Mandie smiled to herself as she thought about the boy and his concern for her. It would be nice to see him again.

At the change of the moon, true to his word, Uncle Ned silently waited for Mandie in the darkness of the trees in the backyard. When Andrew was asleep, she quietly slipped out the back door and found him there.

"Franklin long moon away. We come, squaw and braves, to take Papoose. When moon rises three times we come here."

"Three days?" she asked.

He nodded.

"I will wait for you right here. Oh, I'm so—"

At that instant the back door opened and Sarah was calling to her as she came out into the yard. "Amanda, are you out there?" Sarah came into view and stopped. "Why, Amanda, who are you talking to out there?" She screamed as she came closer. "An Indian!" She turned to flee back to the house. Uncle Ned ran quickly away.

Mandie followed Sarah, running and calling, "It's all right, Sarah."

Mrs. Bryson appeared in the doorway. "What is going on?"

Sarah ran to her, clutching her long skirts. "An Indian! Amanda was talking to an Indian!"

"What!" Mrs. Bryson was shocked.

"It's all right. That was Uncle Ned. He was my daddy's friend," Mandie tried to explain.

"Your daddy's friend? An Indian?" Mrs. Bryson was white with fright as she turned back into the house.

"'My daddy had lots of friends, all kinds," Mandie added.

"I never heard of Indian friends. What was he doing here?" The woman was furious now.

"He just keeps in touch with me. He promised my daddy he would," Mandie tried to reassure her.

"Keeps in touch with you?" Mrs. Bryson was still unsettled. "Now you listen here, young lady. Don't you dare let that Indian come back here again. Why, I'll have my husband shoot him! He'll steal us blind!"

"Oh, no, Mrs. Bryson!" Mandie broke into tears.

"Well, I'd better not catch him here again." She was very determined.

"You won't, Mrs. Bryson. I promise," she told her, silently thanking God that Uncle Ned was not to return again until he came after her. Then she would slip out and the Brysons would not see him.

The next three days dragged and it seemed as though the Brysons were meaner than usual to Mandie. They couldn't stop warning her about the old Indian. She tried her best to be patient and made her plans for the night when she would leave.

Andrew was more fretful than usual and she had a hard time getting him to go to sleep the night Uncle Ned was to return. She was almost sick with worry, fearing Uncle Ned would come with his friends and one of the Brysons would see them before she would be able to warn them.

At last the baby grew quiet and Mandie hastily gathered up her few belongings and crammed them into the same flour sack she had brought from home. Bending to kiss the chubby cheek of the sleeping infant and to scoop up Snowball in her arms, she picked up her bag and slipped outside into the warm summer darkness.

As soon as she had reached the shadows of the trees she saw Mr. Bryson come out the back door and settle down on the steps with his pipe. Her heart fluttered as she thought of the consequences should he catch the Indians there. She knew there was a pond nearby that was out of sight of the house and the Indians would probably pass it on their way. She hastened to the pond to intercept them.

The water seemed black and dangerous in the darkness, but Mandie sat down on a fallen log nearby to wait. After walking around in circles before deciding to curl up and sleep, Snowball softly purred in her lap.

Uncle Ned saw her first. He came quietly to stand at her side.

"Papoose, why you wait here?" he asked.

"Oh, Uncle Ned! I was afraid the Brysons would see you. They threatened to shoot you if you came back!" She stood up, catching Snowball as he fell. "Did the others come? Are we ready to go to Franklin?"

"Yes, Papoose. Come," he said and led the way back past the pond. There an old Indian squaw and two young braves waited for them.

Mandie ran to the old woman and hugged her tightly. It was so good to hug someone who cared for her. At that moment, a distant yell filled the air.

"Amanda! Amanda! Where are you, Amanda?"

The girl turned to Uncle Ned. "Quick! Let's go! That's Mrs. Bryson looking for me!"

The group ran through the cornfield, up the slope on the other side of the pond, and were soon hidden from the moonlight in the dark woods Uncle Ned led the way and the two braves brought up the rear.

The old woman took Mandie's bag, threw it across her shoulder with her own bag, and grasped the girl's hand tightly as she hurried along.

Snowball stiffened in Mandie's arms, frightened because of the speed at which they were traveling He didn't scratch the girl, but merely sank his claws into the shoulder of her dress and didn't move.

They did not slacken their pace until they reached the Nantahala River. There Uncle Ned stopped them.

"We cross here." He pointed to a narrow place in the river where the rocks rose in the moonlight on the water. There was a foot-log extending from side to side. "Then pass through Charley Gap. Papoose must not be seen there."

"Charley Gap? We're going right by my father's house?" Mandie questioned, her heart pounding.

"Yes. Big trouble if Papoose seen," Uncle Ned cautioned her. "We rest now." He sat down on a boulder nearby.

The two braves drifted, one on each side, and likewise sat down some distance away. Mandie dropped gratefully to the ground. Her feet hurt and her legs were tired. It seemed hours and hours since they had left the Brysons' land, and she was also sleepy and hungry.

There was the clanging of church bells in the distance and Mandie knew, with a sinking heart, that the Brysons must have sounded an alarm when they discovered her missing.

"The bells, Uncle Ned. They are probably getting a search party together."

"Don't worry, Papoose. They not find us," he told the girl. "Now we eat."

The Indian squaw brought forth meat and dark bread from her bag and held it out to the girl. Mandie thankfully took it and turned to the old man.

"She doesn't speak English, does she?" she asked.

"No. She know Indian talk. She good squaw. Name Morning Star."

Mandie turned back to the squaw. "Thank you, Morning Star."

The old woman smiled and bit into her own ration of food.

"Uncle Ned, does each Indian carry his own food? You have yours, and the other two men—do they have theirs?"

"Yes. We bring meat. Long way to Franklin."

When they had finished eating, Uncle Ned urged them on. "We go in dark. Sleep when sun shines. No one see."

The ringing of the church bells grew dimmer and then could no longer be heard as they made their way across the Nantahala River, went down Buckner Branch, and crossed the Tomahawk Trail. They had to stop often for Mandie to catch her breath. It was all up and down hill and through thick underbrush, and the rough rocks hurt her feet.

A long time later they approached Mandie's father's land. Uncle Ned halted the group.

"Careful. Follow me." He indicated that they were to swing out in a circle away from the house.

Mandie kept her eyes wide open, staring toward the darkened house and outbuildings. Evidently everyone was asleep at this hour. She almost wished she could run right past her mother and let her know that she had defied her and had run away from the Brysons. But she obeyed the old Indian, knowing she would be stopped if some of her people did see her.

She came to a sudden halt at the nearest point to the house, gazed at the log cabin with tears in her eyes, and then furiously ran ahead of the squaw in the direction Uncle Ned was taking.

She thought of her father's grave up the mountainside and wished she could visit it, but she knew it was out of their way. She would have to wait until someday in the future.

She would come back someday. She knew she would.

Her tired feet carried her off her father's land and on toward Franklin.

CHAPTER FOUR

THE MANSION

The first streaks of dawn were lighting up the sky when Uncle Ned finally stopped the group to sleep. They had just crossed Wiggins Creek when they finally sat down to rest.

Mandie flopped down on the grass. "Guess I'm plumb tuckered out." She laughed wearily.

Morning Star quickly gathered branches and made a bed for her to lie on, hidden under the trees. The girl used her shawl for a blanket, knowing when the sun came up it would be warm again.

She was so excited she couldn't sleep, but the fatigue overcame the excitement and she dropped off to dream.

The sound of shooting woke her. She sat up quickly and almost smashed Snowball, asleep by her side. For a minute she couldn't remember where she was. Then the old squaw put an arm around her and she relaxed. She could see Uncle Ned standing near the creek. He came to her. She could tell by his shadow that the sun was fast moving into the west. She must have slept all day.

"Braves go see where gun shoot," he told her. "They come, we go."

At that moment there was the sound of voices in the trees nearby.

"Well, I reckon we done searched fur enough. That girl couldn't 'a got no futher than this," a man's voice came to them.

Uncle Ned quickly whisked Mandie behind a laurel tree and he and the squaw slipped behind the rhododendron bushes nearby.

"Yeh, let's go see what's goin' on up yonder. Must be Jed's search party," another male voice replied.

Two men came into view. They were carrying rifles and stomping the underbrush beneath their feet. One was a tall man with a white beard and the other was a short, fat man who was spitting tobacco juice as he went. Mandie peeped around the tree, but she did not recognize either one. She realized they must be looking for her. They paused while the tall man lit his pipe.

"Don't much blame that youngun fer not wantin' to stay at that Bryson house. Hear tell that female is a tiger," the tall one was saying.

"Yep, I hear tell they can't nobody please her. But I shore would like to find that youngun 'fore the wildcats git her. I wouldn't want to take her back to the Brysons, but I wouldn't want her to git lost on this mountain either," the short one said. "I knew her pa. Good man, he was." They walked on, out of hearing, and were soon lost from sight in the tall underbrush.

The squaw went to Mandie and put her arm around her. Uncle Ned followed.

"Be not afraid, Papoose. We go to Franklin. White men not stop Indians," he reassured the girl.

"I know. I know how smart the Indians are. I know you will get me to my uncle's house in Franklin," she replied, grasping the old man's hand. "I'm not afraid. After all, I'm part Cherokee, too."

The two braves came silently up to the old man.

"White men carry guns; coming this way," the taller one said.

"Two passed here," Uncle Ned told them. "Looking for Papoose. We go." He pointed in the direction of Hightower Gap away from the way the two men had gone.

The group slipped quietly through the woods, resting only when Mandie was tired, and they finally reached the Little Tennessee River. They took long detours for safety's sake but followed the banks of the river most of the way. They came on through Burningtown and up the main road that ran through Franklin.

The sight before her was unbelievable to Mandie. All the houses were so close together and there were so many of them. Then there were all the stores. They passed the livery stable. It was barely dawn, but there was the sound of voices and horses. She was speechless as she stared around her.

"John Shaw that way." Uncle Ned pointed down the long main road. "Take Papoose to house. White man must not see Indian."

He halted in front of an immense white house with a huge yard covered with green grass, flowers, and shrubs, and a small summerhouse at one side. A white picket fence enclosed the yard and a hitching post with a stepping-stone was at the gate. Across the road was an old church with a cemetery.

Mandie stood in frozen awe at the monstrous size of the house and the surrounding yard and gardens. So this was Uncle John's mansion. It must have twenty rooms, at least. She at once became nervous and excited at the prospect of meeting her father's brother. What if he didn't like her? What if she had to go back to the Brysons? But then, she would not think of such things, because she would not go back to the Brysons under any circumstances. She would go live with Uncle Ned's tribe if her uncle rejected her.

"Go, Papoose," Uncle Ned urged her. "I come later. Love."

"And love to you, Uncle Ned and Morning Star." She turned to hug the old Indian and the squaw, and then quickly opened the gate and ran up the steps to the front porch. She lifted a shaking hand to knock on the front door.

She could not hear a sound inside. No one seemed to be at home. Her heart sank. She turned to look at the Indians who were half hidden by the shrubbery. Then she heard footsteps coming closer to the door. She looked up to see a big, tall man, barefooted and in workclothes, standing before her.

"Are you John Shaw?" she asked nervously.

"No, ma'am. He's not home." The man scratched his gray head as he stared at her.

"When will he be back? You see, I'm his niece, Amanda Shaw," she explained.

"Well, come in, miss." The man held the door open and Mandie turned to catch a glimpse of Uncle Ned's smiling face.

She entered a wide hallway and followed the man to a room on the right, which she decided must be the company parlor judging from the rich furnishings. She sat down on the edge of a soft armchair and deposited her bag on the floor by her side. Snowball escaped from her arms and went running off into the other part of the house.

"When will Uncle John be back?" she asked.

"Oh, he's gone to Europe. He's been gone since March. I'm the caretaker, Jason Bond." He was still standing as he explained.

"Oh, goodness, to Europe!" She was dismayed to have come all this way and then not find her uncle at home. "What will I do?"

"Where're you from, miss?"

"I lived with my daddy, Jim Shaw, and my mother over at Charley Gap in Swain County until my daddy died in April and my mother got married again. Then they sent me away to live with some awful people at Almond Station and I ran away." She told the man the truth, knowing her uncle would have to know. "I—I don't have anywhere to live."

"Oh, well, plenty of room here. He oughta be back any day now. Come on, I'll find you a room." He picked up her bag and led the way up a long flight of stairs to the second floor, and then down a long hall and opened the door to a room furnished with blue and gold. Mandie stared in delight. Never had she seen such an elegant room.

"How about this one?" Jason Bond was asking as she stood there.

"Oh, it's beautiful! It's wonderful!" She stood in the middle of the room, gazing about.

"I'll get Liza to bring you some fresh water for your pitcher over there, and some breakfast if you ain't et yet."

"Oh, I am hungry," she said. "In fact, I'm starving!" She laughed.

"Well, we'll fix that." Jason Bond went out the door and she removed her wrinkled bonnet, tossed it on the bed and sat down in a big, soft chair. She had a strange feeling that she must be in the wrong house. How could her uncle have so much when her father had had so little?

An enormous old black woman knocked and then came on in with a tray of food, followed by a young black girl with a bucket of water.

"I'm Lou, Aunt Lou, they call me, my child. I keeps this house together." She set the tray on a table nearby and stood before Mandie. "Now, what might be your name?"

"Amanda Shaw, Aunt Lou. My daddy was Jim Shaw, John's brother." She lifted the cloth covering the food and exclaimed, "Oh, thank you, Aunt Lou. I'll eat every bite; I'm so hungry."

"Well, you'd better had if you gonna stay around here. Now this here's Liza. She'll be lookin' after you whiles you here." She beckoned to the young girl who still stood behind her. Liza came forward and poured the water into the pitcher on the washstand.

"Guess you'd better wash that dirty face 'fore you eat." Aunt Lou smiled at her. "Liza, you comb that pretty hair for my child. But let her eat first."

Aunt Lou left the room and Mandie went to wash her face in the bowl of water.

"I be back later, Miss Amanda," Liza told her. "You want anything, all you has to do is pull that cord over there."

"Pull that cord?" Mandie asked, looking to where Liza was pointing toward the drapery beside the bed.

Liza laughed and danced around the room. "That makes a bell ring down at the other end where I hear it and I knows you calling me." She danced on out the door, laughing.

Snowball came running into the room and jumped up into Amanda's lap as she sat down to eat.

"You just wait, Snowball. You have to eat on the floor. Here," she said, putting him down and giving him some milk in a saucer that had been on her tray. She added a bit of bacon. "Now you eat it all up because we're going to take a nap."

True to her word, she, with Snowball's help, ate every bite of the food and then, pulling down the silky bedspread, she flopped onto the big soft bed and fell fast asleep with the kitten curled up beside her.

At noontime Liza came to call the girl to dinner and had to wake her.

"Time to eat, Miss Amanda," Liza said, shaking the girl.

Mandie sat up rubbing her eyes. "Eat? I just ate. Oh, goodness, what time is it?" Snowball rose and stretched.

"It's time to eat again. Wash your face and I'll comb that hair," Liza told her.

The black girl quickly unbraided Mandie's hair, combed out the many tangles and then braided it again.

"I think I'll wash your hair later," Liza suggested.

"Oh, yes, it is dirty," Mandie agreed, remembering the bed of twigs she had slept on and the many miles she had walked through briars, dusty roads and river water.

"Later," Liza said. "Now you just follow me. I'll show you where the food be."

They went back down the long, carpeted hall, down the elaborate staircase and through another long hall into the most beautiful room Mandie had ever seen. A huge crystal chandelier hung over an enormous dining table covered with a crocheted tablecloth and set with one place at the end for her. Silver candelabra stood at intervals along the table. A whole wall was covered by a tapestry of peacocks and flowers. The opposite side of the room had long French doors opening onto a terrace. Mandie stopped to gaze about the room.

"Here, missy, down to this end," Liza beckoned to her as she pulled out a chair with a velvet seat. "You set right here and I bring on the food."

Mandie, still speechless, walked to the chair and sat down. Then she turned quickly as the girl turned to leave the room. "What do you have to eat?"

"Anything you want, missy. Ham, chicken, sweet potatoes, green beans, turnip salat, cornpone, biscuits, honey, preserves, anything you want. Now what must I bring you?" Liza waited.

"You mean you have all those things already cooked? All for one meal?"

"Well, missy, all us servants have to eat too, and there's two more 'sides me and Lou. There's Jenny, the cook, and there's Abraham, the yard man, what lives in the house in the backyard. Lou, she's the boss," Liza went on. "So we just cook everything at one time. That's the way Mr. Shaw tells us to do. Want me to bring you some of everything?" Liza grinned.

"Oh, no, I couldn't possibly eat so much. Just a small piece of ham, a spoonful of green beans, a huge sweet potato, a big piece of cornbread, and milk," Mandie told her. "My uncle must be an awfully rich man if he has all that for one meal."

"Oh, he is, missy. Richest man this side of Richmond, they say. So much money he'll never spend it all. And no one to leave it to—except—"

Aunt Lou came through the door at that moment.

"Liza, git a move on here. Take that cat there and feed it and git this child something to eat. And no more of that gossip, you hear?"

Without a word, Liza took Snowball and quickly left. the room.

"And how is my child feeling after her nap?" Aunt Lou put her arm around Mandie's shoulders.

"Fine, Aunt Lou. Liza says my uncle is unusually rich; is that so?"

"I don't knows about it being unusual, but he shore is rich. Liza ain't got no business meddling in his affairs like that, though."

"She wasn't meddling, Aunt Lou. I asked her. You see, my daddy was never rich."

"Many's a good man that don't git rich."

"You see, you can tell by my clothes that I am not rich. I don't have any pretty, fancy dresses and bonnets." Mandie smoothed her dark gray frock.

"Well, that's one thing we's can fix, my child. We's got a sewing room here that's just plumb spang full of pritty cloth. We'll just make you up some new clothes," Aunt Lou was telling her as Liza came back into the room carrying a silver tray loaded with dishes and the smell of hot food. "Now you just eat up, my child, and Liza can bring you 'round to the sewing room when you git done. I'll see what we can whip up."

"Thank you, Aunt Lou. I'll hurry," Mandie assured her, as she picked up her fork. The black woman left the room. "Don't go away, Liza. I'll be finished in a minute."

"I has to go eat, too, but I'll be right back. Just pull that little cord over there by the window if you want me. It'll ring in the kitchen," Liza told her.

"You haven't eaten yet? I thought I was the only one left to eat dinner," Mandie told her. "Go get your food and come sit right here." She pushed out a chair next to her with her foot.

Liza laughed. "You don't understand, missy. I'se a servant. Us servants has our own table in the kitchen."

"But I'm the only one at this big table. Can't you come and eat with me?"

"Nope, can't," Liza replied. "Nobody exceptin' Mr. Bond and Mr. Shaw eats at that table, and you, of course, 'cause you'se kin."

"Where is Mr. Bond?"

"He et early 'cause he had to go off and tend to some bidness," the dark girl told her. "Now you eat up. I'll go eat and then I'll be back."

Liza laughed and danced out through the door. Mandie, famished as she was, hurriedly ate the rich food in anticipation of getting a new dress made for her—a brand new dress made just for her—one that nobody had ever worn.

When Liza took her to the sewing room, Mandie was again amazed with the wonders of her uncle's house. It looked like a store. Fine materials, laces, ribbons, buttons of every color, were everywhere about the room. Aunt Lou, who was also the seamstress for the household, was waiting for her.

"You just pick out what you want and we make it," the old woman told her.

Mandie immediately spied a roll of pale blue silk in the pile. She stroked the soft material with her fingertips.

"This one, please," the girl murmured shyly. "I've never had a light-colored dress in my life."

"And a bonnet to match." Aunt Lou smiled at her. "We'll just put lots of trimming on it—lace, ribbons, and sech. We'll make a real baby doll out of you, that's what we'll do."

Mandie spent the afternoon in the room while Aunt Lou pinned, measured, and cut material. She just couldn't believe it would all turn into a dress just for her. When Aunt Lou was ready to sew, Liza came to tell Mandie she had a visitor in the parlor.

"Miss Polly, that lives in that big house next-door, she's come to see you, missy," Liza said. "She waiting in the parlor for you."

"In the parlor? I don't even know where the parlor is," Mandie laughed bewilderedly. "I've never seen such a big house in my life."

"Right this way." Liza led her. "Down this hall and on down these steps and it's the big double door on the left, next to the front door. 'Member the room where you first came in?"

"I remember the room, but I didn't remember the way. Thank you, Liza." Mandie went on through the double door and there stood a girl about her own size in front of the sofa.

She had long, dark hair and eyes as dark as chinquapins. She smiled and came forward.

"My name's Polly Cornwallis. I live next door, and Mr. Shaw's cook told our cook that Mr. Shaw's niece had come to visit, and so I came over." She rolled off this long speech without taking a breath.

"I'm glad you live next door," Mandie told her. "Sit down."

They sat on the sofa.

"My name is Amanda Shaw. My uncle is gone off to Europe and I'm here alone, so I'm glad you came."

They were friends at once and before they realized it, Liza was telling them supper was ready. Polly had to go home, but promised to come back the next day and bring her schoolbooks. But the next day brought more than Polly and her schoolbooks for Mandie.

CHAPTER FIVE

THE SECRET TUNNEL

Early the next morning, Jason Bond answered a knock at the front door. He found a messenger there from John Shaw's lawyer's office in Asheville.

"Mr. Wilson sent you this letter, Mr. Bond," the young boy told him.

Mr. Bond took the letter, withdrew a paper from the envelope, and stood there reading.

"What's this? What's this?" Jason Bond was plainly shocked. "Come on in, my boy. I'll get the cook to give you something to eat. I'll have to send an answer back."

He took the boy to the kitchen and left him there with Jenny. Then he hurried to his room and wrote a note. Hearing Mandie singing in her room, he knew she was up, and knocked on her door.

"I see you're up bright and early. Come on downstairs. I have something to tell you." He led the way down to the dining room and yelled through the door to Jenny.

"Send Liza in here with something to eat," he said and went back to sit down by the girl at the table.

"What's wrong, Mr. Jason?" Mandie asked him. She could sense he was disturbed about something.

"Well, it's like this," he began, as Liza brought in the coffee and poured it. He waited until she left the room. "I have a letter here from your uncle's lawyer."

"You do?" Mandie leaned forward.

"Yes, but I'm afraid it's bad news. He says—he says your uncle has—died in Europe and—"

"Died! Oh, no!" she gasped and brought her hand to her mouth. "Please, God, not my Uncle John, too!"

"I'm sorry," Mr. Bond said. "I couldn't think of any way to tell you. The letter says he was buried over there and—"

"When, Mr. Jason?"

"A few weeks ago. It took a long time for word to reach his lawyer and then his lawyer had to let us know," the old man told her.

"Oh, Uncle John, now what will I do?" she sobbed.

Mr. Bond held her hand and tried to comfort her. "Don't worry about what you're going to do. You're going to stay right here. I'm sending a note back to the lawyer, telling him you are here and you are going to stay here until the will is found."

"The will?" she asked.

"Yeh, until the will is found. Lawyer Wilson drew up a will for your uncle last year, but he says in this letter he believes your uncle made another one since then. At any rate, he thinks the will must be in his papers here in the house somewhere, so we'll have to look for it."

"What good is the will if Uncle John is dead?" she asked.

"Don't you know what a will is? It's a paper, a legal paper, stating who is to receive what of the inheritance when a person dies. Your uncle had lots of money and property and someone will get all that, depending on who is mentioned in his will," Mr. Jason told her. "There's a possibility you will be mentioned in his will as a legal heir."

"An heir?"

"Yes, that's the person who gets whatever is left to him by the person who dies."

"But he never even saw me that I know of. He might not have even known that I was born."

"Maybe, maybe not. Anyway, he knew he had a brother, who was your father; and since your father is dead, if he willed anything to him, then you would get it instead."

Mandie finally understood most of what Mr. Bond was telling her, and she became anxious to find the will. She also wanted to talk to someone her own age.

"May I invite Polly to spend the night with me, Mr. Bond?"

"Of course, but her mother will have to agree, you know."

So when Polly came over and heard the news, she returned home to tell her mother and came back to tell Mandie that her mother would come to call later in the afternoon.

Mrs. Cornwallis, a young widow, was very expensively dressed; her clothes were beautiful. Mandie was a little unsure of herself in the presence of such a lady.

"My dear, such a shock for you. And just the day after you got here, too. You must come over to our house and stay until things are settled," Mrs. Cornwallis told her.

"Thank you, Mrs. Cornwallis, but I can't leave. I have to help Mr. Jason look for Uncle John's will," Mandie said. "And I would like Polly to spend the night with me, if you would let her."

"Yes, yes, of course, dear," Polly's mother agreed. "But, doesn't anyone know where John Shaw kept his will?"

"No, not even his lawyer. He says it must be somewhere here in the house, so we have to find it."

"Mandie, can I help you look?" Polly put in.

"That's why I wanted you to spend the night," Mandie replied.

Mrs. Cornwallis rose to go. "Polly can spend the night, dear; but please get some sleep, girls." She laughed as she left.

"Will you have to go home now because your uncle died? I sure hope not," Polly said.

"Oh, no, Mr. Jason said I was to stay here until the will is found; and we're going to find it ourselves. Come on! We'll start right now."

The two girls left Polly's nightclothes in Mandie's room and then in whispers decided to take candles and go up to the third floor. Mandie had not yet been to the third floor of the house, and was anxious to do a little exploring.

They found the door to the stairs, turned the knob and it opened. Silently they gazed up the dark steps, then slowly began their ascent on the creaking stairway. They reached a landing halfway up and stopped to open the window and push open the shutters to let in the light and fresh air before climbing the last flight.

"At last!" sighed Polly, as they reached yet another door at the top of the stairs.

Upon opening it, they found themselves in a long hallway. Holding their half-spent candles at arm's length, they cautiously followed the corridor to the only door they could see in the hall, at the left. Mandie, arriving first, pushed it open.

Before them was a huge, impressive bedroom furnished with two ornately carved four-poster beds. Each was covered with a white crocheted spread and draped with matching canopy curtains. There were two full-length mirrors with heavy wood frames to match the beds. Four tall windows were covered with sheer Priscillas.

Before the girls could take in more in the meager light, the canopy curtain moved slightly on one of the beds and they heard a strange noise. At the same time, a draft from somewhere snuffed out their candles. With this, the frightened girls ran down the hall in search of the stairway. Just as they reached it, the door slammed violently and when they grabbed for the doorknob they discovered there was none.

Mandie gasped and clung to Polly as the two raced down to the other end of the hall. In the darkness they both stumbled into the wall, pushing a hidden panel open which led to yet another descending stairway. Just when they were beginning to wonder if the stairs would end, they came to a short hallway. They could see no door, but more stairs led downward and they took the plunge hand in hand.

To continue the maze, they found another door, opened it and stumbled into a dark room, managing to cross it without bumping into any furniture. A second door in the room led to another stairway, at which point Mandie cried, "Where in the world are we?"

"Don't ask me," was Polly's bewildered reply.

At the end of another hall they came upon a locked door, but this time Polly discovered a large key dangling on a nail beside the door. With a trembling hand she inserted the key in the lock. Exhausted with suspense and fear she handed the key to Mandie and asked her to open the door. To the complete surprise of both the girls there were bushes and vines growing directly in front of them in the open doorway. They pushed through the shrubbery and exclaimed together, "We're in the woods!"

They could barely see the back of the house through all the trees.

"It was a secret tunnel, just like in the storybooks!" cried Polly.

"It's amazing! I can hardly believe this is happening," added Mandie.

"Say, I'm getting awfully hungry," murmured Polly. "It must be close to dinnertime."

"Yeh, me too. Come on, let's run," Mandie called as she bounded toward the other side of the house.

Polly caught up with her. "Let's keep this *our* secret. Then we can explore it all over again."

"All right. We won't tell anyone where we've been," Mandie agreed. "But I sure would like to know what was behind that curtain on that bed. Ooh, it makes me shiver just to think of it!"

"I know," agreed Polly. "Let's get Mr. Bond to go up there with us and see what it is."

"That's a good idea. Come on. Let's hurry and eat dinner." Mandie once again broke into a run.

As they came in the back door Aunt Lou greeted them. "Land sakes! Where you all done been? Vittles bein' put on the table. Git a move on and git washed. Quick!" She shooed them on through the kitchen with a big grin, as they obeyed.

They washed, hurried to the dining room and slipped into their chairs just as Mr. Bond came in right behind them.

"Well, well, where have you two been for so long?" he asked.

"We've been looking for the will," Polly said, quickly.

"On the third floor," added Mandie, watching for his reaction.

"On the third floor, eh? Well, did you find anything up there?" He began slicing the ham.

"Yes," Polly said.

"But we don't know what it is," Mandie reminded her.

"Well, what's that supposed to mean? How did you find something if you don't know what it is?"

"We found a big bedroom with ghost-white curtains and spreads over two big four-poster beds on the third floor, with white curtains all over all the windows. It makes chills run down my spine!" Mandie exaggerated.

"Mine, too! It made a noise, Mr. Bond, and made the curtains move and then it blew out our lights," Polly told him.

"Well now, if you'll eat up, we'll just go back up there and see what it is."

They were soon finished and Mr. Bond went to get some matches and an oil lamp.

Mandie absentmindedly slipped her hand into her pocket. "I still have the key to that tunnel," she whispered.

"Listen, let's tell Mr. Bond about it—just him—nobody else?" begged Polly.

"All right, but not till we see what the ghost is," cautioned Mandie as Mr. Bond returned.

They followed the kind man up the stairs silently, darting glances all around. When they reached the landing where they had opened the window, he closed it, commenting that the draft might cause their lamp to go out. Arriving at the top of the stairs he opened the door into the center hall of the third floor.

"Land sakes! Gotta replace that knob," he said, as he noticed the other side of it was missing.

The girls followed more closely behind him.

"It was in that room," Mandie said, pointing to the door on the left.

"All right, we'll just see what's in there," the caretaker told them. He walked over to the bed and the curtains moved. And there was that noise again!

As he touched the curtain a bat flew out from behind it. The girls screamed and ran into the hall. After a long chase, Mr. Bond finally ran the bat out through the window in the hall and closed it again, leaving the shutters open to allow some light from outside.

"Come on back in now and see for yourselves, girls. It's gone," he assured them.

The two slowly entered the room, looked cautiously around and were satisfied.

"Mr. Jason, we found a secret tunnel today right here in this house," Mandie blurted out.

"A secret tunnel?" the old man asked.

"Yes, come on! We'll show you!" Mandie fairly danced about.

"It goes into the woods," Polly said.

"I don't know anything about a secret tunnel in this house," Mr. Bond said.

The girls explained how they had found it. They led the way down the hall and searched for the loose panel. Instead, they found a door they hadn't seen before, which opened to a small room containing steps which led to the attic.

"Well, reckon that's it," Mr. Bond said. "We've looked everywhere and haven't found it yet. There's only one more door left and it's locked." He indicated a door near where they were standing.

"Oh, we missed that one," Mandie jumped.

"I've got the key. I know what's in there," Mr. Bond said.

"Here," Mandie pulled the key from her pocket. "I have the key to the door at the other end of the tunnel. We can come in from that end."

"Too late tonight for such things," Mr. Bond said. "We'll try it tomorrow in the daylight."

"Well, if you have the key to this room, can we see what's in there?" Polly asked.

Mr. Bond took out his keys and fumbling through them came up at last with the key that unlocked the door. The girls stepped ahead of him into the room and looked around in surprise.

There were shelves on three sides of the room filled with books. In front of a large stained-glass window was a huge desk with papers strewn about on it. All the shutters were open, letting in the moonlight from outside. On the opposite side of the room was a beautifully carved couch with big soft cushions. On the three sides with shelves there were wall sconces holding candles, as many as could possibly be placed between the rows of books.

Mandie noticed a smaller door in one corner which she tried to open and found locked. The caretaker had no key for it. She also noticed an ashtray with ashes in it on the desk and a pen in a bottle of ink.

"Wonder what your uncle used this room for—a private library?" Polly asked.

"He did his private book work up here," Mr. Bond told them. "None of the servants are allowed on the third floor."

"Do you know what's on the other side of that locked door, Mr. Jason?" Mandie wanted to know.

"Nope, can't say I remember ever seeing it before. Believe those curtains may have been pulled over it when I've been in here, and that's not been many times."

"Can we light the candles, Mr. Bond, so we can see how they look all burning at one time?" Polly begged.

Mr. Bond struck a match, lighted one candle, and the one on either side of it automatically burst into flame. He repeated this around the room.

"You see how close they are? That's what makes 'em all light up magic-like," the old man told them.

The room was brilliant, and Mandie's attention was drawn to a paper on top of the pile on the desk.

She picked it up and read aloud, " 'March 1st. Dear Brother Jim'—This is to my daddy!—'I am going on vacation to Europe for the summer and since one never knows what the future on a ship can hold, I would like to make peace with you while I can. I am an old man now, fifteen years older than you, you know, and I have no one to leave my belongings to, except you. I am taking the blame entirely for the disagreement between us all these years. I want you to know that Elizabeth is still in love with you, and she says she will never love anyone else. All that matters to me now is—' " Mandie looked up, puzzled. "That's all; it's unfinished. Who is Elizabeth?"

Mr. Bond took the paper and read it over again. "I'm afraid I have no idea who Elizabeth is."

"I wonder why it's not finished," Mandie mused.

"Might have been written over again on another piece of paper. See that ink blot?" He showed her a black smear of ink on the paper, which she had not noticed.

"You're right, Mr. Jason," Mandie's blue eyes filled with tears. "I hope my daddy received that letter before he—passed away."

"He probably did." Mr. Bond put the paper back on the desk and reached for a long rod.

"What's that?" Polly wanted to know.

"It's a snuffer, to put out all these confounded candles," he said, as he swung it around the room extinguishing each one as he went.

"Imagine doing this every day," Polly remarked.

"Yeh, and I'm glad I don't have to," he said.

Once in her room for the night, with only Polly for company, Mandie studied the paper again, which she had taken from the library. She was glad Polly's mother had agreed to let her stay with her until her uncle's missing will was found.

"I hope my daddy got this," she said again. "I have to find this Elizabeth who loved him."

"In the meantime, tomorrow we'll show Mr. Jason the tunnel," Polly reminded her. "What did you do with the key?"

"I put it on the bureau over there." Mandie pointed to it.

But, in the morning the key was gone. It was nowhere to be found.

CHAPTER SIX

THE GHOST

One morning, later that week, the two girls had wandered across the road through the cemetery, reading stone markers and commenting about the names, when they perceived someone knocking at John Shaw's front door.

They hurried across the road to find a tall young man with big hazel eyes, standing there with a black traveling bag in his hand.

He looked down at the girls, smiled, and asked, "Is this where Mr. John Shaw lived before he died abroad?"

"Yes, sir," Mandie told him. "I'm his niece, Amanda Shaw."

"You are?" he questioned her. "I'm his nephew. You live here?"

"Yes, come on in and sit down. I'll get Mr. Bond." She opened the door and met Mr. Bond in the hallway. "Mr. Bond, this is Uncle John's nephew."

The old man quickly looked the young man over and said slowly, "Mr. John Shaw didn't have any nephews."

"Well, I'm Bayne Locke, his sister's son. And since I *am* his nephew, I have come to claim my part of his property," the young man told him.

"I said, Mr. Shaw did not have any nephews; in fact, no living relatives, except his brother, Jim, and his family and they live in Swain County," Jason Bond was emphatic.

"I am John Shaw's *nephew,*" the stranger insisted, standing there in the hallway. "My mother died when I was born and I never have seen my uncle, but I'm sure I can claim at least part of what he owned. Where's his will?"

Mr. Bond looked puzzled, scratching his head thoughtfully. "To tell you the truth, we haven't found the will yet. But we have received word from his lawyer concerning the property—"

The young man interrupted, "I have as much right to stay here as anyone else until the will is found, if it *is* ever found." He plopped his bag on the floor.

"Oh, it'll be found all right," Mr. Bond told him.

"Well, until it is found, please show me my room. I've been traveling all the way from Richmond and I'm tired," Bayne Locke demanded.

"I suppose you can stay here tonight, but I'll have to have proof as to who you are," the old man said.

"I have it right here." Bayne pulled a paper from his inside pocket and handed it to Mr. Bond.

"All this says is that you are the son of Martha Shaw and Caro Locke. It does not prove you're John Shaw's nephew."

"Anybody that knows the Shaw family knows that he had a sister who died twenty-two years ago giving birth to a son in Richmond," Bayne told him.

Mr. Bond still stood there scratching his head. Mandie was left speechless with the matter. Then Polly suddenly looked from Bayne to Mandie and spoke up.

"Well, Mandie, you have a cousin!" she exclaimed.

"Well, sort of, I suppose I do," Mandie agreed. Then she turned to Mr. Bond. "I'll show my cousin to a room, Mr. Bond. Which room should I put him in?"

"Either one down the hall upstairs. I'll get Liza to go up and get things ready." Mr. Bond turned back down the hallway toward the kitchen.

The girls led the young man up the stairs, past Mr. Bond's room, to an unoccupied bedroom.

Mandie pushed open the door and peered into the room. It was well furnished with heavy furniture, red rugs and gold draperies.

"This will have to do," she said, standing aside for Bayne Locke to enter the room. "It's on the front of the house and won't get the afternoon sun."

"Fine, fine," Bayne muttered, throwing up the windows and opening the shutters.

Liza danced in with a broom and a dustmop.

"Shoo, shoo! You-alls just git out of the way now, so's I can git this place shuck up," the black girl ordered the girls.

Mandie turned back as she went out the door, followed by Polly.

"Dinner's at twelve o'clock on the button. Don't be late."

"Never been to dinner on time in my life, but I'll turn over a new leaf just for you," Bayne called back to her.

As the two girls sat in the swing on the front porch, Polly asked, "What are you going to do now? That man says he's your cousin, and he'll take what he came after, if you ask me."

"We'll see about that! Just leave him to me!" Mandie teased.

"But what can you do about it?" Polly wanted to know.

"Tonight's the night for Uncle Ned to come visit," Mandie said.

"Uncle Ned? Who's he?"

"He's the Indian who brought me here. Remember I told you?"

"Yeh, but so what? What can an Indian do about this Bayne Locke?"

"I'll ask Uncle Ned to get the Cherokees to check up on this so-called cousin. Uncle Ned has his own ways of finding out things."

The screen door opened and Aunt Lou stuck her head out. "Got that new dress done fuh you, my child."

Mandie quickly followed her back into the house with Polly close behind. The blue dress was finished and pressed and was hanging in the sewing room. Mandie could only stand and gasp. She had never owned such a garment in all her life.

"Well, don't just stand there, my child. We'se got to put it on to see if it fits." Aunt Lou smiled as she began to unbutton the dress Mandie was wearing.

The dress fit perfectly and Mandie turned and twirled in front of the long mirror with oh's and ah's and Polly admiring.

"It's beautiful, Aunt Lou." Mandie was tearful as she turned to hug the old woman tightly. "Thank you, Aunt Lou! Thank you!"

"It takes a pretty girl like you to make a dress pretty," Aunt Lou told her. "You look mighty fine, my child."

"Positively heavenly, Mandie," Polly agreed.

"Will you unbutton me now, Aunt Lou?" Mandie asked.

"Unbutton you? What for? There's more acomin' from where that one came from. Now you just keep it on and enjoy it, my child." The old woman patted her on the head.

"More, Aunt Lou?"

"Sho' 'nuff. Next one will be ready 'fore you git that one dirty," Aunt Lou assured her. "Gonna be the lady of the house, you is. And you gotta look like the lady of the house—no more countrified looks. You'se a city girl now. Gotta dress like city folks."

"But, Aunt Lou, I hate to make so much work for you. You have other things to do, I know."

"Ain't just me working on these dresses. Got help from old Miz Burnette over on the hill, too."

"Mrs. Burnette makes my clothes too, Mandie," Polly told her. "Mother says she does the best work in town."

"Somebody has to pay her," Mandie said.

"Oh, never you mind about pay. Mr. Bond done arranged all that. Now git on 'bout your business. I'se got other things to do," Aunt Lou gave the two girls an affectionate shove out the door.

Thank you, dear God, Mandie whispered to herself. Thank you for all these nice things.

That night, when Mandie met Uncle Ned in the summerhouse nearby, she wore her new blue dress. The old Indian was happy when she told him about all the nice things that had happened to her, but he was greatly disturbed when he heard that her Uncle John had died and Bayne Locke had come to the house saying he was his nephew.

"Bayne Locke. You know where he come from?" he asked.

"He said he had come all the way from Richmond, Uncle Ned," Mandie told him. "I suppose he must have lived there before he came here."

"Cherokee go to Richmond. Find out. I know by next full moon," he promised.

"Thank you, Uncle Ned. I seem to ask you for so many things, but I don't have anyone else to ask," the girl said.

"No, no—is all right. You one of us. Cherokee keep watch over Papoose. I promise Jim Shaw. Anything you ask, I do," Ned reminded her. "You Cherokee, too."

"Isn't that wonderful, Uncle Ned? That I have such people, people who will always look out for me. Tell all the Cherokees I am grateful. I'm happy that I'm one of you and I long for the day when I can visit my people."

Not only was Mandie planning to check up on Bayne Locke, but Mr. Bond had immediately sent a messenger to Lawyer Wilson's office, requesting information concerning the young man.

Later that night when he thought everyone was sound asleep, Mr. Bond climbed the stairs to the third story in a determined effort to locate John Shaw's will and settle the matter once and for all as far as Bayne Locke was concerned.

John Shaw's library was directly over the room that Mandie and Polly occupied on the second floor and he tried to be very quiet, but despite his efforts, he stumbled into a chair in the darkness.

"Polly, did you hear that?" Mandie shook her sleeping friend.

"Yes," Polly said, sitting straight up in the bed.

"A ghost!" Mandie whispered.

"In Uncle John's library. Let's go see what it is," Polly said, jumping from the bed.

"This time of night?" Mandie was leery of such adventures.

"Ghosts only walk at night. Didn't you know that?" Polly informed her. "I read a book about ghosts once. They can't do you any harm. So why be afraid? We're more powerful than they are. Want to go see what one really looks like?"

"Oh, Polly, you aren't afraid of anything, are you?" Mandie reached for her slippers. "Let's go, if you insist."

Polly led the way up the dark stairs while Mandie carried the oil lamp from her room. They crept along the hall and found the door open to Uncle John's library. As they cautiously peeped in, Mandie began to laugh.

"Some ghost that is!"

Mr. Bond turned at the sound of her voice. "Why, what are you two doing up this time of night?"

"We heard a noise, so we came up to see who it was," Polly answered. "We had kinda hoped it was a ghost."

"Well, I'm not a ghost," Mr. Bond chuckled. "But I'd advise you two to be quiet and not disturb the rest of the house. I don't want that Mr. Locke poking his nose in here."

"No, that wouldn't do," Mandie agreed. "He might find the will before we do. Can we do anything to help?"

"Well, start at the comer there and look through every book on the shelves. If you find any piece of paper at all, or any handwriting in the books, let me see it," Jason Bond told them.

So the real work began on the search for the important paper.

CHAPTER SEVEN

SEARCH FOR THE WILL

The search for the will was more involved than anyone had dreamed. Jason Bond and the two girls covered every inch of the house—except the tunnel. The missing key had not been found either, after it had disappeared from Mandie's bureau.

Mandie spoke to Mr. Bond about it, "I've asked Aunt Lou, Liza, Jenny, and even Abraham, and nobody has seen a key of any kind."

"Could be that Mr. Bayne Locke has been in your room, Mandie, but don't ask him about it. We don't want him involved in what we're doing around here. The less he knows the better," Jason Bond told her. "You two girls just keep your eyes peeled. Maybe it'll turn up somewhere."

No one had been able to find the entrance to the tunnel from the inside of the house, and with the key lost, the door could not be opened from the outside.

Mr. Bond was leaving the dining room after breakfast one morning, when there was a knock on the front door. He went to see who it was, followed closely by the two girls.

A tall, middle-aged woman with gray, staring eyes, and a tall, brunette girl were standing there.

"I'm Mrs. Gaynelle Snow and this is my daughter, Ruby. I've come to claim my part of my uncle's estate," the woman announced to Mr. Bond.

"Well, dad-blast it! If everyone in the continent ain't gonna try to claim John Shaw's property!" he shouted angrily.

"What did you say?" The woman stared at him with her sharp eyes, then peered to get a glimpse of Mandie and Polly behind him in the hall. *"Well,* if you're not going to invite me in, I guess I'll just walk in!" She pushed the old man aside and stepped into the hallway. "Where are the servants? Tell one of them to show me to my room!"

"Room! You'd think we was running a hotel here!" Mr. Bond stood there ruffling his white hair, trying to resolve the situation.

Liza was crossing the hall just then and the woman, followed by her daughter, yelled at her, "Hey, you there, find me a room in this mansion."

Liza stopped and stared at the woman and the girl and then looked at Mr. Bond.

"Might as well take them up to a room," he sighed. "Claim they're kinfolk. I'll have to prove them a lie before I can throw them out."

The girl turned her nose up at Polly and Mandie as she followed Liza and her mother up the stairs.

"Stupid ain't the word!" Polly exclaimed.

"Right you are!" Mandie agreed.

After the unexpected arrival of Mrs. Gaynelle Snow and her daughter, Ruby, things took on an even livelier pace at the John Shaw house.

Mandie and Polly took the notion to move into a bedroom on the third floor. They had grown tired of the room on the second floor where Bayne Locke always seemed to be lurking in the hallway watching their every move. Jason Bond warned they would be too frightened up there and wouldn't stay one night, if that long. But they in turn said they would stay no matter what happened.

Polly's mother, young, widowed, and longing for companionship, saw her chance for a trip to Philadelphia without her daughter, as long as the mystery seemed to be prolonged. Polly eagerly moved more of her things over to join Mandie in their new room on the third floor. Liza thoroughly cleaned the large bedroom for them, but was anxious to get back downstairs. All the servants were leery of the third floor and the attic.

The two girls were putting their things away in the drawers and the wardrobe, when Polly handed Mandie a cut glass jar full of powder. "Here's your powder, Mandie." Just as she reached for it, it slipped and fell to the floor, sprinkling the carpet and dusting Snowball, who gingerly jumped across the room, shaking his feet and licking his fur.

Mandie and Polly were doubled up in giggles at Snowball's action, when Mandie suddenly bent closer to the floor. "Hey, look! The key! Here's the key to the tunnel!" She picked it up from the carpet.

"The key to the tunnel!" exclaimed Polly. "You mean it was in the powder jar?"

"It must have been, it's right here in this pile of powder," Mandie told her. "I wonder where Liza got this jar, anyway."

And at that precise moment, Liza came through the doorway, carrying an armful of Mandie's belongings.

"Say, Liza, where did you get this jar of powder?" Mandie questioned, holding up the jar.

"Land sakes! You done went and spilled powder all over this here rug just after I cleaned it! Now why you want to do that?" Liza scolded her as she dropped the things onto the bed and stood there staring at the powder on the carpet.

"Sorry, Liza, it was an accident," Mandie told her, "but look what was in this jar—the key we've been looking for! Where did you get the jar, Liza?"

"Now let me see," she pondered. "I think it was on the bureau in the room that Mr. Locke is staying in. Yes, that's where it was," Liza went on. "I didn't think he needed that good-smelling powder, so I took it for you."

"Liza!" Mandie laughed. Then she turned to Polly. "Then Bayne Locke must have taken it from my room—the key, that is."

"I didn't think we could trust that man," Polly added.

"Hey, come on. Let's find Mr. Jason and take him to the tunnel," Mandie excitedly brushed the white powder off her skirt. "Let's go!"

They found Mr. Bond on the front porch.

"The key! We found the key! Let's go to the tunnel!" Mandie called as she and Polly ran on down the steps. Mr. Bond scratched his head and followed.

Breathlessly, the two girls pushed aside the bushes in front of the door. Mr. Bond reached for the door to unlock it, but it was already unlocked and standing wide open.

"Well, how do you like that?" Mr. Bond said, as he stepped inside.

"Now, we go for miles and miles before we come to the door into the main part of the house," Mandie told him.

And they walked and walked—down halls, up stairs and down again, and no door appeared to lead into the house at all. Instead, they found a panel in the wall slightly ajar.

"Look, that wall is open a little," Mandie whispered.

As Mr. Bond reached to touch it, the panel closed back into place and they could not even tell it had been open at all.

"Well, looks like it's not meant for us to get through," Mr. Bond said.

"I wonder how that panel got loose," Polly speculated.

"You girls probably knocked something loose on your travels down through here," Mr. Bond laughed.

"Guess we'll just have to go back out the way we came in," Mandie muttered. "But we're not going to give up."

"Nope, we're not," Polly confirmed. "Must be somebody on the other side of that wall, the way it closed so fast, and I know it was open, 'cause I saw it."

"Probably one of those ghosts we've been trying to catch up with," Mandie teased.

"Maybe we can find the other side of this tunnel now that we know the panel opens," Mr. Bond told them.

They left the tunnel the way they had entered. Mr. Bond locked the door and put the key in his pocket.

The three of them went back into the house and were climbing the steps to the third floor when they met Bayne Locke coming down. He grinned at them and would have gone on down the steps, but Mr. Bond stopped him.

"Look here, fellow, where have you been up that way?"

"Why, I've been up to the third floor," Bayne sarcastically replied. "Where'd you think I'd been?"

"What reason did you have to go up to the third floor?" Mr. Bond wanted to know.

"Hey, mister, you just work here. I am the nephew of the man who owned this house." Bayne was not grinning any longer.

"And I also happen to be in charge of Mr. Shaw's affairs until the will is located," Mr. Bond replied.

At that moment, Mrs. Snow and Ruby appeared at the top of the stairs to the third floor.

Mandie turned to them, "And what were you doing on the third floor?"

Mrs. Snow hurried down the steps, with her daughter at her heels. "What business is it of yours? I have as much right as you do to this house and everything in it. So, don't bother asking me any questions, because you certainly won't get any answers." She kept right on going down to the second floor, her daughter following and turning to make faces at the girls.

"That woman is no relative of mine!" Bayne Locke loudly proclaimed.

The woman turned back. "And Mr. Locke is no relative of mine." She and her daughter disappeared down the hallway below.

"Well, why don't you throw her out? She's certainly not kin to John Shaw!" assured Mr. Locke.

"Same reason I'm not throwing you out right now. I have to prove you're no kin before I can oust you from this house. But that day will come. You can be sure of that." Mr. Bond passed the younger man and went on up the stairs, Mandie and Polly following.

"Guess we won that time," Mandie remarked.

"Yeh, but who's gonna win the final say-so?" Polly replied.

They climbed the stairs all the way to the attic. It was dark and spooky, even though there were gabled windows to let in the daylight. The floor was covered with boxes, old furniture, trunks, dishes, clothes, and even an old organ.

"Now, the best thing to do is to go around the wall like this and tap on it to see if it will move," Mr. Bond told them as he rapped the wooden wall with his hand. "You two go around that way and I'll go this way."

Mandie and Polly did as he told them, laughing as they went, banging on the wall. They were almost all the way around the attic when they realized Mr. Bond was no longer with them.

"Polly! Mr. Bond! He's gone!" Mandie cried. "Where did he go?"

"I don't know. He was here just a minute ago. Maybe he's behind some of that old furniture. You go that way and I'll go this way and maybe we can find him," Polly told her.

As they worked their way around the room, they kept calling, "Mr. Bond! Mr. Bond! Where are you?"

Finally they met again.

"He's not here!" Mandie gasped.

At that moment, something scampered across the floor and both the girls screamed.

"Let's get out of here." Polly shouted, running for the door to the steps. Mandie, her heart pounding, followed close on her heels, and then she stopped suddenly as she looked back and saw Snowball beating an old piece of wood around with his paws.

"Oh, Snowball! Polly, it was Snowball!" She picked up the kitten.

"Well, anyway, let's get out of here." Polly ran ahead to the door.

They came down the steps into the front hall so fast they almost collided with Liza who was passing through with her arms full of bed linens.

"Hey, where you two going?" Liza stepped out of their way just in time.

"Liza, have you seen Mr. Bond? He disappeared," Mandie told her.

"I ain't seed him since he went up the steps with you two," Liza answered. "Why? What's wrong? Something wrong?"

Mandie immediately tried to compose herself, knowing the black girl would become frightened if they told her what had happened.

"Oh, nothing, we just missed him, I guess," Mandie said.

"Yeh, we stayed too long in the attic," Polly helped out.

"You been in the attic? Lawsy mercy, what you two done been doin' in that spooky place?" Liza's eyes widened. "Ain't you'ns askeered to go up there?"

"We just went up there looking for something, Liza. Come on, Polly, let's go out in the yard."

Once the two girls were out of Liza's sight they ran for the entrance to the tunnel.

"He's gotta be in the tunnel. He must've found the panel that opened up," Polly declared.

"Right. Maybe we can find the way in from the tunnel now," Mandie said as she ran on ahead and pushed at the door. "Oh, no, Mr. Bond locked it when we left, remember? And we don't have the key!"

"Guess we give up and go home and wait for him to come back from wherever he's gone," Polly lamented.

To their amazement, Mr. Bond was sitting in the swing on the front porch when they came around the corner of the house.

"Mr. Jason! Where did you go?" Mandie ran to him.

"Where did I go?" the old man asked.

"Yes, when we were in the attic, you just disappeared," Polly added.

"Oh, the attic—why, I just came on back downstairs."

"But we didn't see you leave," Mandie insisted.

"No, because some of that old furniture is taller than you two, I suppose." He smiled at the girls. "Did you get scared because I left you alone up there?"

"Oh, no, Mr. Jason. We were just trying to find you. We thought maybe you had found the secret panel," Mandie told him.

"The secret panel? Oh, the panel to the tunnel. No, I don't suppose there's an opening into the attic after all," Mr. Bond said.

The two girls looked at him and then at each other and didn't say anything else, but they went on inside the house and up to their room on the third floor.

"I don't believe him!" Mandie was emphatic about it.

"Neither do I!" Polly flopped down beside Mandie on the big bed.

"But why would he lie to us, Polly?"

"Must have a good reason."

"Well, after all, this is my uncle's house and Mr. Jason shouldn't keep secrets from me," Mandie moped.

"Nope."

"Well, don't you have any ideas?"

"I just can't figure this one out, Mandie. Everybody seems to be trying to hide something from everybody else."

"I know. Guess it's the money my uncle has. Money makes people fight sometimes, my father always told me. He always said it was better to be poor. Then you would know who your friends really are."

"Oh, Mandie, I don't agree with that at all. I'd just die if we were poor." Then Polly realized what she was saying. "Sorry, I forgot. I mean, I know you told me how poor your family is. But, anyway, don't you think it's better now, with all those new dresses and so much to eat, and servants to do all the work?"

"Well, I suppose. But look at the difference in things since Bayne Locke and that Mrs. Snow and her terrible Ruby came here. They're all after my uncle's money!"

"So what are we going to do about Mr. Jason now?"

"I suppose we'll have to watch him now, along with the others."

CHAPTER EIGHT

JOE COMES TO VISIT

The people who sat around the dining table at mealtime after that acted like enemies. There was very little conversation between any of the occupants of John Shaw's house.

Mr. Bond tried his best to carry on a conversation at the table one day at dinnertime, but Bayne Locke and Mrs. Snow and her daughter completely ignored him. The girls did not talk either, but continued to listen and watch everyone else. Mr. Bond only got curt answers to any questions he asked in an attempt to draw the girls out.

"Well, if this ain't the quietest bunch I ever seed in all my born days," Liza remarked as she brought in the dessert. "What's the matter—cat got all your tongues?"

Mandie laughed. "No, Liza, we just can't do two things at one time. If we're going to eat, we have to eat, and if we're going to talk, we just can't eat."

"Oh, I sees," Liza smiled at her. "Everybody must be starved to death." She twirled on out of the dining room with her arms full of dishes. "Most nonsense I ever heard of!"

"Well, guess she's right," Mr. Bond remarked, looking straight at the two girls. "But if everyone's starved to death, why is everyone leaving so much food on their plates?"

"Don't include me in that. I eat whatever I'm served," Mrs. Snow haughtily informed him.

"So do I," her daughter piped in.

"I'm always hungry. I always eat anything I can get my hands on," Bayne Locke said. "Food's too good to waste."

"That leaves me to answer, I suppose," Mandie volunteered. "My stomach doesn't feel too well lately. Too much excitement around. Besides, I'm not used to so much food at one meal."

"Well, I think eating is a silly habit and a waste of time when you could be doing something more interesting. Therefore, I only eat enough to keep from starving," Polly told them.

"Maybe the food will taste a little better at suppertime," Mr. Bond said as he rose from the table. "Although I didn't see anything wrong with what we just had."

There was a loud knock on the front door. Everyone was silent and listened. There were indistinct voices in the hall and Liza came hurrying into the dining room.

"Missy, you'se got company—the doctor man and his son," Liza announced to Mandie.

"Joe!" Mandie rushed from the room.

She greeted Dr. Woodard and Joe in the front hallway.

She grasped the old man's hand. "Dr. Woodard, I'm so glad to see you, and you, too, Joe." She turned a little shyly toward the boy. "Seems like ages since I saw y'all. Come on into the dining room and meet everybody. You'll probably want something to eat, anyway."

"Wow! Your uncle sure does have a big house," Joe commented.

"Hope you've been all right, Mandie," the old doctor squeezed her hand.

"Everybody," Mandie addressed all who were still at the table, "these are my friends, Dr. Woodard, and his son, Joe."

Liza was already setting two more plates and she motioned for them to sit down.

"Jason Bond, Doctor," Mr. Bond said, shaking his hand heartily. "Sit down, eat. You, too, young fellow." As the two sat down, Mr. Bond resumed his seat. Mandie took her place again, and then introduced each one around the table. "This is my friend, Polly Cornwallis. This is Bayne Locke, Mrs. Snow, and her daughter, Ruby. Now do help yourselves, Dr. Woodard, there's plenty to eat."

"Yes, I can see there is," Dr. Woodard said, piling his plate high, and turning to Joe who kept his eyes glued on Polly. "Joe, dig in, boy."

"Oh, yes, sir," Joe answered and began filling his plate, still stealing glances at Polly who was openly staring at him also.

"Where are you from, Dr. Woodard?" Bayne asked him.

"We live near where Amanda comes from, in Swain County," he answered between mouthfuls of green beans and cornbread. "Had to come to Franklin on some business and just thought we'd drop in to see how she was getting on."

"You know that Uncle John died?" Mandie questioned.

"Died? Why, no, I hadn't heard. When? What happened?" Dr. Woodard asked.

"He died right after I came here," she told him. "He was in Europe."

"It was very sudden, Doctor, from what his lawyer told me, and he was buried overseas," Mr. Bond added.

"Well, I'm very sorry to hear that," the doctor replied. "Your ma and sister are fine, Amanda. I saw them at the store yesterday."

"Oh, Dr. Woodard, please don't tell them where I am!" Mandie begged, as she quickly studied the doctor's face. "You—you haven't already, have you?"

"Well, as a matter of fact, I have, Amanda. But, now don't you worry. It's all right with your ma, if you want to stay here—but then, what's going to happen now that your uncle is gone?"

"You *told* her?" Mandie felt betrayed.

"Yes, I had to. There was a posse out looking for you all over Nantahala Mountain after you ran away from the Brysons. Just happened you had written Joe where you were going," Dr. Woodard told her. "I didn't want to, Amanda, but I had to. Those men were wasting their time. But like I said, your ma doesn't care if you stay here. She told me so. Will you stay on here, now that your uncle is dead?"

"Yes, I will," Mandie replied. "Mr. Bayne Locke says he is my uncle's nephew and Mrs. Snow says she is his niece. But, we haven't found the will yet, so we don't know what he left to whom."

"Well, that's a nice kettle of fish. Can't find the will, eh?" The doctor continued eating as he turned to Mr. Bond. "Say he has a will to be found yet?"

"That's right. His lawyer believes it's somewhere in this house but we haven't turned it up yet," Jason Bond told him. "And until we do, nothing can be settled."

Dr. Woodard turned to Bayne Locke and Mrs. Snow.

"I don't recollect Jim and John Shaw having any other living close relatives," he told them.

"That's because my mother, who was John Shaw's sister, Martha, died when I was born," Bayne told him.

"When you were born? Now, let me see, you must be twenty-two or twenty-three?"

"Twenty-two."

"Well now, twenty-two years ago I was in school with Jim Shaw and he didn't have a sister. As a matter of fact, I had known the family probably four or five years before that." The doctor was emphatic about this.

"Sorry, but he did have a sister and I am her son," Bayne Locke smiled crookedly at the doctor.

The doctor grunted his disapproval and turned to Mrs. Snow. "And you claim to be a niece? He didn't have any niece except Amanda here."

"Well, I don't know who you think you are, but I guess I know who I am." Mrs. Snow jumped up from the table and threw down her napkin. "Come on, Ruby, we have things to do." And they left the room in a hurry.

"Guess she's mighty sensitive about it," Dr. Woodard mumbled.

"You're absolutely right, Doc," Jason Bond told him. "I know these people are not kin to John Shaw, none of them excepting Amanda here, but I got to get proof before I can put them out. And that proof should be on the way any day."

Mandie finally noticed that Joe and Polly were staring at each other. Thinking they were both just being shy, she tried to start a conversation. "Joe, you just ought to see all the nice clothes Aunt Lou has made for me since I came here."

"Clothes? Aunt Lou? Oh, yes," Joe turned and smiled at her. "I see you have on a new frock. It's awfully pretty."

"Joe, maybe Dr. Woodard would let you visit with us for a while. We have this huge house with all these rooms and all this food," Mandie began.

"Could I, Dad?" Joe turned to his father and watched Polly out of the corner of his eye. "Could I stay here till you come back next week? Please?"

"Well, I don't know about that. There isn't any—"

"Please, Dr. Woodard!" Mandie begged.

Jason Bond tried to help her. "He's welcome, Doc, if he wants to stay. Like Amanda said, plenty of room and plenty to eat."

"What about clothes? What did you bring with you?" his father asked.

"You said we were going to be in Franklin two or three days, so I brought a change of everything," Joe replied. "Please, Dad."

"All right. I'm not sure what your mother will say, but I reckon it'll be all right," his father finally agreed.

"Whee!" Polly spoke at last and jumped up. "Let's show Joe around—all over—you know."

Mandie understood the "all over" to include the tunnel and she quickly left the room with them.

Joe, who inadvertently found himself between the two girls, was speechless with all the finery and rooms in the house, and most of all, the story about the tunnel. Mr. Bond still had the key and Mandie had to return to secretly ask him for it. He smiled and handed it to her.

Curious about the tunnel, Joe was glad that his father had allowed him to stay to visit; but Mandie wanted to talk to him alone and it was near suppertime before she had a chance. Mr. Bond went with Polly to her house next door to get more clothes and Mandie promptly asked Joe to sit in the swing on the front porch with her.

"I sure miss school, with you and everything, Joe," she told the boy.

"Me, too, Mandie. I never go over to your mother's house any-more, but I heard that Irene is getting seriously involved with Nimrod," Joe told her.

"Nimrod! Oh, well, they are two of a kind!" she laughed. "Joe, have you—do you ever—that is, were you ever up at my father's grave since I left?"

Joe reached over and took her hand in his. "Yes, I've been up there several times when I was with Dad in the neighborhood. I've tried to keep it cleaned off. And once in a while, I find some flowers growing along the way and I put them on his grave."

"Thank you, Joe!" She reached over and kissed him on the cheek. "You're the only real friend I ever had."

Joe blushed and squeezed her hand. "You, too, Mandie. You know, we will grow up someday. And I still plan on looking out for you."

"Oh, Joe!" Mandie became shy.

Polly came around the corner of the house suddenly and broke the spell.

"Goodness gracious! Holding hands!" she teased, as she stood in front of them.

Mandie and Joe both blushed then and the boy nervously watched Polly as she went into the house. Mandie caught the look and sensed some feeling between Joe and her friend, and wise beyond her years, did not give away the fact that she was upset over it. After all, Joe was going to be around until the next week. And after all, she had known Joe all her life and she was sure she came first with him.

CHAPTER NINE

UNCLE NED'S MESSAGE

The messenger Mr. Bond had sent to Lawyer Wilson's office returned early one morning, tied his horse to the hitching post at the road and came to the door to give his report.

"Morning, Jason," he said as Mr. Bond opened the door. "I jest got back and came straight hyar."

"Come in, Daniel," Mr. Bond greeted the man. "Come on into the kitchen and I'll see if we can't rustle up a cup of coffee."

"That would be nice, Jason," Daniel said, following him into the kitchen where Jenny, the cook, was washing the breakfast dishes.

"How about some coffee and something to eat with it for my friend here, Jenny? We'll just sit right here," Mr. Bond told her as they sat down at the table where the hired help ate their meals.

"Sho, Mr. Jason, comin' right up," Jenny said, bustling about.

"Did you have a good trip, Daniel?" Jason asked, as the man eyed the food being placed before him.

"Well, Tiddlywinks threw a shoe smack-dab in front of old man George's mansion and that was lucky 'cause his smithy put on a new 'un right then and thar. Otherwise, I tended to my bisness and had to wait fer Lawyer Wilson to come back to town," Daniel told him. "Then when he did git back, didn't do no good. He ain't never heerd of this hyar man, Locke, or that thar woman, Snow. Said they probably thought they could worm their way into some easy money."

"Well, that's exactly what I figured. I didn't believe a word of their stories. Now, what did he say I should do about it?" Jason Bond asked.

"Hyar, he writ you a letter." Daniel pulled out a folded envelope from his shirt pocket.

Jason took it, withdrew a letter on the lawyer's stationery, and read parts of it out loud. " 'Just leave things alone for the time being and I will begin a thorough investigation in order to get the proof we will need to evict them from John Shaw's house.' "

"Sounds like you gonna hafta put up with 'em a whit longer, eh?" Daniel gulped down the last of the strong coffee.

"I 'spec so. We'll have to do things legal-like so there won't be no repercussions," Jason agreed. "Dad-gum, I was hoping I could put them out in the street when you got back. Well, reckon I'll have to wait."

"They been causin' you any trouble?" Daniel asked.

"Not really. It's just that I don't trust them and I can't keep them in my sight all the time."

"Does the girl keep a lookout on 'em, too?"

"Yeh, Mandie and Polly follow them around some—that is, when they're around. I sorta figure Mandie has decided not to trust *me* either. She won't talk about things anymore. And we've got Doc Woodard's boy staying here for a few days from over in Swain County. The girls are more interested in him right now than in our impostors."

"Well, I gotta be ramblin' on home 'fore Sadie hyars I'm done back and ain't come home yit." Daniel rose and turned to Jenny. "Thet was right good, Jenny—good food."

"Yessuh," Jenny replied, smiling.

"You comin' back to town on Saturday?" Jason asked as he led the way to the front door.

"Yeh, reckon I'll have to git some things from the store," Daniel answered, walking on out to his horse.

"Stop by and I'll have the money then to pay you for the trip," Jason told him.

Daniel waved and was off down the road on his horse.

Mandie and Polly came out the front door while Jason still stood there on the porch. Joe was close behind them.

"Well, 1see Mr. Daniel got back," Mandie remarked.

"Yep, and Lawyer Wilson don't know nothing atall about these people we got staying here," Mr. Bond told her.

"Does that mean you can make them leave?" Polly asked.

"Nope, he's got to do some investigatin' first."

"Well, I hope it won't take long," Mandie said.

Mandie remembered this was the night that Uncle Ned was supposed to return with his information on the Snows and Bayne Locke. She also knew tomorrow was the day that Polly's mother was supposed to return home, and she was glad because jealousy had sprung up between the two girls over Joe. Not a word had been said, but each one sensed it. Mandie had been subconsciously possessive of Joe from the first day he had smiled at her, and she always felt he had eyes for her only.

Joe was attracted to Polly, but he did his best to remain loyal to Mandie. Polly was attracted to Joe and did nothing to disguise the fact.

"We're going over to my house, Mr. Jason. Mother is coming home tomorrow and I have to tell the cook," Polly told him, as the three went on down the front steps.

"Well, be sure you get back in time for supper," the old man called after them.

Polly bounded along the lane to her house. "Can't wait to see what Mother brings me."

"Is this the first time your mother ever went off and left you?" Joe asked.

"She didn't exactly leave me. I didn't want to go, so I persuaded her to let me stay with Mandie. I've always gone on trips with my mother, but this time I just didn't want to go. Too many interesting things going on," Polly told him. She turned to Mandie. "We sure fell down on our job of finding the will, didn't we?"

"Yeh, but it's bound to be somewhere. It will eventually be found," Mandie said.

"If we could only find the way into the tunnel from inside the house!" Polly sighed.

"Let's try again tonight. Three heads are better than two," Joe suggested.

"All right, except it'll have to be real late, because Uncle Ned is coming as soon as it gets dark," Mandie warned.

"Uncle Ned is coming? How do you know?" Joe asked.

"Because I sent him to Richmond to find out about Bayne Locke and this is the night he said he'd be back. He never fails to keep his word," Mandie assured him.

"Can I see him, this time? Please?" begged Polly. "You always tell me about him but I've never seen him."

"Oh, he's just a real old Indian," Joe told her.

"He's also kin to me somehow. I told you I'm part Cherokee," Mandie put in.

"That's right. I forgot you're an Indian papoose," teased Joe.

"That's not funny, Joe," Mandie snapped.

"Sorry, Mandie, I didn't mean any harm. It's just that I can't get used to the fact that your father was half Cherokee," he said, taking her hand in his, causing her heart to flutter.

"Well, you didn't answer my question. Can I see this kinfolk of yours, Mandie?" Polly tried to break the mood.

"I guess so. But you'll have to wait until I talk to him and tell him you want to meet him. Otherwise he'll run away if someone besides me shows up."

"Well, here we are," Polly said, as the huge house she lived in came into view behind the trees. "Come on, we'll beat Cook out of something good to eat."

Mandie met Uncle Ned that night in the summerhouse after dark, while Joe and Polly waited in the swing on the front porch.

"Uncle Ned, I knew you would come. You always do," she greeted the old man as he appeared from behind the big walnut trees shadowing the porch. "Sit down, Uncle Ned."

The Indian sat across from her and smiled. "Papoose have visitor, doctor son?"

"How did you know?" Mandie asked, smiling.

"Cherokee knows all," the old Indian told her. "Cherokee find people named Locke in big city."

"In Richmond?"

"In Richmond. People know Bayne Locke. People *not* know if Bayne Locke kin to John Shaw."

"They don't?"

"Cherokee stay in Richmond. Find people who know. Then I tell Papoose," Uncle Ned told her.

"So he did come from Richmond and he has relatives there. Well, at least we know that much," Mandie said.

"Must go now. Morning Star send love to Papoose," he said.

"Give her my love, too, Uncle Ned. But, before you go, please, wait a minute." Mandie grasped his arm as he rose. "My friend, Polly Cornwallis, wants to meet you. She and Joe are on the front porch. Is it all right if I bring them out here to see you?"

"Yes, but hurry," he grunted.

Going around the corner of the house, she beckoned to the two and they came hurrying toward her.

"Polly, this is Uncle Ned," Mandie proudly introduced him. "And Uncle Ned, you know Joe already."

Joe nodded and held out his hand to Uncle Ned. The Indian solemnly shook hands with a grunt.

Polly smiled up at the tall Indian. "How do you do, Uncle Ned? I've heard so much about you that I wanted to meet you."

"Pleased to see Papoose number two," the old man said.

Everyone laughed at his name for Polly. The sound carried to the house. Jason Bond stuck his head out of the upstairs window directly above.

"What's going on down there?" he yelled.

"Nothing, we're just getting some fresh night air," Mandie quickly replied, looking up at him.

At the sound of the other man's voice, Uncle Ned darted out of sight, whispering as he went, "Must go. See Papoose next moon."

Mandie silently waved to him as he disappeared into the shadows.

The three walked back to the front porch and sat down in the swing.

"Say, that was close, Mandie," Joe sighed.

"Sure was, but somehow I don't believe Mr. Jason would mind if I had an Indian friend—unlike the Brysons, who were out to kill every Indian they could find."

There was a slight stirring in the doorway behind them.

"No, I don't mind, Mandie," Mr. Bond said. "I see him every time he comes. And I know who he is."

"Oh, Mr. Jason, you scared me," was all Mandie could say.

"I'm sorry, didn't mean to frighten you. Did he get any information for you?"

"Well, how did you know that?" Mandie was surprised.

"I heard you talking to him the night you asked him to find out about these people," the old man said.

Mandie dropped her voice to a whisper and told him what the Indian had told her.

"That's good. I'll let Lawyer Wilson know. Now are y'all going upstairs? The parties in question are already turned in for the night."

"Let's do," Polly said.

"Sure, Mr. Jason. We haven't given up. We're going to look upstairs again for an entrance to the tunnel," Mandie chirped.

"Well, get to it then. I'm going back to my room. See you tomorrow." And he disappeared back into the dark hallway.

"Well, what are we waiting for?" Joe laughed.

The three softly crept up the steps to the third floor on their unending mission, being careful not to be heard by their mysterious visitors.

CHAPTER TEN

THE SECRET DOOR

Joe led the way, carrying an oil lamp, Mandie close behind with matches in her pocket in case it went out. Polly brought up the rear as they noiselessly tiptoed on up the steps to the attic. Even the old door cooperated by not creaking this time when Joe pushed it open. They moved very slowly and carefully around, whispering softly to each other as they made an inspection of the attic. Joe, still in the lead, held the lamp at arm's length, the light picking up the debris, as the girls closely peered at everything in their path.

Joe carefully inspected the walls and the ins and outs of the eaves and the dormer windows.

"It seems to be awfully solid. I don't see how this wall could open up anywhere and there isn't room for any steps behind it," Joe whispered to the girls.

"But, it has to open somewhere," Mandie insisted.

"Well, look at it. You can see the wall all the way around the house up here, except where it goes into the eaves and the eaves are not high enough to have steps going down," he insisted.

"All right, maybe that's the way it looks, but there's sure an opening somewhere because we found it on the other side in the tunnel," Polly told him.

"Well, if you want to, we can keep moving and check the wall out all the way around," Joe said.

The three silently pushed on the wall as they went, reaching high and low, examining every foot of it. They were all tense with the spooky atmosphere when suddenly there was a loud noise on the third floor.

"Sounds like someone is below us!" Mandie whispered.

"Could be that Mr. Locke or Mrs. Snow," Polly added.

"Come on, let's slip up on them and see who it is," Joe suggested, as he moved toward the door to the steps. "Stay close behind me, because I'm going to blow out the light."

"All right," Mandie said softly, as she and Polly held hands and Joe put out the lamp.

They felt their way down the dark steps to the door leading into the hall of the third floor. Joe put out his hand to caution them to be quiet as he slowly pushed the door open. It was still dark on the third floor hallway and there was no sign of a light or anyone around.

Mandie pulled at Joe's shirt. "Psst! Go left toward Uncle John's library."

Joe followed her directions and the three slipped along the passageway to the door of the library Mr. Bond had shown them the other day. As they reached it they heard a slight movement in the room.

"There's someone in there!" Joe whispered, putting his hand on the doorknob, the girls close behind him.

"Push it open," Mandie urged him.

With that, the three burst into the room which was in total darkness. A man's figure outlined by the moonlight from the window moved quickly toward the small door that had been locked the day Mr. Bond was with them, and to which no one had the key. Just as the figure reached the door, the three dived at him, pulling him to the floor.

"All right, we've got you!" Joe cried, as he held onto the man's coattail. The girls were snatching for his sleeves and kicking him in the shins.

"Hey, wait a minute! Let's get some light in here!" the man said quickly.

"No!" Joe shouted. "Here, Mandie, take the lamp and light it. I'll hold onto him!"

The man quit struggling and Mandie quickly lit the lamp with a match from her pocket. Then, holding the lamp, she stared into the man's face, her hand shaking violently.

"Oh, no!" she cried, unable to move.

"Mandie!" the man said, smiling at her.

"You can't be my Uncle John!" Mandie shook her head.

The man reached for her and took her into his arms as he passed the lamp on to Joe.

"But, I am!" He kissed her hair. "My dear little niece!"

"Then, you really are my Uncle John?" Mandie's voice trembled with excitement.

"Yes, I guess I played a mean trick on you," he told her.

Joe and Polly stood there staring and listening.

"But, Mandie, how do you know this man is your Uncle John? You said you had never seen him," Joe insisted.

"Yes, it is Mr. Shaw, Joe. My next-door neighbor, remember?" Polly assured him.

"He's just like my daddy! Can't you see that, Joe? You knew my daddy. He looks just like him, except maybe a little older." She leaned back to gaze into the smiling face—so familiar, yet different.

"Good guess. I'm fifteen years older," Uncle John said.

"But why did you make us think you were dead, Mr. Shaw?" Joe asked.

"Well, I guess I just wanted to see what would happen to my property when I do die. When I heard of my brother Jim's death, it was too late to see him, of course, but, thank the Lord, I had written him a letter before he died," he said, sitting down at the desk. "You see, there's been hard feelings between the two of us since before you were born, Amanda. Then when I learned that he—was gone, I knew you were my only living relative, and since you are so young, I had to find out just whom I could trust to look out for you if anything happened to me."

"Then Bayne Locke and the Snows are no kin to you?" Mandie sat on the floor at his knee, while Joe and Polly hovered nearby fascinated with their discovery.

"Absolutely none! And I want them out of my house immediately! I had to take my lawyer into my confidence to send the message of my demise and of course he knows they are no kin, but he would have to prove it to stand up in court."

"But, Uncle John, where have you been all this time?" Mandie wanted to know. "That is, since I've been here."

"I've been living with my people—the Cherokees." He smiled at the girl. "Remember, we *are* part Cherokee."

"You've been living with the Cherokees? Then Uncle Ned must have known all along what was going on!" she reasoned.

"Yes, I came home with him when he saw you out in the yard earlier tonight. I could see things were getting out of hand, with no one able to find my will and all. However, I didn't know you children were occupying rooms on the third floor, and you almost caught me when you got the lamp from Amanda's room and went to the attic."

"Well, where is that will?" Polly put in.

"It's under the carpet over there by the door," he said, pointing toward the small door which was still closed.

"Under the carpet?" All three gasped and then laughed.

"What a good place to hide it!" Joe exclaimed.

"Where does the door lead to, Uncle John?" Mandie questioned. "Mr. Jason tried to open it, but it was locked and he didn't have the key."

"Oh, he has no idea where that door leads. He has never had a key. I have the only key." He pulled it from his pocket and got up to walk to the door. "Here, you want to see what's behind here?"

Mandie scrambled after him, Polly and Joe crowding closely behind her. John Shaw put the key in the lock, turned it with a click, and pushed open the door. Behind it was a paneled wall. Reaching to one side he pushed a latch and one panel swung aside. And there before them was the entrance to the tunnel.

He smiled as the three gasped in surprise.

"Uncle John!" Mandie covered her mouth with her hands.

"If we only could have found a way to unlock that door!" Polly moaned.

"And all this time you have been trying to open a wall in the attic!" Joe laughed.

"The tunnel stops here. It doesn't go up to the attic," Uncle John told them.

"But, what is the tunnel for?" Mandie asked.

"My grandfather, your great-grandfather, Amanda, who was also named Jim Shaw, built this house at the time the Cherokees were being run out of North Carolina. He didn't believe in the cruel way the Indians were being treated and he had this tunnel built for them. He hid dozens of Cherokees in there, fed and clothed them, and then helped them on their way when things calmed down along about 1842, and they could set up living quarters somewhere else," John Shaw told her. "That was the way my father met my mother. He was twenty-eight years old and had never been married when he met my mother. She was only eighteen, a beautiful young Indian girl."

"She was beautiful, Uncle John?" Mandie grasped his hand.

"Very beautiful, Amanda. I have her portrait. The frame needed redoing. It's in Asheville now, being refinished. You'll see it when it comes back."

"Oh, Uncle John, I'm so happy!" Tears filled Mandie's eyes as she looked up into her uncle's face. "I'm so happy you are—not—are still alive!"

At that moment, there was the sound of footsteps in the hall. Jason Bond appeared in the doorway and almost dropped the lamp he was carrying when he saw John Shaw standing there.

"Mr.—Mr.—S—Shaw!" he stammered.

"Yes, it's me, Jason. Sorry I couldn't let you in on the secret, but no one knew I was really and truly alive except Ed Wilson," John Shaw told him. "And I must say you've played your part well, Jason. You can be trusted." John Shaw explained everything to Jason Bond, who still stood there gaping and trembling.

"Oh, dear," Jason muttered as he learned the truth. "I—I'm sure glad you're back, Mr. Shaw. It sure straightens out a lot of problems. Like these people that moved in here—"

"Yes, I know. I knew about them as soon as they arrived. Uncle Ned kept me informed as to what was going on. Sorry you had to put up with them, but as soon as the sun rises they will be hitting the road."

And that was the way it happened. Upon being confronted by the real, living John Shaw, Bayne Locke, Mrs. Snow, and her daughter were all too glad to pack up their belongings and leave the next morning.

Mandie stood on the porch holding her uncle's hand as the three made their abrupt exit. She breathed a sigh of relief.

"Now maybe things will simmer down!" she exclaimed.

"Well, no, actually things are just beginning to happen! I'm expecting company from Asheville." He squeezed her hand.

Joe and Polly, standing nearby, looked at each other and Polly said, "Well, my mother is coming home today. So that eliminates one more guest from this house."

Joe scratched his head. "Don't know when Dad will come back for me, but it should be sometime this week."

John Shaw turned to them and said, "Well, let's not everybody leave at once! I thought we could have a little party when the company arrives from Asheville."

The three young people grinned at each other. *A party? What fun!* Mandie had not the faintest idea as to the importance of the party or the people who would be visiting. She merely knew it would be her very first *real* party.

CHAPTER ELEVEN

THE TRUTH REVEALED

The return of John Shaw was truly a happy event in the household. Every piece of furniture in the house was polished, silverware was cleaned, the best linens laid out for use, and two guest rooms readied for the two mysterious visitors who were coming from Asheville.

Mandie moved back to her room on the second floor. Joe also moved his things down to a room on the same floor. Everyone was excited, but no one could find out the names of the expected guests and John Shaw remained secretive about the whole thing.

Polly's mother returned and Polly moved back home, but came to visit Mandie every day. Joe received a note from his father saying there was a sudden outbreak of fever and he was needed so badly he couldn't come for him until things were under control.

Early one bright, sunshiny morning John Shaw drew Mandie off into the parlor.

"Today is the day the company's coming. Now, I want you to put on your loveliest dress and brush your hair until it shines—that is, if it will shine any more than it does already."

"Oh, Uncle John, I'm *so* excited! I don't even know these people, but I'll do my best to look and act like a lady," she promised him.

"That's all I ask, and I know you will." The old man smiled and her heart melted as the memory of her father's smile flooded back to her.

Mandie hurried off to her room and enlisted the aid of Liza to button her up in the newest dress that had been made for her. It was made of snow-white muslin covered with sprigs of bluebells that matched her blue eyes. Liza combed out her long blonde hair and let it hang loose in ringlets.

"Miss Amanda, you are really and truly beautiful today," Liza said, admiring the finished product.

Mandie laughed nervously. "Why do you say that, Liza, because you made me that way with all your fussing?"

"Nope, you just got that natural bloom today. Wouldn't doubt but that Joe boy tries to put some sugar on them lips if he catches you by yourself," Liza teased her.

Mandie blushed. "Oh, Liza, quit that silly talk. You know Joe has been my friend all my life. But, he's *not* my boyfriend."

"No, he ain't no boyfriend yet, but I can tell he'd *like* to be," Liza answered solemnly. "One of these days you'll know."

"Do you really think so, Liza?" Mandie turned to stare at the black girl.

"Sho as I'm astandin' here." Liza crossed her arms over her bosom. "You wait and see. And 'member I told you so."

Mandie's cheeks were still rosy. "Liza, do you think Uncle John will approve of the way I look?"

" 'Course he will. Now, you'd best be gittin' on down there to the parlor and act like a lady. Company comin' any minute now." Liza hurried her down the steps to the parlor where Uncle John was waiting.

"Where's Joe? Isn't he dressed yet?" Mandie looked around.

"First of all, my dear niece, you are absolutely lovely," her uncle told her. "As for Joe, I sent him on an errand. He won't be back for a while."

"Oh," was all she could say. She had been counting on Joe's support at her side to meet these important strangers who were coming to visit.

At that moment, there was the sound of creaking wagon wheels and horses stopping out front, and John Shaw turned quickly to her. "Supposing you wait right here, my dear. I'll meet the company at the door and bring them in to meet you shortly."

"Yes, sir, Uncle John," she agreed and he quickly left the room.

Mandie could hear women's voices at the door, one sounded older and one quite young; there was also the soft speech of a black woman, and Aunt Lou was directing them inside with the baggage.

"John Shaw, you could give a person more time to get things together for such a trip," the younger voice was teasingly greeting Mandie's uncle.

"My, yes, you'd think someone was dying, instead of it being a party we are coming to," agreed the older woman.

"Well, I think you'll find the party well worth your sudden trip. Come on in here to the parlor. I want you to meet my other guest," John Shaw was saying.

"Really, John, we should freshen up a bit first," the younger woman was hesitating.

"Nonsense, you never looked lovelier. Come on," he insisted.

John Shaw appeared at the doorway to the parlor, accompanied by the most beautiful young woman Mandie had ever seen. She was dressed in rich silks, with diamonds sparkling on her fingers, and the scent of perfume came with her into the room. She had piles of shining golden hair, sparkling blue eyes, and a complexion that looked as though it had never been exposed to the sun's rays.

Mandie could hardly take her eyes off the younger woman, but snatched a look at the heavy-set, bustling matron, also dressed in the finest and most fashionable clothes Mandie had ever seen.

John Shaw hesitated. "Amanda, this is Elizabeth—you read about her in my letter to your father that night—"

The young girl was overwhelmed. So, this was the woman who had loved her father. She rushed forward to take her dainty hand. Elizabeth kept staring at Mandie and the older woman caught her breath and stood as if frozen to the spot.

Elizabeth was quite flustered as she turned to John Shaw. "John, who is this girl?"

John Shaw put one arm around Elizabeth and the other around Mandie.

"Elizabeth, this is your daughter, Amanda Elizabeth—"

The young woman trembled violently and John led her to a sofa to sit down, while Mandie, not quite comprehending the situation, trailed along, still holding onto her hand.

"Sorry it had to be such a shock, but I only found out the truth myself just a few months ago," John told her.

The older woman had finally found her voice. "John Shaw, just what kind of trick are you playing?"

"It's no trick, Mrs. Taft. You, of all people, know that. You knew that Elizabeth's baby didn't—"

John was interrupted by Mandie's urgent tugging at his coat. "Uncle John, what—who—"

Elizabeth and Mandie were staring at each other, speechless.

"John, it can't be. You know my baby died," Elizabeth kept repeating. Then she turned to Mandie, "Do you know your birthdate, child?"

"Oh, yes, I was born June 6, 1888," Mandie managed to say.

"Your baby did not die, Elizabeth. This is your baby—grown to a full twelve years old, never knowing who her real mother was," John was telling the young woman.

"John Shaw, you are only making trouble, you know that," Mrs. Taft was warning him as she sank into a deep chair.

"Uncle John, please—" Mandie begged.

"Yes, my child, this is your real mother, and this dear woman is your real grandmother," John finally turned to Mandie.

"It is quite a long story. Your mother, Elizabeth Taft, ran away and married your father thirteen years ago, but her parents opposed the marriage because your father was half Indian. Your father had lived here with me before that. Elizabeth's parents managed to have the marriage annulled and moved to Asheville to get away from your father's influence. Then, they discovered Elizabeth to be expecting a child. So, they sent her to an aunt's house in Madison County where you were born. They told your mother you died at birth, and persuaded your father to take you, telling him that Elizabeth had agreed she had made a mistake and didn't even want to see you. Then Jim pulled up stakes—"

"Oh, no, no! It must be a lie! To think my own mother and father could have done such a thing to me!" Elizabeth sobbed.

"Jim took you, Amanda, off to Swain County and had the misfortune of meeting Etta McHan, a widow with a daughter, who immediately latched onto him and got him to the altar. He never came to Franklin again, that I know of. You see, he and I were both in love with Elizabeth and he figured I had a hand in breaking up his marriage, but, so help me God, I never even knew you existed until a few months ago," John Shaw continued.

"That, that—woman—in my father's house—is not my real mother?" Mandie could hardly believe it.

"That's right. Not one whit kin to you, nor is her daughter. And I have Uncle Ned to thank for informing me of your father's death and of your existence. And, Amanda, he did get my letter about Elizabeth before he passed on and after I put two and two together, he wrote me about you."

"Then, you actually didn't know about me, Uncle John?"

"No, not until just before your father passed away. You see, Jim never came back to the house here. He just went off without ever seeing me and I had no idea he had taken a baby with him. I also fell for the lie about your death," her uncle said.

"Honor thy mother," Mandie was mumbling to herself.

Elizabeth, trying to recover from the shock, suddenly stretched out her arms to Mandie. "I've always had a strange feeling—Come to me, my—my daughter!" Mandie rushed into her arms and their tears mingled, as Mandie babbled incoherently, "Oh, Mother, Mother, my very own *real* mother! I'm so, so glad! I'm so happy! Thank you, dear God! Thank you, dear God!"

John Shaw turned to Mrs. Taft who was silently wiping tears from her chubby cheeks. "I'm sorry I had to do that but, but I had to. Let's leave them be, now. Come on, I'll show you to your room where you can be comfortable." He offered his arm and without a word the old lady rose and left the room with him.

"Let me look at my beautiful daughter!" Elizabeth held Mandie at arm's length. "And all those years I've missed being with you. Oh, my baby!" She held Mandie close. "I won't miss another minute away from you. You can be sure of that, my darling. And your father, Amanda—I loved him so much." Tears glistened in her eyes. "It's too late now for that, but it's not too late to claim my own daughter."

"My father never loved that—that woman. I'm sure of that," Mandie told her. "She never loved him either. Oh, *why* didn't my father tell me who my own mother was?"

"Don't blame him, my child. If anyone is to blame, it's myself. I shouldn't have given him up so easily," Elizabeth told her as she stroked the girl's soft, blonde curls. "And believe me, I will never give you up."

"Oh, Mother!" Mandie cried.

"And you know—we have the same name. Your father named you Amanda Elizabeth, which is my own name. That proves he loved me, doesn't it?"

"Yes, yes, 1know he must have loved you, Mother, because he never loved anyone else."

Upon learning who the visitors were, Joe was overwhelmed and Polly could only stare at the beautiful young woman. And Mandie would not let her mother out of her sight, and was reluctant to go to bed that night, even though she would be close by.

Mandie knelt by her bed that night and thanked God. "Oh, God, you are so good to me! I know now that you do love me. All the trials and troubles I had to go through were necessary to bring back my own real mother. Please forgive me for ever doubting that you loved me. I should have remembered—*'The Lord is my Shepherd, I shall not want!'* "

And while Amanda tossed and turned in her bed, too excited to go to sleep, John Shaw and Elizabeth Taft were alone in the parlor. Mrs. Taft had retired early, complaining of being tired from her journey, but, actually, glad to get away from the two who had stirred up the secret past.

It had started to rain after supper, and John lit the fire in the parlor to keep out the sudden, damp chill that so often came in the mountains. He and Elizabeth were sitting on a low sofa in front of the fireplace, silently watching the flames jump and sing as they raced up the chimney. Neither had spoken a word after bidding Mandie and Mrs. Taft good night.

Finally, John leaned closer, covering her small white hand with his larger rough one. "Elizabeth—"

"Yes, John—" Elizabeth breathed softly, placing her other hand on top of his.

"It's—it's been a long time—" John faltered.

"Too long, John. And even now, Mother didn't want to come to your house. I threatened to make the trip by myself and then she gave in. I really believe she was afraid to face you after all these years," Elizabeth said.

"Well, I imagine she must have realized that somehow your trip here concerned Jim."

"Yes, an old friend of thirteen years ago doesn't just suddenly invite you to 'a most important occasion' at his house without good reason, and what good reason it was, John!" She smiled at him as tears of happiness filled her eyes.

"Elizabeth, I wish I had known the truth years ago. Even though I was in love with you, I would have done anything I could to get you and Jim back together."

"John, I can never thank you enough for giving me back my daughter," she said, squeezing his hand between hers.

John turned to her, "Then, Elizabeth, would you consider sharing her with me, now that—"

"Oh, John, no, don't say that. I don't want to hurt you, but you know how much I loved Jim. I've never looked at another man."

"I know that, Elizabeth. But he was my brother and he is no longer with us. I would be willing to take a chance because I love you so much."

"But that wouldn't be fair to you—" she hesitated.

"That's for me to decide. It would be enough to know that you were finally mine."

"John, I just don't know. I really am truly fond of you, but in a different way from the way I loved Jim."

"I know that. But, I'm hoping that with time you will love me, too. It would be wonderful to share Amanda with you, too. She is the only living relative I have left, except some distant Cherokee cousins."

Elizabeth was silent for a few moments. "Let me think it over tonight. And I'll see you at breakfast—early," she said, rising as he still held both her hands.

"Fine, Elizabeth. I hope you sleep well and have pleasant dreams of me." He laughed. "I don't imagine you will sleep a wink after all the excitement, but, anyway, you are right. It is time to retire. I'll be up with the birds in the morning, and I hope I have something to sing about." He bent and kissed her lightly on the lips.

Elizabeth looked solemnly up into his face. "Until then, John."

CHAPTER TWELVE

THE WEDDING

After hours of tossing, unable to sleep, Mandie finally slept soundly for two hours then awoke with a start. She sat straight up in bed, trying to remember what was so special. The first streaks of light were in the sky and she could hear the twittering of the birds in the tree outside her window.

Then it suddenly came to her. Her mother—her real mother—her very own mother was here in this house!

She bounced out of bed and hastily snatching clothes from the drawers and the wardrobe she was quickly dressed. She quietly opened her door and crept down the long stairway.

The smell of fresh coffee was in the air and she knew Jenny must be up. Slipping into the kitchen, she found Aunt Lou busily giving the day's instructions to Jenny, who was rolling out the dough for the morning's biscuits.

"Aunt Lou, is my mother up yet?" Mandie quickly asked the old woman, who was startled by the sudden presence behind her.

"She ain't been in here if she is, my child," Aunt Lou smiled and put her arm around the girl. "Set yo'self down over there. I'll get fresh milk for you while you wait on dat important lady."

Mandie smiled and sat down at the table. Aunt Lou wiped one hand on her apron and poured a glass of milk from the pitcher on the sideboard.

"Here, you drink this. You ain't et a bite since them people come here. Your stomach's gonna be stuck to your backbone, first thing you know."

Mandie laughed and gulped the milk down. "Thank you, Aunt Lou. My stomach does feel kinda hungry."

Liza breezed into the kitchen. "Lady's in the dining room. Mr. John, too."

Mandie scrambled to her feet and ran for the door, "Oh, I have to go. Thank you, Aunt Lou. Thank you, Liza." Then turning back, she added, "And thank you, Jenny! *Thanks, everybody!*"

She hurried through the door, then slowed down to approach her mother and Uncle John who sat at the table. They both turned to smile at her.

"Good morning, Mother. Good morning, Uncle John," she greeted them, slipping into a chair at the side across from the two of them. The thought of her real mother being present still seemed a bit strange to her.

"Good morning, my darling. I hope you slept well." Elizabeth reached over to pat her hand.

"Good morning, my dear," Uncle John said, watching the two.

"Mother, I thought about it all night last night. Where are we going to live?" Mandie questioned.

"Why, we'll go back to Asheville, of course," Elizabeth told her.

"But, couldn't we stay here with Uncle John? You see, I've just found him, too, and I'd like to get to know him. He looks so much like my father." Mandie looked from one to the other.

"Well, Elizabeth?" John queried.

"Well, John—" the young woman began.

Mandie nervously interrupted. "I was thinking about this so much I couldn't sleep last night and I think I have a good solution to our problem."

"Why, what's that?" Uncle John asked.

"Well, it's like this," Mandie began, and then paused to look from one to the other. "Mother, if you and Uncle John would just get married, then we could all stay together here for always!"

Elizabeth laughed hysterically. "And here I was afraid to express my own mind for fear my daughter wouldn't like it."

John laughed, too. "Has Amanda answered my question, then, Elizabeth?"

Mandie was confused by the conversation, and was trying to figure out what they were talking about, when Elizabeth turned to her daughter. "You see, dear, your Uncle John asked me last night to marry him—"

"He did? Oh, Mother! Oh, Uncle John!" Mandie cried, and got up and ran around to embrace them both.

Elizabeth finished her sentence. "And I told him I had to think about it overnight. I was really afraid you wouldn't approve."

"Oh, Mother, he's my father's brother!" Mandie exclaimed.

"Amanda, my child!" Uncle John got up to put his arms around the girl. She looked up into his face and saw the strong resemblance of her father. She buried her face against his chest.

"You have my answer, John dear," Elizabeth told him.

Just then, Mrs. Taft came through the doorway. Mandie ran to her, grabbing her hand and leading her to the table.

"Guess what, Mrs.—Grandmother—you are my grandmother, you know," she told her as she pulled out a chair across the table from her mother.

"Yes," the old lady grudgingly admitted as she sat down.

"Guess what, Grandmother?" Mandie plopped down beside her. "My mother and my Uncle John are going to get married!"

Mrs. Taft darted a glance at the two. "This is quite sudden, isn't it, Elizabeth?"

"Not as sudden as you think, Mother. You see, John has been asking me to marry him for the last fifteen years, through the mail," Elizabeth told her mother, and winked at John.

"That's right, Mrs. Taft. I never gave up," John laughed.

Mandie cut in. "But it was my idea, really. I told them if they would just get married, then Mother and I could live here. We wouldn't have to go to Asheville."

"Oh—so you won't live in Asheville?" the old lady asked. "Well, Amanda, you haven't seen our home in Asheville yet. Your grandfather was one of the richest men in the country and when he died ten years ago, he left a fortune to your mother and me."

"Oh, that's very nice, Grandmother, but I'd really prefer living here where my father used to live," Mandie told her. She looked around the huge room. "Just think. He used to eat in this very room. Oh, I loved him so much."

Elizabeth turned to her mother. "You don't really need me, Mother. You have all the servants. I think Amanda has a good idea. We'll just live here and be on our own."

"Don't tell me you are allowing a child to make such important decisions for you!" the old lady rebuked her daughter.

"No, Amanda did not make any decisions for me. John asked me last night to marry him and I was ready to say yes this morning, provided we lived in this house. You are welcome to stay, Mother, of course, but this will be our home."

"Well, I was just—I didn't—" the old woman was quite ruffled at having her daughter speak to her in such a way.

"It is better this way, Mrs. Taft," John added. "I would never think of parting with this house. It's to be Amanda's at the time of my death, and I trust she keeps it in the family."

"Have it your way, then. I'll go back to Asheville where I have friends," Mrs. Taft replied curtly, then added, "After the wedding, that is, so I hope you won't delay too long with your plans."

Plans were indeed rapidly made. Dresses were ordered, the house refurbished, and guests invited. Elizabeth insisted on having Uncle Ned come to the wedding. After all, he was kinpeople to her new family.

Dr. Woodard finally came for Joe, but promised to return with Mrs. Woodard for the wedding. Mandie was surprised to learn that Dr. Woodard and her mother seemed to know each other from way back.

Polly and her mother paid them a formal call and Mandie was again surprised to find that Polly's mother also knew her mother from long ago. Actually, Mandie's mother had been born and raised and lived in Franklin until her father moved to Asheville when she was sixteen. And there he had built their mansion.

It seemed to Mandie that everyone in town was talking about the forthcoming wedding and had been invited to attend. Things moved along quickly and the day soon was upon them.

Uncle Ned arrived and was given a guest room, even though he felt very uncomfortable among the white people. Mandie and Polly were the bride's attendants. Joe and his father stood for Uncle John. The ceremony took place on a warm September afternoon in the chapel of the church across the road where John Shaw was a member and where Elizabeth Taft had belonged before moving out of town.

Everything seemed like a dream to Mandie—all white, full of clouds and scents of flowers, soft music, and whispering voices. Her feet never seemed to touch the floor as she floated down the aisle with her bouquet. She was so happy, she was afraid she would awaken and find it was not true. She faintly heard the wedding march. She barely understood the words of the pastor. And when her mother and her uncle floated back down the aisle together and out through the door of the church, she pinched herself to be sure it was real.

The drawing room of Uncle John's house had been transformed into a wonderland for the reception. There were flowers, greenery, and candles everywhere. Mandie darted in and out through the room to keep from missing anything. She had never known there could be such happiness. She caught a glimpse of her grandmother sitting alone in a corner and tried to talk to her, but the old lady had little to say to anyone except Jason Bond, whom she had charmed.

"Hey, slow down, Mandie," Joe said as he caught her arm at the corner of the long table holding the cake and punch bowl. "Where're you going in such an all-fired hurry?"

"Ain't goin' nowhere," she teased him.

"Ain't goin' nowhere? I think you'd better go somewhere—back to school if that's the way you're going to talk," Joe laughed.

"Oh, yes, I'm going back to school, all the way through, with years and years of education," Mandie continued to joke with him.

"But not *too* many years," Joe said, as he moved closer. "I don't want you to know more than I do."

"Know more than you do?" she asked, twirling her long silk skirts.

"That's right. I don't want my wife to be smarter than I am," he said, reaching to grasp her hand.

"Wife?" Mandie shot back.

"You heard right. I said my wife. I'm asking you now to become my wife—that is, when we get all educated and grown up, and all that, of course," he said, looking seriously into her blue eyes.

"Oh, Joe Woodard, you're not old enough to propose," she teased.

"I'm old enough to know what I want," he said. "Well, what is your answer? Will you be my wife—someday?"

Mandie became solemn. "I'll have to think about it, Joe. Too much has happened lately."

"I'll wait for your answer. Whenever you make up your mind let me know," he said, squeezing her hand hard.

"Holding hands in public! Shame! Shame!" Polly appeared at Mandie's side.

"Well, shame on you for being so nosy!" Mandie retorted.

"I have to look where I'm going, don't I? I couldn't just close my eyes as I passed," Polly scolded.

"Let's go talk to Uncle Ned. He looks kinda left out over there in the corner," Mandie remarked, and the three moved across the room to where the old Indian was sitting on a stool quietly taking in the whole scene.

Mandie was so happy she was giddy. As she approached the old man, she laughed, "Uncle Ned, will you come to my wedding? Joe has asked me to marry him!"

Polly stared at Joe in disbelief. Joe blushed and slipped away across the room.

"When Papoose gets to be squaw, then I come to wedding," Uncle Ned smiled.

"Joe!" Mandie called after him. "I didn't mean—don't be angry with me!" But he ignored her and kept going.

"Uncle Ned, I guess I said the wrong thing, but everything is so out-of-this-world right now, I can hardly cope." Mandie put her arm around the old Indian. "I'm so glad you came."

Mandie didn't get a chance to see Joe again, alone, and he and his father left early the next morning. Then she learned that her mother and her new stvepfather were going to Swain County to visit her father's grave and his Cherokee kinpeople, and she was to go with them.

Uncle Ned went ahead to prepare the Cherokees for the visit. Mandie still could not comprehend; so much was happening. All her young life she had never known what it was to be really and truly happy. She thanked God every night for being so good to her.

To top off the excitement, they went by train. Mandie had never been inside a real train before. It was stuffy and dirty, but to her it was like a chariot from Heaven. At the station, Dr. Woodard, his wife, and Joe met them, and they went to spend the night at their house. Mandie knew she would get a chance to see Joe alone, sooner or later.

After supper, as the older people were sitting around discussing old times, Mandie asked Joe to show her his dog's new puppies. They went outside and into the barn where Samantha was giving her four offspring their supper. She flapped her tail when she saw Joe approaching, but kept right on with her duties. She was a golden brown mixed breed and her puppies were a variety of colors.

"Joe, they are beautiful! But, they're so little! Watch that black one! What a little pig. He keeps rooting the others away," the girl laughed.

"They might let him push and shove, but they get their share," Joe assured her. Then he turned abruptly to her, "Well, did you make up your mind?"

Mandie blushed. "Oh, Joe, I'm really and truly sorry for the way I acted at the wedding. I was just plain in the clouds during the whole time. I acted so foolishly."

Joe dropped his head and kicked at the straw on the floor. Then he looked straight into her eyes. "That's all right, Mandie. I understand. After all, it isn't every day one finds their real mother and then gets a stepfather, too."

"It's all so unreal," she said quietly.

"But, you still didn't tell me. Did you make up your mind about us?" He was determined.

"I've been thinking about it, Joe. I'll—I'll let you know tomorrow," she promised him.

"All right, tomorrow I'll expect your answer," He turned to the doorway. "Let's go back to the house. I'm hungry. How about you?" He took her hand and they laughed together.

The next day was like opening an old scrapbook and reliving the old memories. They all piled into the Woodards' wagon and began their journey up the mountainside. They approached the cemetery from the opposite side and did not pass Jim Shaw's house.

At the sight of the graveyard, Mandie jumped from the moving wagon and hurried to kneel at her father's grave. There were several withered bunches of wild flowers which Joe, true to his word, had put there. The Woodards stayed in the wagon while John helped Elizabeth down and together they joined Mandie in silence, standing hand in hand, and gazing at the mound of dirt which had settled considerably from the rain.

Mandie's memories of the day of the funeral came flooding back and tears flowed down her cheeks. If only her father could see them all now. She suddenly burst into uncontrollable sobs, and in a flash Joe jumped from the wagon and flew to her side.

Elizabeth blinked back the tears as John squeezed her hand and pulled out a clean white handkerchief, carefully wiping first her tears and then his own.

"We all loved him, John," she whispered as she moved closer.

"Yes, we all loved him, my darling," John replied, holding her tightly.

Joe was whispering. "Mandie, he can't hear you. He's in Heaven."

"I know that! I know that!" she sobbed.

It was a silent group who came down the mountain through Charley Gap in sight of Jim Shaw's house. As soon as she spotted the house, Mandie reached instinctively for Joe's hand.

"Joe, I'll marry you when we get grown, if you'll get back my father's house for me." A sob caught in her throat.

Joe put his arm around her. "I will, I promise I will, Mandie." He roughly planted a kiss on her cheek as the wagon jolted them along the bumpy trail and Amanda slid closer and smiled.

"Guess we'll be seeing your Cherokee kinpeople next," Joe said.

"Yes," Amanda whispered, afraid to breathe for fear she would awaken and find it all a dream. "Thank you, God. Thank you for everything. My cup runneth over." She lifted her face to the morning sun.

Somehow, the secret tunnel back home seemed far away and unimportant.

MANDIE

AND THE

CHEROKEE LEGEND

For My Brother and My Sisters,

James Matthew Leppard,
Margaret Louise Leppard Langer,
Sibyl Belle Leppard Langford,

In Memory of Our Childhood Joys and Sorrows.

CONTENTS

MANDIE AND THE CHEROKEE LEGEND

"Blessed are they which are
persecuted for righteousness' sake;
for theirs is the kingdom of heaven."
(Matthew 5:10)

CHAPTER ONE

MANDIE AND THE PANTHER

Mandie sat with her feet dangling in the cool water of the Tuckasegee River. Her white kitten, Snowball, played at the edge of the rocks. It was a hot day for the North Carolina mountains and Mandie was tired. Slipping away from the others, she had hastily pulled off her shoes and stockings, thrown her bonnet on a nearby bush, and run down the bank to the river.

She had left her fine clothes at home and traveled in calico. Mandie and her new family were on their way to visit her Cherokee kinpeople, none of whom she had ever seen. She was wondering if the Cherokees would like her. After all, she was only one-fourth Cherokee herself, and not only that, she didn't even look like an Indian with her long blonde hair and bright blue eyes.

It was so important to Mandie that the Cherokees like her, because they were her father's people, and her dear father was now in heaven.

A faint sound behind Mandie startled her, bringing her out of her reverie. She was so frightened, it took all her willpower to turn her head to see what it was. To her horror, directly behind her the beady eyes of a panther watched as it crouched menacingly in a chestnut tree, ready to spring. She froze, her heartbeat pulsating wildly in her throat as she gasped in fright. The others were all up at the wagon on the road. There was no one to help her. No one, that is, but God. *Please, dear God, make the panther go away,* she silently prayed, her eyes never leaving the animal. She knew she shouldn't have slipped away by herself. The beady eyes still watched her.

Then out of the corner of her eye, she caught a glimpse of a young Indian boy standing in the nearby bushes. He looked at her, then at the panther, then turned to walk away.

"Help me! Please!" she whispered hoarsely.

The boy glanced back but continued on his way. Never in her life had Mandie hated anyone as she did that boy right then.

Suddenly, from another direction, an arrow winged through the air striking the beast in the tree. Mandie held her breath—appearing through the trees was Uncle Ned! The thrill of relief flooded her body.

"Don't move, Papoose." the old Indian cautioned, as he quickly moved forward.

The panther, severely wounded, loosened its grip and fell from the tree. Mandie scrambled up the bank, her white kitten leaping after her.

"Uncle Ned! Where did you come from?" she asked as she paused to put on her shoes and stockings over her wet feet.

"Papoose take too long to get to Cherokee house. I come see why," he replied, turning the panther over. "Go back to wagon, now. I come soon. Wait there."

The girl snatched her bonnet from the bush where she had left it, calling back as she ran up the hill, "Hurry, Uncle Ned. We'll wait for you."

She hurried through the trees, and as she caught sight of the others at the wagon on the road, she called out, "Mother! Uncle John! Uncle Ned is here!"

Her mother and Uncle John, standing under the shade of the trees, turned to look at her. Her friend, Joe, came from around the wagon.

"Where, Mandie?" asked Uncle John.

"Down there—down at the river," she replied, pointing back at the way she had come. "Oh, it was awful! I was washing my feet and this panther was up in the tree getting ready to attack me when all of a sudden Uncle Ned came out of the woods and shot him with one of his arrows!"

The other three looked at one another, startled.

"Slow down, Amanda," her mother told her. "You're out of breath."

"Oh, and there was this Indian boy standing there in the woods, but he wouldn't help me at all; and he saw the panther, too," she continued. "He just turned around and walked away, leaving me there helpless and alone."

Uncle John lifted a rifle from the wagon and started down the hill. "Let me go see what Uncle Ned is doing. He might need some help."

"Guess I'll go, too," called Joe, hurrying after John.

"Amanda, dear, please don't *ever* go off alone like that again," her mother pleaded. "Something awful could have happened to you."

"I'm sorry, Mother," Mandie said soberly, putting her arm around her mother's waist. "But it was so hot I just had to wash my feet to cool off a little. It has been such a long journey all the way from Franklin. Wonder how much farther we have to go?"

"I know, I know," her mother replied, stroking the blonde curls. "We are all hot and tired. It shouldn't be much farther. Uncle Ned will know."

When the men came up the hill with Joe, Mandie ran to meet them. She hugged the old Indian. "You always come just in time, Uncle Ned."

"I promise Jim Shaw I see after Papoose when he go to happy hunting ground," the old Indian reminded her.

"I know, Uncle Ned, but now that I have found my real mother and she has married my Uncle John, you don't have to worry about me," the girl replied.

"May be fine, but I promise. I keep promise. Even when Papoose get to be squaw and marry Joe here, I keep promise," he told her, with a twinkle in his eyes.

Joe blushed and kicked at the stones under his feet. He intended to marry Mandie when they grew up, but he certainly didn't want people talking about it. He stole a quick glance at Mandie. She was looking at him.

"I'm glad, Uncle Ned. If you had not come along when you did, I don't know what might have happened to me. I probably wouldn't be here to tell about it," Mandie admitted. "Did you see that Indian boy in the woods there? He just looked at me, and then at the panther and walked away."

The old man turned quickly toward her, his eyes squinting. "I no see Indian boy. Where he go?"

"I don't know. He just disappeared into the woods," she replied.

The old man tightened his lips and murmured, "Mmm."

"All right, let's get going," Uncle John said, changing the mood. "We want to get to Uncle Ned's house before sundown."

The road they traveled on ran parallel to the Tuckasegee River for many miles. After a while Uncle John turned the wagon onto an old wooden bridge and crossed to the other side, traveling upward along the banks of Deep Creek.

"Oh, how I'd love to get into that water!" Mandie exclaimed, as she peered at its clear, shallow stillness.

Joe leaned out to look. "There're enough rocks to walk plumb through it."

"Won't be long now," Uncle John called back to them from his seat at the front.

And it wasn't long before cornfields started showing up along the way. Here and there tobacco was growing. At one place a hog ran grunting across the road in front of the wagon, causing the horses to buck and snort. There was an odor of food cooking, and as they came around a sharp bend in the road, a settlement of log cabins came into view. Mandie and Joe became excited.

"Looks like we're here!" exclaimed Joe.

"I can't wait to meet all my kinpeople!" Mandie cried.

"Just better not be any boys among them casting their eyes on you," Joe warned.

Mandie's mouth dropped. "I do believe you have a jealous streak in you, Joe Woodard."

"Remember, you promised. I get your father's house back from that woman he was married to, and you'll marry me!" Joe reminded her.

"Oh, Joe, it'll be years and years before you'll be old enough," Mandie replied.

"Not so long. I'm past thirteen already."

They were slowing down in front of the largest cabin in the group. There was a barn at the rear and horses could be seen behind a split-rail fence. The house looked very similar to the one in which Mandie had lived with her father. It was made of logs chinked together, with a huge rock chimney at one end. The door stood open, and they could smell the strong odor of food cooking.

"This is where Uncle Ned lives," Uncle John called back to the two young ones. He stopped the wagon by the barn and helped Elizabeth down as Uncle Ned took the reins to unhitch the horses. Mandie and Joe jumped down and looked around. There, standing across the road, was the Indian boy she had seen in the woods.

"Uncle Ned, look! There's the boy I saw in the woods!" she called, pointing to the boy.

Uncle Ned turned to look. "Oh, that Tsa'ni. He go to school. He not good Indian. I not know why he not kill panther."

An Indian squaw with a red kerchief tied around her head appeared at the door of the cabin. Mandie ran to hug her.

"Morning Star! I'm so glad to see you!" she squealed.

The old Indian woman grunted and held her tightly.

"She can't speak English, but she understands what we say pretty well," Uncle John told Mandie.

"I know. She came with Uncle Ned when he brought me to your house in Franklin," she replied. "But how did you know?"

Uncle John winked and smiled. "I stayed here at Deep Creek with the Cherokees while you were at my house hunting for my will, remember?"

"Oh, yes, of course," she laughed.

Uncle Ned and Morning Star motioned for them to come inside the log cabin. Mandie set Snowball down and looked around. It was very similar to her father's house in Charley Gap. There was a huge rock fireplace with the kettles hanging in it. A homemade table nearby was draped with a cloth, and when Morning Star removed the cloth, Mandie saw that the table was set and supper was ready and waiting.

At the far end of the room were several beds built into the wall and covered with cornshuck mattresses. Curtains hanging between them could be pulled around each one. Over in the other corner was a spinning wheel and a loom. And against the wall was a ladder going upstairs where Mandie knew there would be more beds.

"Food sure smells good!" Joe exclaimed.

Uncle Ned was speaking Cherokee to Morning Star, explaining who Mandie's mother was. All the Cherokees had known her father and now Morning Star embraced her mother. With tears in her eyes, Elizabeth smiled at the old woman.

In his Indian fashion, Uncle Ned tried to make the white people feel welcome. "Wash! Eat!" he told them, pointing to a washpan on a shelf. A clean towel was hanging on a nail beside it. A bucketful of fresh drinking water was also nearby with a gourd dipper hanging on a nail over it. Ned was a full-blooded Indian, but he knew how the white people lived.

"Save food for Snowball," Uncle Ned told Mandie, handing her a pan from the shelf. She understood they were to save the scraps from their plates for the kitten.

A beautiful young Indian girl about Mandie's age came through the open door. She was wearing a long, full skirt with a ruffled blouse; multicolored beads hung from her slender neck. Her long, black hair was held back by a red ribbon. Moving silently in her soft moccasins, she smiled as she came forward.

Uncle Ned put his arm around the girl. "This my son's papoose. She Sallie," he told the others.

"Hello, Sallie, I'm Amanda Shaw—Mandie for short," Mandie greeted her. "This is my mother, Elizabeth Shaw; my stepfather, who is also my uncle, John Shaw; and my friend, Joe Woodard, the doctor's son."

"Welcome," Sallie replied. "I know John Shaw. We are so excited to have you all visit us." Her speech indicated she was well educated.

Elizabeth took her small brown hand in hers. "Sallie, we are so happy to be here."

"Yes, we are, Sallie," John Shaw added.

Joe stole a glance, admiring her dark beauty, and then put in his greeting. "Sallie, we love your grandfather, Uncle Ned."

Morning Star spoke quietly to Uncle Ned and he announced loud and clear, "We eat now! Eat! Sit! Sit!"

The adults gathered at one side of the table and were soon deep in conversation. Mandie found a place on the other side between Joe and Sallie. Morning Star took the plates to the kettles over the fire, filled them, and brought them back to the table. Uncle Ned passed them around.

"Give thanks, John Shaw," Uncle Ned spoke again, as Morning Star sat down.

They all bowed their heads as Uncle John raised his voice in thanks. "We give thanks to thee, O Father, that we are all together, and for the wonderful food prepared for this meal. Bless this house and the people that dwell here. Amen."

"Guess we can eat now," Joe remarked.

"Yes," Sallie told him and then turning to Mandie, she said, "I was very sorry to hear about your father. I remember Jim Shaw. He used to visit us now and then."

Mandie was surprised. "You knew my father! Well, yes, I suppose you did. Uncle Ned said my father used to come to visit his people here."

"All the Cherokees loved Jim Shaw. He was a good man," the Indian girl said. "My father is dead also. I live here with my grandfather and my grandmother."

"And I have known your grandfather all my life. At least, ever since I can remember. He always came to sell the baskets the Cherokees made. And I never even knew I was part Cherokee until Uncle Ned told me, after my father went to heaven. My grandmother was Talitha Pindar, a full-blooded Cherokee," Mandie told her.

"I know. The Cherokees all know who you are," Sallie said. "Eat. It is owl stew. It is very good."

Joe, who was listening to their conversation, almost choked as he stuttered, "Owl—st-stew?"

"Yes, it is something special Morning Star makes."

Mandie swallowed hard and lowered her spoon into the delicious-smelling bowl of stew in front of her. She sipped it, blinked her eyes, and smiled. "It *is* very good." Then she dug in, thinking, *This is what the Cherokees eat and I am part Cherokee.*

Joe had to follow suit. There was no way he could let a girl outdo him. Then he also smiled and said, "Say, we'll have to get Morning Star's recipe for this to take back home." He reached for a piece of beanbread and washed it all down with a huge swallow of coffee.

"I suppose you know Tsa'ni?" Mandie asked Sallie.

"Of course. He lives right down the road. He is the grandson of your father's uncle, Wirt Pindar, who lives in Bird-town," the Indian girl told her.

"Now, let me think that one out. In other words, he is my great-uncle Wirt Pindar's grandson? That would make him my cousin!"

"Yes. He goes to school and is very intelligent, but has no common sense about him," Sallie said. "He—he thinks too much."

"I see. Well, I guess he was thinking too much, or something, today, when he left me with a panther staring at me." Mandie told her about the incident by the river.

"You might as well know. He does not like white people," Sallie said. "The English for his name is John, but he refuses to use it and goes by his Cherokee name. Most of us are called by our English names."

"He doesn't like white people? Why?" Mandie wanted to know.

"Because the white people destroyed our nation and took our people's land and homes and forced them to move away," Sallie said.

"I know that was wrong, terribly wrong, but that was a long time back in history. The white people living today had nothing to do with it," Mandie protested. "Besides, it was my grandfather who rescued my grandmother and her people."

Joe leaned forward. "Oh, Sallie, you've got to come to Franklin and see Mandie's Uncle John's house. It's complete with tunnels and hidden rooms, and all. Her grandfather had all this done to hide the Cherokees who didn't want to leave that area."

"I must see it, then," agreed Sallie. "It sounds very interesting. Is that where you live now, Mandie?"

"Yes, since my father died," she replied. "Uncle Ned helped me get to Uncle John's house. And then Uncle John found my real mother, and here we are!"

"Most of your kinpeople live in Bird-town," Sallie said.

"That's what Uncle Ned said. After we visit with you a day or two, we'll be going over there. Is it far to Bird-town?"

"No, but by wagon you have to follow the road instead of cutting through the woods and that makes it longer. Probably two, three hours."

The grown-ups were getting up from the table.

"You men go sit and visit and you young ones go along with Sallie outside. I will help Morning Star clear the table," Elizabeth volunteered.

"I have to feed Snowball first," Mandie told her, and holding out the pan Uncle Ned had given her, she waited for her mother to fill it with food left on the plates, which was very little, except for Joe's. He had not eaten all the owl stew, she noticed. She took the pan over to the hearth and the kitten purred contentedly as he hastily ate the food.

"He was hungry!" Sallie laughed.

"Come on. He'll follow us outside after he finishes," Mandie told her.

"Yeh, you sure can't lose that cat. He follows you like a shadow," Joe said as they went out into the yard.

Tsa'ni was sitting on a log under a hickory nut tree nearby. Sallie steered them in his direction. He stared at them silently as the group approached. Mandie could sense hate emanating from his dark eyes.

"Tsa'ni, this is your cousin, Mandie Shaw, and her friend, Joe Woodard," Sallie told him.

The boy looked from one to another and merely nodded his head without saying a word.

Mandie did not like the boy, but she knew she must at least speak to him because he was her cousin. She could still visualize the panther sitting in the tree and Tsa'ni walking away.

"Hello, Tsa'ni. Could we sit with you?" she ventured.

He immediately moved all the way down to the end of the long log.

"Sit. The log belongs to Sallie's grandfather. It is not mine," he told them.

They sat down, Mandie next to Tsa'ni.

"Mandie lived at Charley Gap with her father before he died," the Indian girl told him.

"Charley Gap? Tsali, our great warrior, whom you white people call Charley, lived in a cave near here before you white people killed him," Tsa'ni said.

"He did? I know the story of Charley, how he fought with the soldiers during the removal and killed one—" Mandie told him.

Tsa'ni interrupted, "—and how your soldiers forced Cherokee prisoners to shoot him down when he surrendered. You killed his brother and his two sons."

"I didn't kill anyone, Tsa'ni. Let's get this straight. What we are talking about was long ago in history—" Mandie's voice raised.

"I know, I know," he interrupted again.

"That was something I was not responsible for, nor my family," continued Mandie. "You can't live in the past, and you can't change history. As far as that goes, the Yankees killed my grandfather during the War of Northern Aggression, but I don't hold a grudge against the people living in the North now. They had nothing to do with it."

"Cherokee blood must be thicker than white blood then," Tsa'ni said.

"Well, just remember my grandmother was a full-blooded Cherokee," Mandie reminded him.

Joe, anxious to smooth the feelings between the two, spoke up, "Could we go see this cave, Tsa'ni?"

The Indian boy hesitated a moment, looking at Mandie. "Sure. It is not far. I will take you there tomorrow, all of you."

Mandie spoke up, "I'd really like to see it, Tsa'ni."

"I will go with you," Sallie added.

The sky was almost completely dark and the air was becoming much cooler. Snowball came bouncing across the yard and jumped into Mandie's lap.

"And so will Snowball," Mandie laughed, snuggling the kitten on her shoulder.

Tomorrow would be a day long to be remembered.

CHAPTER TWO

LOST IN THE CAVE

Mandie awoke the next morning to the sound of a rooster crowing, and she had to think for a minute before she knew where she was. Sallie was asleep on the cornshuck mattress next to her, and she knew Joe was sleeping on the other side of the rough hand-sawed wall dividing the room. She pulled the long cotton nightgown over her head and quickly reached for her dress hanging on a nail. Today was not a day to be wasted sleeping. She was in Uncle Ned's house, among the *Cherokees!*

The Indian girl looked up at her and smiled.

"You are in a hurry," she said.

"Yes, I don't have a minute to spare. I want to enjoy everything I can about our visit," Mandie replied.

From beyond the wall, Joe called to them, "Right. We gotta get going so we can go with Tsa'ni to the cave. Remember?"

"Of course," Mandie agreed.

"I smell coffee. Someone else is already up," the Indian girl commented as she, too, pulled on her skirt and blouse.

The three hurried down the ladder and found Uncle Ned, Uncle John, and Elizabeth sitting at the table. Morning Star was tending a pot over the fire.

"Good morning," Mandie called, as she came down the ladder.

"Come, eat," Uncle Ned said as they lined up at the washpan to wash their faces in the cool creek water from the bucket.

"You won't have to say 'eat' twice to me this morning. I'm starving!" Joe joked as he sat down across from Uncle Ned.

The girls joined them, and the Indian woman placed bowls of steaming hot oats and slices of homemade bread, with thick slices of ham between, in front of them. Elizabeth filled the coffee cups and passed them around.

"Good morning, Morning Star," Mandie smiled as she caught the old squaw's hand. The Indian woman smiled too and patted the girl's long blonde curls.

"Love," she whispered, and Mandie returned the word.

"Love. Oh, Morning Star, you are learning English!"

Sallie was listening. "She can understand some of what you say in English, but I have never heard her say an English word before. You are a good influence, Mandie."

After the chores were done and the noon meal eaten, the three wandered outside, waiting for Tsa'ni. Soon he arrived, carrying a lantern.

"Sallie, get the lantern from your grandfather's barn, too. It will be dark in the cave," Tsa'ni told her.

Sallie got the lantern and gave it to Joe to carry.

"Ready?" Tsa'ni asked.

"Yes, but I should tell my mother that we are going now," Mandie told him.

"Never mind. I will tell your mother, and your grandfather, Sallie." The Indian boy hurried up to the open door of the cabin with Mandie right behind him. Looking inside, he said, "I am taking the boy and the girl to see the mountain, the woods, and the creek. Sallie is going with us."

Elizabeth spoke up. "How kind of you, Tsa'ni. Amanda, you won't be long, will you?"

"No, Mother," she replied, turning to join the others waiting in the yard. "Tsa'ni, you didn't mention the cave."

"That is all right. The cave is included in the mountain and the woods. Come, let us go." He started off down the road toward the creek.

Mandie picked up Snowball and carried him on her shoulder. At first it was great fun, skipping along by the creek bank, throwing pebbles at the fish, plucking wild flowers, chasing butterflies, but after a while it became an uphill climb, and it was beginning to get hot. There was no definite trail, but Tsa'ni seemed to know the way all right. The other three grew more quiet and slowed their pace as they became more and more exhausted.

"Whew! Tsa'ni, how much farther?" Mandie complained, holding her skirt close to her legs through the thick undergrowth.

The Indian boy laughed. "Not far."

"Not far to you must mean miles to us," Joe sighed, as he pushed a brier away from his pant leg.

"Tsa'ni, where *are* you taking us?" Sallie demanded.

"To the cave, Sallie. I know the way," the boy replied.

Mandie turned to the Indian girl. "Don't *you* know where the cave is, Sallie?"

"No, I have only heard of it. I do not wander around the way the boys do." Sallie smiled. "And I have not lived long with my grandfather, so I do not know this land."

"Do not worry. I will not get you lost. I know exactly where we are going," Tsa'ni assured them.

A long time later a rushing, roaring waterfall came into view. Mandie stopped to admire it.

"Oh, how beautiful!" she exclaimed.

"That is where we are going," Tsa'ni told her.

He ran ahead of them and when they reached the falls, he stopped and gave them directions. "Now, you must walk across the rocks in the creek behind the waterfall. The entrance to the cave is behind the falls," and he started forward.

"We'll get all wet!" Mandie screamed above the noise of the water.

"No, you will not get wet if you stay against the cliff away from the water when you walk through. Just watch where you step. The rocks are slippery sometimes," Tsa'ni yelled back and continued on.

Mandie followed, with Sallie behind her, and Joe bringing up the rear. Snowball was frightened of the water and clung desperately to Mandie's shoulder.

Once under the falls, Mandie looked up and could see a ledge protecting the walkway as the water cascaded down into the creek. It felt terribly damp under there and the rocks were awfully slippery. There was no use trying to talk. No one could be heard above the sound of the water.

Joe lost his footing once, and if the girls hadn't grabbed for him, he would have fallen into the creek. The slip caused the girls to almost lose their balance, and Mandie felt her free hand scrape a rock as she grabbed for a hold. Regaining her footing, she stuck her hand out into the waterfall to wash away the grit and slime. The water was ice cold.

Tsa'ni had stopped ahead of them, and when they caught up they found him waiting in front of a huge, dark hole in the cliff which appeared to be the mouth of the cave. He had taken a match from his pocket and was lighting his lantern, motioning for Joe to light the one he carried, and then he entered the cave.

Once inside, the loud roar of the falls became a muffled sound and Mandie looked around, afraid to go any farther. Joe, right behind her and Sallie, swung the lantern around, lighting up the cave. They could see huge, moss-covered boulders around the entrance. The floor seemed to be solid rock.

"Come." Tsa'ni called, going deeper into the cave. "I want to show you something."

The three hurried on, passing into another part of the cave with enormous, long spears of rock hanging from the ceiling and sprouting up from the floor. They looked around in wonder.

"What are those things?" Mandie asked, breathlessly.

"That is what I wanted to show you. The ones hanging from overhead are stalactites and the ones sitting on the ground are called stalagmites," Tsa'ni explained.

"Well, what caused them?" Joe asked.

"They are formed by the water dripping from above," the Indian boy replied.

"It must have taken an awfully long time," Sallie remarked.

"Hundreds of years, maybe thousands," Tsa'ni nodded.

Mandie set Snowball down, and he began to check out the scent of the floor.

"You mean this cave has been here that long?" Mandie asked.

"And this is the cave where Tsali lived?" Sallie queried.

"Yes. People are born, live, and die, but mountains stay forever," the Indian boy replied. "This cave has several tunnels and other sections. Come, I will show you."

The group followed as he went down a long tunnel which led into another section of the cave, and then continued into another tunnel. It was all so dark and cold. The lanterns made a soft glow and cast eerie shadows. Snowball seemed nervous. He leaned against Mandie's skirt and meowed to be picked up. She consented and he snuggled against her shoulder.

"Oh, Snowball, I think you are lazy today," she laughed.

"Look, there is a stream over there. Look closely and you can see minnows in it," Tsa'ni told them, pointing to the other side of the large cavern they were in.

Everyone hurried over to the stream and huddled on the ground to watch for minnows in the flowing water.

Tsa'ni, with a sly grin on his face, silently crept away, heading for the entrance. He knew his way around inside, and the trail for home, but he knew the two white children didn't know the way, and neither did Sallie. *The white girl claims to be part Indian*, he thought. *Well, we'll just see how much Indian she is. A real Indian could find the way out. White people—always coming to mess in Cherokee business!*

Joe turned to speak to Tsa'ni. "I don't see any minnows." And then realizing the Indian boy was nowhere in sight, he called, *"Tsa'ni, where are you?"*

The girls were startled at the alarm in Joe's voice. They saw no sign of Tsa'ni. Mandie once again felt the hatred rising in her heart.

"He has left us," Sallie spoke angrily.

"Oh, no, Sallie! How will we ever find the way out—and home?" Mandie cried.

"We can only search around and hope to see familiar things," the Indian girl told them.

"Thank goodness, we have a lantern," Joe added.

Mandie sighed. "Well, let's be on our way." She started forward and then stopped. "Joe, you'd better go first with the lantern so we can watch our step."

"Please, be careful," Joe warned them. He stepped ahead and flashed the light into the next section of the cave. "Did we come in from here or over there? There's another opening over there." His voice echoed.

The girls turned to look. There *was* another opening. They were both puzzled.

"This one, I—I think," Mandie said, indicating the one nearest where they stood.

"No, I think it is that one over there," Sallie disagreed.

"Hey, now, we can't go two ways at once," Joe said.

"All right, which way do you say, Joe? We'll go the way two of us agree on," Mandie said.

"I just don't know!" Joe sounded confused. "I suppose we could *try* this way and then come back if we don't find the way out."

"And maybe get thoroughly lost doing it!" Mandie moaned.

"But there is nothing else we can do but try," Sallie reasoned.

"Agreed," Joe said. "So here we go." He led the way into the next cavern, and to their dismay it had several openings.

"Listen for the sound of the water," Sallie told them. "If we can get headed toward the water, we will find our way out."

The three stood still, holding their breath, listening for the faint roar of the waterfall. Simultaneously they pointed in three different directions. Then they all laughed.

"I've always heard two heads are better than one, but I'm not so sure three heads are any good at all," Mandie sighed.

"Let's do it this way," Joe suggested. "We'll take turns deciding which way to go."

"All right, you choose first," Sallie replied.

"This way," Joe said, pointing to his right, and the girls followed.

Now they were in a long tunnel with no end in sight within the dim light of the lantern.

"Mandie, you choose next," Sallie said, as they stumbled along the rough floor.

"Right now I would choose to go back the other way. It looked smoother and I don't remember a floor as rough as this one. No, wait! I see a dark place on the right up there." She hurried forward. "It's an opening."

"Well, let's go through it," Joe said, flashing the lantern light inside the next cavern. At that moment it seemed like hundreds of dark birds came flying at them. Flapping wings buzzed around their heads and a wild cackling sound filled the air. Joe and Mandie froze in terror.

"Bats." Sallie yelled. "Get down low and go back out!"

The three almost crawled out of the cavern into the tunnel they had just come down. Two of the bats circled here and there, and then disappeared.

"Sorry, I picked the wrong way," Mandie said breathlessly, as they ran through the tunnel.

"Here is another opening on the left," Sallie said.

"Joe, hold the light inside first so we can see."

Joe flashed the lantern around but no bats appeared. Directly across the passageway was yet another opening.

"There's another tunnel over there."

The girls followed him on through. It was a large cavern with a huge hole in the middle of the floor. They gathered around to look. Even though Joe held the lantern as far over the hole as he could bend, they could not see the bottom.

"Oh, how spooky!" Mandie shrieked.

"Do not get too near the edge!" Sallie warned them.

Joe turned to look at the girls. "I think we are completely lost."

"That Tsa'ni! Just wait until I tell my grandfather what he has done to us!" Sallie cried.

"There's only one thing left to do," Mandie told them. "We must pray. In fact, we should have prayed long before now."

"Pray?" asked Sallie.

"Yes. I know you must go to church, because Uncle Ned does. Whenever I am afraid or confused I ask God to help me," Mandie told her. "And He always does."

"Yes, I go to church and I believe in God," the Indian girl replied.

"Then, let's all repeat this verse together: 'What time I am afraid I will put my trust in Thee.' " And the three did as Mandie suggested.

"Oh, dear God, please help us! We need your help now!" Mandie pleaded, turning her eyes upward.

"Now let's not worry anymore. God will help us find the way out," Joe added.

"Yes, but I cannot hear Him telling us which way to go, can you?" Sallie was serious as she looked at the other two.

"No, but we have to trust Him to put it into our heads which way to go," Mandie explained.

"I think I'll check what's over on the other side," Joe said, walking slowly around the huge hole in the floor.

The wall on the other side had stones of all shapes and sizes piled up against it, and there was no opening.

Mandie, following Joe, accidentally stubbed her toe on a rock near the bottom of the pile, and all of a sudden the whole stack seemed about to tumble. She jumped out of the way and bent to look closer at the stones. As she was straightening up, her eyes caught a glitter in the pile.

"Joe, hold the lantern over here! I saw something shiny in the rocks!" she exclaimed.

"Oh, it's probably mica," Joe said.

As he swung the lantern the light revealed more glitter and the three began pulling at the rocks to see what was there, breaking fingernails and rolling rocks onto their shoes. All at once a large stone rolled down, uncovering a pile of gold nuggets.

"Gold!" whistled Joe, furiously digging away the loose stones.

"Gold!" murmured Mandie.

"Gold!" repeated Sallie.

Then the three of them broke into hysterical laughter.

"Here we are, lost to civilization, with a fortune in gold at our feet!" Mandie cried, picking up a nugget.

"Yes, we'd better be trying to find our way out," Sallie reminded them.

"Find our way out? Oh, Sallie, aren't you interested in seeing how much gold is here behind the rocks?" Joe asked, as he kept digging.

"Gold—that is what caused the Cherokees to lose their land, their homes—everything!" Sallie replied, sadly

Mandie turned to her, understanding. "I know, Sallie. If that gold had not been found in Georgia, the white people might not have ever made the Cherokees move out." She dropped the nugget into her pocket.

"Daylight! I see daylight!" shouted Joe as he continued to pull away at the rocks. "There's an outside opening behind all these rocks!" In his excitement he broke the lantern on a rock he was rolling away and they were suddenly in the dark.

But he was right. Together the three soon had a hole dug big enough for them to squeeze through to the outside. The terror of being lost in the dark, cold cave was over.

"It's a little uphill out there, I think. Let me go first and then I can help you two crawl out," Joe suggested.

All thought of the gold left their minds. Joe climbed through the hole they had dug and pulled the two girls after him. Snowball scrambled ahead of Mandie. Sallie went through last and barely cleared her foot when the whole side of the cave seemed to come tumbling down and the opening disappeared.

"Thank you, God! Thank you!" Mandie cried.

"Amen!" Joe added.

"Me, too!" Sallie said.

They stood up and looked around. They were in a thick forest of balsam firs and it seemed to be growing dark rapidly. Hours must have passed since they left Uncle Ned's house and now they were lost in the woods. There was no sign of the waterfall or the creek. It would be dark soon, and they had no lantern.

CHAPTER THREE

CAPTURED IN THE DARK

Tsa'ni waited for hours outside under the waterfall for the three to find their way out of the cave, but they never came out. He smiled to himself. *That white girl claimed to be part Cherokee. If she was part Cherokee she would find the way out.* He sat down to whittle on a piece of pine he took from his pocket. It got later and later and then began to grow dark, and still there was no sign of the three!

Suddenly he heard voices and saw lights flashing through the waterfall in front of him as they came nearer. He stood up and put his knife and the piece of wood back into his pocket. Evidently a search party was coming and he had better be prepared for them.

A group of men appeared through the trees, swinging lanterns in the dark. One stepped forward and Tsa'ni recognized him as Uncle Ned.

"Cave under water," he said, motioning to the waterfall. "Papooses might go there."

Uncle John walked to the edge of the creek, swinging a lantern. "Where is the cave, Uncle Ned? I can't see a thing beyond the water."

"Follow me," the old Indian told the others. He took them across the rocks and under the waterfall.

Then they were face to face with Tsa'ni.

"Tsa'ni! Where Papooses?" Uncle Ned demanded.

"We went into the cave and they ran off and left me. I went back inside to look for them, but could not find them," the Indian boy lied to the old man.

"Lost in cave!" Uncle Ned muttered.

"Do you know your way around in there?" asked Uncle John as the old Indian approached the entrance and flashed his lantern light inside.

"Little," Uncle Ned replied. "Big place, many rooms. Drumgool, pull trees. We make trail." He spoke in Cherokee to another Indian in the group.

Drumgool, understanding his friend's language, turned back and ordered the other men to gather small branches from the trees. Soon they returned with their arms full, while Uncle Ned and Uncle John waited at the entrance to the cave.

"We make trail," the old Indian repeated, entering the tunnel into the cave. The other Indians, understanding perfectly what he meant, began breaking twigs from the branches they carried and dropping them on the floor as they followed him.

Tsa'ni followed along in the rear. Now that the three were really lost, he was afraid of what they might tell. He had better prepare a good argument for when they were found. *Palefaces, why didn't they stay out of Cherokee territory? Always causing trouble!* He thought to himself.

Led by Uncle Ned, with Uncle John close behind, the search party thoroughly combed the cave.

"No one come to cave anymore. Rocks slide," Uncle Ned said, pointing to a rockpile that had evidently fallen from above in one of the sections.

"But Tsa'ni, knowing this, took them inside?" Uncle John questioned.

"Tsa'ni bad brave." Uncle Ned was angry.

"I don't think the boy likes us, even though we are kinpeople," replied Uncle John as they entered another tunnel.

"Tsa'ni no like white people," Uncle Ned explained. "He have no heart." He swung his lantern up and another rockpile came into sight. "Rocks dangerous."

"Where, oh, where can those kids be?" John sighed. "Tsa'ni said they ran off and left him while they were in the cave. Maybe they are already outside somewhere, or have already gone back to the house."

"Papooses come home; Morning Star send word. No, Papooses not home," the old man said as he flashed his light into the room with the huge hole in the floor. The opening the young ones had dug in the wall to escape through was now completely obliterated, and a pile of rocks hid the gold nuggets. "Papooses not here."

They went into the other sections and surprised the bats as the three lost ones had done.

Tsa'ni, still tagging along at the rear, was growing more and more positive that the three had just completely disappeared. He knew only the one way in and out of the cave, and they had certainly not come out. On the other hand, they weren't to be found in the cave. They had just vanished.

It was a big cave and the men were tired, but Uncle Ned insisted on going through the entire place one more time. This time the men laid bare twigs for their trail. They walked slowly and poked into every crevice, looked into every nook and cranny, and finally ended up back at their starting place.

Uncle Ned shook his head in dismay. "Not here. Now we look in trees, bushes," he told the men, explaining how they would work.

"Please, God, let us find them before some harm comes to them," Uncle John implored, as they gathered to leave the cave.

Mandie, Sallie, and Joe stumbled along in the darkness after they left the cave. It was some time before their eyes became accustomed to the dark night so that they could detect outlines of bushes and trees.

"Where do you think we are, Sallie? Do you have any idea?" Joe asked.

"I do not know this land, but I think we should keep going downhill because we went uphill all the way to the cave," she replied, pushing the limbs of a bush out of her face.

Mandie, carrying Snowball on her shoulder, was having the roughest time of all because the kitten insisted on clinging to her dress; and every time she took an uneven step because of unlevel ground or rocks and underbrush in the way, Snowball tightened his claws. And with the nightfall, it had become cold on the North Carolina mountain.

"I hope we're not too far away from food. I'm hungry!" Joe exclaimed.

"Me, too," Mandie added. "And I'm cold."

"Here is food," Sallie said, stopping by a huge bush and pulling berries from its limbs. "Serviceberries. They are good to eat."

"Oh, yes," agreed Mandie as she and Joe joined the Indian girl for a berry supper. They sat down on a boulder nearby. She offered one to Snowball. He turned his nose away from it. "Snowball, if you don't want these berries, you're going to have to wait, and no telling how long."

"Cats don't eat berries, Mandie," Joe laughed at her.

"Well, Snowball eats tomatoes, so why can't he eat berries?" Mandie told him. "Goodness gracious, I'm tired." She took a deep breath and stretched.

"Me, too, but we must keep moving on. There may be dangerous animals here," Sallie told them as she stood up.

"Of course! And we don't have a thing to defend ourselves," Joe said, as he and Mandie got to their feet and Snowball clung to the shoulder of Mandie's dress.

"Joe, what did we do in that cave?" Mandie admonished him. "We said we would trust in God. Have you forgotten so soon?"

"Well, no, but it would help if we had a rifle," he answered.

"Since we do not have one, I suggest we make haste," Sallie said, going ahead downhill through the bushes. The other two quickly followed.

It was a cloudy night with no moon to light the way. The three hurried along, slipping, sliding, sometimes falling over huge boulders along the path they took, sometimes getting caught in the briers of a bush, sometimes being struck in the face by an unseen branch. On Sallie's advice they tried to keep on a downhill route, but it was so dark and the trees and brush were so thick, they could not be sure which way they were going.

A small animal brushed by Sallie's legs in the darkness, and in her fright she lost her balance and went sliding downhill straight into a stream. Mandie and Joe ran after her.

"Here I am. Here!" the Indian girl called to them as she rose from the edge of the water. Luckily the wet sand had stopped her and only her feet had gone into the water.

"I can't see you," Joe called.

"Keep talking," Mandie told her. "We'll follow your voice." She put Snowball down so she could hurry.

"I landed in a stream down here," Sallie called to them.

"I can hear you," Joe yelled back to her. He went running down the hill and suddenly ran into what sounded like a bunch of huge tin cans.

Mandie, frightened by the noise, called out. "Joe, are you all right? What was that noise?"

"Looks like a whole lot of big cans," he said, as Mandie and Sallie both got to his side.

The Indian girl walked slowly around, feeling the cans and trying to see in the darkness. "I think it is a still."

"A still?" asked Mandie.

"A real moonshine still?" asked Joe.

"That means someone has been here and may be somewhere close around," Mandie figured.

"Sure does, and it means they must be bootleggers," Joe laughed.

Sallie did not understand his language. "Bootleggers?"

"Yeh, that's people who make liquor illegally," the boy said.

"Bad Cherokees make liquor, but not here," Sallie replied.

They were talking loudly enough that their voices carried in the dark, still night.

Mandie cautioned them. "The bootleggers might be around. We'd better be quiet. You've already made enough noise banging against those tin cans."

Out of the darkness a pair of hands grabbed Joe from behind and at the same time another pair latched onto Sallie, pushing her against Mandie and causing the girls to fall. The two dark forms were barely visible.

"Hey, what are you doing to me?" Joe demanded, as he felt his hands being tied behind him. He put up a struggle but the hands were too strong.

"They ain't nothin' but younguns, Snuff," a woman's coarse voice said as she held onto the two girls.

There was a strong, sickening smell about the two strangers. Evidently they had been drinking what they made in the still.

"Ne'er mind what they be, they done found somethin' that ain't none of their bidness and they's aliable to be atellin' the wrong people 'bout it," Snuff replied as he finished tying Joe's hands, and with the end of the long rope started to tie Sallie's as well, leaving a short piece of rope between the two.

"Please, Mr. Snuff, we won't tell anyone we saw you, or whatever it is you don't want us to tell," begged Mandie, the woman still holding her tightly.

"No, we'll just do as you say, Mr. Snuff," put in Joe.

"Shet up!" Snuff replied.

'Ysee, Snuff, they don't even know what we're atalkin' about," the woman told him.

"Shet your smacker, too, Rennie Lou," the man said. He jerked Mandie's hand from the woman, causing the girl to slip as he jerked her around. She almost fell head first into a bush. As she stumbled, her hair ribbon fell out and caught on a twig unnoticed.

Snuff pulled Mandie's hand behind her, and leaving a short space in the rope for Sallie's hands, he tied Mandie's, letting the long end of the rope dangle. Now all three were tied to the same rope.

"We are lost," Sallie tried to explain. "We do not even know where we are. If you would just show us the way back to Deep Creek, we would be most grateful."

Snuff turned quickly to look at Sallie in the darkness. "An Injun, by George! We've captured an Injun here!"

"Now, how do you know?" It's so dark I can't even tell what color hair they've got," Rennie Lou said.

"Don't you catch that Injun accent? No matter how much eddication they git, you kin always hear that kind of lisp they have," Snuff said, trying to look closely at Sallie in the dark.

"Yes, you are right. I am Cherokee," Sallie proudly told him, as she tried to straighten up in pride.

"Well, well, well, whadda ya know!" Rennie Lou slapped her skirt and laughed hoarsely. "And is the udder two Injuns, too?"

Snuff was trying to see what the other two looked like but it was too dark.

"Nope, don't think so. That 'un has got yellar hair," he said. "Well, now that you'ins can't git away too well, mind tellin' me whar you thought you was goin' this time o' night?"

"Sallie told you the truth, Mr. Snuff. We are lost," Joe replied.

"That's right. We are," Mandie added.

"Lost? Everybody that believes that stand on your head," the man growled. He pulled the rope, almost causing the three to lose their balance. "Now, where was you'ins goin'?"

"We were in the cave and got lost," Sallie told him. "There are probably search parties out right now looking for us."

"In the cave? What cave?" the man asked.

"The cave where the Indian Charley hid," Mandie told him.

"The cave whar the whut?" he howled and stomped his foot. "Now that's a good 'un. Ain't no cave nowhere 'round hyar, much less an Injun called Charley."

"Well, we were in a cave," Joe said, "whether you believe it or not. We were in a cave."

"I know every leaf and stone in these hyar woods. Ain't no cave hyar," the old man argued.

"But Joe's right. We were in a cave. The Indian boy with us ran off and left us and we got lost," Mandie insisted.

"Snuff," the woman said as the old man jerked Mandie around on the rope. "Make 'em show us if thar's a cave. A cave might come in handy sometime."

"All right. We'll keep 'em in the barn till daylight and then they will show us the cave," Snuff agreed, pushing the three together in front of him. "This way. Rennie Lou, lead the way and watch out for any sudden-like tricks."

O God, please help us! Mandie prayed silently as they were herded forward. She had never been so scared in all her life. The old man and woman didn't seem to have any common sense about anything, and there was no telling what they might do to them. Besides, everyone would be out looking for them, and her mother would be awfully worried.

They stumbled about in the darkness trying to follow the woman as they were ordered to do. Snowball, unseen by the man and woman, scampered along near Mandie. All three were already tired, hungry, and worn out. Now they were about to collapse from their weariness in avoiding the branches that scratched their faces and the thorns and briers that tore their clothes. Mandie slipped on a rock and pulled the other two down with her as she fell.

"Now, look ahyar. None of that stuff!" the old man yelled, jerking cruelly at the rope. "You're agoin' to the barn whether you like it or not. Git up! Now! Rennie Lou, give 'em a hand!"

The old woman tried to help in the dark but she wasn't much help. They finally managed to get to their feet.

"I'm sorry, Sallie, Joe. I accidentally fell. I didn't do it on purpose," Mandie apologized.

"It's all right, Mandie," Joe calmed her.

"It could have happened to either one of us," Sallie said, as they moved on.

Soon they could make out the blurred outline of a building in the clearing ahead. As they came closer they could see it was a rough log cabin, and to their dismay they were pushed on past it. Snowball followed.

"Go on! This ain't the barn," Snuff told them.

"Ain't far," Rennie Lou looked back and informed them.

After passing a clump of bushes behind the house, another structure showed up in the darkness. Rennie Lou walked on toward it and stopped at the door. She swung it open on creaky hinges.

"All right, inside!" Snuff prodded them on through the doorway into the darkness.

"Want me to light the lantern, Snuff?" the woman asked.

"Course not, woman. You want them to see us?" the old man growled. He pushed the three forward. "There's a pile of hay over thar. You kin sleep thar till it gits daylight!"

"Could we have a drink of water?" Joe asked. "We haven't had any food or water since noon yesterday."

"Water? Well, reckon you kin. Rennie Lou, git the water bucket over thar," Snuff said.

The woman picked up something in the darkness and came toward them, Joe felt a metal bucket in her hands as she pushed it in his face. "Hyar you air. Sorry we ain't got no dipper," she said. "But I tell you whut. There's apples in that haystack if you kin manage to eat one without usin' yer hands!" She laughed hysterically, holding the bucket to Joe's mouth.

"Rennie Lou, leave 'em be," Snuff warned her. Turning back to the three captives, he said, "Now we'll be back as soon as the sun cracks that darkness. Meantime you'd better rest good 'cause you're gonna find that cave for us, or else."

The man and the woman left the barn then, slamming the door behind them. The three prisoners gave a sigh of relief. Snowball moved around Mandie's feet.

"Now, we've got to think fast," Joe whispered to the others. "How can we get loose? We've got to get loose before they come back, so we can get away."

"Yes, they are definitely drunk," Mandie agreed. "I'm afraid of people who drink liquor."

"You never know what they will do when they have been drinking spirits," Sallie said. "But what can we do?"

"Oh, I don't know offhand but I suggest we start thinking," Joe replied. "I have no idea how you go about sitting down when you are all tied together like we are, but why don't we just take a plop all together?"

"All right, on count of three we'll all sit at once," Mandie agreed.

"One, two, three!" Together they landed in a pile of hay in the dark. Snowball prowled around them and started playing with the end of the rope hanging from Mandie's hands.

"We'll never be able to get up again," Sallie told them.

"We've got an awful lot of thinking to do first," Joe said.

"Yes, we've got to get back to Uncle Ned's, so we can go back to the cave and get the gold," Mandie reminded them.

"I do not want any of that gold, but I will go with you," Sallie told her.

"Yeh, we've got to get back to that gold somehow. There must be a fortune there," Joe said.

"I wonder who put it there," Mandie mused as she twisted her hands in the rope. "Do you suppose these people here did?" Snowball's paw caught at the rope behind her.

"No, because they don't even know about the cave," Joe said.

"Maybe some bank robbers left it there," Mandie suggested.

"I doubt it because it is too hard to get to the cave from any road or trail," the Indian girl replied. "Besides, they would probably guard it. And Tsa'ni seems to know his way around in there."

"You don't mean *he* could have put it there?" asked Mandie.

"No, he would never have gold like that," Sallie answered. "I mean someone would have seen him around if they were guarding the gold."

"You're right. But how did it get there? And who put it there?" Joe asked.

"We could ask Uncle Ned about it," Mandie said.

"First, we have to get away from these people, so we'd better concentrate on that," Joe reminded the two girls.

It was going to take an awful lot of thinking to get them out of their predicament.

CHAPTER FOUR

DIMAR

Elizabeth Shaw could sit still no longer waiting for her daughter to come back or to be found. It was a long time after midnight and no word had come from anyone. She decided it was time she helped in the search.

"Morning Star," she began, trying to talk to the old squaw. "You and me—" she pointed to the squaw and to herself—"let's go to Bird-town and get Mandie's kinpeople to help find them."

Morning Star understood part of it. "Bird-town," she said.

Elizabeth smiled and made motions like she was riding a horse and then pointed to the old woman and to herself again. "Bird-town," she said again.

The Indian woman grinned as she understood what Elizabeth meant. She got up and motioned to Elizabeth to follow her. She went outside to the barn. There was a small cart inside and Morning Star hastily opened a door to a stall and led out a pony. Elizabeth helped her harness it to the cart and they started out for Bird-town.

Meanwhile the three prisoners in the barn were still talking and trying to figure out a way to escape from the old man and woman.

"If we could only see in this darkness, we might find something we could cut the rope with," Mandie said.

"How is either one of us going to cut the rope when all our hands are tied?" Joe wanted to know.

"If one of us had something we could hold in our hands, we could back up to each other and cut each other's ropes apart," Sallie said.

"That's right," Mandie replied and then jumped as Snowball clawed her hand as he played with the rope. "Oh, Snowball, you stuck me with your claws!" Then she caught her breath. "Snowball! Snowball! He can do it!"

"Do what, Mandie?" Joe asked.

"Untie the rope. If I shake it for him to play with, he can claw at it.until it comes undone!"

"Oh, Mandie, how could a cat untie a rope?" Joe asked.

"Well, it does feel looser and besides, I am the last one on the rope." She shook her hands behind her, and Snowball jumped and began playing and clawing at the rope.

"Mandie, it'll never work," Joe told her.

"Snowball is smarter than you give him credit for. Don't forget, I am the one who educated him," laughed Mandie, still shaking her hands as the kitten played. "It's looser! It's looser!"

"Please keep trying," Sallie told her as she shifted from her cramped position to lean back against a post. Then she jumped forward again. A nail had scratched her back. "Mandie, there's a nail behind me. If Snowball has the rope loose enough, you might be able to hang it on the nail and pull it apart."

"Where, Sallie, where?" Mandie was excited.

"Do not lose your sense of direction. It is directly behind me on the post. I am going to move so you can slide over here in my place," the Indian girl said, moving slowly closer to Joe, who began edging farther away to give the girls room to move. Mandie kept sliding until she felt the post behind her. She leaned back trying to locate the nail.

"I've found it!" she cried. "Now if I can just catch the rope on it!" She maneuvered her hands until her fingers found the nail, and then she slid her wrists around until the nail caught the rope.

"Did you find it?" Joe wanted to know. "Or I should say, did the nail find the rope?"

"Yes, now I have the rope caught on it. If I can only catch the right loop so it will start untying."

"Be careful. You might hurt yourself," Sallie warned her.

Snowball had followed Mandie and was again pulling at the rope with his claws. One foot caught and he pulled with all his might trying to get his paw free. Mandie felt the rope give way. She rubbed her wrists together and slipped one hand out of the noose.

"It worked! I have my left hand free!" she cried. "There! I have it all off! Now, let me get you two untied."

She slipped behind Sallie and freed her hands and then removed the rope from Joe's hands. The three sat there rubbing their bruised wrists in the dark.

"That man must not have tied the knots very tight," Joe said.

"Probably because he was too drunk to realize what he was doing," the Indian girl said.

"Well, let's get going!" Mandie stood up, picking up Snowball.

"I will leave a signal for our people if they come here looking for us," Sallie said, as she removed the beads from around her neck and hung them on the nail. "My grandfather will see these and will know we were here."

"I hope we find them before they get this far," Joe said.

"We'd certainly better be careful going by the log cabin," Mandie reminded them as they stepped out of the barn. The first signs of dawn were in the sky.

"We will circle the clearing and stay away from the house," the Indian girl told them. She led the way, keeping the house at a distance as they tried to find their way back into the woods and downhill.

While the three were trying to find their way, Uncle Ned's search party had fanned out across the mountain. He and Uncle John stayed together while the other men scattered out. Sometime later the old Indian found the bright blue ribbon from Mandie's hair hanging on the bush by the creek where she had lost it in the scuffle with the old man and woman.

"Papoose ribbon!" he cried excitedly as he pulled the ribbon from the bush. "They been here!" He looked around on the ground. "Feet make marks!" He pointed to the footprints in the soft sand by the water.

Uncle John anxiously bent to look.

"Looks like quite a few different feet," he remarked.

"Yes," the old Indian said, as he straightened up to follow the direction of the footprints. "Go this way." He walked on up the hill, bending low to see the prints as he continued. The old cabin came into view.

"At least we know they got out of the cave," Uncle John said.

"I hear people coming," Uncle Ned said, listening as he turned his ear toward the sound. "Walk like white people."

Snuff and Rennie Lou appeared in the distance, their heavy shoes noisily clopping on the rocks here and there. Uncle Ned stepped behind a tree and motioned for Uncle John to do the same.

As the couple drew nearer, the old Indian stepped out directly in front of them. They stopped in their tracks.

"Where Papoose—wear this ribbon?" Uncle Ned held up Mandie's ribbon for them to see.

"What papoose?" Snuff asked. "We ain't seen no papoose, Injun."

"Papoose feet make prints to your house," Uncle Ned said, pointing to the tracks in the dirt. "Where Papoose?"

Rennie Lou held tightly onto Snuff's arm. She was frightened of the old Indian. Snuff tried to bluff his way out.

"I told you we ain't seen no papoose. Now git out of our way!" Snuff gave Uncle Ned a shove.

At that instant Uncle John, his rifle in his hand, stepped out from behind another tree and Uncle Ned gave a loud whistle to round up his braves. The man and woman stood still without saying a word. Indians came from every direction out of the woods as they heard their leader's call for help. Snuff and Rennie Lou, quaking in their boots, were soon surrounded.

"Hold man, woman," Uncle Ned ordered. "Me and John—we go look." The circle of Indians closed in around the frightened pair.

Following the footprints, Uncle Ned and John went on past the cabin and into the barn. The old Indian looked around and grunted as he picked up Sallie's beads from the nail on the post.

"Papooses been here," he said to Uncle John, holding up the beads.

"But evidently they are gone now," Uncle John replied.

"Left different way. Prints going opposite way," Uncle Ned said, motioning to the footprints left by the three as they had detoured around the house.

Suddenly the dark, cloudy sky broke loose and the rain came pouring down. The old Indian looked up in dismay.

"Rain wash feet marks away!" he exclaimed. "Must hurry!"

"And the children are out in this," Uncle John fretted. "Unless they found the way back, which I doubt very much."

The old man whistled for his braves once more and they came on the run, pushing the man and woman along with them in the downpour.

"Must hurry. Rain clean trail," Uncle Ned told them. "We follow feet marks now!" He pointed to the footprints remaining in the sand.

"What we do with palefaces?" Drumgool asked, pushing the two forward.

"Let go. Must hurry," the old Indian instructed him.

"I think we should send the authorities back up here, Uncle Ned," John said. "These people are kidnappers."

Uncle Ned nodded in agreement.

Snuff and Rennie Lou heard all that was said and looked at each other anxiously. They were sober this morning and the realization of their crime began to dawn on them.

"Look, we ain't meant no harm. We didn't hurt the younguns," Snuff pleaded. "In fact, we'll hep you hunt 'em if you want."

"No! We don't need your help," Uncle John told them, firmly. "You have broken the law. It will all be taken care of as I said. I am reporting this to the authorities. You're not going to get away with it."

"Please, mister," the woman begged. "We won't never do it again. I 'spect we jest had too much partyin' 'fore they showed up. We didn't hardly know whut we was doin'. Can't you unnerstan' that?"

John shook his head and ran to follow Uncle Ned, with the braves bringing up the rear. The rain was quickly obliterating the tracks of the three, and they were hurrying as fast as they could go. Their clothing was heavy with the dampness, and the wet rocks had become slippery, but they knew they were on the trail of the missing children.

Far ahead of them, Mandie, Joe, and Sallie pushed their way through the dripping bushes and mostly slid downhill when they came to huge boulders now and then. Snowball registered his complaint by clinging tightly to Mandie's dress.

"Sallie, do you think we are heading in the right direction?" Mandie asked.

"I am not certain but I do know we are headed toward the foot of the mountain, and once we get down there we'll be able to find the way home," the girl replied.

"Whew! I'm still hungry!" Joe complained as he led the way. "We sure were dumb not to load up with apples from that barn."

"It's too late now," Mandie replied. "When we get back to Uncle Ned's I'm going to eat everything in the house." She laughed, tossing her long, wet hair back out of her face.

"Even owl stew?" Joe teased her.

"I said everything," she replied.

"Everyone must be worried about us by now," Sallie said. "I am certain my grandfather has a party searching—if we only knew which direction they were coming from."

"Looks like a level place for a while here," Joe remarked as they came down into a meadow.

At that moment an arrow suddenly shot through the trees near Mandie, who was carrying the kitten. Snowball, frightened by the sudden movement, jumped down and darted ahead. He ran up the first tree he came to and peered down from a limb.

Mandie, not noticing the kitten, stared and pointed to the arrow imbedded in another tree. "Joe! Sallie! Look!"

"Land o'Goshen, don't stand there! Come on!" Joe grabbed her hand and turned to grip Sallie's hand. They ran along until they came to a thick clump of bushes, where they hid. From there they saw a young Indian appear in the clearing and go to the arrow in the tree.

Sallie immediately felt relief. She was certain the boy would help them. She broke out of the bushes, calling back, "That is an Indian boy. He will help us. Come on!" She ran toward the boy. "We are lost! Please help us!"

Mandie and Joe, not trusting the boy, stayed behind the bushes. The boy turned to look at Sallie. "Where did you come from?"

"I am Sallie Sweetwater. My friends and I are lost. Will you help us?" she asked as she stood before the boy who seemed to be not much older than she was.

The boy looked around. "Your friends? Where are they?"

"They are behind the bushes because you almost hit us with your arrow and they are frightened," she told him.

"I am very sorry. I will not harm any of you. Tell them to come out," he said.

Sallie called to her friends. "Come on, Mandie, Joe. He will help us find the way!"

Mandie and Joe reluctantly appeared from their shelter and came forward. The boy's eyes lit up when he saw the blonde-haired girl.

She is the most beautiful girl I have ever seen, he was thinking as she came nearer. *And blue eyes! How beautiful!*

Mandie returned his stare, thinking what a handsome boy he was!

"Where are you going?" the boy asked.

"We are trying to find the way to Deep Creek where I live with my grandfather," Sallie told him.

"Deep Creek." he repeated. "You are going in the wrong direction!"

"Oh, no!" Joe moaned. "I'm starving to death!"

"Yes," the boy said. "My name is Dimar Walkingstick. I live with my mother not far from here. I will take you to her for food and dry clothes. Come!" He turned, expecting them to follow him.

"I am certain my grandfather has a search party looking for us by now," the Indian girl said. "We shall leave a trail for him."

"Of course. I will go ahead and break the twigs as we go. He will see them and find the way to my house," Dimar said, as he began marking their way.

"Food!" Joe murmured. "At last, some food!"

"That's what he said," Mandie replied, following along with Joe as Sallie stayed with Dimar, marking their trail. "And a fire to dry our clothes. This rain will never stop!"

Snowball was completely forgotten in the excitement. He clung desperately to the limb of the tree, too frightened to descend.

CHAPTER FIVE

UNCLE NED TO THE RESCUE

Elizabeth and Morning Star arrived at Bird-town, hurriedly told Mandie's great-uncle, Wirt Pindar, what they had come for and in no time flat they were riding toward the mountain with Wirt leading a group of men. Elizabeth insisted on going along and was given a pony to ride, but Uncle Wirt reminded her that she would have to climb the mountain on foot when they reached it.

By the time the foot of the mountain was in sight, the rain began.

"Well, looks like we're going to have a wet hike," she remarked as she dismounted. Gathering her long skirt about her, she tucked the hem into the waistband so as not to be slowed down by the weight of the wet material about her feet.

"Yes, will be hard find trail in rain," Uncle Wirt told her. He motioned for his men to come together and then gave them directions to spread out up the mountain as they climbed.

Morning Star took Elizabeth's hand and motioned toward the men. Together they followed Uncle Wirt up the incline in the downpour.

"Morning Star, pray," Elizabeth told her, clasping her hands together and looking toward the sky. She knew the Cherokees always looked up to God in the sky rather than bowing their heads when they prayed. "Pray!"

Morning Star understood and stopped to raise her face and hold her hand on her heart as she prayed in Cherokee.

"Please, God, guide and direct us to our lost children!" Elizabeth implored. "We put our faith in you!"

They quickly caught up with Wirt as he climbed through thick, wet underbrush. Morning Star was experienced in this kind of thing, while Elizabeth was hardly a match for the dense undergrowth in the pouring rain. But in her determination to find the children, she quickly adapted to the way the Indians were stepping and making their way.

"We climb opposite side. Ned climb from Deep Creek. We climb from Bird-town," Wirt explained as they kept going.

"Yes, I realize that," Elizabeth replied, pulling a brier from her skirt. "That is good; we will be covering two sides of the mountain between us,"

It was a long, tedious journey up the mountainside in the heavy rain. The Indians were watchful for any sign of a trail and now and then paused to send a loud whistle through the woods in hopes of being heard by the children.

Covered with bruises and scratches, Elizabeth forced herself to keep up with Morning Star who, in spite of her age, was as agile as the men in the party. She paused only a second to catch her breath after a steep climb over boulders that were constantly in their way. She kept a prayer in her heart that no harm come to the missing ones. She had lost her twelve-year-old daughter when she was a baby and had only recently been reunited with her. Those memories kept her diligent on the path now.

Wirt, worried about the white woman trying to keep up with the Indians, called for a rest stop at the bottom of a huge boulder.

"We sit," he commanded, pointing to a clearing under a ledge projecting from the boulder above. "Rest."

"Please don't stop on my account," Elizabeth called breathlessly. "I can keep up with you."

"Sit, rest," he told her. "Morning Star need rest, too." He pointed to the old Indian woman who sat down on the rocky floor under the ledge.

Elizabeth followed her, glad for the rest. The men also came under the shelter to get out of the rain.

"While we rest, we send message," Wirt told them. Stepping back out into the rain, he gave his loud whistle that rang through the trees. Turning, he instructed the men, "You next, then you, until all give message."

The men, one at a time, stepped out and repeated the loud call through the woods. As the last one turned to sit down, there came an answering call in the distance, barely discernible through the sound of the rain.

"Ned near us. His call." Wirt cried excitedly as he ran up the face of the boulder, whistling again. His men followed.

Morning Star and Elizabeth smiled joyfully. Maybe Uncle Ned had some good news. They lifted their skirts and ran after the men as fast as they could manage.

Uncle Ned, hearing the call and answering, turned to Uncle John as they stopped beneath a tree.

"Wirt must be near. That his call," the old Indian said.

"Someone must have let him know," Uncle John replied. Then he spoke up excitedly. "Elizabeth! Of course—she wouldn't sit there all this time and do nothing. She has rounded up our kinpeople at Bird-town."

Uncle Ned grunted and the two men, with the others following, started out in the direction from which the call had come.

It didn't take the two parties long to meet. Elizabeth ran forward as John came to meet her.

"Any word?" they both asked at once.

They both shook their heads in the negative as their arms flew around each other.

Wirt was speaking in Cherokee to Uncle Ned. Elizabeth, raising her head from John's shoulder, heard a soft meow. She looked up to see Snowball still clinging to a limb in the tree.

"Snowball!" she cried, pointing.

Everyone turned to look. John quickly scaled the tree, picked up the frightened kitten and brought it down to Elizabeth.

She stroked the wet kitten who clung to the shoulder of her dress. Her voice trembled as she spoke, "Oh, John, where can Mandie be without Snowball?"

Uncle Ned walked over to the tree. There his quick eyes caught sight of the broken branches on the bushes.

"Trail!" he said, quickly pointing to twigs jutting out at angles on the bushes ahead. "Quick! Follow trail!" He hurried ahead, watching for the marked bushes.

The two parties of searchers fell in behind him and made their way through the brush.

Meanwhile, the three children arrived at Dimar's mother's house and were welcomed in to dry by the fire and to partake of a meal. As soon as they had gotten inside the log cabin, the rain stopped.

"This is my mother, Jerusha," Dimar told them, and turning to his mother, he said, "These are friends I found lost in the woods—Mandie, Sallie, and Joe."

"Ah, my papooses," she said, hurrying to them. "Come." She took the girls by the hand and led them behind a curtain at the far end of the room. "You wrap in blanket," she said, handing them each a blanket from the beds.

Sallie explained in Cherokee that they must find the way back to her grandfather's house as soon as their clothes had dried and they had eaten.

The girls went back to the fire, and Jerusha spread their dresses to dry. Dimar helped Joe find a blanket and hung up his wet clothes.

"Now, we eat," the woman said smiling.

She brought them tin plates filled with ham, corn, and beanbread, and cups of steaming hot coffee were set on the hearth. The three ate as though they had not eaten in a week.

"Oh, how good." Joe said, with his mouth full as he continued to cram in the food.

"This is the best meal I think I've ever had," Mandie added.

"Good food," Sallie agreed.

Dimar and his mother sat nearby, having their meal and watching the three. Jerusha kept turning the clothes so the heat would dry them.

"Eat. Much food," she told them. She rose and refilled Joe's plate but the two girls refused.

"I just can't eat anymore," Mandie told her. "I'm full up to here." She touched her throat and laughed.

"Me, too. The food was very good. We thank you." Sallie smiled as she pulled the blanket closely around her.

Even though it was summertime and terribly hot during the day, the rain cooled the air considerably. All the homes had a fire in the fireplace for cooking, and today it felt especially good.

Everyone jumped at the sound of voices outside. Mandie was the first to look out.

"It's Uncle Ned!" she cried and, securing her blanket, ran to open the door. Joe and Sallie joined her.

Uncle Ned cried with joy as he took the three into his arms. John and Elizabeth crowded in behind him.

"Uncle Ned! Mother! Uncle John!" Mandie cried excitedly.

Elizabeth handed the wet kitten to Mandie.

"Snowball! How could I not have missed you?" she said, cuddling the kitten to her blanket. She ran to the fireside and fed him the scraps on her plate, which he swallowed at once and began searching for more. Jerusha was quick to comply.

It was a joyous occasion and everyone was talking at once. Jerusha made them all feel welcome and brought out more food. The cabin was filled with so many people, there was only room to stand. Tsa'ni sulked over in a corner, afraid to mingle with the crowd. His eyes kept darting from Mandie to Sallie to Joe. Mandie ignored him. She could feel the hatred in the air between them, though she knew she shouldn't hate him. She shouldn't hate anyone. But it was so hard to be nice to an enemy. She was afraid all her Cherokee kinpeople would be like Tsa'ni and would not like her because she was mostly white.

Uncle John grabbed her hand and led her to Wirt Pindar.

"Mandie, this is your Great-Uncle Wirt. He is your grandmother's youngest brother,"

The old man bent to embrace her.

"My real uncle!" she exclaimed, backing off a little to look at him. He was also looking her over. "My very own uncle!"

"Jim Shaw's papoose." the old man said softly. "Look like Jim Shaw, but have Indian thumb." He was holding her hand and examining it.

"Indian thumb?" the girl questioned him.

"Short, blunt thumb," he explained, holding his own next to hers. They were similar in shape.

"I have a Cherokee thumb!" she cried. "I'm so glad!" She turned to John. "Uncle John, let me see your thumb."

He held out his thumb and laughed. "We both have one like Uncle Wirt's."

"Little one come to Wirt's house," the old man said.

"Oh, yes, Uncle Wirt. We *are* coming to visit you," Mandie replied.

"Today," he said. "Not far to Bird-town."

Uncle Ned was standing nearby listening. "Close to Bird-town. Far to Deep Creek. We go to Bird-town."

"Now," began Elizabeth as the three gathered around her, "I want to know exactly what happened. *Where* have you been?"

Tsa'ni, wide-eyed and listening from across the room, moved in closer to hear what they would say. Mandie saw him and took pity on him. She thought, *I won't tell a lie. I just won't tell everything.*

She looked back at her mother. "We got lost in the cave and couldn't find Tsa'ni," Mandie told her.

"And we couldn't find the way we came in so we dug our way out," Joe added.

"Yes, and then those strange people in the woods tied us up and left us in the barn," Sallie explained.

"But how did you get separated from Tsa'ni?" Uncle John asked.

"Well, we stopped to look into a pool of water and I guess it was then we got separated," Mandie replied.

Tsa'ni was holding his breath as he eavesdropped. He did not understand why the girl did not tell the whole story.

"Do not see how got lost from Tsa'ni," Uncle Ned said.

Sallie answered her grandfather. "I suppose he thought we were right behind him, but we stopped to look into the water and then we lost him."

"And how did you dig your way out of the cave?" Elizabeth wanted to know.

"Well, there was a pile of rocks and—" began Joe.

"—and a pile of gold," Mandie interrupted. "And I mean a pile of gold! And then we could see the daylight through the rocks, so we dug with our hands until we had all the rocks out of the way."

"Gold?" Uncle John asked as he looked at Uncle Ned. "You saw gold in that cave?"

Tsa'ni moved a little bit closer. They had found gold in the cave? They must be lying.

"Yes," Mandie affirmed. "It was all under the rocks we dug through to get out."

"But then the rocks all fell in and the hole closed up as soon as we got through it," Joe added.

"Do you know of any gold in that cave, Uncle Ned?" John asked.

"No. No gold. Maybe mica in rocks," Uncle Ned said.

"But it was *gold*, Uncle Ned. We saw it!" Mandie insisted, forgetting about the nugget in her pocket.

"No one goes in cave. Dangerous. Rocks fall in," the old Indian said.

"Maybe it was mica you saw, but, anyway, we're so thankful you are all safe," Elizabeth told them. "Now, don't you think we'd better get going so we can get to Uncle Wirt's house before dark?"

The three scrambled for their clothes. As Mandie put on her dress behind the curtain, the gold nugget fell out of her pocket and lay unnoticed on the floor by the bed.

Tsa'ni, breathing a sigh of relief that he was not implicated by the three, swaggered up to Mandie and said in a low voice, "You have no Indian blood in you. You could not even find your way back. You are just white, that is all."

Dimar, standing nearby, overheard and spoke up, "Tsa'ni, you are a disgrace to the Cherokees, talking like that to your own blood."

Joe advanced toward Tsa'ni. "You look here, Tsa'ni, Mandie is a well-seasoned traveler. She made a journey all the way from Almond Station to her Uncle John's house in Franklin, through the woods, across the rivers, and over the mountain. And that is rough terrain. Why, she even—"

Mandie caught him by the arm and interrupted. "Never mind, Joe. We have to go now. Come on." She turned to Sallie who was also listening. "Just ignore him."

Sallie nodded in agreement.

Wirt came over to Tsa'ni, who was his grandson. "You go to Deep Creek; bring John Shaw's things to my house. They stay with me. Make haste."

Tsa'ni looked at the old man. "I am on my way," he said. He turned and gave the three a know-it-all look and walked out the door.

Tsa'ni had no plans to do what his grandfather had asked. He had plans of his own.

CHAPTER SIX

CHEROKEE KINPEOPLE

Uncle Ned and his group went to Bird-town with the others. They were all tired and it was the closest place to go.

Mandie, who had ridden behind her mother on the pony from the foot of the mountain, looked around, her eyes taking in everything. This was part of the Cherokee Indian Reservation here at Bird-town. This was the original land where her Indian ancestors had lived. It was like a small town with a wide dirt road running through it. Rows of log cabins were spaced apart by crops.

There seemed to be an unusual number of women and children waiting along the road. Most of the men had gone with the search party, and they were now returning to their families.

Elizabeth followed Wirt Pindar to his house. It was the largest in the group and was in the center of the community. Aunt Saphronia, Wirt's wife, embraced them and made them welcome. She was a tiny Indian woman with a million wrinkles in her face. She had food cooked and waiting. Her neighbors, some of whom were relatives, opened their doors to the extra men from Deep Creek.

Saphronia then spotted Mandie.

"Jim Shaw's papoose!" she cried as she hugged the girl. "Love!"

"Mandie, this is your Uncle Wirt's wife, Aunt Saphronia," Elizabeth told her as John Shaw came up behind her.

"I love you, too, Aunt Saphronia," Mandie said, blinking back tears as her father's name brought back memories.

"Aunt Saphronia." John Shaw smiled as he put his arms around the little woman.

Saphronia looked up into his face. "Take care Jim Shaw's papoose."

"Yes, I will, Aunt Saphronia, together with her mother Elizabeth here," he replied.

"You forget," Elizabeth reminded him. "I have already been here. When we came to get Uncle Wirt, I met Aunt Saphronia then." She smiled at the old squaw.

"Right. I'd forgotten in all the excitement," he replied, grinning as he put one of his arms around Elizabeth and tried to include Mandie.

The girl laughed. "I don't think your arms are long enough to hug three of us at one time."

"Eat. Food ready," Saphronia told them, leading them to the table.

As they sat at the long table Mandie turned to her Uncle Wirt. "Tell me about my grandmother, Uncle Wirt, when she was a young girl. What did she look like'?"

Uncle Wirt cleared his throat as he strove for the right words. "Talitha beautiful—more than others. She sing, she dance, she smile. Braves follow her. She like everyone. Everyone love her. She born here."

"She was born here?" Mandie was surprised. She had never thought about that. "Before our people were made to move out and give up their land?"

"Yes. She oldest papoose. Me youngest. All gone to happy hunting ground, but me," he said sadly.

"I love you, Uncle Wirt. I thank God that I am able to come to see my Cherokee kinpeople. He has been good to me," she said.

The old man's face brightened. He smiled. "Love, Papoose. Jim Shaw's papoose."

The others had been listening and now Uncle John spoke up.

"Talitha was my mother, you know, Mandie. But I didn't know her well because I had to go away to school as a small boy, and she was very ill. It was a long time before I had a chance to come back, but I have been back many times since then. Your father also came to visit, at least once a year, but he never knew our mother. She died not long after he was born.

"When she died our father lost all interest in life. He just pined away. He died when your father was only five years old," he said.

"Five years old," Mandie said thoughtfully. "Then you took care of my father while he was growing up."

"Yes, Jim and I lived in the house in Franklin until he got married," Uncle John said. "Uncle Ned and Morning Star lived with us for several years. He taught us both how to fish, swim, and how to use a bow and arrow."

"They lived with you and my father" Mandie was surprised. She turned to the old Indian. "Uncle Ned, you never told me that."

Uncle Ned smiled. "Take many moons tell Papoose many things."

Dimar Walkingstick came in through the doorway and went straight to Mandie. Everyone was surprised to see him because they had left him at home with his mother when they came to Bird-town.

He held something out to Mandie. "Here. I think this is yours. It was on the floor where your dress was hung to dry."

Mandie took the gold nugget and gasped, "Oh, Dimar, thank you! I had forgotten about it entirely."

"Sit. Eat," Uncle Wirt told the boy, sliding closer to Uncle Ned to make room for him. Dimar squeezed into a place between the two old Indian men, directly facing Mandie. His eyes fastened on her and remained fixed as she showed the others what he had brought.

"You *did* take a nugget with you!" Sallie exclaimed.

"Holding out on us, huh?" Joe teased.

"You see, Uncle John," she said, handing him the nugget. "There *is* gold in the cave. It *is* gold, isn't it?"

"It certainly is," Uncle John said, passing the nugget on to the two Indian men. "Look at that!"

Uncle Ned grunted. "Cherokee not know gold in cave."

Uncle Wirt agreed. "No, Cherokee not know."

The two old men looked at each other and seemed to be concerned.

"How much do you think was there?" Uncle John asked.

"Probably a bushel basket full, wouldn't you say, Joe, Sallie?" Mandie answered.

Sallie nodded. Joe said, "Oh, probably more than that. I'd say several tote sacks full."

"Let's see, you said you found it under some rocks when you were digging a hole to get out of the cave?" Uncle John questioned.

"Yes, sir," Mandie said. "We found this pile of rocks and could see the daylight through a tiny hole in the middle of them so we started digging to see if there was an opening. There was only a small layer of rocks over the pile of gold."

"Between the three of you, could you find the pile again?" Uncle John wanted to know.

"I don't know. You see, as soon as we got through the hole all the rocks came tumbling down from above and covered up the opening we'd dug," Mandie said.

"Unless the rockslide changed things drastically inside the cave, I think I would recognize the place," Joe added.

Uncle John turned to Sallie. "What about you, Sallie? Would you remember where it was?"

"Gold has always been bad luck for the Cherokees. I would rather not look for it," the Indian girl replied.

Everyone turned to look at Sallie.

"I know what you are referring to—the removal of Indians because of the discovery of gold in Georgia. But it wouldn't be like that now," John reminded her.

Uncle Ned spoke up. "Cave dangerous. Cherokee not need gold."

"But, Uncle Ned, there must be a fortune there," John said.

"Cave not too dangerous. Tsa'ni go there many times," Uncle Wirt put in.

"That's right. Tsa'ni goes there. Has he ever found any gold'?" John asked.

"No," Wirt said. "We go to cave when sun up."

"Uncle Ned, will you come with us?" John asked.

"Papoose go, Ned go. I promise Jim Shaw." He nodded his head. "But—gold bad for Cherokee."

"May I go, too?" Dinar spoke up.

Everyone had forgotten about him.

"Of course, if you want to," John told him.

Dimar rose. "I must return home now. I will meet you at the cave tomorrow morning."

So plans were made for another search—this time for a pile of gold. And this time they wouldn't get lost.

Meanwhile, Tsa'ni had gone straight to the cave from Dimar's house. He did not bother to go on to Deep Creek and deliver the Shaws' belongings to Bird-town as his grandfather had asked. He felt sure the others would return to look for the gold and he wanted to beat them to it.

He didn't have much oil left in his lantern, but he would hurry before the light went out. He knew his way around inside the cave pretty well. He hurried from one room to another, swinging the light close to the wall as he went. According to what he had heard them say, they had found the gold next to a wall.

Once, as he paused to look carefully at a pile of rocks, he thought he heard voices. He stood still and listened but could hear nothing.

"Hmm, probably the echoes of old Tsali," he said to himself, and went on about his search.

He knew which room the bats lived in so he carefully avoided them. He was certain gold couldn't be in there anyway. They would never have stayed long enough to dig out a hole in the wall with the bats flying about their heads.

As he carefully searched tunnel after tunnel, the light in the lantern began to grow dim as the oil was being used up. He shook it and gave a sigh. He would have to leave, go home and refill the lantern before he could continue his search.

As he wound his way back toward the entrance, the light finally sputtered and died, leaving him in total darkness. He felt his way forward slowly. As he crossed the cavern with the huge hole in the middle of the floor, he stumbled on a broken rock. Losing his balance, he grabbed desperately for the rocks, but slid back and fell directly into the pit. Just as he thought he'd never hit bottom, he landed with a splash, his head cracked against a stone, and he knew no more.

CHAPTER SEVEN

THE PIT

"Are y'all ready to go prospectin'?" Joe called through the wall in the upstairs room the next morning as the rooster crowed in Uncle Wirt's yard below.

"Yep!" Mandie yelled back as she jumped out of bed and stretched. Snowball followed her.

"I will go with you," Sallie said as she rose to reach for her dress hanging on a nail.

"Beat you downstairs!" Joe called, and the girls could hear him scrambling down the ladder.

The adults were already sitting around the table. It seemed no matter how early the young ones got up, the older ones were always there first.

"I was just going to wake you," her mother said. "On this trip to the cave we are going prepared. You must eat a good breakfast, and we will carry more food. I understand we have an uphill climb on a footpath after we leave the wagon on the road, so we can't carry anything heavy."

"Besides, we have to carry lots of lanterns," Mandie told her. "It's awfully dark in that cave."

"Yes, and I have lots of rope handy, too," Uncle John added.

"Shouldn't we take something to bring the gold back in?" asked Joe as he sat down to eat beside the girls.

"Oh, yes, the men will take something to put it in—if we find it," John smiled.

"Gold—bad luck," Uncle Ned mumbled as he rose from the table.

"Hurry. We go soon," Uncle Wirt told the young people as he also stood up. "Eat."

Mandie laughed. "That's one English word my Cherokee kin-people all know—eat." She dug into her bowl of cornmeal mush.

"Eat—that's a good word to know," Joe said.

"Do you like what our people eat? Do you eat the same thing when you are at home?" Sallie asked the two as she began eating her mush.

Mandie and Joe looked at each other.

"Well, yes, almost the same thing." Mandie paused. "Everything I have eaten since I came to Cherokee country has been delicious."

"At home we have fatback and red-eye gravy sometimes, and grits," Joe added.

Elizabeth was packing meat and bread in several separate pack-ages. "Let's make haste now," she called. "We don't want to be too late coming back." Turning to John, she asked, "Tsa'ni never came with our things from Uncle Ned's house, did he?"

"No," he replied. "We can stop and get them on the way back."

As they went through the community at Deep Creek, they asked several people, but no one had seen Tsa'ni. They left Morning Star at her cabin and said they would stop for their things on the way back. Tsa'ni's mother was not in her cabin as they stopped by.

Uncle Ned mumbled, "Bad Cherokee."

Uncle Wirt, his grandfather, agreed, "Tsa'ni not good."

However, there was one Indian boy they could depend upon. Dimar was sitting on a rock near the waterfall waiting for them when they got there. His eyes fastened on Mandie again. He rose and came forward.

"Good morning," he greeted them.

"Good morning, Dimar," Uncle John replied. "You haven't seen Tsa'ni around, have you? He never did come to Bird-town."

"No, I have not seen him," the boy said. "I have not seen anyone around here."

"Tsa'ni—bad Cherokee," Uncle Ned muttered. "Go." He motioned for the others to follow him under the waterfall and into the cave.

"Since we aren't sure what direction to take, we'll all scatter out in different directions, but you three be sure to stay together," Uncle John told them. "Now let's all go looking for a pile of rocks!"

Elizabeth took one look at the cave and shuddered as she turned to the three children. "To think you were lost in here! I would have been frightened to death!"

"It sure wasn't any fun," Joe answered, shifting the coil of rope he was carrying over his shoulder.

"No, it wasn't." Mandie agreed.

Sallie took a lighted lantern from one of the men. "Come, we will look together." She motioned for Mandie and Joe to follow her.

"I'm glad you decided to come with us," Mandie told the Indian girl.

"Since my grandfather was coming, I decided I should try to help, too," she answered.

"Please be careful," Elizabeth warned them.

Uncle John called after them. "Yes, you be *very* careful. We don't want to have to go looking for you again."

"We will," Mandie promised as she picked up Snowball. "I think we can find it."

"Don't worry, Mrs. Shaw. We can't get lost with everyone in here," Joe said.

With Sallie leading the way with the lantern, the three went off down a tunnel. This time they were laughing, feeling very secure with the grown-ups nearby. They stopped to look at every little pile of rocks they could find along the way.

"That can't be it," Joe said as Mandie and Sallie walked over to a rock-covered wall. "The place we went through had a smooth wall all around except for the pile of stones covering the gold."

"No, Joe, it had lots of rocks stacked all along the wall," Mandie disagreed.

"Now wait a minute, Mandie. It did not!" Joe countered. Turning to the Indian girl, he asked, "Didn't it, Sallie?"

"I do not know, Joe. Do you not remember the lantern went out and we were digging in the dark?"

Mandie and Joe looked at each other.

"That's right, Sallie," he said.

"Yes, you dropped the lantern, Joe! It must be wherever you dropped it," Mandie reminded him. "We'll find the broken glass—"

"Aw, now, come on, Mandie. All those rocks fell on top of it. It's probably well buried by now," Joe interrupted.

"We have not passed the room with the bats in it yet," Sallie said. "The bats flew at us before we found the gold."

"Oh, goodness, I had forgotten about the bats," Mandie groaned. "Do you suppose we could pass quietly so they won't get stirred up again?"

" 'Course not, Mandie. There's no way you can sneak up on bats. They are very sensitive," Joe admonished her. "We'll just have to watch out and get away fast when they come out."

They rounded a corner and a whirring, cackling noise greeted them.

"Here they come!" Sallie yelled as they bent low and ran down the passageway.

The terrifying black creatures circled and circled before they finally roosted again in their hiding place.

"Whew, that was close," Mandie said, breathlessly, pulling Snowball's claws loose from her shoulder, "Snowball, calm down. Let go!"

"We are getting close to the place," Sallie said. "Remember, it was not long after we saw the bats that we found the opening."

"There was a large hole in the floor of that room where the gold was," Mandie reminded them. "We walked around it before coming to the pile of rocks."

"Right," Joe agreed.

Meanwhile, Uncle Ned was leading Elizabeth and John around another way. Uncle Wirt had taken Dimar with him in still another direction.

Uncle Ned pointed to cracks in the walls and ceiling and kept muttering, "Dangerous! Cave not good!"

"But Uncle Ned, these cracks look like they have been here a long, long time," John replied, examining them closely.

"Long time. Ready to fall now," the old Indian said.

"John, if this thing started caving in we'd never get out," Elizabeth fretted.

"This is a huge cave, Elizabeth, and the walls look like pretty solid rock. Even the floor is mostly rock," John said. "Anyway, we'll hurry." He put his arm around her tightly.

"John, I wonder where the children have gone," she said.

"Papooses not lost," Uncle Ned reassured her as he continued on through the tunnel they were in.

"I would like to know what happened to Tsa'ni," John remarked.

"Tsa'ni—bad Indian," Uncle Ned repeated.

They wandered on through the tunnel, searching for the pile of rocks that might be covering a pile of gold.

In another tunnel Joe was leading the way with the lantern when he yelled, "Here's the room with the hole in the floor!"

The girls joined him to look at the place. There it was—the hole in the floor of the cavern where they had found the gold.

"Now, our opening must have been over there," Joe said, pointing across to the other side.

At that moment the three heard a low moan and then a weak cry, "Help!"

They stood absolutely still with fright.

"W-w-w-wh-what was th-that?" Joe whispered.

"It may be the spirit of Tsali," Sallie replied.

"But Charlie didn't die in this cave," Joe said.

Again there was a call for help, this time a little louder.

"Sounds like it came up from that hole in the floor," Mandie said, not moving an inch.

"Who is it?" Sallie called in a loud voice.

"It is me, Tsa'ni. Please help me!" he answered, more clearly now.

Mandie was suddenly seeing another day, another call for help. She was remembering the panther and her terrible predicament. Tsa'ni had turned and left her alone. But she couldn't do that to him. No matter how mean he had been, she would have to help him now.

"Where are you, Tsa'ni'?" Mandie called to him.

"I fell in the opening in the floor. I am down here at the bottom of it," the boy said.

"Tsa'ni!" Joe ventured to the edge of the hole, and swinging the lantern he could faintly see something at the bottom of the pit. "Why should we help you after what you did to us?"

Mandie hesitated, fighting with her own feelings.

"No, Joe, we must help him," she said, coming to his side.

"He must have come back here looking for our gold." Joe frowned. "He's not honest. I won't help him."

"Oh, but Joe, the Bible says we should return good for evil," Mandie reminded him. "You know that."

"Well, anyway, there's nothing we can do to help him. The hole is too deep," the boy argued.

"Are you hurt, Tsa'ni?" Sallie called down to the boy.

"Yes, I cannot move," he answered in a weak voice.

"Joe, let's tie our rope around that stalagmite over there and I'll scoot down to see what's wrong with him," Mandie suggested.

"Are you crazy? There's no telling what's down in that hole," Joe argued.

"I will help," Sallie told Mandie.

"You can't climb down a rope," Joe reprimanded.

"I can so. It's not much different than climbing a tree, and I've climbed quite a few trees in my life," Mandie said, as she put Snowball down and began to pull the end of the rope from Joe's shoulder, "Come on. Unroll the rope."

Joe set the lantern down and did as Mandie asked. They fastened the rope as tightly as they could knot it and pulled it over to the hole as Mandie prepared to descend.

"Go very slowly," Sallie warned.

Pulling up the slack in the rope, Mandie finally wriggled around on the edge of the hole so that she was swinging down. Joe held the lantern as far out as he could over the hole.

Snowball, watching Mandie slide down the rope, reached over with his paw and started to claw at it.

"Snowball, stop that!" Mandie commanded, looking up at him.

Sallie picked up the kitten. "I will hold him. He might fall."

Mandie slid on down until her feet touched the bottom. She looked around in the dim light until she saw Tsa'ni lying on his back watching her. She let go of the rope and bent over him.

"What's wrong, Tsa'ni?" she asked. "Where are you hurt?"

"I do not know. I cannot move," he said.

The girl saw a stream of water near where he lay. She took off her apron and dipped it.

"Here, let me wash your face," she said. "But I'll warn you. It's pretty cold."

She wiped his face gently and he didn't move.

"Tsa'ni, we have to figure out a way to get you out of here," she said.

"Please, go for help," he begged. "Get some strong men to help me."

"Uncle Ned and Uncle John and your grandfather are all in the cave somewhere," she told him. "You just lie still and we'll go find them. It shouldn't take very long." She dipped her apron into the water again, squeezed it out, and placed it across his forehead. "There, I'll leave that right there. Maybe it'll help. Now I'll go back up the rope and get help."

"Please hurry," the Indian boy moaned.

"We will," Mandie called back as she caught the rope. By pulling it tight and bracing her feet against the wall of the pit, she was able to work her way back up to the top. Sallie and Joe pulled her onto the floor at the top.

"Well, what's wrong with him?" Joe asked.

"He can't move, Joe. We must find the men as fast as we can."

Mandie picked up Snowball as they hurried through the tunnels and caverns calling the men's names. It was a few minutes before they finally got an answer.

"Here, Papoose. Stay there. We come," Uncle Ned called from somewhere out of sight.

"That's Amanda," Elizabeth said.

"Maybe they've found the gold," John said as they followed Uncle Ned in the direction of the voices.

Turning a sharp corner they were met by a flood of light from Mandie's lantern.

"Uncle Ned, Uncle Ned, we found Tsa'ni! He's hurt—bad. He's in a deep hole. It will take some strong men to get him out."

"Show us, Mandie," Uncle John said, and turning to Uncle Ned, he added, "So he came back here looking for the gold."

Uncle Ned nodded his head and grunted. Then he gave his whistle for help. Uncle Wirt and Dimar were not far off and came on the run. Soon they were all in the cavern with the hole in the floor.

"There!" Mandie said, pointing. "He's down there. I went down to see what was wrong with him. He can't move."

She showed them the rope still fastened in place.

"Papoose good Indian," Uncle Ned said, putting his arm around her.

Mandie, pleased beyond expression by the compliment, looked up in his face with a big smile. "Thank you, Uncle Ned."

"This is the room where we found the gold," Joe told them. "I think it was over there where all those rocks are spilled all over the floor."

"Over there?" Uncle John was trying to distinguish the rocks he was talking about in the dim light from the lanterns.

"But first we have to get Tsa'ni out!" Mandie reminded them.

The two Indian men were already making a rope ladder to get down inside the pit.

"If he can't move, Uncle Ned, it's going to take some doing to get him out," John said, helping with the rope.

"Make basket. Put basket down hole," the old Indian replied. He was busy weaving the rope they had been carrying into a crude basket. Wirt and Dimar were helping, evidently knowing exactly what he had in mind. Uncle John finally understood. He walked around the hole to the other side, carrying the end of the rope from which they were making the basket. The other end stayed on the other side. The rope was fastened on each side to the basket so it could be lowered into the pit and then pulled back up.

Dimar volunteered. "I am young and strong. I will go down and put Tsa'ni in the basket."

"Go," Uncle Ned told him, and he slid down the rope Mandie had used.

"I am at the bottom," Dimar called. "Send down the basket."

The crude basket was lowered and Dimar pulled it flat on the rock floor of the pit. He and Tsa'ni were about the same size, and it was no easy job to lift the other boy and lay him on the rope basket. Neither spoke a word.

"All right, pull! He is in the basket," Dimar called.

The men carefully pulled on the rope from either side of the hole, and soon the basket with Tsa'ni in it appeared.

"That way," Uncle Ned motioned to the men on both sides to walk to the far end of the pit, holding the rope taut as they went. Then they lowered the basket carefully to the floor. Uncle Wirt bent to examine the injured boy.

"I cannot move," Tsa'ni told his grandfather. His face was pale and he looked frightened in the lantern light.

"We take Tsa'ni to wagon," Wirt told the others.

Tsa'ni turned his head away.

Joe protested as they prepared to leave. "What about the gold?"

"We'll have to use the wagon to get Tsa'ni to a doctor. We'll just have to come back tomorrow," Uncle John told them.

Mandie sighed. "Oh, me. All this work all over again." She was feeling hatred again toward Tsa'ni for interfering with their plans. After all, he had fallen into the pit because he was trying to beat them to the gold.

"Yeh, all because of that stupid boy," Joe said.

Sallie looked at the two, "He will be sorry."

"I hope he is," Joe said. "First thing you know, someone else will get the gold, and we'll never know what happened to it. So many people know about it now."

Mandie and Sallie agreed. Too many people knew about the gold. They must hurry back the next day.

CHAPTER EIGHT

THE BROKEN WAGON WHEEL

Uncle Ned pulled the wagon to a halt in front of his cabin and motioned to the others. "Wirt and me take Tsa'ni to doctor. You stay here. Morning Star make food."

"Are you sure you won't need any help?" Uncle John asked as he helped Elizabeth down from the wagon.

"No. You watch papooses," Uncle Ned said, laughing.

"I don't think they'll go anywhere. It's past suppertime and I know they're hungry," Uncle John told him.

Mandie, Joe, Sallie, and Dimar jumped down and headed for the cabin. Dimar had told his mother he would be gone for a day or two, so he decided to stay at Uncle Ned's house for the night.

Morning Star had the food cooking and Elizabeth helped her finish. The four young people sat on the doorstep with Snowball.

"Where are they taking Tsa'ni to a doctor?" Mandie asked Sallie.

"To Dr. Carnes. He is a white doctor. He lives between here and Bryson City," the Indian girl replied.

"He probably won't find anything wrong with him. I think it's all put on so he won't get into trouble for trying to steal the gold," Joe remarked, as he drew lines in the sand with a stick.

"But, Joe, he didn't say a word all the way back. He had his eyes closed," Mandie said, secretly thinking the same thing as Joe. She was desperately trying to rid her mind of the mean thoughts.

"Well, I could do that, too. Saves answering a whole lot of questions," Joe chided.

"I do not think so, Joe," Sallie disagreed. "I really believe he was hurt. He looked pale and weak."

"Well, he sure slowed things down for us."

"You're right there, Joe," Mandie said.

"Your uncle said we would return tomorrow," Dimar reminded her. His eyes never left her face. His admiration was plain to see, but Mandie was not aware of it.

"But, Dimar, we have to go all the way back up there to the cave and then all through those spooky rooms until we find the right one again," Mandie said.

"That will not be hard this time. I think I can remember exactly which way we went." Sallie was confident.

"Yeh, like that." Joe drew a rough diagram of the cave in the sand. "Here's the entrance, and we went this way." He pointed. "Then this way and that way," He sketched a line through the outline.

"That is right." Sallie was watching.

"But there's still the problem of actually finding the gold. It's buried somewhere under all those rocks, and they all look the same," Mandie reminded them.

"That should not take long with so many people to help dig," Dimar said.

Elizabeth came to the doorway. "Eat!" She laughed.

"Eat! That word is good in any language!" Joe exclaimed as they stood up and hurried to the table for their evening meal.

"Amen!" agreed Mandie.

Dimar managed to sit between Mandie and Sallie with Joe on the other side of Mandie. Joe was beginning to notice Dimar's behavior around his friend. He didn't say anything, but kept a watch on the two of them during the meal. Mandie still did not seem to notice the extra attention.

Uncle Ned returned after a while, alone. Everyone looked up, anxious for news of Tsa'ni.

"Tsa'ni go home. Wirt go with him," the old Indian told them as he sat down to eat. "Doctor say—stay in bed."

"Well, did he think it was serious? I mean, can Tsa'ni move now?" Uncle John asked.

"No," the old man replied. "Hurt back, legs."

"Well, I hope he doesn't have a *bad* back injury. He may never walk again," Elizabeth said.

Everyone became serious. Mandie was fighting elation over the fact that Tsa'ni really was injured. In the back of her mind she knew she should feel sorry for him. But she couldn't help feeling he deserved it.

She spoke up to clear her thoughts. "Can we go to see him tomorrow?"

The old Indian nodded. "Yes—Tsa'ni bad Cherokee."

"You mean because he tried to get the gold?" asked Joe.

The old man nodded again. "Gold bad for Cherokee. Tsa'ni bad, too."

Mandie turned to her Uncle John. "Are you still going back to the cave tomorrow?"

He turned to Uncle Ned. "What do you think? Should we go back up there tomorrow?"

"Go tomorrow. Be done!" the Indian grunted.

Uncle John laughed. "You still aren't happy about looking for the gold. Uncle Ned, the Cherokees could use the gold for a lot of things they need—a hospital, a school closer by, even a new church. Depending on how much is there, the gold could buy lots of things which would take years and years to get otherwise."

"Gold make people crazy. Bad for Cherokee. Bad for Tsa'ni." He was very firm about it.

"I know, but we'll see what good we can do with it," John continued.

"You mean we can't *keep* the gold?" Joe asked, surprised at the conversation between the two men.

"Of course not, Joe," Uncle John told him. "This is Cherokee territory, so it rightfully belongs to them."

"But the cave is not on the Cherokee reservation," Joe argued.

"I know that, but it's almost one hundred percent Cherokee territory around here. Besides, that cave belongs to their history. Remember, Tsali hid in there," John added.

"Couldn't we just keep a little sample for a souvenir?" Mandie ventured.

"Depends on how big the sample is," Uncle John laughed. "Anyhow, we'll cross that bridge when we come to it."

Morning Star had been sitting at the table listening to the conversation. No one had any idea how much she had understood until she spoke up with great conviction, "Jim Shaw's papoose have gold!"

Everyone turned to look at her, startled.

She tried to explain. She pointed to herself and then to Mandie. "My gold Papoose's gold."

Mandie jumped up to hug her. "Oh, Morning Star, you are learning to speak English! I wouldn't take your gold. Like Uncle John says, it belongs to the Cherokees living around here."

Morning Star shook her head furiously and rattled off something in Cherokee. Uncle Ned listened and turned to explain.

"Morning Star say gold bad for Cherokee. Morning Star remember Cherokee move. I remember, too."

"Times have changed, Uncle Ned," John insisted. "I can guarantee you no harm will come to the Cherokees when the gold is found. It won't be like it was before."

The old man grunted and got up to go outside. John followed him.

"Early to bed, early to rise," Elizabeth told the children.

The four went to bed early, but there was a great deal of talking going on over the wall. Dimar and Joe were on the one side and the girls on the other. Joe, knowing the Indian boy was interested in Mandie, tried to monopolize the conversation.

"Mandie, this is even more exciting than looking for your uncle's will, don't you think?" Joe began.

"Well, I don't know about that," she said. "I suppose it is just *as* exciting. Of course, I've never seen so much gold before."

"Neither have I," Sallie put in.

"I sure hope we find it," Dimar said. "There must be a pile of it if it can buy a hospital and all that other stuff your Uncle John was talking about, Mandie."

"A *huge* pile of it. I have no idea how much it's worth, though," said Mandie.

"Your uncle will know," Dimar assured her.

"I'm sure glad he's around to handle everything because Uncle Ned is certainly not interested," she said.

"He can remember the removal," Dimar reminded her.

Joe, becoming jealous of the boy, faked a yawn and said loudly, "Well, time to go to sleep. Have to get up early."

"Yes, we have to get up early," Sallie agreed.

"I almost forgot something. If we are leaving early in the morning for the cave, how are we going to see Tsa'ni?" Mandie asked.

"Well, I have no intention of going to see Tsa'ni. You will just have to wait until we come back if you insist on visiting him," Joe replied.

The question was settled at early dawn when the four, wide awake with excitement, went downstairs for breakfast. Uncle Ned and Uncle John were just coming in the door from outside. They looked disturbed.

Seeing the four youngsters at the table, Uncle John explained, "Well, it looks like we won't be going back to the cave today. The wagon has a broken wheel and we have to get the part from Bryson City, which is going to take some time."

The four spoke as one, "Oh, no!"

"It wasn't broken when you came home last night, was it, Uncle Ned?" Mandie asked.

The old man shook his head. "Broke today."

Uncle John explained. "No, it wasn't broken last night. It looks like someone has been prowling around and deliberately damaged the wheel."

The four looked at one another.

"Well, since Tsa'ni can't walk, it couldn't have been him this time," Mandie said.

"How about the old man and woman that captured us in the woods?" Joe asked

"Snuff and Rennie Lou?" Mandie asked.

"Yeh, maybe it was them."

"I hardly think they would come down here and do a thing like that," Uncle John said.

"You said you told them you were going to report them to the authorities," Sallie reminded him.

"Yes, as a matter of fact, I did tell them that."

"But why would they want to do something like that?" Uncle John added.

"Maybe they know about the gold," Dimar suggested.

"And maybe they know we are going after it," added Mandie.

"Well, anyway, however it happened, we will have to wait until the wagon is repaired," John Shaw said.

"Couldn't we borrow a wagon from one of the neighbors? After all, Uncle Ned knows all of them," Mandie said.

"No, we'd rather not do that. We'd have to keep it all day, and we'd have to explain where we were going. Uncle Ned and I are going to ride into Bryson City when we get the horses saddled up and see what we can get to fix the wheel."

"Are you going to talk to the authorities about the old man and woman?" Joe asked.

"I suppose we'll do that while we're there," John said.

"They must have a still up there. Remember, we told you they thought we were spying on their still," Mandie added.

"I remember."

"May we go visit Tsa'ni while Uncle John is gone, Mother?" Mandie asked Elizabeth.

"If you want to, but you mustn't stay too long. Tsa'ni is probably too sick to be bothered with company," her mother told her.

As the men rode away to Bryson City, the four waved good-bye from the front of the cabin.

"Anyone want to go see Tsa'ni now?" Mandie asked.

"I will go with you," Sallie replied.

"I don't know. I think he is dishonest with us," Joe mumbled.

"I will go," Dimar said, eager for the chance to be with Mandie.

Joe was quick to notice, and he thought he'd better go along just to keep an eye on the two. He shuffled his feet around in the sand and looked up. "All right. I'll go, too, but I won't have anything to say to him."

Tsa'ni lived about a mile down the road from Uncle Ned's house, but the road had such a sharp curve that it was easier to cut through the backyards of several neighbors. Mandie had already decided that all the Cherokees' cabins were alike and so she was not surprised to find Tsa'ni's home a duplicate of Uncle Ned's. The door of the log cabin was open and as they approached, a kind Indian woman came to welcome them.

"Come in. I am glad you could come to see Tsa'ni," she said, as they entered the house.

The boy was on a bed at the far end of the room, and Mandie could feel him staring at her.

"I am Amanda Shaw, and you must be Tsa'ni's mother," Mandie introduced herself.

"Yes, I am Meli," the woman said. "Your father was my husband's cousin."

Mandie nodded. "That's right. How is Tsa'ni today?"

"Not good. But, go—see," she said, directing the four over to the bed.

Tsa'ni stared but did not speak.

"We came to see how you are," Mandie spoke cheerfully.

There was no answer.

"What did Dr. Carnes tell you about your injuries?" she asked.

Tsa'ni seemed determined not to speak.

"You could at least answer," Dimar told him. "You are being rude."

Tsa'ni took a deep breath. "Why should I speak to the white girl? White people! They are always causing trouble for the Cherokee!"

"No one caused trouble for you, Tsa'ni," Dimar retorted. "What happened to you was your own fault. And you *were* rescued because Mandie cared about what happened to you."

"The white people come here poking into the Cherokees' affairs," Tsa'ni said. "I do not want to see any more white people!" He turned his face toward the wall.

"You are a very narrow-minded person, Tsa'ni," Mandie told him.

"Tsa'ni, if you had not been trying to find the gold first, you would not have been injured," the Indian girl said.

"Go away! I do not wish to communicate with white people! I do not wish to have any company!" He still kept his face turned away from them.

Joe was filled with anger. "You may not wish to communicate with white people, but you must admit you tried to get the gold which we found first."

"The gold belongs to the Cherokees, not the white people!" Tsa'ni turned to glare at Joe.

"We found it and we will do what we please with it!" Joe insisted.

"Do not be too sure about that! Now, get out!" Tsa'ni yelled, flushed with anger.

The four backed off to leave. They stopped to say good-bye to his mother who had been watching the whole scene.

As they walked back through the yards to Uncle Ned's house, Mandie asked, "I wonder what he meant when he said we shouldn't be too sure about doing what we please with the gold?"

"Just talking," said Joe. "He wants to frighten us away from it."

"He could have told someone else about the gold," Sallie suggested.

"Yes, and they could be looking for it right now," Dimar added.

"I hope not," Mandie said. "You all heard what Uncle John said could be done with the gold, and I sure hope the wrong people don't get it."

They all felt their plans were strangely threatened. Mandie hated Tsa'ni more that ever in spite of her intentions to forget the wrongs he had done them. He was such a revengeful person. How could anyone like him?

CHAPTER NINE

TSALI'S MESSAGE

Uncle Ned and Uncle John were back from Bryson City in time for the noontime meal. As they all sat around the table, they discussed their journey.

"Did you get the piece to fix the wagon?" Mandie asked before anyone had eaten a bite.

"Yes, as soon as we finish eating, we'll get it back in working order, and tomorrow we'll go back to the cave," Uncle John told her.

The four looked at one another and smiled.

"Eat," Uncle Ned commanded.

"Yes, sir, Uncle Ned," Mandie replied, picking up her fork, and starting on the beans. The other three followed suit.

Elizabeth turned to John. "Did you talk to anyone about those two people up in the mountain?"

"The old man and woman? Yes, we told everything we knew about them. There will be men scouting the mountain looking for a still in a few days," he said.

"We went to see Tsa'ni and he was rude to us," Mandie said. She related the conversation between them. Uncle Ned listened closely.

"Tsa'ni bad Cherokee," he mumbled. "Up to no good."

"Bad," echoed Morning Star.

"Well, there's nothing he can do if he can't get about," Uncle John told them.

"I don't trust him at all," Joe said. "I think if he *could* walk, he wouldn't let us know it."

"Joe!" Elizabeth admonished him.

"Sorry, Mrs. Shaw, but I don't trust him," Joe told her.

"I don't either, Mother," Mandie said. She had decided to give up believing the Indian boy.

"I cannot trust him either," Sallie added.

"Neither can I," Dimar joined in.

"Well, in that case, maybe there *is* some reason not to trust him," Elizabeth replied.

"Reason—Tsa'ni bad," the old Indian repeated.

"Oh, Uncle Ned, you've been saying Tsa'ni is bad ever since we got here. How about telling me why you say that?" John asked Ned.

"Leave Papoose with panther. Try to steal gold. No bring things to Bird-town," the old man explained. He took a deep breath. "Now he make bad talk to Papoose."

"The Bible says repay evil with good, remember, Uncle Ned?" John reminded him.

"Big Book not say Tsa'ni can be bad Indian," the old Indian muttered.

Everyone smiled.

Mandie couldn't understand why one should keep on doing good to a person who kept on doing bad things in return. She was quite exasperated and was losing her determination to be kind. Then she remembered her father had taught her to pray for her enemies, so she decided she would start praying for Tsa'ni. In the meantime, she hoped he would recover from his accident—but not in time to beat them to the gold!

Uncle Wirt went with them the next morning to the cave. He was still angry with his grandson and would not talk about him. He had gone on to his house in Bird-town the day before and had not seen Tsa'ni since.

After arriving inside the cave, Sallie led them straight to the cavern where they had seen the gold.

"Here is the place," she told them, pointing to the pile of rocks along the far wall.

Mandie agreed. "Yes, this is it."

"Well, let's start digging," Joe said, pushing up his sleeves.

With the three men to help them, it didn't take long to move the piles. Elizabeth watched from a safe distance as they threw the rocks behind them out of the way. Sallie found the first nugget.

"Gold," she said, handing the nugget to Uncle Ned who was working beside her.

He turned it over in his hand, didn't say a word and passed it on to John. The others crowded around.

"The real thing," John Shaw said. "Let's see how much we can find."

Mandie and Joe were moving the rocks at the bottom of the pile when she stooped and squealed. "Here it is! All of it!" They had uncovered the gold they had found before.

"At last!" Joe gasped.

The men bent to inspect the gold.

"You were right, Mandie. It is about a bushel," her uncle told her. "Now let's get it into these sacks and get out of here."

Everyone was stuffing the sacks with the gold when Sallie, cleaning off the floor under one end of the pile, called out, "Look! Writing!" She was pointing to the wall of the cave behind the rocks.

The group gathered to see what she had found. They all worked to clean the wall and the rest of the writing. Soon large Indian sign language appeared and also some words in English.

Sallie bent close to read it. "This gold left here for good of Cherokee after white man makes peace. This gold belongs to us who are hiding here to save our lives. Curse on the white man who takes it. Tsali." She gasped as she finished the words.

All were speechless as they stared at the crude letters on the stone wall.

Joe turned to Ned. "Could it really have been Tsali who wrote this message and left the gold?"

The old Indian nodded. "His name." He pointed to the symbol under the English "Tsali."

"He did not forget his people," Dimar said very solemnly. "He gave his life and left them a fortune."

"After all these years!" Mandie exclaimed. "And to think we were the ones who discovered it!"

"Someone else must have written the message for him," Uncle John said.

"Probably the white man, William H. Thomas, who came to ask him to surrender to save his people," Sallie added. "He was the trusted friend of the Cherokee people."

"Of course," Uncle John agreed.

"Would it be possible to take the message, too, with the gold?" Mandie asked.

"You don't mean that?" Joe laughed. "That's a stone wall."

"I just don't know. I suppose we could get somebody to look at it to see if the piece of stone could be chiseled out," Uncle John suggested.

Elizabeth asked, "Wouldn't it be better to leave it here for history's sake?"

"Well—" began John.

"On, no, Mother," Mandie protested. "You see, the wall caved in on us when we climbed through the hole we dug, and sooner or later rockslides will completely cover it again and maybe even break it up. Besides, we don't want to spread word about the gold yet, do we?"

"You're right," her uncle said. "We'll see about getting it chiseled out."

"We take message out," Uncle Ned told them.

Wirt nodded.

"Please, could I help?" Dimar asked.

Uncle Ned nodded. "Strong brave."

"Let's hurry," Uncle John said, bending to help fill the sacks. "We want to get back before sundown. Uncle Ned, you and Uncle Wirt can come back whenever you get ready and see what you can do about cutting out the message."

Carefully sorting through the rocks to be sure they got it all, they finally finished filling the sacks and carried them to the wagon. It was time-consuming and back-breaking work, but it seemed worth the effort. With all this gold the Cherokees could accomplish a lot.

As they prepared to return to Uncle Ned's cabin, Uncle John warned them, "It's better that we don't discuss this with anyone outside our little group here until we can come to some decision as to how to give this gold to the Cherokee people."

Uncle Ned looked fiercely at the others. "No talk!"

Uncle Wirt added, "No talk."

The others agreed. Some plan would have to be made for distributing the gold to the Indians, and until something was finalized, it would be safer not to let anyone else know about what they had found.

It was dark when they arrived at Uncle Ned's cabin. Morning Star had the table set with food to greet them. They hurriedly unloaded the gold in the barn and covered it with hay.

"Should be safe here until we can decide something further," Uncle John said as they shut the door. He took the nail hanging on a leather strap and dropped it into the hook, the only way there was to secure the door.

They were all happy as they walked toward the cabin, not realizing they were being watched in the darkness.

CHAPTER TEN

THIEVES IN THE NIGHT

The four young people were talkative and restless long after they had gone to bed. Snowball sensed their mood and bounced around between them. There was a small window next to Mandie's bed, and she and Sallie kept peering out at the barn.

"Just think what's in the barn!" Mandie exclaimed.

"Yes, and think of how much fun it will be giving it to the Cherokees," Joe called over the dividing wall.

"It is such a dark night. If the moon were only shining, we could see the barn more clearly," the Indian girl said.

"I do not think we need to stay up all night watching the barn," Dimar said from the small room he occupied with Joe.

Sallie tensed up suddenly. "Mandie! Look! Is that someone out there?"

Mandie pressed her face against the windowpane. "Where, Sallie?"

"At the corner. There!" Sallie poked at the window.

"I can't see anyone, Sallie," Mandie was getting excited.

"Oh, I suppose it was just my imagination," Sallie admitted. "We should go to sleep."

"I can't believe those girls," Joe sighed.

"Hey, wait, I see a light! Look!" Mandie shouted.

The two girls stared hard into the darkness. Then gradually the light grew stronger.

"It's a fire! The barn is on fire!" Mandie screamed. She ran to the ladder and screamed again. "Uncle Ned, Uncle John, the barn is on fire!"

Dimar and Joe hastily pulled on their trousers and ran to see. They took one look through the window and flew down the ladder. The girls, pulling their dresses on over their heads, followed, Snowball close behind.

Uncle Ned and Uncle John were already out the door by the time the boys' feet hit the floor. Elizabeth and Morning Star were getting dressed.

"Bell!" shouted Uncle Ned to Dimar as he ran. The boy understood and ran to the huge iron bell hanging in the tree and pulled the rope. The clapper sent out a loud gong and in seconds neighboring Indians began appearing from all directions carrying water buckets.

"Oh, please, dear God, don't let it burn up," Mandie prayed as she was held back by her mother.

There were so many men fighting the fire that it was soon extinguished with little damage done, thanks to the girls who had seen it start. Uncle Wirt had gone to his son's house for the night, and he was among the fire fighters who had answered the call of the bell.

The volunteers all went home and Uncle Ned, Uncle Wirt, and Uncle John stood surveying the damage.

"Thank goodness we caught it in time," John said. "That was deliberately set. I just hope whoever it was doesn't come back tonight."

"I will guard the barn," Dimar offered as he stepped forward. "I will stay out here."

Joe, not to be outdone, spoke up, "I'll help you. One of us can sleep inside while the other one watches and then we can switch."

So it was agreed. The boys stood watch for the rest of the night. The girls, more restless than ever, kept watching at the window.

"Who do you suppose set that fire?" Mandie asked as they lay by the window.

"I do not know," the Indian girl said. "But whoever it was I wish we could catch him."

"I have a feeling whoever did it knew about the gold," Mandie said.

"Yes, I think so, too," Sallie agreed.

"Tomorrow Uncle John will repair the barn and Uncle Ned and Uncle Wirt will go back and start work on chiseling out the message in the cave. And when they get done, we can do something with the gold. Uncle John said they wanted the message to show the people when they present the gold to them."

"That will be a great day for the Cherokee!" the Indian girl said.

Tired and worn out, the two girls were soon asleep in spite of their excitement. But while they slept peacefully, things were not so peaceful in Uncle Ned's yard.

Joe was trying to sleep inside on the haystack, while Dimar was on guard outside the barn. He couldn't get comfortable, his ears attuned for intruders. Finally he gave up trying to sleep and went outside to join Dimar.

"I might as well forget it," he told the Indian boy. "I can't go to sleep in there."

"I can't sleep either," Dimar said.

"How about if you stay in the front here and I'll stay at the back?" Joe asked.

"All right. Sounds good to me." Dimar was too tired to argue.

Joe walked around to the back and stretched out in the grass. He had been lying there for what seemed like hours to him, when he heard the soft snap of a twig. He didn't move, but his ears perked up to listen. The night was so dark it was impossible to see very far. Then he heard another pop in the underbrush behind the barn. Now he was certain someone was there. He waited, his heart pounding furiously. Whoever it was, he must be out of sight lying in the tall grass.

Quietly turning on his side with his eyes trained on the brush in front of him, Joe finally distinguished the figure of a man. He took one step forward, pausing to listen, took another, then paused again. Joe waited until he was almost within reach, then bolted upright.

He could hardly believe his eyes, "Tsa'ni! You liar! You're supposed to be in bed!"

Tsa'ni stared in surprise at the sudden outburst. As he turned to run, Dimar, having heard the commotion, joined the chase. He was as surprised as Joe to see Tsa'ni.

"Tsa'ni! You are a disgrace to our people!" Dimar shouted at the fleeing Indian, who, knowing the area so well, was soon far from the reach of his pursuers.

The two boys finally gave up the chase. "Looks like we lost him," Joe said, exhausted and gasping for air.

"Yes, but now we know who started the fire, don't you think, Joe?" Dimar replied, wiping the perspiration from his forehead.

"Shall we wake up his mother and Uncle Wirt and tell them?" Joe asked. "We must be somewhere near his house. I'm sure he's the culprit all right."

"No, I think it best we wait until daylight. We can keep watch until morning, and then we'll tell Uncle Ned," thy Indian boy said.

"Yeh, Uncle Ned will know what to do," Joe agreed, as they returned to the barn.

In spite of their good intentions, they both fell fast asleep and didn't awaken until daybreak, when they heard Morning Star open the door of the cabin.

They waited until everyone was gathered around the table, and then relayed the excitement of the night before.

"Uncle Ned, we think we know who set fire to your barn," Joe told the old man.

Every head turned in his direction. Just then, Uncle Wirt came in through the open door, unnoticed.

"Who?" Uncle Ned asked.

"Tsa'ni," Joe replied.

Uncle Wirt stopped in his tracks, his presence still undetected.

"Tsa'ni?" Uncle Ned repeated, shaking his head There were a few seconds of shocked silence; then the questions began.

"How do you know, Joe?" Uncle John asked.

"We caught him prowling around the barn last night, only he escaped," Joe said.

"Joe caught him by surprise. We know it was Tsa'ni We chased him a long time," Dimar added.

Uncle Wirt stepped forward to the table and everyone noticed him for the first time.

"Tsa'ni?" Uncle Wirt asked incredulously.

"Yes, Uncle Wirt," Joe replied.

"Tsa'ni—gone last night," Uncle Wirt nodded.

"I'm sorry, Uncle Wirt. I know he's your grandson," Uncle John sympathized.

"No. Tsa'ni bad Indian," Uncle Wirt affirmed. "He make lies."

"We chased him all through the woods, but he didn't go home," Joe said.

"But, we didn't actually *see* him set fire to the barn," Mandie spoke up. "We couldn't say for sure that he was the one who did it unless we actually saw him, right?"

"You are absolutely right, my dear," Uncle John agreed. "We are jumping to conclusions. Just because Joe and Dimar saw him near the barn last night doesn't mean he was the one who started the fire."

"But what other reason would he have for lying about not being able to walk and then showing up at Uncle Ned's barn the night of the fire?" Joe argued. "If he were just curious, he wouldn't have taken off like the wind when he saw us."

" 'Judge not, lest ye be judged,' " Mandie quoted. "Do you remember our Sunday school lesson not long ago, Joe?"

Elizabeth gazed admiringly at her daughter and smiled.

"I don't understand why you are always defending him, Mandie, after all the things he has done to us." Joe shook his head.

Uncle Ned pushed a plate of food toward Uncle Wirt. "Sit. Eat. We go get message in cave."

Uncle Wirt sat down and began eating.

"I would like to talk to Tsa'ni if anybody sees him," Uncle John said.

"No one is going to be seeing him around for a while. I'm sure of that!" Joe was emphatic.

"You boys better get some sleep," Uncle John told them.

"Sleep? We want to help fix the barn!" Joe said between mouthfuls.

"Sure thing," Dimar added.

"All right, but you must both be terribly tired—or did you sleep some last night?" He looked at the boys with a knowing grin.

They both dropped their heads. Joe told him, "I guess I dozed off a little after we lost Tsa'ni."

"So did I," Dimar admitted.

Uncle Ned got his tools from the barn, harnessed up the horses to the wagon, and he and Uncle Wirt set out for the cave.

The boys went out to work on the barn with Uncle John.

Mandie and Sallie helped Morning Star and Elizabeth with chores around the house. Everyone was occupied for the day, though constantly on the alert. But just as Joe predicted, the day passed peacefully with no sign of Tsa'ni.

Inside the cave Uncle Ned and Uncle Wirt began hammering away at the stone wall. After hours and hours of work, they had made a continuous crack around the carved message and stood back to survey their work. Then there was a soft rumble. The two men held their breath listening. The rumble became louder and louder until the whole cave seemed to tremble.

"Rockslide!" gasped Uncle Ned, snatching his lantern and tools as he stumbled backward to the other side of the cavern.

The two men were temporarily stunned, and then suddenly the whole wall broke into pieces and a portion of the ceiling came crashing down. They ran for their lives. The noise was deafening. They had barely reached the entrance when the whole cave seemed to collapse. They ran without stopping until they were safely on the road. When they gazed back, it seemed the entire mountainside had changed in appearance. Huge boulders had slid down the side, dragging trees and brush with them into the waterfall. Everything in view was in shambles.

"Cave—gone!" Uncle Ned gasped.

"Gone!" echoed Uncle Wirt.

"Tsali message gone!" Uncle Ned wiped tears from his eyes as he thought about the great Indian hero who had remembered his people even in death.

Uncle Wirt could not speak. He simply turned toward the wagon on the road. Uncle Ned followed him and together they rode silently back to tell the others the news.

It was late afternoon when Mandie and Sallie saw them coming and ran to meet them. The girls could tell immediately that something was wrong.

"Uncle Ned, what happened?" Mandie asked as he stopped the wagon in front of the barn and stepped down. John and the boys came out at once.

"Cave gone. Tsali message gone," Uncle Ned shook his head in sorrow.

"Gone? How could it be gone?" Mandie asked.

"Rockslide. Cave gone. Message buried," Uncle Ned replied.

"A rockslide? Are you all right?" Uncle John asked, checking them over. "How did you manage to get out?"

"Run. God with us," Uncle Ned explained.

"Cave gone," Uncle Wirt repeated, shaking his head in bewilderment.

"That message Tsali left would have meant so much to our people," Sallie stated sadly.

"Now no one will ever believe us when we tell them about it," Joe said dejectedly.

"Part of our history has been lost," Dimar added.

"But we still have the gold," Mandie reminded them.

"Yes, and we still must decide what to do with it," Uncle John said.

As they sat around the table for the evening meal, they discussed the matter at length.

"I'll watch the barn again tonight," Joe offered after a lull in the discussion.

"So will I," Dimar said.

"You boys need a good night's rest," Uncle John told them.

"We can take our blankets and roll up in them on the grass outside. If anyone comes around, we will surely wake up," Joe insisted. Dimar nodded in agreement.

"Well, I certainly hope so," Elizabeth said. "It could be dangerous."

"Gold bad luck," Uncle Ned muttered.

"Not the gold, Uncle Ned. It's the greedy people," Mandie said.

Elizabeth spoke up. "What *are* we going to do about the gold? We can't keep it here forever."

"I know," Uncle John replied. "We'll have to decide what to do very soon."

"Why can't we put the gold in the bank?" Mandie asked.

"Good idea! Have you ever heard of bank robbers, Mandie?" Joe protested sarcastically.

"Bank robbers don't ever come to Bryson City." Mandie was sure of herself.

"I suppose the bank *is* a possible solution," John said. Turning to Wirt and Ned, he asked, "Do you think we could get it to the bank early tomorrow morning before the town is stirring?"

Both the old men nodded affirmatively.

"Well, if the people decide to storm the bank and take it, it belongs to them anyway," Joe conceded.

"No. Gold bad luck to Cherokee," Uncle Ned insisted. "Cherokee not steal gold."

"But what about Tsa'ni?" Dimar asked. "He wanted the gold."

"Tsa'ni!" Uncle Wirt spat out. "Bad Cherokee!" He rose to leave.

"Don't be too hard on him, Uncle Wirt," Elizabeth told him. "We don't know for sure who set fire to the barn."

But Uncle Wirt was angry, it was plain to see.

"He lied about not being able to walk and he should be punished for that," John said. "Will you be back tomorrow to help us move the gold to the bank?"

"Early tomorrow," the old man nodded as he waved good-bye.

As darkness began to fall, the two boys took their blankets to spread on the grass by the barn. The girls went up the ladder to their room and watched from the window until they were too sleepy to stay awake any longer. Snowball curled up contentedly at Mandie's feet.

It was long after midnight and both boys were sleeping soundly. The figure of a man appeared out of the brush and came stealthily toward the barn. He stopped at the corner of the building and lowered the flame of his lantern to the grass against the wall.

Joe stirred uneasily in his sleep, unseen by the intruder. Then his subconscious registered the distinct odor of burning grass mixed with the stench of liquor. He was awake in a flash, taxing his brain to orient himself to the situation. Then he saw the blaze not ten feet away, and he lunged to his feet. The figure, still not aware of Joe, darted around the corner. Joe headed the other way to alert Dimar who was already awake.

"He's on that side of the barn," Joe whispered softly, pointing to the north side.

They crept around the building in opposite directions and were both surprised to find themselves face to face with Snuff and

Rennie Lou. With one fell swoop Joe had Snuff on the ground. Dimar kept his eyes on Rennie Lou, who stood there in a daze.

"We got you this time!" Joe shouted as he held him to the ground.

"Hey, wait a minute. I ain't done nothin'," the man protested, his speech slurred.

Dimar took a deep breath and gave his loud Indian call for help. Within seconds Uncle John and Uncle Ned came rushing out of the cabin.

Noise of the scuffling woke the girls and they slid down the ladder and watched at the door.

"Why, it's the man and woman who captured us on the mountain," Mandie said, as she watched Uncle John "handcuff" Snuff with his belt.

Morning Star slipped past the girls without a word and joined the others outside. Rennie Lou had come out of her stupor and saw a chance for escape while Dimar and Joe went to stomp out the fire. But she was no match for the strong Indian woman, who subdued her after a short struggle.

"I ain't done nothin'!" the woman was yelling. "Leave me alone, squaw!"

Morning Star ignored her threats and kept a firm grip on her arm.

"Hey, you're a white man," she directed to Uncle John. "You gonna let this Injun woman bully me?"

"Anything she wants to do to you will be all right with me," Uncle John replied. "Don't you realize these young people are the ones you kidnapped on the mountain? You two are going to jail as soon as we can get the law to take over."

"Take palefaces to Bryson City," Uncle Ned said as he went to hitch the wagon.

"This time of night, Uncle Ned?" Elizabeth asked as she joined John.

"Yes," the old man nodded.

"He's right, Elizabeth. We can't keep them here, and they should have been behind bars before now," John told her.

"Please, mister, don't do that," Snuff begged.

Uncle John ignored him as he called to the girls, "Mandie, can you bring us some rope? We need to secure these two for the trip to town."

Sallie and Mandie came out with several coils of rope. The boys helped Uncle John tie the couple up and get them into the wagon.

"Could we go along, Uncle John?" Joe asked.

"Oh, yes, please!" Dimar joined in.

Uncle John hesitated but then added, "Well, I suppose we do need you two as witnesses of the kidnapping and the arson."

"Right!" the boys exclaimed together.

"What about us?" Mandie protested.

"This is man's work, child," Uncle John told her. And they were off.

"Mmm, so it wasn't Tsa'ni after all," Mandie said as they walked back to the house.

"No, I do not think he was the one, Mandie, and I am glad it was not a Cherokee," Sallie said.

"But he was prowling around here for some reason—probably knew we had the gold." Mandie continued. "Tsa'ni really is strange, pretending to be hurt when he isn't. I wonder if he ever went back home."

Tsa'ni had never reached home. He was at that moment caught in an abandoned hunter's trap in the woods. This time he was really hurt.

CHAPTER ELEVEN

SPREADING THE WORD

"Well, we might as well all go back to bed," Elizabeth told the girls. "It'll take them a long time to get through in town and get back here."

The girls reluctantly went back upstairs, but soon were fast asleep. Snowball curled up close to Mandie. It seemed no time before the rooster was crowing and they could hear Morning Star in the kitchen. The girls quickly got dressed and went downstairs. Elizabeth was setting the table.

"I hope they got to town all right." Mandie stretched and yawned. "Those people are awfully mean and rough."

"I'm sure they got there all right. They tied those two with enough rope to wrap around the house," Elizabeth said.

"Eat." Morning Star smiled, pointing to the table.

The girls laughed and at that moment Uncle Wirt came through the door. He glanced around for the men.

"Where are Ned and John?" He looked puzzled.

"Joe and Dimar captured the people who set fire to the barn last night," Mandie said matter-of-factly, "and they've all gone to Bryson City to turn them over to the authorities."

Uncle Wirt stood there listening in amazement while they explained what had happened the night before. He breathed a loud sigh of relief and sat down at the table.

"Not Tsa'ni!" He could hardly believe it.

"Did he ever come home, Uncle Wirt?" Mandie asked.

"No," the old man replied. "Never come home."

Everyone looked at one another, wondering where the boy could have gone. Mandie thought, *He must be ashamed for what he has done and is staying away long enough to get the nerve to face his family.*

Uncle John, Uncle Ned, and the boys arrived back from town before they had finished eating and sat down at the table to join them. Joe and Dimar began eating as though they were starving.

"I'm glad you are all back safely," Elizabeth said. "Aren't you going to tell us about your trip?"

"Yes, yes, the law was mighty glad to get our hoodlums. Seems they were wanted in quite a few counties for several different offenses," John related. "Now we can all breathe a sigh of relief."

"We take gold to bank," Uncle Wirt reminded them.

"As soon as we can eat and get it loaded, Uncle Wirt," Uncle John replied.

"Hurry, take away gold," Uncle Ned said.

"Once it's safe in the bank, we'll inform the Cherokees of its existence," Uncle John stated.

"How do you plan to do that?" Mandie asked.

"Council pow-wow," Uncle Ned told her. "They tell people."

"How will all the people decide what they want to do with the gold?" she asked.

"They will take a vote. A place will be set up in the council house on the Cherokee reservation," Uncle John explained

Joe finally laid down his fork. "Boy! That sure was good! Now I have the strength to help load that gold."

Uncle Ned rose and took a rifle from the wall. Uncle Wirt examined his own gun, and John picked up his from the other end of the room.

"Guns?" Elizabeth looked alarmed.

"We need all the protection we can get to get this load in to town. You never know what kind of trouble we might run into," John assured her.

"I know how to use one of those rifles," Joe spoke up. "Can I carry one, too?"

"I do have one more. You and Dimar can decide between you which one will carry it," John said as he reached for the other gun standing by the bed.

Joe took it and then looked at Dimar. "Here, you carry it the first half of the way to town and I'll carry it the second half."

"Fair enough," the Indian boy said, taking the gun.

"Careful, now. The guns are already loaded," John cautioned them.

The girls wanted to help, of course, but were waved aside as the men and boys loaded the gold into the wagon. It didn't take long. Morning Star brought out several quilts to cover the sacks scattered on the floor of the wagon. Joe and Dimar perched on top of them, while the three men climbed onto the driver's seat.

"Please don't be too long. We'll be worried," Elizabeth called to them.

"We'll hurry back," John promised, waving to her. Then he instructed everyone to keep his gun out of sight. "We don't want to appear too well-armed. It could look mighty suspicious."

Mandie stood watching them pull into the road. Then she lifted her face to the sky. "Please, God, get them there and back safely."

"I trust God to take care of them, too," Sallie said, touching Mandie's shoulder. "I have asked Him into my heart."

"Oh, how wonderful, Sallie!" Mandie hugged her. "Isn't it good to be able to pray and trust God for everything?"

"It sure is, Mandie," she answered, smiling happily.

The men arrived at the bank in Bryson City just as Mr. Frady, the banker, was opening up for the day. He was a short, fat, nervous little man and he jerked around to look at the wagon pulling up at the door. *Three men and two bogs—that could mean trouble,* he thought, but then he spotted a familiar face under a wide-brimmed hat.

"John Shaw!" Me hurried down the steps to greet him. "It's been a long time!"

"Wilbur, it's good to see you, old man," John returned his greeting. "We are in desperate need of your bank right now." He lowered his voice. "We have about a bushel of gold under these quilts, and we need a safe place to keep it."

Wilbur's gray eyes grew round behind his spectacles. *"A bushel of gold?* Are you joshin' me, John?"

"No, sir, it's real gold," John replied, chuckling at the banker's reaction.

"If I didn't know you, John Shaw, I'd say you had just pulled off a big robbery," Wilbur told him. "Come on in." He opened the door and the two of them stepped inside.

"Let me open the safe before you bring it in," the banker said, stepping to a large heavy door at the back.

"How about if we drive around to the back door? It won't be so public that way," John suggested.

"Of course. That's the safest way," Wilbur agreed.

They swung the wagon around to the back door and hastily unloaded the gold into the bank's safe. No one was about and Wilbur kept the front door locked until they were finished.

"Now that we have it all in here, tell me, where in the world did it come from and what are you planning to do with it?" Wilbur asked John, as the others returned to the wagon.

"It's very confidential right now, Wilbur, but we'll have it off your hands in a few days. We want to keep it quiet so there won't be a robbery."

Wilbur wiped the sweat from his furrowed brow. "Well, I should hope not! How many people know about it?"

"Just Uncle Ned and Uncle Wirt and the rest of my family—and Dimar, the Indian boy with us," John told him. "I have promised not to discuss our plans right now, but if you do hear anything about a mysterious pile of gold, pretend you never saw it. Is it a deal'?"

"You bet!" Wilbur agreed. "But please don't leave it here too long. I would like to sleep at night."

"We'll see you in a few days then," John waved as he left by the back door and joined the others in the wagon.

"Glad job done," Uncle Ned said, with a sigh of relief, as he picked up the reins and they moved through the alley and into the main street.

"Well, it's up to you and Uncle Wirt now to get the word out," John reminded them. "But don't tell anyone where it's being kept."

The two Indians left John and the boys back at Uncle Ned's cabin and went directly on their mission to tell the Cherokees about the gold.

"Shucks, we didn't even get to use the rifle," Joe complained as he handed the gun back to John inside the cabin.

John hesitated and then said, "Go ahead and try it out. You and Dimar can go back into the woods. You'll find more ammunition in the box over there. Just be careful."

The boys were overjoyed. "Thank you, Uncle John," Joe beamed, taking the rifle back.

"Thank you," Dimar added as the two headed for the door.

Mandie called after them. "You be careful, Joe Woodard, and don't go shooting somebody, you hear?" Joe stopped and turned, laughing at her outburst. "Mandie, you know I have my own rifle at home. This won't be the first time I've used one."

"Yes, but this is a strange place and that's Uncle John's rifle— I know you have never used that one before," the girl answered seriously.

Joe's face turned red as everyone smiled.

"If I didn't like you so much, Amanda Shaw, I'd say something mean!" With that he and Dimar hurried out the door.

Little did Mandie know how close the two boys would come to shooting someone. They walked on through the woods for a while, looking for an appropriate place for target practice. The trees were dense and it was hard to see very far ahead. Then they came to a small clearing.

"How about here?" asked Joe.

"Good," the Indian boy agreed.

Joe shot at a broken limb, and suddenly there was a loud clanging noise. The boys froze in silence, listening. Then it came again.

"What's *that?*" Joe whispered.

"Sounds like an animal caught in a trap." Dimar returned the whisper. "Careful, it could be dangerous." He slowly crept forward, Joe following. The clanging sound became louder, as if to beckon them on. "I think it's behind that bush over there," Dimar said softly, pointing ahead.

They cautiously moved toward the bush. Then suddenly they caught a glimpse through the leaves of what lay on the other side of the bush and they stopped in shock. There, completely helpless in an abandoned trap, was Tsa'ni, his foot tightly secured by the metal spring. He looked at them with a guilty stare as they came into view. The clanging had stopped.

"Not *you* again!" Joe slapped his hand to his forehead in exasperation.

"It seems all we do is get this boy out of trouble!" Dimar remarked.

"Would you please get this thing off my foot?" Tsa'ni sounded demanding. "That's all I want you to do."

The boys looked at each other and then at Tsa'ni's foot. It had been bleeding and was very swollen. Evidently the boy was in a lot of pain.

Joe stepped aside with Dimar so they could talk.

"I don't see how we can get that thing off his foot," Joe whispered. "We don't have tools, and besides, his foot is all swollen. Let's go for help. He'll think we are just leaving him alone."

Dimar nodded.

They walked back to Tsa'ni and shook their heads.

"I don't think we can help you. If we turn you loose, you'll just get into more trouble," Joe said to him. "This way we know where you are."

"You do not deserve any help," Dimar added.

Tsa'ni looked at them in shock. "Please! Just release my foot. I'll get home somehow by myself."

"No, we cannot help you, Tsa'ni," Joe insisted. "We don't have any tools to release that spring."

Joe and Dimar turned and walked away. When Tsa'ni realized they were not going to help him, he called and called after them, "Please! Please!"

Once out of sight, Joe and Dimar started running toward Uncle Ned's cabin. They were almost breathless when they finally got there. Uncle John was chopping wood by the barn and saw the boys coming. He dropped the axe and hurried to meet them.

"Uncle John, we've found Tsa'ni," Joe told him, handing him the rifle. "He's caught in a trap in the woods."

"We told him we would not help him," Dimar said.

"We didn't want him to know we had gone for help. Let him worry a little after all his meanness," Joe added.

"Let me get some tools and we'll go see what we can do," Uncle John said, shaking his head. "He certainly gets into more trouble than anyone I've ever known."

"We'll need a blanket or something to carry him back. His foot is in pretty bad shape, and I don't think he can walk this time," Joe told him, as John went toward the barn for tools.

"Ask Morning Star for one while I get the tools," John replied.

Morning Star got a blanket, some bottles and a cloth from the shelf, and rolled it all up together inside the blanket.

"I go too," she declared. "Special medicine."

Elizabeth understood. "She wants to go with you to doctor him with her medicine. That's what's in the bottles."

Mandie was thinking aloud. "You see, you should never tell a lie. He said he couldn't walk before and it was a lie. Now he really can't walk. I think it happened to him because he lied."

"Yes, he is a bad Cherokee," Sallie agreed.

"You should see his foot. I know he can't walk this time. He must have been caught in the trap ever since we chased him night before last. We lost him in that direction," Joe told them.

"Go." Morning Star went outside to join John as he came from the barn. The boys followed.

It was quite a job prying the trap from Tsa'ni's foot because it was so tightly secured in the swollen flesh. The foot was extremely painful to the touch, but John tried to be careful as he gently but steadily freed the flesh from the prongs of the spring. When the foot was finally free, Morning Star washed it with liquid from one of the bottles. Tsa'ni winced and bit his lip in pain. Then Morning Star gently wrapped it in a clean piece of cloth and stood up.

"Take him," she said, pointing to the boy.

John and the two boys laid Tsa'ni on the blanket and, rolling the edges of it, made a swing to carry him. Since Uncle Ned's house was much closer than Tsa'ni's, they carried him there and laid him on a bed downstairs. Morning Star administered more of her medicine.

"You boys go tell his mother he is here, and when Uncle Ned and Uncle Wirt come back with the wagon, we'll take him home," Uncle John told them. "I'll be outside."

He went out the door, and Joe and Dimar left on their errand.

The two girls had been watching the whole thing from a distance. Tsa'ni had ignored everyone until now and had not spoken a word.

Mandie came over to his bed now. "I'm sorry you are injured, Tsa'ni, but the Bible says you reap what you sow and you sure have sowed some wild lies. I think you had better pray about it. We'll all pray for you."

Tsa'ni looked at her sullenly. "What I do is my business, not yours!"

"You have been messing in our business, Tsa'ni; that's how you got hurt!" she reminded him, standing up and straightening her skirt. "Now that you are really hurt maybe you won't be able to mess in our business anymore."

Elizabeth stepped in. "Amanda, why don't you and Sallie go outside? Let Tsa'ni rest until his grandfather gets back."

"Yes, Mother," Mandie answered as she scooped up Snowball and turned to Sallie. "Come on. We'll see what Uncle John is doing."

Elizabeth did not uphold the things Tsa'ni had done, but she could see how weak he was and she didn't think it was the right time for him to be reprimanded.

Morning Star brought him a bowl of soup, and cradling the boy's head in her lap, she fed him with a spoon. He didn't say a word but greedily swallowed the broth.

Joe and Dimar came back, bringing Tsa'ni's mother with them. She ran to her son, fell to his side and started weeping. Joe and Dimar looked at each other and went back outside.

When Uncle Ned and Uncle Wirt finally came home with the wagon, John stopped them.

"No use to unhitch the wagon, Uncle Ned," John told them. "We'll be needing it. Uncle Wirt, the boys found Tsa'ni in the woods. He's inside. He has really been hurt this time, I'm afraid."

The two Indians went inside and came back out shortly, carrying Tsa'ni in the blanket. They put him into the wagon, and helped his mother climb in beside him.

"Please hurry back," John said as they pulled away in the wagon. "I want to hear what you've accomplished today concerning the gold."

"Soon," Uncle Ned called back.

As they all sat around Uncle Ned's table later that night, the old man told his news.

"Pow-wow tomorrow, council house," he said. "Told Cherokee Papoose found gold. Cherokee no want gold."

"But you did get all the chiefs to agree to let the Cherokee people vote on what to do with the gold, didn't you, Uncle Ned?" John asked.

"Cherokee vote pow-wow tomorrow, council house," the old man answered.

"You mean you can get all the people together to vote on something that fast?" John asked in amazement.

Uncle Wirt spoke up, "Tell one Cherokee. Cherokee tell another Cherokee. News travel fast."

Mandie smiled at the way he put it. "You mean when you tell one Cherokee something, he will tell another and so on, until they all know?"

Uncle Wirt nodded.

"It sure has been a busy day for the Cherokees," Joe whistled. "Imagine passing the word to over one thousand people in one day!"

"Approximately thirteen hundred to be exact," John said. "Of course, the families are large in most cases, and they live in large family groups together."

"That's still a lot of people," Mandie agreed.

"So now all the Cherokee people know about the gold?" John asked again.

"Yes, all know," Uncle Ned nodded.

"Did you tell them to come to the council house tomorrow and vote on what they thought should be done with the gold?" John continued. He wanted to be sure they understood each other.

"Yes," Ned said.

Mandie, Sallie and Joe looked at one another.

"Just think, we are the cause of all this," Joe laughed. "I feel kinda good about it when I think of all the good it will do them."

"I'm glad to be a part of it," Sallie said. "I hope the people decide on a good use for the gold."

"Well, I guess we'll know tomorrow," Mandie said, and then turning to Uncle John, she asked, "Can we go over to the council house to watch tomorrow?"

Her uncle hesitated, looking at Ned and Wirt.

"Papoose go. Papoose Cherokee. Papoose vote," Uncle Ned told her.

"You mean I can vote, too, Uncle Ned?" Mandie was excited.

"Mmm," the old man nodded.

"Can I go along for the ride even though I am not Cherokee and can't vote?" Joe asked wistfully.

Uncle Ned and Uncle Wirt both nodded. "Go."

The four youngsters discussed the matter long into the night after they had gone up to bed.

The next day would hold more excitement for them. It would be a day long to be remembered.

CHAPTER TWELVE

THE CHEROKEES' DECISION

Jerusha, Dimar's mother, came riding up on a pony early the next morning just as Morning Star was putting on the coffee. She walked in through the open doorway, smiling, as she said, "Vote." She put her arms around Mandie, Sallie and Joe and tried to tell them how happy she was that they had found a fortune for the Cherokees.

"Gold," she said, hugging the three. "Find gold. Make Cherokee feel good. People need things."

The three laughed. "Oh, Jerusha, we are so happy for all the Cherokee people. Uncle John says there is enough gold to do a lot of good," Mandie told her. "Maybe you could build a new church, or a hospital, or even a new school."

Jerusha nodded her head. "Vote." Evidently it was a new English word for her and she kept trying it out. She turned to her son and embraced him. "Vote."

"Yes, I will vote," Dimar said, embarrassed by his mother's display of affection.

Morning Star stepped forward. "Sit. Eat." Jerusha sat down and everyone else joined her.

Elizabeth sat next to Dimar's mother. "I'm so glad you could come down to vote. This is such an important thing for the Cherokees. I know you will all agree on something you need."

The woman nodded her head. "We agree what to do with gold."

At that moment more guests arrived. Everyone turned to stare as Tsa'ni was carried into the house by a huge man, who turned out to be his father. His mother, Meli, came in behind them.

"We vote," the man said as he put Tsa'ni on a chair and turned to Uncle Ned. "We vote." Meli took a place at the table.

Uncle John got up from the table and came across the room to shake hands with the man. "Good morning, Jessan. I'm glad to see you."

Jessan replied, "John, long time since we met."

"Where have you been, Jessan?" John asked.

"I take corn to Asheville to sell. Come back to vote," he said.

John turned to Mandie who was listening to their conversation. "This is Jim's daughter, Amanda. Mandie, we call her. Mandie, this is your cousin, Jessan, Uncle Wirt's son."

Mandie got up and smiled at him. "I'm so glad to meet you. I want to get to know all my Cherokee kinpeople."

Jessan laughed, showing perfect white teeth. "Lots of Cherokee kinpeople."

"How is Tsa'ni's foot?" she asked.

"Better," Jessan replied. "Well soon."

Mandie liked her cousin, Jessan, immediately. He seemed too nice to have such a miserable son as Tsa'ni. She was thinking of the many people she would meet when she went with the others to the council house to vote.

Uncle Ned's cabin was practically running over with people, and they soon began loading up for the journey to the council house.

Everyone was in a happy mood except Tsa'ni, who never said a word and tried to ignore what the others were saying.

Mandie was glad she didn't have to ride in the same wagon with Tsa'ni. There seemed to be an air of contempt and sulkiness wherever he was. Uncle Wirt and Jerusha rode with him and his parents.

Joe and Dimar sat on either side of Mandie. Joe was aware again of Dimar's interest in Mandie. She never seemed to notice. Joe was determined Mandie would be his wife when they grew up, and he didn't want anyone else making eyes at her. He liked Dimar, but not when he stared at Mandie.

As they arrived at the reservation center the seven-sided, dome-roofed council house came into view. There must have been several hundred Cherokees milling about it. Every Cherokee in North Carolina must have come to vote. They laughed and talked happily with each other. Almost all the women had red kerchiefs tied around their heads. The young girls looked as if they were wearing their best dresses as they shyly chatted with the young Indian men. It seemed to be a great big party.

When Uncle Ned found a place to leave the wagon and unhitch the horses, they all got down and walked to the council house. All the people turned to look at the group. Mandie smiled at them.

Elizabeth turned to Joe. "Well, I guess we're the only white people around, so we'll have to wait outside," she said, laughing. "Let's stand in the shade here by the doorway."

"Sure, Mrs. Shaw," Joe agreed. Turning to Mandie who was going ahead with Uncle John, he called to her. "Don't forget. Vote for a church, a hospital, or a school. Maybe a hospital would be best, the way Tsa'ni keeps getting himself hurt," he laughed.

Mandie called back to him. "Maybe that would be the best anyhow."

She followed the crowd inside. The Indians moved back to make way for her. She gazed at the inside of the huge building. There were bleachers to sit on. Stout log poles held up the dome-shaped thatched roof and the symbols of the clans adorned the posts. The place of the sacred fire was directly ahead as they entered. Behind the fire sat men with stacks of papers and books.

Uncle Ned was watching her, proud to show off his people's council house. He pointed to the men. "Vote," he said and led them across the room. He explained in Cherokee who Mandie was. Most of the Cherokees knew Uncle John from his visits.

The six men sitting behind the papers got up and smiled at her.

"Jim Shaw's papoose vote," one spoke, indicating the papers.

The second man said, "Papoose find Cherokee gold."

Between Uncle John and Uncle Ned they called the men's names as they spoke to the girl, but Mandie was too fascinated with everything to remember who they were. However, she knew they must be important people to occupy the place behind the fire.

The first man handed Mandie a piece of paper. "Vote," he said.

She took the paper, looked at it, saw that it was completely blank, and turned to Uncle John. "What do I do? Just write down what I think should be done with the gold?"

"That's right. Just write down whatever idea you have about using the gold." Uncle John turned to the first man and took a piece of paper for himself. "Have all these people already voted?"

"Yes," the man answered.

"We must be late, Uncle Ned," John whispered to the old man.

Uncle Ned had a sly smile on his face. He moved away from the others and wrote on his piece of paper and handed it back to the man who was giving them out. The man carefully recorded it in his book.

Mandie sat down on a bleacher and wrote the word *hospital* on her slip of paper and returned it to the man, as Uncle John, Morning Star, Dimar, and Sallie all gave their papers back to the Indian in charge.

"We wait," Uncle Ned told them, pointing to seats nearby.

Mandie turned and saw Tsa'ni being brought in by his father, Jessan. Meli, Jerusha, and Uncle Wirt followed. They took pieces of paper from the men, wrote, and returned them. They turned around and looked at Mandie and her group.

Mandie quickly turned to Dimar and Sallie. "I hope they don't come over here with Tsa'ni."

Before they could reply, the other group headed their way and sat down on the bleachers in front of them. She pulled her long skirt back and moved her feet to keep from touching them. No one spoke. Everyone seemed to be waiting.

The men with the papers began gathering up all their things. The first one, who had spoken to Mandie, stood up. He beat on a drum a couple of times. Silence fell over the crowd.

"Vote is done. We have counted all votes," he said in a loud, booming voice. "I will read the decision of our people on what to do with the gold found in the cave." He picked up one of the open books and began reading from it. "We, the Eastern Band of Cherokee Indians of North Carolina, do not wish to accept the gold found in the cave." He paused and looked up.

Mandie couldn't believe her ears.

He continued, "Even though it was purported to have belonged to our great warrior Tsali and to be left by him for our people, gold has always brought bad luck to our people. Therefore, we hereby designate as the holder of the gold with complete authority to use it as she wishes, the daughter of our beloved Jim Shaw, who has gone on to the happy hunting ground. We leave it in the hands of Amanda Elizabeth Shaw, who found the gold, to do whatever she deems best with it. Signed—The Eastern Band of Cherokee Indians of North Carolina."

Mandie was really in a daze now. She couldn't even think straight. The gold belonged to her Cherokee kinpeople and was worth a fortune, according to Uncle John, but here they were refusing to accept it and were giving it entirely over to her. She didn't know what to do.

The man was still talking. "This decision was made unanimously. There was not a dissenting vote."

Mandie heard that all right. That meant Tsa'ni had voted in her favor also. She just couldn't believe it was happening. She must be dreaming. She pinched herself to see if she was awake.

"Amanda Shaw, would you please come up here and accept the decision of our people?" He was looking straight at her, waiting.

Mandie turned to Uncle John. "Uncle John, I can't walk up there. I'm too scared. Why did they do such a crazy thing?"

Uncle John smiled, got up and took her hand, pulling her to her feet. "Come on. I'll go with you." He walked over to the man, practically dragging Mandie with him. The man extended the sheet of paper to Mandie.

"This is your authorization from the Cherokee people," he said.

Mandie trembled as she took the paper and turned to face the hundreds of Cherokees. "Oh, I love you, my Cherokee kinpeople. I love you." Tears came into her blue eyes. She held the paper against her heart. "I'll do my best, with Uncle John's and Uncle Ned's and Uncle Wirt's help, to use the gold wisely."

Something that sounded like a war whoop went up from the hundreds of Cherokees as they showed their gratitude. Mandie just stood there, unable to move. The first thing she knew Joe was tugging at her hand.

"Mandie, let's get out of here," he whispered.

The crowd started moving. The people passed by to speak to her, some in English, some in Cherokee.

She lifted her face as she moved along toward the others. "Thank you, God. Thank you. My people do love me."

She and Uncle John sat back down. Joe and her mother had taken seats next to them, now that the voting was over. Everyone was saying nice things to her, but she couldn't understand a thing they were saying. She was still in a daze.

She was staring directly into Tsa'ni's face as he turned to look at her. He managed to get up on his good foot and extend his hand to her as he turned around.

"Love, my cousin, love," he said, his face lit up by a big smile. "Please, forgive me!"

"Oh, Tsa'ni, my cousin, love." She smiled and put her arms around his neck and kissed him on the cheek. "My Cherokee kinpeople."

She turned and smiled at the people surrounding her. "I think we will build a hospital for my people!"

The crowd cheered.

She was sure she had made the right decision.

But now she felt that something even greater had been accomplished. She had gained her cousin's love and acceptance as a Cherokee. God had overruled. After having struggled so long with negative thoughts toward her cousin, the battle was won. She was proud to be part Cherokee, and even prouder to be a Christian.

MANDIE

AND THE
GHOST BANDITS

In Loving Memory of
That Dearest of All Fathers,
James William Leppard
(1886–1960)
Who Taught Me What Books Are,
and
My Dear Brother,
Arnold O. Leapard
(1909–1975)
An Artist of Great Renown,
Both of Whom Have Gone on Before,
And Both of Whom Led Me Along the Way.

CONTENTS

MANDIE AND THE GHOST BANDITS

"It is more blessed to give than to receive."
(Acts 30:35)

CHAPTER ONE

JOURNEY ON A TRAIN

In the dark alley behind Bryson City Bank, Mandie Shaw stood on tiptoe to peer over the side of the wagon. Her heart beat faster at the sight of the small leather traveling bags full of gold nuggets.

Mandie's Uncle John and two Cherokee Indian friends loaded bag after bag of gold nuggets into the wagon while Mr. Frady, the short, round banker, watched nervously.

Uncle Ned, Mandie's old Indian friend, plopped two bags of nuggets into the wagon. "Gold bad for Cherokee," he mumbled.

Mandie, with her white kitten, Snowball, on her shoulder, took Uncle Ned's hand and returned with him to the vault for more. "But Uncle Ned," she said, "just think what a wonderful thing we are going to do for the Cherokees with all this gold. Something that could never be done without it. We should be thankful for finding it in the cave."

"Humph! Gold not good for Cherokee," Uncle Ned insisted. "Better left in cave."

"But you know the great Cherokee warrior, Tsali, left a message with the gold where we found it," Mandie argued. "Remember?

He said the gold was for the Cherokees after the white man made peace. In fact, the inscription said it was a curse on the *white* man, not the Indian."

Uncle Ned frowned at her. "Then curse on Jim Shaw's Papoose. And I promise Jim Shaw I watch over Papoose when he go to happy hunting ground."

"My father would not believe in any old curse, Uncle Ned," Mandie assured him. "And neither do I. It's all a bunch of malarkey. God watches over us, remember?"

"Big God not watch over Cherokee when white man take land away," he said, picking up two more bags of nuggets.

Mandie shook her blonde head. "I can't explain that. God sometimes does things that seem bad to us—like taking my father to heaven. But it's to teach us a lesson—how to be better Christians. I don't know what it was, but He must have had a reason for the terrible suffering the Cherokees went through back then." She looked pleadingly at the old man. "Please, Uncle Ned, you believe in God. I know that."

The tall, old Indian set down the bags and hugged the small twelve-year-old. "Papoose right. Must believe in Big God. Now we take gold to Asheville. Build hospital for Cherokees," he relented.

Mandie kissed his dry, withered cheek as he straightened up. Uncle Ned smiled, patted her on the head, and picked up the bags again.

Mandie followed Uncle Ned outside. "And we have to trust God to help us get it there safely," she reminded him.

Tsa'ni, Mandie's Cherokee cousin, sat in the driver's seat of the wagon. "How many more?" he called. "There must be a large amount of gold in there."

Uncle Wirt, Tsa'ni's grandfather, passed a bag to Uncle John at the back door. "You just watch wagon. We load bags," he yelled at Tsa'ni.

Mandie looked startled at the harsh tone of Uncle Wirt's voice. She knew he was still angry with his grandson Tsa'ni for the many bad deeds he had done. But Mandie thought the boy had changed since the time he tried to beat them to the gold. She believed he should be given a chance to prove himself.

Walking to the side of the wagon, Mandie spoke quietly. "There's a little more, Tsa'ni," she told him. "But it's awfully heavy. That's why it's in such small bags. They think it will look more like luggage that way, too."

"Are we taking this gold to the train?" Tsa'ni asked.

"Yes, it's all been kept secret because of the danger involved, but we're going directly from here to the depot. Then we'll take the train to Asheville," Mandie explained in a low voice.

"What happens when we get to Asheville?" Tsa'ni asked.

"We'll put the gold in a bigger bank so it'll be safe. Then we're going to start building the hospital for the Cherokees on some land between Deep Creek and Bird-town," Mandie explained.

"So, it has all been planned," the Indian boy said, "and no one has told me a thing."

Just then Uncle John called to Mandie from the doorway. "Hop in, Mandie. That's all."

Mandie, with Snowball clinging to her shoulder, climbed into the back of the wagon and made a place for herself among the bags of gold. Tsa'ni followed. Uncle John shook hands with Mr. Frady, the banker. "Well, Wilbur, thank you. We've finally got it off your hands," he said.

"Thank goodness!" the short, round man replied. Nervously, he wiped the sweat from his brow. "Maybe I can get some sleep now. That was just a little bit too much for me to worry over, John."

Uncle John turned to the two Indians. "Let's get going," he said. "My wife should be waiting at the depot with the others by now." The three men climbed into the wagon.

"I wish you Godspeed," Mr. Frady called from the doorway.

Uncle John tipped his wide-brimmed hat at Mr. Frady as Uncle Ned shook the reins, and the horses pulled the wagon down the alley past an old drunk and onto the dark, deserted street. It was time for everyone in Bryson City to be at home eating supper.

The train would be in shortly. The whole operation was going smoothly. Their secret seemed well kept.

Snowball nosed around the quilts covering the gold in the bottom of the wagon bed and disappeared underneath in his inspection of the leather bags.

Tsa'ni suddenly made a quick movement and pulled the kitten out from its hiding place, tossing him to Mandie.

"That animal friend of yours knows how to bite," he said, rubbing his leg. Under the quilt his hand touched something. Pulling it out he found an old half-burned candle. He looked at it for a few seconds, then put it in his pocket.

"I'm sorry, Tsa'ni," Mandie apologized. She shook the kitten lightly. "Snowball, you know you aren't supposed to behave like that. Now curl up in my lap and be still," she scolded.

"Where did you get such a cat?" Tsa'ni asked.

"Oh, I've had Snowball since I lived in my father's house at Charley Gap. He goes with me everywhere I go," Mandie said, softly rubbing the kitten's white fur. Snowball purred contentedly. "He's a smart cat. He helped my friends and me escape from the bootleggers who kidnapped us when we got lost in the mountains."

"Now, how did he do that?"

"Well, they tied our hands, and Snowball played with the ends of the rope until it was loose enough for us to get away," Mandie explained. "Snowball also knows when it's time to eat and time to go to bed."

"That is nothing. Most animals know that," Tsa'ni retorted.

A train whistle sounded in the distance and soon the depot came into view.

Uncle John turned around in the front seat. "Remember, Mandie, when we stop, I want you and Tsa'ni to go directly to your mother. She should be right inside. Uncle Ned and Uncle Wirt and I will unload the gold into one of the train cars. We don't want to draw any unnecessary attention."

"Yes, sir, I understand," Mandie answered.

When Uncle Ned stopped the wagon by the depot platform, Mandie stood. "Come on, Tsa'ni. Let's go," she said quietly.

Clutching Snowball, she jumped down. Tsa'ni followed, and they both hurried inside the wooden building where her mother and friends waited.

When Elizabeth, Mandie's mother, saw the two through the doorway, she stood up from the long bench where she and the other young people were sitting.

Mandie looked around the large room. *This place looks like a church with all these benches like pews*, she thought. There was even a wood stove standing in the middle of the floor, just like the one in their church back home in Franklin.

Elizabeth met her daughter with a hug. "I already have all the tickets, so we can get right on the train," she said as the train came puffing up and stopped by the platform.

"Sallie, Joe, Dimar, get your things. Here are yours, Amanda." She gave Mandie a small bag. They were only carrying the essentials for overnight because they planned to go home to Franklin from Asheville.

Together they boarded the first passenger car and sat down to wait for the men.

Since Mandie had been on a train only once before, her excitement was hard to contain. She wanted to see and feel everything. Sitting on a long cross seat at the end of the car and beside the other young people, she rubbed the soft, dark upholstery and looked around in the dim lamplight. There were only a few other passengers.

Sallie, Uncle Ned's granddaughter, straightened her long, dark dress, which had been made especially for this journey. "I have never been to Asheville," she said. "I am excited about going there." She pulled her bright red shawl around her shoulders.

"I've been to Asheville several times with my father," said Joe, Dr. Woodard's son. "It's a beautiful town but it's full of hills. And, boy, does it get cold at night in that place."

"I look forward to seeing the great home of Mr. Vanderbilt," said Dimar, the Cherokee boy who was with them when they found the gold.

"Oh, Dimar," Mandie laughed, as she rubbed Snowball's fur. "We aren't going to visit Mr. Vanderbilt. Are we, Mother?"

Elizabeth smiled at the conversation and said, "I doubt it, but I do know the man."

Mandie sat up straight and the others leaned forward. "Really, Mother?" Mandie asked.

"Well, actually, my father knew him," her mother replied. "Don't forget that I lived in Asheville a long time before I married your Uncle John."

"Why, yes, I hadn't thought of that," Mandie said. She turned to Dimar. "I don't know whether you understand or not, Dimar," she said. "You see, my grandmother had my mother's marriage to my father annulled when I was born."

Dimar looked puzzled but continued to listen. "She told Mother I had died. Then Grandmother gave me to my father and told him that my mother didn't ever want to see him again. So he took me and moved to Swain County where he married another woman. I always thought *she* was my mother until my father died and I found my Uncle John in Franklin. He's my father's brother. Uncle John knew where my real mother was in Asheville, and he asked her and my grandmother to come to his house so we could see each other. Then my mother and Uncle John got married. See?" She took a deep breath.

Elizabeth smiled at Mandie's long explanation.

"I knew some of that by listening," Dimar said. "That is interesting, like a storybook. Are we going to visit your grandmother in Asheville?"

Mandie turned to her mother for an answer. She knew her grandmother didn't like the fact that Uncle John had exposed her long-kept secret. And she wasn't very happy that Elizabeth had married John. "Are we, Mother?" Mandie asked.

"My mother is away visiting relatives in Charleston, and I'm not sure what your Uncle John has planned for us," Elizabeth told her.

Just then Uncle John came up the aisle with Uncle Wirt right behind him. "I've made plans for us to stay at the hotel," he said, sitting beside his wife.

"A hotel? What is a hotel?" Mandie asked.

The other youngsters were wide-eyed with interest. In 1900 few young people in western North Carolina had traveled very far from home.

Sallie and Dimar waited for an explanation, too. With a knowing grin, Joe crossed his arms and leaned back in his seat.

"A hotel is a place where you pay to spend the night," Uncle John explained. "It has bedrooms to sleep in that they rent out by the night and a dining room where you can buy your meals. It's for travelers."

Sallie looked confused. "We are going to buy a bedroom to sleep in?"

Joe laughed. "No, silly, you don't buy a bedroom. You only pay so much money per night to be allowed to sleep in the room."

"And how do you happen to know so much about it, Mister Doctor's Son?" Mandie asked, sarcastically.

Joe straightened his shoulders. "Because I *am* a doctor's son," he said, "and a doctor travels a lot. I have often stayed in a hotel with my father when he allowed me to travel with him."

"You have?" Dimar asked.

"Sure," Joe said. "But it's not that exciting. It's just a room with a bed in it. You just go in the room and go to sleep like you do at home, only the hotel rooms are real fancy, and there are lots and lots of bedrooms in one big building. And there are all kinds of people sleeping in the same building." Joe enjoyed being the center of attention. "When you're hungry," he explained, "you go into this huge room with lots of tables and you tell the lady what you want to eat, and she brings you the food. That's all there is to it, except you have to pay money for it."

Uncle John smiled. "You sound like a well-seasoned traveler, Joe."

Mandie frowned. "Well, who sleeps in the same room with you?" she asked.

"No one, silly, unless you want them to." Joe laughed. "When you pay money for the room, you tell them who is to sleep in the room. That's all," he explained.

"Then we are all going to sleep in one room?" Sallie asked.

"No, Sallie," Uncle John told her. "You see, each room has only one big bed, so we will need at least four rooms—one for you and

Mandie, one for Uncle Wirt and Uncle Ned, another for Mandie's mother and me, and we'll see if all three of the boys can manage in one room."

Sallie was shocked. "Oh, but that is so many rooms, and you have to pay money for each room. Could we not all sleep in one room? It would not cost so much money that way," the Indian girl reasoned.

"That's not the way hotels do business, Sallie," Uncle John replied. "Usually only two people can sleep in a room. But don't worry about the money. It has all been taken care of."

"It sounds like fun, Sallie." Mandie giggled. "You and I get a whole room all by ourselves."

"You must promise not to talk all night, though," Elizabeth cautioned them.

"Uncle John"—Mandie changed the subject—"where is Uncle Ned?"

"He stayed with the cargo back in the baggage car," Uncle John said in a low voice. "After a while Uncle Wirt and I will take our turns looking after it. We thought it would be better if we didn't let it completely out of our sight."

The train gave a lurch and the couplings between the cars clanged as it began pulling out of the station. The sudden movement caught the young people unaware and they fell against each other, laughing.

"Away we go!" shouted Mandie above the noise.

The whistle blew, and the train picked up speed as it rounded the bend, leaving town and safety behind. None of them knew what danger lurked ahead in the dark night.

CHAPTER TWO

GHOST BANDITS IN THE DARK

After a while the journey became monotonous. In the dark there was nothing to look at through the windows, and the train crept slowly around the mountain.

Bored, Mandie came up with an idea. "Why don't we go back and see Uncle Ned for a little while?" she suggested. "He's all alone back there. Want to?"

"Yes!" cried her equally bored friends.

"Could we, Mother?" Mandie asked.

Elizabeth looked at John. "What do you think?"

"Well, I suppose it'd be all right," John answered. "Just don't stay too long," he told them. "And Sallie, tell your grandfather I'll be back in a little while to relieve him."

"Yes, sir," Sallie replied, as they stood up and started down the aisle of the train car.

"And please be careful when you go from one car to the other," Elizabeth called. "It could be dangerous if you don't watch your step."

"We will," they promised as they went out the door at the end of the car. When they stepped onto the platform between the cars, the cold mountain wind whipped around them and the noise of the train was deafening. They hurried into the next car.

Joe quickly shut the door behind them and stood there shivering for a moment. "I thought it was supposed to be summertime," he laughed.

"Yes, but the wind is always cold at night in the mountains," Dimar told him.

"A breath of cold air is good for us," Tsa'ni added.

There were a few passengers in the car they had just entered, but when they moved to the next car they found it completely empty.

Sallie looked around the dimly-lit car. "There certainly aren't many people on this train," she remarked.

Mandie stopped to look out a window. She leaned against the glass. "Look!" she cried, pointing outside. "Horsemen!"

The group crowded in front of the window.

"In the moonlight they look like ghosts," Mandie joked.

Joe cupped his hand against the window to see better. "What are they wearing over their clothes?" he asked.

"I do not know, but they are keeping pace with the train," Tsa'ni answered.

"It is too dark to see their faces," Dimar said.

"Oh, they see us!" Mandie said, waving her hand.

Joe looked away from the window. "I think they're trying to get on the train," he warned.

Suddenly, the train jerked to a stop. All five young people staggered and grabbed for anything to keep from falling. The train had stopped on a hill, and they found it difficult to stand upright. They all looked at each other questioningly.

"Why are we stopping here?" Sallie asked.

"I don't know," Joe answered, "but something is wrong."

Just then, a loud clang came from the direction of the baggage car. Dimar led the way as they rushed to the back door of the car to see what had happened. Dimar tried to open the door. It was stuck. He peered out the window. "The baggage car," he cried. "It has come apart from the rest of the train! It is rolling back down the track!"

"Oh, no!" Mandie yelled. "Uncle Ned . . ."

"Grandfather!" Sallie screamed.

Joe pushed his way to the window to look. At that moment there was a deafening crash. He turned slowly. Both girls were in tears, and a sick look of realization covered the faces of Dimar and Tsa'ni.

Mandie ran for the front door of the train car and threw it open. Joe hurried after her and the others followed.

Outside, Mandie hopped off the train and blindly started in the direction of the baggage car. Snowball clung to her shoulder in fright. Joe and the others stepped off the train more cautiously.

"Mandie! Wait!" Joe called. "Look! We're right on the edge of a steep ridge."

Mandie stopped. In the dim moonlight she could see the sharp drop-off just a few feet away. Her heart thumped louder as she realized the danger she was in.

Joe rushed to her side and took her hand. "Come on, all of you," he commanded. "Let's get back to the others on the train. We can't find that baggage car by ourselves."

But just as they turned to get back on, there was a loud noise and the train started up again.

They all froze in panic. By the time they could think clearly enough to run, it was too late. The train was going too fast and all five of them could never get on board without someone getting hurt.

Mandie hid her face in her hands and cried.

Sallie began to shake all over. "Grandfather!" she wailed. "Now, how will we get help for my grandfather?"

Tsa'ni put his arm around her shoulders. "Do not cry, Sallie. We will, somehow," he said.

Sallie pulled away and bumped into Dimar. Dimar grabbed her arm to keep her from falling.

"Do not move. It is steep here," Dimar told her.

"Doo-oo not moo-oove at a-a-all-ll," said a spooky voice behind them.

The young people whirled to see one of the horsemen seemingly float toward them. As he drew nearer they could see he was wearing a flowing, ground-length, light-colored cape and a light wide-brimmed hat. A tiger mask covered his face, and he carried a dimly-lit lantern. He looked huge.

The young people stood speechless with fright. They huddled together as he approached.

The ghostly man swung the lantern up to light their faces and spoke in an angry, eerie voice. "Wha-a-at are you-oo do-oo-inng he-e-ere?" he asked.

Dimar, with a protective arm around Sallie, looked him boldly in the face. "We were on the train when the baggage car wrecked," he answered. "And when we came out to see what happened, the train pulled away. But who are you and what do you want?" Dimar asked.

The creature spat tobacco juice on the ground and held the lantern closer to Dimar's face. "We-ell-ll-ll, what da ya kn-now-w, ah In-n-n-ju-u-un!" he taunted in his spooky voice. He swung the lantern in front of the other faces. "Thr-ree-ee In-n-ju-u-uns! Well-ll now-ow, wha-a-at air you-oo two-oo whi-i-ite young-un-ns do-oo-in-n' with the-e-ese hyar In-n-ju-u-uns?"

Mandie stepped forward, angry about the insinuation. "The three Indians happen to be our friends. Not only that, I am one-fourth Cherokee myself," she retorted, flipping her blonde hair.

At Mandie's sudden movement, Snowball dug his claws into her shoulder. Mandie winced and took the kitten into her arms.

"Too-oo ba-a-ad you-oo got offuh that trai-ain-n."

Just then, two other ghostlike figures materialized out of the darkness. They were both dressed exactly like the first.

One of them cleared his throat. "Watcha got hyar?" he asked. "By grannies, we're agonna hafta do sump-umm with these hyar younguns."

The third creature pulled a rope from under his long, flowing costume. "Better tie their hands behind 'em, and git 'em on the wagon and take 'em so fur away they cain't innerfear."

He grabbed Dimar's hands and tied them behind him as the first creature tied Tsa'ni's and Joe's. The other one tied the girls' hands behind them. Afraid to fight back or run away, the young people shivered on the edge of the mountain in the semi-darkness. They had no idea whether or not the men were armed.

The first creature spoke again, dropping his spooky voice disguise. "Tiger number two, you and Tiger number three take 'em away. I'll git back to work. Hurry up and git goin'."

Joe spoke up. "Mister, if you'll just let us go, we'll find our way home and won't bother you."

"No, we won't bother you," Mandie agreed. "We only want to find my family and Sallie's grandfather. Whatever your work is, we won't interfere."

"I say you won't innerfear," the first creature replied. "Git goin'."

He disappeared into the darkness. The second creature motioned with his lantern for the young people to follow him. The third creature brought up the rear.

Silently, they walked single file along the railroad track for a few yards. Then Mandie stopped suddenly, turned her face to the sky, and spoke, "What time we are afraid," she paused and Joe joined her in the last part, "we will put our trust in thee, dear God," they said.

The creature bringing up the rear overheard them and gave Joe a shove.

"Git a move on!" he muttered. "Ain't no God up thar gonna hyar you."

"Oh, but God does hear us, and He does answer our prayers," Mandie insisted.

The creature leading the way walked back to "take care of" Mandie when Joe stepped between them.

"You leave her alone, mister," Joe demanded.

"Well, then, you'd better tell her to shet up. And keep yourself quiet, too," the creature replied. "Else all of ya gonna git whut's comin' to ya."

Mandie whispered in Joe's ear. "Sorry. I'll be quiet, but I'll still pray."

Joe smiled at her.

"Up this trail! Git!" the creature ordered as he led the way.

The group stumbled silently among the brush and rocks as they climbed the mountainside. They stayed close to one another, having no idea what their fate would be, and worried about what had happened to the others.

After a short time they came to what looked like an old wagon trail. There, all alone, stood an old wagon with two horses hitched to it.

"In the wagon!" yelled the creature leading them.

The young people looked at one another silently. With their hands still tied, they managed to climb into the back of the wagon. The two creatures sat on the seat—one sitting backwards to watch them; the other, whipping the horses into a run. The trail was terribly rough. The wagon lurched over rocks and bumps and holes in the darkness, jostling the youngsters from side to side.

Snowball, still clinging to Mandie, protested loudly. Mandie tried her best to hold onto him by turning her head sidewise and raising her shoulder.

The wagon finally came to a halt in front of a deserted hut with a low, steeply-slanted roof. In the woods, Mandie had lost all sense of direction and wondered how they would ever find their way back.

The driver stepped down from the wagon. "Out and inside!" he ordered.

They could do nothing but obey. Inside the dark hut the first creature swung his lantern around, inspecting the interior. The other one stayed outside. The dim light showed no windows and only one door. The hut was just one big room with a huge rock fireplace. The young people looked around in dismay, afraid to speak. A nearby shelf held an old coffeepot, tin plates, and utensils. A pile of dirty, ragged quilts lay in one corner on the floor. That was all they could see.

The creature turned to go. "Now we're gonna put an iron padlock and chains on the door outside so thar ain't no way ya kin git out of hyar, and thar ain't no use yer tryin'," he sneered. "That'll teach ya to poke into other people's business."

"Please, mister, if you'd just let us go, we'll go straight home," Mandie begged.

"Yeh, go home by way of the wrecked train to see what happened to thet gold, eh? Ain't no way we gonna let ya go. We gonna git thet gold and be gone 'fore ya ever git out of hyar, *if ever*." He gave an evil laugh. "Ya may never git out of hyar. This is a deserted part of the mountains. Ain't no one ever comes this way. So we done got y'all tuck care of." He laughed again, stepped outside, and closed the heavy log door.

With the sound of a metal padlock and chains fastening on the outside, Mandie and her friends became prisoners with little hope of ever being rescued.

CHAPTER THREE

THE LITTLE BIRD

With the lantern gone, the hut became dark as pitch. The group huddled together in the center of the floor and helped one another untie their hands.

"If we only had a light," Sallie wished out loud.

With that reminder, Tsa'ni thrust his hands into his pockets and triumphantly produced the candle he had found in Uncle Ned's wagon. "Wish granted," he said smartly, although no one could see what he had. He stood up and felt his way to the huge fireplace on the back wall.

Sallie heard him moving about. "What do you mean?" she asked.

"Tsa'ni, where are you going?" Joe stood up, trying to find him.

"I am going to make a light for Sallie," the Indian boy said from near the fireplace. "If I can only find something to strike a flame."

"Are you going to build a fire in the fireplace?" Dimar asked.

"No. It might smoke and suffocate us because there is no ventilation in here," Tsa'ni replied.

The others could hear him striking stones. Suddenly a spark caught a piece of straw in the fireplace and flamed. They gathered around him and then saw the candle in his hand.

"Where did you get the candle?" Dimar asked.

"That's the candle you found in Uncle Ned's wagon!" Mandie cried. "He found it in the wagon after we loaded the gold at the bank," she explained.

"Yes," Tsa'ni said. He lit the candle, stomped on the burning straw, and set the candle in one of the tin plates on the hearth. "See what I did for you, Sallie?"

"Thank you, Tsa'ni," Sallie answered gratefully.

The flame threw a dim light around the room. They all gathered near the candle and sat down once more. Snowball curled up on Mandie's lap for a nap.

Sallie sighed. "Oh, my poor grandfather!" she said sorrowfully. "I wonder where he is!"

"And I wish I knew where my mother and Uncle John are right now," Mandie added. "How did all this happen, anyway?"

"Somehow those ghost creatures must have known about the gold on the train and caused the wreck," Dimar mused.

"I'm sure your folks are all right, Mandie," Joe comforted. "Don't worry."

There was a long silence. Tears came into Sallie's eyes as she envisioned her grandfather at the bottom of the ravine.

Mandie reached over to take Sallie's dark hand in her own small white one. "We have to trust God to take care of all of them, Sallie," Mandie said, "and figure out a way to get us out of this place." She glanced around the cabin, hoping to find some way to escape.

Snowball stirred and jumped out of Mandie's lap. Prowling around the cabin, he uncovered an old rope among the dirty quilts and played with it, scooting the end across the floor.

"Look what Snowball found!" Mandie cried.

"What good is a rope to us?" Joe asked.

"Maybe we could think of some plan to use the rope to escape," Dimar suggested. "Let us all try."

The young people grew silent again, trying to think of possible uses for the rope. Suddenly there was a twittering noise and a small bird flew down from the rafters. Snowball, at once alert, began chasing it.

"A bird! Snowball, come back here and leave that little bird alone!" Mandie scolded.

But Snowball had other plans. He chased the bewildered little bird around the room until it finally beat its wings against the huge fireplace and found the chimney opening. The bird disappeared. Mandie tried to grab the kitten, but she was a few seconds too late. Hungry for the little bird, Snowball clawed his way right up the inside chimney wall.

Mandie stood at the fireplace trying to see up the chimney. Soon the scratching noises stopped, and the frightened meowing began.

"Snowball! Come back down here, you silly cat!" Mandie called. "Kitty, kitty! Snowball!"

"He must have thought the chimney was a tree!" Joe laughed.

Mandie cocked her head in an effort to see where the kitten was. "Joe, it's not funny! How in the world will I ever be able to get him down?" Mandie wailed.

Dimar came and stood beside her. "I will go up and get him!" he offered.

"Go up the chimney?" Sallie frowned.

"Yes, it is quite wide. I think I can manage," Dimar insisted. "Snowball must be holding onto the rocks inside the chimney." Dimar stooped to pick up the candle and tried to shine the light up the chimney.

"I think he has gone too far up, Dimar. You can't reach him," Mandie moaned, clenching her fists.

"Dimar can climb the chimney," Tsa'ni said. "I know how, too."

"Climb the chimney?" Mandie questioned. "Dimar, you might fall!"

"I will not fall," Dimar told her. "You see, by bracing my toes on one side of the chimney and my backside on the other, I can push myself up and reach Snowball. I will not fall."

"If you can do that," Mandie reasoned, "maybe we could all climb the chimney and get out of here.—What do you think, Sallie?"

"I think we should try it," the Indian girl agreed.

Mandie picked up the rope Snowball had been playing with. "What if we tied the rope up on the roof like we did in the cave when we rescued Tsa'ni from that pit?" she asked.

Tsa'ni examined the rope. "It might work if the rope is long enough," he said.

Joe grabbed one end and stretched the rope across the room. "It's a lot longer than this room is wide," he said.

Dimar took the rope from Joe. "Yes, it looks long enough," he said. "I will take the rope with me and climb all the way to the top. After I secure it there, I will throw the end back down the chimney for you to use in climbing," he told them.

The others anxiously watched as Dimar, with the rope coiled around his shoulder, disappeared into the black recesses of the chimney.

Snowball continued to meow for help.

"Let us know when you find Snowball *and* when you get to the top, please!" Mandie called.

After a few moments Dimar yelled down to them. "I now have Snowball on my shoulder," he said.

"Oh, thank you!" Mandie said gratefully.

They all waited around the fireplace in silence. Then there was a loud clattering noise, and the girls cried out in fear.

"Dimar! What was that?" Joe called up the chimney.

"It is just me on the roof. It is made of tin." Dimar's voice came faintly down the chimney. "I have Snowball out, too. I am fastening the rope around the top of the chimney and will throw the end down to you. Here it comes!"

There was a swishing sound and the end of the rope appeared in the dim candlelight in the fireplace. Joe lunged forward and grabbed it.

"We have it, Dimar," he called. He turned to the others. "Girls first. Sallie or Mandie?"

"Sallie, you go first," Mandie told her Indian friend.

"All right, but, Mandie, please be careful when you come up. It looks rather frightening," Sallie told her. She took the end of the rope, stooped to put her head up the chimney, and then stood up. Grasping the rope tightly, she swung herself off the stone floor. As her feet touched the side of the chimney she kept moving her hands up the rope. The rope was rough and her hands burned as she climbed. Her arms felt as though they were going to pull out of their sockets, but with determination she made her way up.

At the top Dimar helped Sallie climb out of the chimney onto the steep, tin roof. Her legs trembled as she stood, but she breathed a sigh of relief. She smelled the soot on her skin and clothes and tried to brush it off with her hands. "I made it, Dimar, but I must be rather dirty," she said.

Dimar laughed. "It does not matter. We will all be dirty," the Indian boy said. Leaning over the top of the chimney, he called, "Who is next?"

Stooping carefully on the slick roof, Sallie picked up Mandie's kitten from where he sat licking himself. "Snowball doesn't like the dirt either," she said.

Inside the hut, Mandie grasped the end of the rope and worked her way up the chimney as Sallie had done. Soot, loosened by the rubbing of the rope, fell into her face and hair, and she squinted to keep it out of her eyes. Suddenly, she felt her skirt catch on something. She tried to wriggle free, but it tore. *Mother will—She* stopped mid-thought. *Mother will be glad I'm alive*, she decided, *if I ever get out of this chimney.*

When she finally got to the top, Mandie felt Dimar's strong hands lift her out of the chimney and onto the roof next to Sallie.

"Do not move!" Sallie warned, handing the kitten to Mandie. "The roof is very steep."

Mandie tried to stand still as she smoothed Snowball's dirty, white fur.

Dimar called for one of the boys to come up.

Joe offered the rope to Tsa'ni. "You go next."

"I will wait. I must put out the candle before I leave," Tsa'ni replied. "I will go after you."

"Well, if you insist," Joe said, grasping the end of the rope.

When Joe arrived safely at the top, Dimar called for Tsa'ni.

Tsa'ni blew out the candle, rolled it in some old ashes for it to cool, and then put it in his pocket. Taking hold of the rope, he pushed himself up and began the climb easily. Suddenly, about halfway up, he felt something give.

"The rope is about to break!" he called to the others on the roof.

Mandie bit her lip. "Please, dear God, don't let it break now!" she cried.

Dimar called down to him, "Try to hurry. Maybe you can get up before it breaks."

But it was too late. At that moment the rope snapped. Tsa'ni braced his feet against one wall and his backside against the wall behind him. He was going to have to work his way up without the rope. It was a miracle he hadn't fallen.

The young people waited fearfully on the roof. Hearing nothing more, Dimar leaned over the top of the chimney. "Tsa'ni, are you all right?" he called.

"Yes, I am all right," Tsa'ni answered. "The rope broke, but I can work my way up."

They could hear the scuffling noise as the Indian boy moved on up the chimney.

Dimar pulled on the remaining piece of rope. Excited, he called down to Tsa'ni. "There is quite a long piece of rope left. If you can manage to get far enough to reach it, you can use it the rest of the way," he said as he tossed it back down the chimney.

"I will try," Tsa'ni replied.

"Poor Tsa'ni. He is always getting into trouble," Mandie moaned.

"Usually through his own doings, though," Joe added.

"But this is not his fault," Sallie defended him.

"I guess not. In fact, it could have been me on the broken rope. He wanted to be last so he could put out the candle and bring it with him," Joe explained.

Just then Tsa'ni called from inside the chimney. "I have the rope!" he said.

Dimar checked to see that it was secure. "It seems to be all right at this end," he answered.

In a few moments a scratched and bruised Tsa'ni appeared at the top of the chimney. He, too, was covered with soot. Dimar and Joe helped him out onto the tin roof.

"Good exercise!" Tsa'ni laughed, rubbing his scratched back.

"Now all we have to do is slide down this roof and jump to the ground," Dimar told them. "Thank goodness the cabin has a low roof. It will not be so far to jump."

"Sounds like fun when we can't see what we're jumping into," Joe laughed.

"I will go first and see what is beneath," Dimar told them. "Listen for me. I will look all the way around the cabin and pick the best side for you to jump."

"I do not mind going first," Tsa'ni offered.

"Neither do I," Joe chimed in.

"No, you two stay with the girls and help them slide down when I call to you," Dimar said, lying down on his stomach. Pushing himself off with his hands, he started sliding down backwards. It was too dark to see much, but the others heard the thud when Dimar landed on the ground.

"I am down!" Dimar yelled.

He walked all around the cabin. "I think the best place is where I came down. There is more grass and weeds here. Not so many thorny bushes."

"All right, we'll send Sallie first," Joe called to Dimar.

Sallie looked at the steep roof and took a deep breath. Twisting her heavy skirt around her, she lay on her stomach and gave herself a backward push as she had seen Dimar do. Before she could plop onto the ground, Dimar broke her fall.

"Mandie coming next," Joe called to Dimar.

"What will I do with Snowball?" Mandie protested. "How will I get him down?"

"Here," said Tsa'ni, pulling the rope off the chimney. "We will tie this around him and you hold onto the end of the rope as you slide down. He will have to come with you whether he likes it or not."

"It won't hurt him?"

"No, it will not hurt him," Tsa'ni replied. "Hold him still while I roll this rope around him."

Snowball did not like the idea, but Tsa'ni rolled the rope around and around the kitten until he couldn't get loose. He gave the end of the rope to Mandie.

"Snowball, be still!" Mandie ordered. "We have to slide down to the ground." She rubbed his head, and he purred. But he would not be still.

Lying down on the roof as she had seen Sallie do, she grasped the rope and slid down, pulling the protesting kitten with her. Sallie caught him as he came off the roof and Dimar broke the fall for Mandie.

Mandie took the howling kitten in her arms and untied the rope. "You shouldn't carry on so, Snowball. Remember, this was all your idea," she told him as she stroked his ruffled fur. He was soon purring softly.

Tsa'ni came down next, with Joe following.

At last the young people, grimy with soot, were safely on the ground outside the cabin. They stood close together in the dark.

"Now what do we do?" Sallie asked.

"We have to find everybody, so we'll just start walking, I guess," Mandie replied.

"But my grandfather is probably in one direction and your mother and the others in the opposite direction. Remember?" Sallie said, trying to brush more of the dirt from her dress.

"I think we should find our way back to the wrecked train," Dimar suggested. "When your mother and Uncle John and Tsa'ni's grandfather can get off the train, I think they would head back toward the wreck to find us."

"Yes, you're right, Dimar," Joe agreed, adjusting the suspenders on his trousers. "That sounds sensible."

"I know my grandfather would come back to find us," Tsa'ni said.

"And *my* grandfather may still be in that wrecked baggage car!" Sallie cried.

Poor Uncle Ned, Mandie thought, *he may have been killed when the baggage car wrecked. Please, God, let him be all right.*

"Then it is agreed. We will try to find our way back to where the train wrecked," Dimar said.

"Yes," the others answered.

"I will walk in front," Dimar declared, "and Tsa'ni, you and Joe walk behind the girls. That way they will be protected." He turned to go.

"Protected?" Mandie asked shakily.

"Yes, from anyone or any *thing* we might meet on our way," Dimar explained.

Mandie shivered as she remembered the panther she had encountered on her first visit to her Cherokee kinpeople. "Thank you, Dimar," she replied and took Sallie's hand. Her other hand clutched Snowball to her shoulder.

So the group went down the vague trail with only a little moonlight to illumine their way. Worry showed on their faces as they hastened their steps to find the others. They didn't know what they would find, but they had to get back to the wrecked train car.

CHAPTER FOUR

RUNAWAY TRAIN

When the train stopped, the adults heard the noise of the wrecked car but didn't know what was happening. Then the train started up again and began picking up speed. Uncle John went back to look for the young people and found the baggage car missing and no sign of Mandie and her friends. The other passengers were frightened, too. They said they had seen the youngsters go on into the next car but they hadn't returned.

Terror gripped Elizabeth. She didn't know whether Mandie and Uncle Ned and the other youngsters had been in the wrecked car or not. Uncle Wirt and Uncle John tried to comfort her, but the engine was going so fast around the curves it was all they could do to stay on their seats. The train was so noisy they couldn't even talk.

Elizabeth practically screamed in her husband's ear. "John, we've got to get off this train and go back to see what happened to Amanda, and Uncle Ned, and the other children!" she cried.

John, with his arm tightly around her, nodded his head in agreement. He was too worried to talk.

Uncle Wirt sat opposite them with a furious expression on his old face. He, too, was worried.

The train came to a sudden, screeching halt and almost threw them to the floor. They looked out the windows. It was so dark outside they couldn't see a thing. Everything became still. Everyone was waiting to see what was going to happen next. There was the sound of a horse galloping away into the distance.

The engineer opened the door at the end of the car and came inside. "I am very sorry, ladies and gentlemen," he began, as he wiped the sweat from his round, red face. "A bandit left his horse and climbed on board when they stopped the train a ways back, and he forced me to open up, full-throttle. Then, a little while ago, he jumped off."

"Why?" Elizabeth managed to ask, shakily.

"I don't rightly know, ma'am," he replied. "You see, they uncoupled the baggage car when they stopped the train back yonder and it went down into the gorge—"

"—Amanda, Uncle Ned, the children!" Elizabeth cried, unable to stop shaking.

John held her tightly against him. "Is that the only car that went off the track?" he asked the man.

"Yes, sir, far as I could tell in the dark," the engineer replied.

"Maybe the children got off when the train stopped," John suggested. "You know how curious and adventuresome they are."

Uncle Wirt clasped his hands together. "But we not sure, and Ned in baggage car, and baggage car in gorge for sure," he reminded them.

"I'm afraid he was. But maybe he managed to get out," John said, grasping for hope.

"What are we going to do?" Elizabeth asked the engineer.

"We're almost in Asheville, so we'll go into the station," the man replied. "If you'll all be patient, I'll go back up front and get this train—what's left of it—into the depot."

He turned and went back out the door.

"We must remember not to mention the gold to anyone," Uncle John cautioned Elizabeth and Uncle Wirt.

"Of course, John," Elizabeth replied, still in tears. "If this train can't go back, how are we going to get back to where the car went off the track?"

John still tried to comfort her. "We'll get some horses in Asheville and head toward Franklin. From there we'll go up the mountain. It's too steep and dangerous to ride back in from Asheville. Besides, I'm hoping the youngsters and Uncle Ned will head for our house in Franklin if they are able to."

Uncle Wirt leaned forward. "We get help, find lost ones. Find bad men, too," he told Elizabeth.

She managed a weak smile through her tears and put her hand over the old man's. "Thank you, Uncle Wirt," she said.

The train slowed as it came into Asheville. John, Elizabeth, and Uncle Wirt picked up their belongings and prepared to leave the train.

There was no one around except the baggage boy and the stationmaster. When the stationmaster heard what had happened, he was very upset. "There won't be another train going back that direction until tomorrow," he said.

John asked him about the local livery stables. "We need a light wagon or buggy to take up to Franklin," he said.

Elizabeth interrupted, "No, John, get three horses. You know I can ride astride as well as anyone. It'll be much faster."

"The trip will be awfully rough for you," John warned.

"Don't worry about that," she said. "All I want right now is speed. We must hurry."

"All right, if you say so." John disappeared with the baggage boy and soon returned with three horses from the livery stables.

Uncle Wirt led the way through shortcuts he knew in the woods. Some of the trails were so overgrown they didn't look like trails anymore, but the old Indian knew every step of the way.

Well into the morning they arrived in Franklin. Tired and dirty, they tethered the horses in front of the house. John helped Elizabeth dismount.

Jason Bond, the caretaker, came to the front door when they rode up. He couldn't believe what he was seeing. They were supposed to be in Asheville. "Mr. Shaw, what has happened?" he inquired, hurrying down the walkway.

While John explained, Elizabeth stood by the horses, trying to adjust her heavy skirts that had become twisted and wrinkled during the hard ride. She was a little shaky, but proud to have kept up with the men.

"We only need a bite to eat, Jason, and fresh horses and we'll be off," John told him, as they all walked to the front porch.

"Let me get a horse and go with you, Mr. Shaw," Jason begged.

"No, Jason, we need you here in case they come home," John told him. "Uncle Wirt and I will go."

Elizabeth stopped and touched John's arm. "You aren't going anywhere without me," she said.

"But there's nothing you can do. You're all worn out, darling. Let Uncle Wirt and me take care of things," John replied.

"Absolutely not! I am going with you!" Elizabeth was adamant.

"Dr. Woodard, Joe's father, is in town," Jason said. "He came by last night. Said he wouldn't go back home until tomorrow. He'll probably want to go with you."

"If he's not here on a life-and-death case, I hope he *can* go with us. We might need a doctor," John told him. "While we're eating, see if you can find him, or get word to him to come over at once."

Aunt Lou, the housekeeper, heard the commotion and was waiting for them at the front door. Elizabeth told her the news, and the large black woman wiped tears from her round cheeks with her apron.

"Lawsy mercy, my chile, she done got lost!" Aunt Lou cried, "and all them other 'lil ones, and that pore old Mister Ned." She put her arm around Elizabeth. "And Miz 'Lizbeth, you looks like you gonna drop any minute."

"I'll be fine as soon as I eat," Elizabeth told her. "I'll run upstairs and change into some riding clothes. You get Jenny to set out some food for us."

Uncle Wirt stood silently at the door. He, like the others, was worried about what they might find when they got back to the wrecked train car.

A short time later, while they were hastily eating, Liza ushered Dr. Woodard into the dining room. "Well, John, what brings you back so soon? I thought you all were going on to Asheville," he said.

John rose to pull out a chair at the table. "Sit down, sit down," he invited. "Liza, bring Dr. Woodard a plate."

As they informed Dr. Woodard of the situation, he assured them that he would go with them. His son, Joe, was among those who discovered the gold. Dr. Woodard was the only other person who knew about the transfer.

Within minutes the four adults left on horseback. They were well equipped with extra blankets, ropes, lanterns, and food, and Uncle Wirt guided them through the trails he knew.

Some time later they came upon an old cabin by a stream in the woods. Uncle Wirt slowed his horse to dismount. "I send word to Bird-town," he said.

"That's a good idea, Uncle Wirt, and Deep Creek, too," John suggested.

A young Indian man who evidently knew Uncle Wirt came from behind the house. They exchanged Cherokee greetings, and Uncle Wirt explained where they were going.

"You go Deep Creek and Bird-town. Need braves at train," the old man ordered.

"I go like lightning," the young man replied. Instantly he ran to the pony tied by the side of the house and was on his way.

"Braves find bad men," Uncle Wirt told his three companions.

All four were silent as they traveled on. What would they find when they got to the wrecked train?

CHAPTER FIVE

TSA'NI IN TROUBLE

"Won't we ever get there?" Joe complained, as he stumbled over the exposed root of a huge tree in the darkness.

"The railroad track is not very far now." Dimar spoke from the front of the group. "When we find it, we will walk down the tracks until we come to the place where the train wrecked."

"Dimar, are you serious?" Mandie asked. "You know part of the track is high up in the air. We could fall off in the dark."

"We will hold hands. Then if one slips, the others can keep him from falling," Dimar explained as they continued through the woods.

"But if we hold hands we will have to walk sideways," Sallie informed him.

Tsa'ni spoke up. "I still have the piece of rope," he said. "We could hold onto the rope together."

"Hey! Remember that time we got lost in the mountains and those bootleggers tied us up? We could tie all of us together the way they did," Joe suggested.

"That sounds like a good way to do it," Sallie agreed. She held her dark, full skirt above her ankles in an effort to avoid the briars in the underbrush.

"Yes, that's the best idea yet," Mandie said, holding tightly to her kitten.

"Well, we must begin using the rope then, because there is the railroad track. Up the hill there," Dimar told them, motioning in the darkness.

"I can't see a thing," Mandie said.

"Neither can I," Joe added.

"Dimar, how do you see that far?" Sallie asked.

"Now I see the tracks," Mandie said, excitedly.

"Yes, they were there all the time," Tsa'ni said sarcastically.

When the young people reached the tracks, as Joe had suggested, they began working with the rope. Dimar fastened one end around his waist and gave the free end to Sallie. She, in turn, wrapped it around her waist and passed it on to Mandie, who did likewise, then Joe, and then Tsa'ni.

"It is just barely long enough," Tsa'ni said, securing the rope around his waist. "Now if one falls, we all fall."

"Oh, no, Tsa'ni," Mandie disagreed. "You see, there would be four of us left standing to pull the other one back up."

"Then we had better be quick if one of us falls," Tsa'ni replied.

Dimar carefully stepped onto the tracks and the others lined up behind him. But before Dimar could give the word to start, Mandie spoke up.

"I think we should ask God to protect us," she said. "I'm scared."

"The rope will protect us," Tsa'ni retorted.

"Tsa'ni!" Sallie rebuked. "Of course the rope will help us, but we need God to watch over us."

"I do not believe in the white people's God," Tsa'ni said vehemently.

Dimar was shocked. "But you go to church with your father and your grandfather," he said.

"Yes, but that is only because they make me go. When I am grown I will not go to church anymore. They will not be able to force me," Tsa'ni answered.

Mandie's heart cried out in pain. *Tsa'ni did not believe in God!* What could she say to him to convince him he was wrong? She knew he was quite stubborn and sometimes quite mean, so she would have to be very careful with whatever she said.

"Tsa'ni, just say our little verse with us. We always say it to God when we're afraid, and then we just leave everything in His hands. He takes care of us, no matter what happens," Mandie tried to convince him.

"But I am not afraid," Tsa'ni rebelled.

"I'm not afraid either, really," Joe spoke up. "But I always say the verse with Mandie and the others, just to tell God I'm depending on Him."

Mandie tried to turn around and look directly at Tsa'ni at the end of the line, but the rope was too tight.

"Please, my Cherokee cousin, believe that God will protect us from harm if we ask," Mandie begged.

"No, I will not say it!" Tsa'ni snapped.

"Then we will say it without you," Dimar told him, reaching behind to take Sallie's hand. Sallie took Mandie's, and Mandie put Snowball on her shoulder to reach for Joe's hand.

The four spoke together. "What time we are afraid, we will put our trust in thee, dear God."

In a whisper Mandie added, "And dear God, please help Tsa'ni."

"Are we ready to go now?" Tsa'ni asked angrily.

"Yes, we are ready to go," Dimar answered. "Please, be careful and go very slowly. If we come to one of those places where the tracks go over a gorge, we will have to walk on the crossties."

After what seemed like hours of little progress, Dimar spotted a dangerous place ahead. "Here is one of those places," Dimar called over his shoulder. "We will have to go very slowly."

They all stopped. The tracks spanned the deep gorge in midair. And as he had said, there were only the crossties to walk on. The track was open. There was no dirt beneath it and nothing alongside it—just the width of the track supported by a bridge framework.

As they started across, Mandie made the mistake of looking down. The ground beneath dropped clear out of sight in the darkness. Her stomach turned over, and she shivered in the chilly night air. *Suppose someone's foot slipped, could the others save him—or her? It would be horrible to fall through the tracks.* She could almost feel the pain. Then she silently rebuked herself. *I told God I would trust Him and here I am worrying about what might happen. Please, dear God, forgive me. I do put my trust in you.*

"This is nerve-racking work," Mandie said, trying to fit her steps to the distance between the crossties without pulling or pushing the others. Everyone seemed to be holding his breath and concentrating on his feet. Snowball clung to Mandie's shoulder.

"I have done this before, lots of times," Tsa'ni bragged.

"Well, I don't think I ever want to do it again," Joe said.

"It is exhilarating up here in the air," Tsa'ni replied, throwing his hands over his head.

Mandie glanced quickly over her shoulder. "Tsa'ni!" she cried. "Please be careful!"

At that moment the Indian boy lost his footing and slipped between the crossties. Thrown off balance, he dangled in the air, trying to grasp the framework beneath the tracks.

The sudden fall jerked the others. Joe, being next to Tsa'ni, had to sit down on the crossties to keep from being pulled down with him. Mandie frantically clutched Snowball and swayed as she tried to keep from falling. Sallie and Dimar, ahead of her, did not feel the jolt quite as badly.

Dimar immediately took over. "Please sit down!" he told Sallie and Mandie. He unfastened the rope from his waist. "Hold on, Tsa'ni, hold on. I will help you."

The girls carefully sat down on the crossties next to Joe.

"Why does Tsa'ni always have to make trouble?" Joe muttered.

"Because he is a bad Cherokee," Sallie replied.

"Pray for him," Mandie urged, "so that he doesn't fall."

Dimar gingerly stepped past the other three to get to Tsa'ni.

Sallie hung her head in shame, then raised her face toward the sky. "Please, God, do not let him fall."

Mandie was looking heavenward, too. "Please take care of him, dear God," she prayed.

As Dimar knelt on the tracks and tried to reach Tsa'ni's hand below, Joe knew he had to help, too, even though he didn't like Tsa'ni.

"Untie the rope from around y'all," Joe told the girls.

"But we might fall, too," Sallie protested.

"You won't if you sit perfectly still," Joe answered. "I need the rope for Tsa'ni."

"Of course," Mandie answered, as Sallie quickly untied the rope from her waist and passed the end to Mandie, who immediately pulled it loose from herself and passed it on back to Joe.

Dimar changed positions. "I still cannot reach you, Tsa'ni," he said.

"Wait. I'm getting the rope free," Joe told Dimar. "Then we can pull him up." He rolled up the rope and crawled back to where Dimar was stooping, trying to reach Tsa'ni.

The other end of the rope was still around Tsa'ni's waist, but it wasn't doing any good because he was hanging onto the bottom of the track with his hands, and his feet were kicking at the huge wooden post supporting the track. He kept trying to catch his toes on the post to take some of the pressure off his hands. So far he had not said a word.

Dimar helped Joe tie the rope around a crosstie and then called down to Tsa'ni.

"We have the rope secured up here and we are going to throw the end down to you. Watch for it," Dimar called to him.

Tsa'ni did not answer except to call out, "Hurry up!"

The first streaks of light began to brighten the sky. The two boys could see Tsa'ni hanging below and they threw the rope down over the side of the tracks, but it didn't go anywhere near Tsa'ni. They tried again and again but it wouldn't fall near enough for him to grab it.

"I cannot hold much longer," Tsa'ni finally said in a hoarse voice.

Mandie and Sallie sat holding hands, helplessly watching as the boys kept throwing the rope toward Tsa'ni. They silently prayed that he would be able to reach the rope.

Suddenly, Tsa'ni's hands gave way and he fell. The rope, too, broke, and the others watched in terror as he disappeared into the gorge below.

"Tsa'ni!" the boys yelled in terror.

Mandie and Sallie burst into tears, holding onto one another for comfort. Dimar and Joe looked at the dangling piece of rope. Dimar silently pulled it up and unfastened it from the crosstie.

Joe took command. "We've got to get across this thing," he said. "Then when the track is back on the ground again, we can get off and climb down there and see if we can find Tsa'ni."

"That is exactly what I was thinking," Dimar replied.

Mandie wiped her tears on her apron with one hand and held tightly to Snowball with the other. "Are Sallie and I going down after Tsa'ni, too?" Mandie asked.

Dimar looked at Joe. "Joe and I will search for him as soon as the track gets back on the ground," he answered.

"If you and Joe are going, then so am I," Mandie insisted.

"Me, too," Sallie added. "I do not wish to be left alone."

Joe looked at Dimar. "I suppose it wouldn't be safe to leave them alone, would it?"

"I guess not. They will have to go with us," Dimar agreed. "However, it will probably be very steep and rough down there."

"I'll be all right," Mandie assured them.

The sky had begun to lighten and in the growing daylight they could see that they were about halfway across the gorge. The crossties were more visible now, but the young people could also see how far below the land was.

The remaining piece of rope was not long enough to tie around them again, so they held onto it between them as they carefully walked single file down the tracks. It was a slow, scary process, but they were even more afraid of what they would find in the ravine.

CHAPTER SIX

SEARCHING

As the young people neared the end of the railroad bridge, the ground gradually came up to meet them, and they breathed a little easier. The awesome trek in open space was over.

Dimar stepped from the tracks onto the ground and led the others to safety.

"Whew!" Mandie blew out her breath. "Dimar, is there any more of that kind of tracks between here and where the baggage car wrecked?"

"I do not think so," Dimar assured her with a smile. "It will get steep down the side instead." Now that it was daylight he looked at her with admiration. *She is beautiful, in spite of her grimy, tear-streaked face,* he thought.

Dimar had often looked at Mandie that way, and Joe was jealous. He spoke up quickly. "Well, suppose we try to find Tsa'ni now," he suggested.

Suddenly there was a noise on the gravel. They all turned to see Tsa'ni climbing up the hill through the thick brush.

"That will not be necessary," he said, coming toward them. He was swinging the piece of rope that had been tied around his waist when he fell.

Everyone stared at him, unable to speak. Was that really Tsa'ni?

"I told you the rope would protect me," he laughed.

"Oh, Tsa'ni, what do you mean?" Mandie asked.

"When my hands slipped, the rope broke and I fell a great distance. But luckily, I landed in the top branches of a tree. All I had to do was get untangled and climb down," he explained, still swinging the piece of rope. "I escaped with hardly a scratch."

"And here we've been mourning for you all the time," Joe complained. "What a waste of tears!"

"You see, God did protect you," Sallie told him.

"I didn't need God. The tree broke my fall," Tsa'ni tossed back at her.

"No, Tsa'ni. God protected you. He used the tree to save you," Mandie explained.

"The *tree* saved me," the Indian boy insisted.

Joe began to walk ahead on the tracks. "There's no use in arguing with the ignorant dumbhead," he said. "We've got more important things to do, like finding Uncle Ned and the gold. Besides, I'm hungry. Let's go."

Dimar agreed. "Yes, we must hurry."

The girls followed Joe and Dimar, trying to keep up with their rapid pace. Tsa'ni lagged slightly behind the others.

"I wonder if my mother and Uncle John and Uncle Wirt got to Asheville all right," Mandie said.

"I don't imagine they stayed in Asheville if they got there," Joe told her. "They'll be out looking for us and Uncle Ned."

"I pray that my grandfather is all right," Sallie said, her voice shaking.

"Do you think he was still in the baggage car when it went off the tracks, or do you think the bandits captured him?" Dimar asked.

"I do not know what to think. It was all so sudden," Sallie answered. "But either way is bad. If my grandfather was still in the baggage car when it derailed, he may have been badly injured." She swallowed hard. "But if the bandits captured him, they may have harmed him."

"Especially since he is an Indian," Tsa'ni said bitterly.

"I can't understand why people are so prejudiced against certain other people. God made us all, and in His sight we are all equal," Mandie reasoned as they hurried along the railroad tracks.

"There are lots of people who think they are living as Christians, but they commit that sin," Dimar joined in.

"I do not claim to be a Christian, so I can say that I think the Indians are much *better* than the white people," Tsa'ni declared.

The other four were shocked.

"How can you say such a thing, Tsa'ni?" Dimar questioned.

"I am ashamed of you, Tsa'ni—as one Indian to another," Sallie told him.

"Why did you come with us in the first place?" Joe asked.

Tsa'ni did not answer.

After several moments of awkward silence, Mandie spoke. "I think the best thing we can do is to quit talking until we get to where we're going. That way, there won't be any hard feelings," she suggested.

The others agreed. Tsa'ni remained silent and trailed along behind.

At last the sun came up and the air grew warmer as the young people trudged along. Birds sang their greetings as they flew hither and yon among the trees. Now and then a butterfly flitted across their path, and once in a while a colorful wildflower peeked out of the underbrush. It was a beautiful day, but the youngsters were tired, hungry, and worried.

After a while the river and the railroad tracks came together and traveled side by side. The rushing water invited the young people to soak their tired feet, but they could not relax.

Ignoring their blisters, scratches, bruises, and sore limbs, they marched forward. At last they came around a curve where the tracks turned away from the river. And there, in the ravine below, lay the wrecked baggage car, splintered against the mountainside.

"There it is!" Mandie cried.

As exhausted as they were, they all broke into a run.

Sallie ran ahead of the others. "Grandfather!" she exclaimed, racing to the edge of the ravine.

Mandie was right behind her. When Mandie's father died, Uncle Ned had promised that he would look out for "Jim Shaw's Papoose," and now it was her turn to look out for Uncle Ned. "Please, dear God, let him be all right. Please let Uncle Ned be all right," she prayed silently.

Dimar and Joe came up behind the girls as they paused to look.

"We must go down together," Dimar told them.

"Yes," agreed Joe. "It looks kind of steep."

Tsa'ni stood alone on the tracks and watched as the others descended into the ravine. They slipped and slid until they finally reached the train car. The car lay on its side. It looked as though it had rolled over several times.

"It's so broken up I don't see how we can get inside to look for Uncle Ned," Mandie said.

"Simple," said Joe. "Dimar and I will crawl in through that hole in the side."

"But, Joe, suppose it turns over while you're in there. It's just hanging on the side of the mountain," Mandie cautioned them.

"Let it turn over," Joe answered. "It won't hurt us. We'll just tumble with it."

"May I go with you? My grandfather may be in there," Sallie begged.

"No, it is too dangerous," Dimar said. "If we find him inside we will bring him out."

The girls waited and watched while the two boys went through the hole in the train car. As the boys disappeared inside, Mandie, with Snowball on her shoulder, reached for Sallie's hand and held it tightly.

After what seemed like hours, the two boys reappeared, empty-handed. They shook their heads as they approached.

"Grandfather!" Sallie began to cry.

"Uncle Ned, where are you?" Mandie moaned.

Joe stepped forward and took Mandie's hand in his.

"I'm sorry, Mandie. He isn't there," he said to her softly. "And neither is the gold. Everything inside is completely smashed. Uncle Ned must have managed to get out somehow. Either the bandits took him or he got out on his own."

Tsa'ni, listening from where he stood, came forward to join the group. "I suggest we search immediately. If the old man is injured, he cannot be very far. That is, *if* he is still alive," he added.

At Tsa'ni's cruel remark, Sallie began to cry louder.

"Let us separate and search the surroundings," Dimar said.

"Immediately, please," Sallie begged through her tears, still holding Mandie's hand.

"Dimar, suppose you take Sallie with you, and Joe and I will go with Tsa'ni," Mandie suggested.

"Fine," Dimar replied. "If you find anything, Tsa'ni, give me a call. I will do the same. And please do not forget to watch for the bags of gold, also. They may be hard to find since they are so small."

"I would think the bandits took the gold," Joe said. "That is probably why they wrecked the train. But it wouldn't hurt to keep our eyes open."

"I will give you a whistle, Dimar, if we find anything," Tsa'ni agreed. "We will go to the left of the car and you and Sallie go right. We will meet back here when we have covered all the ground," he said.

The group separated. Mandie, with Snowball on her shoulder, followed Joe and Tsa'ni down the incline, through bramble bushes and rocks. She didn't mind the pricks and scratches. She was set on finding her dear friend, Uncle Ned.

Tsa'ni walked bent over to watch the ground for footprints or other clues. Joe and Mandie watched the bushes and trees for any sign of a trail. In the dense forest the trees grew so close together it took time to look at all of them.

"No one has come this way," Tsa'ni called over his shoulder. "But maybe we will find a trail ahead."

Mandie turned to Joe, who was walking behind her. "Then Uncle Ned could not have come this way," she said.

"What Tsa'ni means is that no one came directly down the path we're taking," Joe explained. "Uncle Ned could have taken a path even two feet from where we are. We just have to keep walking up and down in order to cover all the area around the wrecked car. Don't give up yet."

"I won't give up. God will help us find him," Mandie said as they walked slowly forward.

"Don't say that too loudly, or we'll get a few smart remarks from Tsa'ni," Joe warned her.

"We'll have to see what we can do about Tsa'ni," Mandie said.

"I think he's hopeless," Joe replied.

"No one is hopeless, Joe. There is always hope," Mandie argued.

As they neared the river, the ground was steep and covered with slippery green moss. Mandie, trying to look all around for any sign, was not watching her step. Suddenly, her feet went out from under her and she sat down hard. Snowball, frightened by the jolt, jumped free and ran into the weeds nearby.

Joe helped her to her feet. "Are you all right?"

Mandie laughed nervously. "I'm all right," she said. "I should have been paying more attention to where I was walking. Oh, goodness, where did Snowball go?" she asked, brushing off the back of her skirt.

The two looked around quickly, but there was no sign of the white kitten. Tsa'ni did not notice their predicament and went on ahead.

Mandie searched the tall weeds. "Snowball! Kitty, kitty, kitty!" she called. "Come here, Snowball!"

The kitten meowed loudly. Joe and Mandie stood still to listen.

"He sounds either angry or hurt," Joe remarked.

"This way, Joe," Mandie said, turning to the left. "Sounds like he's over this way—toward the river."

She went on through the bushes, looking for the kitten, with Joe right behind her. The meow grew louder.

Then Snowball hopped out of the weeds in front of them. With his fur up, he meowed loudly.

"Snowball, you shouldn't run off like that," Mandie scolded. She stooped to pick him up, but he was too quick for her. He bounded into the bushes. Mandie and Joe followed. But as they came through the underbrush into the open area by the river, a terrible sight greeted them.

There on the sandy riverbank lay Uncle Ned on his back. His head was covered with blood. His bow and arrows were by his side.

Mandie, blinded with tears, rushed forward. She dropped to her knees at his side.

"Uncle Ned! Uncle Ned!" she cried, touching the still face. "Please, Uncle Ned, don't be dead! Please speak to me, Uncle Ned! Oh, dear God, please don't let him be dead!"

Joe knelt by her side and tried to find a pulse in the old man's wrist. He held his hand over Uncle Ned's mouth to see if he was breathing. He couldn't feel a thing. Jumping up, he yelled for Tsa'ni.

"Tsa'ni! Quick! Here by the river!" Joe called.

In seconds the Indian boy came rushing through the bushes.

Mandie cried as she held Uncle Ned's wrinkled hand in hers.

"Move, woman!" Tsa'ni ordered. He pushed Mandie aside to kneel by the old man. He, too, felt for a pulse and breathing with no results. "I am afraid he is very near death."

Tsa'ni stood up and gave a loud Indian call for help. Dimar and Sallie quickly joined them. When Sallie saw the condition of her grandfather, she sobbed uncontrollably.

"We must get him out of here at once!" Dimar ordered.

"Oh, dear God, how? Show us how!" Mandie said through her tears.

At that instant a faint Indian call answered Tsa'ni's. Speechless, the five young people looked at one another.

"God has sent help!" Mandie cried.

Tsa'ni gave a shrill whistle and again received an answer.

"Keep it up. Whoever it is will find us," Dimar told him.

They all waited silently, listening for the response. Each time it grew louder.

Then suddenly, Uncle Wirt burst through the bushes, followed by Uncle John, Elizabeth, Dr. Woodard, and four young Indian braves from Deep Creek and Bird-town.

Mandie rushed to Dr. Woodard, grasped his hand and pulled him down beside Uncle Ned. "Dr. Woodard, quick!" she cried.

The others gathered around as the doctor carefully examined the old Indian. Dr. Woodard looked up. "He's not dead, but he's close to it," he said gravely. "I cannot help him here, but if we don't treat him immediately, he probably will not live."

"We take him home," Uncle Wirt told them.

"It would be better if we could get him to John's house in Franklin," Dr. Woodard said. "We could care for him better there."

"Then we'll take him to my house," Uncle John declared.

Elizabeth put her arms around her daughter and tried to comfort her. But Mandie's whole body shook as she sobbed. Uncle Wirt put his arm around Sallie. It was a sad moment, always to be remembered—Uncle Ned, the dear old man, lying there helpless, and close to death.

Uncle Wirt turned to the braves and spoke rapidly in Cherokee. The young Indians immediately unrolled the blankets they carried and prepared a hammock-type bed to carry the old man over the mountain. Gently lifting him, they placed him on the blankets. Each brave took hold of a corner and lifted him from the ground. The old man did not move or utter a sound.

"Speed is the important thing," Dr. Woodard cautioned them. "We must get him to Franklin as quickly as we can."

The braves nodded in understanding.

"Braves, run!" Uncle Wirt ordered. "Quick!"

Without hesitating a second, the braves took off through the bushes, carrying the old man. Mandie and Sallie tried to follow, but Uncle John held them back.

"Wait! We have horses up at the tracks," Uncle John told them. "Since the braves left their horses, we'll have enough for all of us to ride back home."

"Braves run faster through woods than horses," Uncle Wirt said.

"Yes, they'll be there by the time we arrive," Uncle John agreed. "Thank goodness Aunt Lou and Jason Bond can help."

Mandie looked up at her mother. "Ever since we found the gold, Uncle Ned has said the gold was bad luck to the Cherokees, and now he may die because of it," she said shakily. "Oh, how could we have been so greedy that we ignored his beliefs?"

Elizabeth held her daughter tightly. "Now, don't blame yourself, dear," she said. "The gold will eventually be a good thing for the Cherokees when we get the hospital built."

"The gold is nowhere to be found," Joe informed them as they all climbed the steep side of the ravine.

The adults stopped and stared.

"So the bandits got away with it!" Uncle John said angrily.

"Cherokee catch bad men," Uncle Wirt vowed as the group hurried on up the mountainside.

Sally looked up at Uncle Wirt. "Please catch the bad men who hurt my grandfather," she said.

Uncle Wirt took her hand in his and squeezed it gently in reply.

Riding double on some of the horses, the group galloped off toward Franklin.

Mandie fought back the tears. "Please, God, don't let him die!" she implored.

CHAPTER SEVEN

MANDIE KEEPS WATCH

Uncle Ned, bathed and dressed in a clean nightshirt, lay very still in a bedroom across the hall from Mandie's room. Dr. Woodard tried everything he knew, but there was no improvement in the old man's condition. Finally, he sent the braves to Deep Creek to bring back Uncle Ned's squaw, Morning Star.

Everyone hovered around Uncle Ned's doorway, waiting for some word.

"I have an idea he was thrown out of the train car and landed on his head," Dr. Woodard told them. "I can't find any broken bones, though. Now that his head has been washed, you can see that there are several large cuts in the scalp."

Mandie tugged at the doctor's hand. "Dr. Woodard, will—will he—live?" she asked.

"Will he, Doctor?" Sallie echoed.

"I don't know," Dr. Woodard replied. "Only the Lord knows that. I have done all I can. I'd say it's up to the Lord now."

Mandie noticed that Sallie was crying and gave her Indian friend a hug. Their tears mingled in love for the old man.

Sallie pulled Mandie across the room with her to the bed where her grandfather lay. "We will stay with him," she managed to say.

"Yes, and we will pray." Mandie said. "I know God will heal him." She held her friend's hand and they knelt by the bed.

"I think we should all pray. Come on," Elizabeth told the others. She led the way into the room and knelt behind the girls. Only Tsa'ni remained outside in the hallway. Aunt Lou, Liza, Jason Bond, and Jenny joined the others. The room was soon full of people on their knees, praying for Uncle Ned to be healed, and thanking the Lord that he had lived so far.

As the group became silent and got to their feet, Dr. Woodard spoke. "We must arrange a schedule now. He shouldn't be left alone, and I have other patients I must see now."

"I am not leaving Uncle Ned, not for one second," Mandie declared.

"Neither am I!" Sallie told them.

"But you were up all of last night, and you only ate a snack while Dr. Woodard was working with Uncle Ned," Elizabeth objected. "You two girls didn't even take a good bath when you changed clothes. You'll be Dr. Woodard's patients next if you don't take care of yourselves."

Mandie shook her head angrily. "No, no, no! I won't leave him! He would never leave me! I love him!"

"I know. I know, dear," Elizabeth said. She tried to put her arm around Mandie, but the girl pulled away. "Let's go take a nap and then you can come right back," her mother suggested.

Mandie stomped her foot. "No! I am not leaving this room!" she cried.

Elizabeth looked at her husband in despair.

"Mandie," Uncle John said firmly. "I know how much you have grown to love Uncle Ned since your father died and how Uncle Ned has been watching over you—"

Mandie wiped at her tears with her apron.

"—but we cannot permit you to throw a temper tantrum like this."

Mandie felt badly for the way she had acted and began to cry softly. Dr. Woodard understood the situation and stepped forward. "John, may I make a suggestion? Why don't you let Mandie and Sallie rest in here tonight?" He pulled one of the big, plush arm-chairs to the side of the bed. "That way, they can keep watch and still rest a little, too."

John thought for a moment. "Well, I suppose that would be all right. Elizabeth?" His wife nodded.

Dr. Woodard pulled a second big chair to the other side of the bed, and the girls scrambled into them. Snowball hopped up beside Mandie and curled up in a corner of the big seat. Joe took his place behind the big chair as if watching over both Uncle Ned *and* Mandie.

Elizabeth looked at John again. Mandie was her daughter, but she didn't know how to discipline her. They had never even met each other until a few months ago. She hardly knew how to be a mother. John, sensing how Elizabeth felt, and knowing Mandie didn't normally act like this, put his arm around Elizabeth and moved her toward the door.

"All right, girls," Uncle John told them. "We are going to get some sleep, but we'll be back. If you get too sleepy, Aunt Lou or Liza will take over for you."

Mandie jumped up from the chair and ran to put her arms around her mother, wiping tears from her face.

"Mother, I'm sorry." Her voice was trembling. "I love you. I do. It's just that I love Uncle Ned, too, and I have to stay here and wait. I want to be here when God heals him," she said.

Elizabeth squeezed her tightly. "I understand, dear. You and Sallie get comfortable in the chairs. We'll be back later."

As Mandie went back to her chair, John turned to Uncle Wirt, Joe, Dimar, and Tsa'ni, who was watching them from the doorway. "Come on, Uncle Wirt, boys," he said. "Aunt Lou will show you some rooms where you can rest."

Joe started to leave with the others, but quickly returned to Mandie's side.

"Do you want me to stay with you?" he asked in a low voice. "I can lie down on the rug there."

"Thank you, Joe," Mandie told him. "I appreciate your offer, but why don't you come back after you sleep?"

Joe squeezed her hand and started to go. "I'll be back soon," he promised.

Out in the hallway, Dr. Woodard gave John a slip of paper. "Here are the names of the patients I'll be seeing," he said. "If there is any change in him at all, send for me immediately. Otherwise, I'll be back as soon as I can. I'll plan on spending the night here."

"You don't really think there is any hope for him, do you?" John asked.

"Well, as I said in there, it's up to the Lord now," the doctor replied. "He does still work miracles."

"I know. We'll all be praying for him."

After everyone was settled, Aunt Lou and Liza went down to the kitchen.

"We'se gotta git my chile somethin' to eat, Liza," Aunt Lou told the young black girl.

"Think that Injun man gonna live?" Liza asked.

Aunt Lou whirled on her heels. "Liza, don't you let me hear you talk like that agin," the old housekeeper said firmly. "That man is Mister Ned what loves my chile and watches over her. And you don't go callin' him Injun man no more. You hear that?"

"Yessum," Liza replied, looking down at the floor.

Aunt Lou pushed through the kitchen door. Jenny, the cook, was stirring something on the big iron cookstove.

"Jenny, I wants two trays loaded with some of everything you got in this kitchen," the big woman ordered.

"Two of everything, Aunt Lou?" Jenny frowned.

"Yep, two of everything you'se got cooked already, that is," Aunt Lou said. "Right now!"

"Yessum!" Jenny answered. Taking two trays from the shelf over the stove, she placed dishes on them and called for Liza. "Here, Liza, help me fill these up."

Aunt Lou supervised as Jenny and Liza opened each pot on the stove and dished up its contents.

"Now, I wants a pitcher of sweet milk," the big woman told Jenny.

"Who all's gonna eat all dis stuff?" Jenny asked, filling the milk pitcher as ordered.

"Jest my chile, and that other poor li'l girl and that smart little cat," Aunt Lou said. "He's the one what found Mister Ned. You oughta heerd what kind of troubles they done gone through."

"Yessum. Miss Amanda done told me 'bout them creatures what wrecked the train—look like ghosts," Liza told her.

"Well, shake a leg, girl. Them chillen's hungry." Aunt Lou picked up one tray and Liza got the other one.

"I don't 'member them sayin' they'se hungry," Liza answered as she followed Aunt Lou through the doorway. "They done et one time since they got home."

"Et? They ain't et enough to keep a bird alive. I knows when my chile is hungry. She don't hafta tell me," Aunt Lou said, climbing the winding stairway to the second floor.

As they entered Uncle Ned's room with the trays, the two girls looked up.

"We'se brought my chile and her li'l friend some food," Aunt Lou said quietly. Setting the tray on a table by Mandie, she motioned for Liza to take the other tray to Sallie. Aunt Lou filled two glasses with milk and set the pitcher aside.

"Now here's enough milk for y'all and the cat," Aunt Lou said, putting the glasses on each tray.

"But, Aunt Lou, we just ate not long ago," Mandie protested.

"See what I done said? They jest et 'while ago," Liza chimed in.

Aunt Lou scowled at Liza. "Liza, you jest hesh your mouth. These chillen's gonna eat what we done brought 'em," she said.

Mandie inhaled the tempting aroma of the food. "We'll try, Aunt Lou," she said.

"Liza, go git two pillows for these chillen so's they kin curl up in dese big chairs and rest after they done et," the old woman said.

"I be right back," Liza promised, dancing quietly out of the room.

Sallie took a bite of fried okra. "The food tastes delicious, Aunt Lou," she said.

"Jenny be a good cook," Aunt Lou replied.

"Jenny is the best cook in the whole world," Mandie added.

Liza danced back into the room with two frilly pillows. As the girls sat in the big chairs eating, Liza plumped up the pillows behind them. Snowball, for once too tired to eat, stayed curled up sound asleep in the corner of Mandie's chair.

"Now, you chillen eat. We'se got work to do, but we'll be back," Aunt Lou said, waving Liza to the door.

Mandie set her tray aside and got up to give the big woman a hug. "Thank you, Aunt Lou. I love you."

The old woman bent to hug her. "I loves my chile, too, and we'se all aprayin' the good Lord spares Mister Ned's life," she said.

"Thank you, Aunt Lou," Sallie replied.

"You go finish eatin' now, Mandie," Aunt Lou ordered. "We'll be back." She closed the door quietly behind them.

When Mandie and Sallie could eat no more, they pushed their trays aside and curled up in the chairs. In spite of their determination to stay awake, before long, both of them were sound asleep. Aunt Lou, knowing this would happen, slipped back inside the room and sat down near the foot of the bed to keep watch.

CHAPTER EIGHT

PRAYER CHANGES THINGS

When Morning Star arrived during the night, she fell weeping upon her husband's bed. Only Mandie and Sallie could calm her.

Mandie knelt with the old squaw and Sallie by the bed. "Morning Star, Uncle Ned is not going to die," she said. "God is going to heal him."

Morning Star couldn't understand everything Mandie was saying, so Sallie translated it into Cherokee.

"God is testing our faith, Morning Star. We must put our faith in God to heal Uncle Ned," Mandie continued. "I believe He will answer our prayers."

As Morning Star calmed down, she took her husband's hand and began to pray in the Cherokee language. Refusing to leave the room to eat or sleep, she stayed with Mandie and Sallie as they watched and waited.

Every day Dr. Woodard came to examine Uncle Ned. But on the third day he sadly shook his head. He turned to John Shaw who was standing nearby.

"I'm afraid we're going to lose him," the doctor said.

Hearing his words, Mandie ran to the bedside and began to cry. She grabbed the old man's hands in hers and shook him.

"Uncle Ned! Uncle Ned! Come back to me. Please don't die!" she cried hysterically, tears streaming down her cheeks.

Sallie knelt beside her grandmother to explain in Cherokee what the doctor had just said.

Morning Star looked up at Dr. Woodard. "God heal. No die," she said firmly.

Uncle John tried to settle Mandie down. But as he reached to pull her hands away from the old man's, Mandie cried out in joy.

"Uncle Ned! Uncle Ned, I knew you wouldn't leave me," she exclaimed.

They all hovered closely around the bed, astonished to see his eyes open. Uncle Ned looked directly at Mandie, then curled his fingers around her hand.

Dr. Woodard reached for the old Indian's wrist, waited silently for a moment, then smiled. "His pulse is normal," he announced. "God still works miracles."

"Grandfather, I love you," Sallie whispered.

Morning Star gently rubbed his forehead. "God heal," she muttered.

Uncle Ned managed a slight smile for his wife and grandaughter. "Eat," he said softly.

Everyone laughed and began to praise God. Aunt Lou hurried Jenny into making some hot broth for the old man. Before long Morning Star was holding his head and feeding him with a spoon.

Uncle Ned continued to improve a little bit each day. As soon as he was able, he told them what had happened to him. Propped up on his pillows, and with everyone gathered around him in great anticipation, he began his story.

"Ghosts ride horses," he said. "Train stop. They unhook train. Baggage car roll backward. Go off track. I jump out. Hurt head. Get water. No more remember."

There were lots of questions, and the young people told him what they had been through. But no one knew what happened to the gold.

Several days later, when Uncle Ned was well enough to sit up in a chair, Mandie waited until everyone else was out of the room, and then came to sit on the rug at his feet. Leaning her head against his knee, she said, "Uncle Ned, I need to talk to you. Are you well enough to talk?"

He nodded and smiled. "Well enough to get up and go," he said.

"I've been thinking a lot since you got hurt," the girl began. "You know, the gold is all gone. I guess the bandits stole it. But you know what I think?" She looked up at him very seriously. "I think God took it all away from us because we forgot to tithe. We forgot to give Him ten percent of it."

Uncle Ned was startled with her thinking. "No, no, no, Papoose!" he said anxiously. "Big Book say Big God throw blessings out window to people if people tithe."

"But we didn't tithe," Mandie said.

"Then we no get blessings," the old man replied. "But Big God not punish. Papoose find gold, but bad men take it away—not Big God."

"Do you really think so? I've been so worried about it," she said.

"So. Bad men take gold—not Big God," the old Indian repeated. "Cherokee find bad men, get gold back for Papoose."

"Oh, I hope we can get it back. I want so much to build that hospital for the Cherokees," Mandie told him. "And if we get it back, we will most certainly give ten percent of it to the Lord."

The old man smiled and patted her blonde head. "Then we must watch so we catch. Blessings fall down on us from window up there." Uncle Ned pointed upward.

Mandie felt better after her conversation with her dear friend. She knew Uncle Ned was right. And now that he was so much better she had time for her friends.

During those first trying days, Joe had more or less been her shadow, and of course, Sallie was always with Mandie and Uncle Ned. But it seemed that Dimar and Tsa'ni had done nothing but sit around and eat. Leaving Morning Star with Uncle Ned, Mandie decided to round up her friends. She found them all together in the parlor.

As Mandie entered the room, Polly Cornwallis, her friend from next door, rushed up and put her arms around her.

"Mandie, I was so sorry to hear about everything," she said, shaking her black curls out of her eyes. "Mother and I have been in Nashville. We just got back this afternoon."

"I'm glad you came, Polly," Mandie told her. "Have you met all my friends?"

Whirling about to smile at Joe, Polly replied, "Yes, Joe just finished introducing all of us."

"Well, then, since Uncle Ned is so much better, and Morning Star is staying with him for a while," Mandie explained, "I thought you might all like to see the secret tunnel Joe and I have told you about."

The others were on their feet immediately.

"Yes, yes," Dimar answered.

"Oh, please," Sallie chimed in.

"It would be interesting," Tsa'ni said.

Joe came to Mandie's side. "I'll be the guide for you," he laughed as he led the way into the hall. "Hadn't we better get the key from your Uncle John?"

Sticking her hand in her apron pocket, Mandie withdrew a large key and held it up. "I already have."

Snowball bounced along under their feet as Joe led the way up the stairs to the third floor and into Uncle John's library. The young Indians were fascinated with the beautiful house. They had never seen such a large mansion before.

Joe walked over to the heavy draperies in the corner of the room and pulled them aside, revealing a door. Mandie inserted the key and swung it open. Behind the door was a paneled wall. Pushing a latch, she waited for the panel to swing aside and then showed them steps going down.

Dimar was impressed. "That is very clever," he said.

"I think so, too," Mandie said with pride. "Uncle John said my great-grandfather built this house when the Cherokees were being moved out of North Carolina. He didn't like the way they were being treated, so he had this tunnel built just for them. He hid as many Cherokees as he could in this tunnel until things became peaceful. It was about 1842 when the Indians moved out and set up their own living quarters," Mandie explained. She turned to Tsa'ni. "That's how my grandfather and my grandmother met," she said. "He was twenty-eight, and she was a beautiful eighteen-year-old Indian girl. So you see, my family not only married Indians, they helped them survive when no one else would."

Tsa'ni only tightened his lips and said nothing.

Sallie sighed. "What a beautiful romance!"

"Yes," Mandie agreed. "My grandmother was Uncle Wirt's sister, you know. So he is really my great-uncle."

"Let's go," Tsa'ni complained.

Joe led them through the door to the steps. "It's kind of dark in places," he cautioned, "so be sure to watch your step."

Snowball meowed at Joe's feet. Joe picked up the cat and handed him to Mandie.

As they made their way through, Sallie and Dimar were thrilled, knowing the tunnel had once protected their people. When they finally emerged in the woods, almost out of sight of the house, they were really excited.

"What an adventure!" Dimar exclaimed, looking back to the exit door concealed by bushes.

Sallie turned to Mandie. "You know that my grandfather and my grandmother lived here at one time, don't you?"

Mandie set Snowball down and the kitten rubbed around her ankles. "Yes, Uncle John told me. Morning Star and Uncle Ned came to live with them after my grandfather died. He said my father was only five years old then," Mandie replied.

"My grandfather has never mentioned this tunnel to me," Sallie said. "He lived here, so he must have known about it."

"Your grandfather is the world's greatest keeper of secrets!" Mandie laughed.

"The old people do not like to talk about the Cherokee removal, or anything that reminds them of it," Dimar volunteered.

Tsa'ni changed the subject. "When are they going to look for the gold?" he asked.

Everyone stared at him.

"Who is going to look for the gold?" Joe asked.

"My grandfather and Mandie's uncle are planning to," Tsa'ni answered.

Mandie stood up straighter. "The Cherokees put me in charge of the gold, so I will go with them to hunt for it," she told them.

"So will I," Joe put in.

"And I," Sallie said.

Dimar was again admiring Mandie's pretty blue eyes. "I also would like to go with you," he said.

"Could I go, too?" Polly asked. "I'd just love to look for those creatures that stole it."

"Oh, Polly!" Mandie replied. "It won't be fun. They were awfully dangerous looking."

"Joe already told me about them," Polly said. "Do you think I could go with you?"

"I suppose. You'd have to ask your mother and also my Uncle John," Mandie said.

"Then let's go find out," Polly said, turning to go up the hill to the house.

The young people found Uncle John with Uncle Wirt and Elizabeth in the parlor. Not waiting for any greeting or explanation, Polly walked straight to Uncle John and asked, "Could I please go with y'all to search for the gold?"

Uncle John looked at her and then at the other youngsters.

"Do what?" he asked.

"You are making plans to hunt the gold, and everyone else is going, so I'd like to go, too," Polly explained.

"Now wait a minute," Uncle John said, addressing the anxious young people. "This business about the gold must be kept absolutely secret. No one is to know about it outside of our immediate group here. If it got to be public knowledge, we'd have half the country out here looking for it. We'd never find it. Do you all understand?"

They nodded in agreement.

Mandie sat down on a low stool near her uncle. "But, are we going to look for it?" Mandie asked.

"Uncle Wirt and I will," John answered.

"But, Uncle John, I am responsible for the gold. My Cherokee kin-people put me in charge of it, so I must go, too," Mandie pleaded.

"It's too dangerous," Uncle John told her.

"I'm not afraid," Mandie protested. "I have to find it so I can give ten percent of it to the Lord, and we can receive His blessings."

"You can give the ten percent after Uncle Wirt and I find it," he reasoned.

Just then Snowball came into the room and jumped into Mandie's lap. That gave Mandie an idea. "I have to go so Snowball can go," she said. "Remember, he was the one who found Uncle Ned. Maybe he can help us find the bandits."

No one dared to laugh.

"Amanda, darling," Elizabeth said gently, "I want you to stay here with me to help take care of Uncle Ned. Please."

"But, Mother, Uncle Ned said we must find the gold so we can tithe," Mandie told her. "And he can't go, so I have to."

Uncle John finally relented. "All right, you youngsters can go with us to the wrecked train car, but I don't make any promises after that," he told them. Turning to Joe, he added, "If we get that far we'll stop at your father's house, Joe. He must be home by now."

"John, are you going to permit this?" Elizabeth asked in disbelief. "You know I don't want Amanda to go."

"I never could resist blue eyes!" he laughed. "Especially when they're so much like yours."

The young people dashed out of the room and ran over to Polly's house to ask her mother's permission. After a lot of talking, they finally convinced her that it was not dangerous, and that they were only going to the wrecked train car. Polly went home with Mandie to spend the night so they could start out early the next morning.

Mandie was excited about the trip to the wrecked baggage car, but would they ever really find the gold again?

CHAPTER NINE

OFF TO FIND THE GOLD

Before sunrise the young people quietly slipped out of bed and gathered in the kitchen. Jenny was busy preparing breakfast and food for the journey. Since Elizabeth was not going, Uncle John had told Liza she could go along to look after the three girls. Liza was so excited she danced around in circles among them while their conversation grew louder and louder.

Aunt Lou heard the commotion and came into the kitchen. "You best be quietenin' down or Mr. John'll be in here to see what's goin' on! Liza, 'member youse jest goin' to take care of my chile and these heah other li'l girls."

"Yessum," Liza calmed down. "I behave. I see to Miss Amanda and Miss Sallie and Miss Polly. I see they behave, too."

Mandie laughed. She knew the trip would be more fun with Liza along. "And I'll see that Liza behaves," she said mischievously.

"Lawsy, Missy," Liza said. "I ain't got nobody sweet on me to go smoochin' with."

Everyone broke into laughter.

"Git outa heah," Aunt Lou said, shooing the young people out through the door. "Git yo' breakfast in the dinin' room. Liza be bringin' it in a minute."

Mandie was the last one out of the kitchen. "Can Liza eat with us, Aunt Lou?" she asked.

"Hesh yo' mouth, chile. Liza don't belong in the dinin' room," the big woman told her.

"But, Aunt Lou, Liza's going to eat with us on the trip. She has to, or eat somewhere by herself," Mandie insisted.

"Well, that won't be under the roof of Mr. John's house," Aunt Lou told her. "While she under Mr. John's roof, she gonna act like the servant girl she be. Now, git on in there wid yo' friends."

"I just don't understand it, Aunt Lou," Mandie argued. "Why can't she eat with us? When I lived at my father's house in Swain County everyone ate at the same table."

"You'll understand some day, my chile. Now git!" the old woman said.

Mandie sat down at the big dining room table with her friends. Before long her mother and Uncle John and Uncle Wirt joined them.

"Uncle John, why can't Liza eat breakfast with us?" Mandie asked, as soon as her uncle was seated. "After all, she'll have to eat with us on the trip."

Liza came through the doorway with huge platters of scrambled eggs, bacon, ham, and grits. "Oh, you want Liza to eat with us?" Uncle John asked. Looking up at the young servant girl, he said, "Liza, you get a plate and sit down over there next to Mandie. We're all in this thing together beginning today."

Liza almost dropped the platters as she set them down. "What, Mister John?" she gasped.

"Mandie wants you to eat with us since you're going on the journey too. So get yourself a plate and sit down," Uncle John told her.

"Yes, Liza, sit right here next to me." Mandie used her foot to push out the chair next to her.

"Missy, I can't do that. Aunt Lou, she git all over me," Liza protested.

"But Uncle John is the boss here. You heard what he said. Get your plate," Mandie insisted.

Liza gave up. "Yes, Missy, I git me a plate and be right back," the black girl said, returning to the kitchen.

Elizabeth looked at John.

"I told you I just can't resist those blue eyes, especially when they look so much like yours," John told her.

"First thing you know, you'll have all the servants in an uproar," Elizabeth protested. "The other servants won't like the idea at all."

"Leave it to me. I'll take care of it if and when that time comes," John told her. "After all, I'm half Indian. I'm not expected to act in the usual 'white people' fashion," he laughed.

"Oh, John, you can be funny!" Elizabeth smiled.

Polly was sitting next to Mandie and gave her a nudge. "Mandie, you have some great parents!" she said.

"One parent," corrected Mandie. "Uncle John is still my uncle, even though he is married to my mother."

"They are very much in love," Dimar said, helping himself to more eggs and bacon.

She missed her father so much, it was hard to sort out her feelings about all that happened.

Uncle John was the "richest man this side of Richmond," according to Liza. Why hadn't he shared his wealth with her father who was desperately poor? She would always wonder about that.

Liza came back through the door with a plate in one hand and a platter of hot biscuits in the other. After putting the biscuits in the middle of the long table, she sat down next to Mandie.

"Here," Mandie said. She reached for the platter of eggs and passed it to Liza.

Joe passed the bacon and ham.

Dimar watched in amusement from the other end of the table. "Eat," he said.

"That's one word that's good in any language—eat," Joe laughed.

Liza nervously helped herself to the food, and then sat there pushing the food around with her fork. She cast a sheltered glance now and then at the others at the table.

"Liza, eat," Uncle John's voice boomed from the other end of the table. "We've got to get going."

"Yes, sir. Yes, sir, Mister John," Liza answered and quickly shoved her mouth full of food.

Sallie looked across the table at Liza and felt sorry for her. *Poor Liza!* she thought. *She's so nervous sitting at the big table that she can't eat.* She almost choked on the food and hurried to wash it down with coffee that was too hot.

"Please do not worry. We are all on your side," Sallie told her. "I felt the same way the first time I sat at this great table in this fancy house. You see, I live in a log cabin with my grandfather and grandmother."

"I ain't never lived in a log cabin, Miss Sallie," Liza replied. "I wouldn't know how to act in a log cabin."

All the young people laughed.

"I also live in a log cabin," Dimar told her.

"And so do I," Tsa'ni added.

Turning to Mandie, Liza asked, "Where all these log cabins at?"

"Liza, haven't you ever seen a log cabin?" Mandie asked. "You know I lived in a log cabin with my father, too. That's how people live out in the country away from town. Log cabins are scattered all over the woods and fields."

"I ain't never lived in de country either. I be born right heah in this house," Liza told them.

"You were?" Mandie said. "Where are your mother and father?"

"They be done dead with de new-moanie, long time ago, when I was a li'l tyke. Aunt Lou, she tuck care of me after that," Liza told them.

"My father died from the same thing," Mandie said.

Uncle John's voice boomed out again. "Eat up, everyone! Whoever is going with me, be ready in fifteen minutes."

He got up and left the table, with Elizabeth and Uncle Wirt following.

"You heard him. Eat," Joe said. "Let's hurry and get done!"

Liza tried her best to swallow the food. She *was* hungry, but to have to sit here with "Miss Amanda" and her friends was too much for her. She pushed her plate away and stood up.

"I'se done," she said. "Let's git our things and go."

Mandie looked at the girl's plate. "But, Liza, you hardly ate anything at all," Mandie objected.

Liza turned to her and spoke softly. "To be honest 'bout it, Miss Amanda, I jest didn't wanta eat in here with all these people. It'd be like you eatin' with Mr. McKinley in the White House."

"You really mean that, don't you, Liza?" Mandie replied. "I'm sorry if I spoiled your breakfast. I won't do it again."

"That's all right, Missy. Next time I eat in the kitchen where I belongs," Liza replied.

When they got outside, Uncle John had horses and ponies tethered at the front gate, loaded with blankets, rope, lanterns, and food. The adults stood waiting on the front porch. Elizabeth caught Mandie by the arm.

"Amanda, you haven't put on your riding outfit," she reprimanded.

"But, Mother. Sallie doesn't have one on, and neither do Polly and Liza," Mandie protested.

"I told my mother we were riding in a wagon," Polly explained. "I didn't know we were going to ride ponies. But it's all right. She won't mind."

Elizabeth frowned at her husband. "John, we need to teach Amanda some proper manners for young ladies," she said.

John laughed. "Why don't we let it go this time? It'll be quicker and safer in that rough mountain terrain if they all ride astride. Seems like I remember *you* saying the same thing not too long ago." He kissed Elizabeth on the cheek.

Elizabeth gave in. "It seems like I always come out on the losing end," she said with a little laugh.

Mandie took her mother by the hand. "Please tell Uncle Ned we'll be back soon," she said. "I didn't want to wake him this early in the morning to tell him good-bye."

"Of course, dear," Elizabeth answered. She gave her daughter a squeeze. "Be a good girl."

"Everybody ready?" Uncle John asked. "Run and find yourselves a pony."

Mandie picked up Snowball and rushed out to the road with the others to claim her pony. Mandie knew she had to help Liza feel comfortable with them. "Liza! Here! Get this pony next to mine!" she called.

Liza gratefully did as Mandie said.

Waving good-bye to Elizabeth, Aunt Lou, and Jenny, the group took off down the road.

A long time later, they approached the place in the railroad tracks where they knew the wrecked baggage car would be. As they drew rein and looked down the ravine, they spotted the wrecked baggage car still hanging onto the side of the mountain.

"We walk from here," Uncle Wirt told them.

Dismounting, they followed him carefully down the slope.

"Watch for trail marking," he said.

"Here is where we went down to the wrecked car," Dimar said, pointing to the spot. "Then we split up, and Sallie and I went over this way," he continued. "Tsa'ni took Mandie and Joe over that way and we all met at the river where we found Uncle Ned."

"When we came in answer to your call, we must have taken almost the same path then, Dimar," Uncle John replied. "That's a lot of shoes making prints in the dirt."

Suddenly, Uncle Wirt stooped to examine the ground. "Boot make this mark," he said, pointing to a firm print in the dirt. "We no wear boot!"

Uncle John bent to look at it. "You're right. That's the print of a hard heel and pointed toe, like riding boots."

"Him go this way." Uncle Wirt walked closer to the baggage car. "Then on. All way to train car."

"Great!" Joe said.

Mandie started looking around, holding Snowball tightly in her arms. "Now if we can find the same prints going *away* from the car . . ."

The group fanned out and soon Dimar called, "Here is the same print going toward the river."

Uncle Wirt found more. "Horses been here. Go up riverbank," he said.

"Yes," Mandie told him. "There were three of them. They came from all different directions."

"Do you want to look inside the baggage car in case we missed something?" Joe asked.

"It looks like it might roll away," Uncle John speculated.

"We went inside, and it did not move," Dimar told him. "It is leaning against big bushes on the other side."

Uncle Wirt headed for the broken place in the side of the car where the young people had entered before. He tried to shake the car, but it wouldn't move. He climbed up and went inside. Uncle John, Dimar, and Joe followed right behind him, but Tsa'ni stayed outside with the girls.

Liza surveyed the wreck. "Lawsy mercy, Missy. Thank the Lawd youse didn't go down the mountain wid dat car," she said.

"Yes, we have plenty to be thankful for," Mandie replied.

"Did you see it fall down the mountain like that?" Polly asked.

"No, but we heard the crash. This is the car my grandfather was in," Sallie told her.

"Oh, dat pore man!" Liza moaned. "So now we's gonna find the bad men what wrecked the train and hurt your grandfather?"

"We will *try* to find them," the Indian girl said.

"Won't you be afraid if we do?" Polly asked.

"No, I will not be afraid. We have all these big, strong men with us now," Sallie replied.

"I'd just like to catch up with them, for all the trouble they've caused," Mandie said.

Tsa'ni clenched his fists. "But they were white men and we are Indians," he said to Sallie. "We cannot do anything to them."

"That's what you think," Mandie told him. "You just wait and see what happens if we find them. Uncle John will see to that."

"Well, since he is living as a white man and not like an Indian, he can prosecute them, I suppose," the Indian boy replied.

"You know he is half Cherokee, but he can live as he chooses. So can you and all the other Cherokees," Mandie informed him.

"You certainly do not know much about it, do you?" the boy told her. "Someday you will find out what it means to be Indian by white people's standards."

When the men and the other boys came out of the wrecked car, the girls stared in amazement. Joe ran toward them wearing a tiger face mask like the bandits had worn.

"Joe, stop that!" Mandie gasped. "Was that mask in there?"

He nodded.

"It does not look so scary in the daylight," Sallie told them.

"Well, I'd sure hate to meet that thing in the dark," Polly declared.

"I'd be done passed out if that thing come toward me in de dark," Liza told them, moving away from Joe.

Joe took another step toward her and raised his arms.

"Liza, there were three of them. And it was dark. And they wore long, flowing cloaks and big hats," he teased.

Liza backed off. "Git 'way from heah!" she squealed.

Dimar came up and took the mask from Joe. "We did not find this mask when we went inside last time, because everything was broken and thrown around. But the railroad must have come since then and taken all the broken baggage out. All that is left is trash," he told the girls.

Uncle John and Uncle Wirt joined them in their discussion.

"That mask proves the bandits were in the baggage car," Uncle John reasoned.

Uncle Wirt nodded. "We trace hoof prints," he said.

Uncle John started for the horses. "We're going to see if we can follow their trail," he told the young people. "Coming?"

No one had to be asked twice. Back at the riverbank, they began the tedious job of tracking the bandits' horses.

The closer they got to the gold, the more danger awaited them.

CHAPTER TEN

A VISIT TO CHARLEY GAP

Uncle Wirt managed to pick up enough tracks in the dirt to follow the bandits' trail. Slowly and carefully, he led the way over the mountain.

The trail ride was fun for the young people. And, as Mandie had expected, Liza turned out to be the life of the search party.

"I ain't never been outside Franklin," Liza told them. "I thought the whole world was a city with lots of houses and people, but we ain't seen a soul 'cept us since we left the road. I wouldn't wanta live out heah." Her eyes opened wide. "I'd be askeered them bears and panthers and things would come and git me."

"When we see one, we'll let you know, Liza," Joe teased.

The black girl looked startled. "You mean we might come close to some of them things?"

"We might see anything in a forest like this," Dimar answered. "But I brought my bow and arrows. So did Tsa'ni and his grandfather. You are well protected. We will not let anything harm you."

Joe patted the rifle slung over his pony. "And Mr. Shaw and I are carrying rifles," he assured her.

Tsa'ni sat up taller in his saddle. "I also have a rifle, as well as my bow and arrows," he said.

"So you double smart," Liza told him. She turned to Mandie. "Missy, don't you think we oughta brought us a gun, too?"

Mandie laughed. "No, Liza, we might shoot somebody."

"But we could shoot the bandits," Liza said.

"No, no," Sallie protested. "We only want to capture them and turn them over to the law."

Polly gradually maneuvered her pony through the group until she was riding ahead next to Joe.

Seeing this, Liza leaned over to Mandie and whispered, "You better watch Miss Sweet Thing. She be after your Mister Joe."

Mandie laughed and then strained her neck to watch the two ahead. They seemed to be joking and talking as they rode along together. A pang of jealousy cut through her, but she could not let Liza know it.

"Oh, Liza, he's not my Mister Joe," Mandie told her. "He can talk to anybody he wants to."

"It ain't him, Missy, that I'm a'talkin' 'bout. It's that Miss Sweet Thing. She shore is tryin' to latch onto him," Liza warned.

"Polly is my friend, and she's also Joe's friend," Mandie replied.

"You jest watch what I'm a'sayin'," Liza insisted. "She layin' it on so thick the bees git drownded in it."

Mandie smiled but did not answer. Adjusting Snowball to a higher position on her shoulder, she petted the kitten thoughtfully. She knew Polly was interested in Joe, but she wasn't worried. She had known Joe all her life. Of course, Mandie was jealous when Polly flirted with Joe, but she tried not to let it bother her. She was sure

Polly would eventually find someone else to "latch onto," as Liza called it.

Up ahead, the men stopped, and the young people hurried to catch up. John and Uncle Wirt dismounted and stood in a grassy spot, by a sparkling spring where the horses could drink.

"Eat now!" Uncle Wirt announced. "Must water ponies."

Taking their food bags from their ponies, the young people tethered the animals where they could graze near the water. Sitting on the rocks by the spring, they enjoyed the ham and biscuits, boiled eggs, and apples that Jenny had packed for them.

Uncle John came to sit by Mandie. "Uncle Wirt has tracked them this far, but we thought we'd better stop to rest and eat." He paused, then looked directly at her. "Do you know where we are?" he asked.

Mandie glanced at him and then around the forest, trying to find a familiar landmark.

"Uncle John!" she cried, grabbing his big hand. A tear trickled down her cheek.

Her uncle took out a big handkerchief. "Don't cry, dear," he said, wiping her tears. "You do know where we are, don't you?"

"Yes, yes, Uncle John." Mandie's voice trembled. "My father's grave is right over the hill up there and—and—his—house is not far away."

"I wanted you to know before we got there. I didn't want it to be a sudden shock," Uncle John said. "We'll stop when we get there, and I'll help you find some flowers to put on his grave."

Mandie buried her face on his chest as he hugged her to him.

Joe overheard the conversation, but had already realized where they were. He passed the word to the others, and they all became silent.

Uncle John got up and spoke to Joe. "We're planning to spend the night at your father's house tonight."

"Great!" Joe exclaimed.

When the others began to talk among themselves, Joe slipped away from the crowd and went to Mandie, who was sitting alone now, except for Snowball. He took her hand in his and squeezed it.

"Mind if I ride beside you?" he asked. "I know you've been trying to stay with Liza to make her feel comfortable. But if you don't mind, I'd like to be with you when we ride up over that hill," he said gently.

Mandie leaned forward and took his other hand in hers. "Of course, Joe. I want you to," she said with a smile.

After they mounted again, Joe and Mandie rode directly behind Uncle John. At the top of the hill, when the cemetery came into sight, the others stopped and waited. They knew Mandie wanted to be alone.

Mandie slid down from her pony, handed Snowball to Uncle Wirt, and took Joe and Uncle John by the hand. Together they walked among the graves until they came to the one with a home-made marker reading: "James Alexander Shaw; Born April 3, 1863; Died April 13, 1900." The mound had flattened some, and it was covered with grass. A handful of wilted flowers stuck out of a clay pot next to the marker.

Mandie let go of their hands and fell on her knees by her father's grave. Tears blurred her vision.

"Daddy, I still love you. I haven't forgotten you. I never will!" she cried softly.

Uncle John knelt by her side and put his arm around her. "Just remember that he's in heaven, darling. And one day you can see him there," he assured her.

"I know, I know! But I miss him! I loved him so much!" she said between sobs.

"I loved him, too, dear. He was the only brother I had." Uncle John stood up to pull a handkerchief from his pocket and wiped his eyes.

Joe squatted next to Mandie. "I'm sorry those flowers are dead," he apologized. "I know I promised you I would keep flowers on the grave, but I haven't been home for a long time. Want to look for some now?"

Mandie nodded, wiping her tears on her apron as Joe helped her up. "Yes, let's find some pretty flowers," she said, taking their hands.

Strolling around the edge of the cemetery, they picked several bunches of Indian Paintbrush and carried them back to replenish the clay pot.

Uncle John stared at the grave with its crude marker. "Mandie, we're going to have a real tombstone put on your father's grave, a granite one," he said.

Mandie smiled up at her uncle with tears glistening in her eyes. "One with a flower pot attached, so we can keep lots of flowers here?"

"Anything you want, darling. As soon as we can get time we'll go to Asheville and look at some," he promised. "Now I think we'd better go back and join the others. We have to pass awfully close to your father's house in order to get to Dr. Woodard's."

"We do?" She looked surprised and then added, "I suppose you do have to go down that road to get to Dr. Woodard's house."

"Yes," Uncle John replied. "But I know how much trouble your stepmother has caused. We're going to try to stay out of sight."

Joe helped Mandie mount her pony. "I haven't forgotten, Mandie," he said. "I'll get your father's house back for you when we grow up. Remember, I promised I would?"

"Oh, I hope you can, Joe," the girl answered.

Joe stayed close to Mandie from then on.

In her mind, Mandie relived the day their old horse, Molly, had pulled the wagon bearing her father's coffin up the hill to the cemetery. She also painfully remembered the empty ride back down. Silently, she thanked God for sending Uncle Ned to her. He had promised her father to watch over her and he kept his promise. He always turned up just when she needed him. Mandie wished he could have come with them, but Uncle John had insisted he was not well enough for the rough journey.

"Ps-s-st!" Joe leaned over and pointed. Her father's house was barely visible through the trees. They stopped their ponies and those behind them waited. The men looked back and slowed down.

"Just think," Mandie sighed, "all my life, I grew up believing that woman living there was my mother. Then my father died, and Uncle John showed me the truth. But I will always wonder why my father didn't tell me," she said sadly.

Joe's pony snickered and bumped into Mandie's pony, giving it a jolt. Snowball didn't like being jostled around on Mandie's shoulder, and he jumped down.

"Snowball! Come back here!" Mandie called. She slid down from the pony and tried to catch him. Joe quickly dismounted to help. But the kitten wanted to play games. Snowball ran and stopped until he thought they were going to try to pick him up. Then he ran again, too quick for them to catch him.

Everyone watched silently. Uncle Wirt had warned them that they must not be seen or heard by anyone at the log cabin in the hollow below.

"Snowball, come here!" Mandie tried to coax him. "Here, kitty, kitty, kitty!"

But Snowball had a mind of his own. He turned to look at her, meowed loudly, and then bounded through the trees toward the house below. Mandie and Joe started after him, but stopped in the shelter of the bushes at the edge of the clearing. The kitten went on.

As they watched from the bushes, they could see and hear someone talking. Moving to get a better view, Mandie's heart beat wildly. Her stepsister, Irene, and her boyfriend, Nimrod, sat on a stump by the side of the house.

"Nimrod, quit holdin' onto me so tight. It hurts," Irene protested.

"I jest wanna be near you," Nimrod answered.

Mandie looked around in despair. How would she ever get her kitten back? Snowball was roaming the yard below. Glancing up the hill, she noticed Uncle John motioning for her to come.

"We'll get Polly to go down and get Snowball," he said. "They've never seen her, so they won't know who she is."

"Maybe she can slip down there and get him before they see her," Mandie suggested.

"She can try, and we'll watch from here," Uncle John said.

Polly gladly consented, and cautiously made her way down the hill into the yard. The two on the stump had not seen the kitten. Snowball was nosing around a flower bed nearby. Polly eased up to him, but when she reached to pick him up, he let out a yowl. She quickly squeezed him in her arms so he couldn't get down. Irene and Nimrod immediately turned around and saw Polly with the kitten.

Irene jumped up. "Who are you? What you doin' here?"

"I just lost my cat," Polly mumbled as Nimrod towered over her. She turned to go, but Irene grabbed her by her black braid.

"Not so fast. This jest don't sound right to me," Irene told her.

The group on the hill watched breathlessly. Mandie was about to go down and rescue Polly when a loud yell startled her.

"Irene! Irene, where you at?" Irene's mother called from the back door. "Irene!"

Irene immediately let go of Polly. "Quick, Nimrod! Behind the barn!" she whispered. "Don't let Mama see you! I'll be back out soon as I kin git away from Mama. Wait fer me." Her mother continued yelling as Irene ran to the house.

Quick as lightning, Polly ran up the hill and disappeared into the trees. She didn't stop running until she reached Mandie and handed her the kitten.

Polly laughed. "Whew! That was a close call!" she said, trying to catch her breath.

Mandie put her arm around her friend. "Thank you, Polly. You don't know how much I appreciate that," she told her.

"That woman is your stepmother?" Polly asked.

"Yes, and that's her daughter, Irene," Mandie replied. "I lived in that house with them most of my life."

The weary group continued on. By the time they passed through Charley Gap and stopped in back of Dr. Woodard's house, the sun had disappeared beyond the mountains. When the doctor and Mrs. Woodard heard the commotion outside, they came into the yard to greet them.

"Light and come in!" Dr. Woodard called.

"Oh, Joe!" Mrs. Woodard cried, "it's so good to have you home."

Joe gave his mother a hug as his dog, Samantha, and her four puppies excitedly ran rings around him. Mandie had to back away from them and hold her kitten. Snowball didn't like the dogs at all, so Mandie hurried inside.

Dr. Woodard's house was made of logs like the others in the area, but it had two stories. Upstairs, there were four bedrooms, crammed full of huge beds with headboards that almost reached the ceiling. Mr. and Mrs. Miller, who lived in a cabin down the hill on the Woodards' property, helped out around the house.

Before long, Mrs. Woodard and Mrs. Miller had a delicious supper cooked and on the table. The young people ate as though they hadn't had a bite to eat for a month. Liza was still uncomfortable eating with the others, and offered to clean up the kitchen.

But Mrs. Woodard shooed all of them out.

"No, we don't need any help," she told them. "You young people just go out on the porch, or make yourselves comfortable somewhere, and rest. I know what you've been through today."

Mandie wandered outside to sit on the porch steps in the bright moonlight. Liza sat down beside her.

"Lawsy, Missy, if Aunt Lou knowed whut I be doin', sittin' at other people's tables and eatin' and then not even cleanin' up the dishes, she'd wring my neck. I could've at least put the vittles up instead of lollygaggin' around here doin' nothin'," Liza told her.

Sallie and Dimar came out and sat in the porch swing while Tsa'ni walked into the yard to play with the dogs.

"You see, Liza, I told you everybody sits at the same table to eat where I come from," Mandie said happily.

"Well, that ain't my style, I guess," Liza replied. "I think dat woman oughta let me do sumpin'."

Just then, Joe came out the door, overhearing what Liza said. "Liza," he said, "my mother considers you a guest in our house same as all these other people, and you sure don't go letting guests wash dishes."

Polly stood at the doorway. "Hey, Joe, how about showing me your horse that you told me about?"

"All right," he said. "Mandie? Liza? Y'all want to go, too?"

Before Mandie could answer, Uncle John called to her from inside. "Mandie, will you come inside for a minute?"

"Of course, Uncle John," Mandie answered. "I'll catch up with you later, Joe."

Mandie glanced at Liza, who made a face. Mandie sighed and then went inside. Joe and Polly were off to the barn. She felt that pang of jealousy again, and wished Liza would go with them.

Inside, Mandie looked around the finely-furnished living room.

Mrs. Woodard motioned toward the settee between her and Uncle John. "Sit down, dear. I won't keep you but a minute," she said. "I just wanted to give you some information for your mother."

"Yes, ma'am," Mandie replied as she sat down by the gentle, attractive woman who looked just a little older than her mother.

Mrs. Woodard handed her some papers. "This is information about the school your mother asked me to look into when I went to Nashville last week."

Mandie took the papers, noting the bold letters across the top. "Miss Tatum's Finishing School for Young Ladies," she read aloud. "Why, what is this for?" Her heart fluttered in fear of what it might mean.

"The school, dear, that your mother is thinking about sending you to," Mrs. Woodard replied.

Mandie sat there in shock.

Mrs. Woodard looked embarrassed. "Did you not know?" she asked.

Mandie shook her head, fighting the tears in her eyes that threatened to spill down her cheeks. "Leave home and all my friends, and go away to a strange school?" she whispered.

Uncle John walked over to Mandie and knelt beside her. "I'm sorry, Mandie. I thought your mother had discussed it with you," he said. "We've been trying to decide what's the best way for you to get your education since you live with us now."

Mandie's voice trembled. "Please, Uncle John, don't send me away," she begged. "I can go to school in Franklin."

"We talked about that, but they don't seem to teach everything your mother thinks you ought to learn," he replied.

Mrs. Woodard put her hand on Mandie's shoulder. "This school— Miss Tatum's—is one of the best schools in the southeast," she said. "Several of my friends have sent their daughters there. They all liked it, and they seemed to learn all the necessaries."

Mandie squeezed her eyes shut and swallowed hard to keep from crying.

"Put the papers with your things, Mandie, and go on back to your friends," said Uncle John, giving her a little hug. "We'll discuss this with your mother when we get back home."

"Yes, sir," was all Mandie could manage to say. She took the papers upstairs and put them in her bag, then rushed back downstairs and out onto the porch.

Liza sat alone on the steps, while Sallie and Dimar talked together on the swing and Tsa'ni played with the dogs. That meant Polly was still with Joe in the barn. But now, the sinking feeling in her stomach made her lose all interest in joining them. She flopped down on the steps beside Liza.

"Better ya git down to dat barn and see whut's goin' on," the black girl warned her.

Mandie didn't answer. She was fighting tears.

Liza frowned. "Missy, what de matter?" she asked. "You done give up on dat Mister Joe? Dat Miss Sweet Thing might jest be spreadin' some of that syrup on him."

Mandie tried to smile and took a deep breath.

"I guess they'll be back soon," Mandie replied.

"Sound like you done wore plumb out," Liza said. "Ain't got enough fight left in you to do battle."

"Liza, why did I have to ask Polly to come along anyway?" Mandie fussed.

"Yeh, I'd like to know that m'self," Liza said.

"She is my friend, but I don't like everything she does," Mandie complained. "She's such a pest. I wish I hadn't asked her to come."

But Mandie would soon regret her unkind words.

CHAPTER ELEVEN

POOR POLLY!

At daybreak the next morning, Joe was in the kitchen starting a fire in the big iron cookstove when he was startled by heavy pounding at the back door. Rushing to answer it, he found Morning Star and two braves standing there.

"Ned send message for John Shaw," one of the men announced.

Joe opened the door wide and asked them to come in. "Sit down. I'll get Mr. Shaw," Joe told them. He pointed to the chairs by the cookstove.

The heat felt good to the Indians. Even in the summertime the mornings were chilly.

Joe darted upstairs, but met John Shaw coming down. Uncle John had heard the pounding and came to see what was happening. Uncle Wirt and Dr. Woodard were right behind him.

"Morning Star is here with two of Uncle Ned's Indian friends. They have a message for you," Joe explained.

As John came into the kitchen, one of the Indians rose, pulled an envelope from his belt and handed it to him.

Opening it, John recognized Elizabeth's handwriting. Silently, he read:

I am writing this for Uncle Ned. Uncle Wirt's son, Jessan, has brought him word that the bandits were seen in the woods near Asheville. There are several abandoned huts near Mr. Vanderbilt's property, and they are believed to be hiding out in one of these. Jessan said that someone found one of the long cloaks the bandits were wearing hidden in a woodpile near there. The braves and Morning Star will give you the exact directions. Uncle Ned is much better and insists on going out. Please take care of yourself, and Amanda and the others, of course.

I love you. God keep you for me.

Your wife,
Elizabeth

"Look at this," John said, handing the note to Dr. Woodard. Realizing Uncle Wirt could not read English, he gave him the details.

"Must go at once," Uncle Wirt said.

Joe sprang into action. "I'll wake the girls and Dimar and Tsa'ni."

Racing up the stairs, he pounded on the door where the four girls were sleeping. Then he burst into the room where the other boys were.

"Hey, everybody, get up! We gotta go! Uncle Ned knows where the bandits are!" Joe yelled.

Dimar and Tsa'ni, already dressed, rushed downstairs.

Mandie stuck her head out of the room. "We'll be right down!" she called.

Hearing the noise, Joe's mother came out of her room and hurried to investigate. Joe followed her down the steps.

Mandie pulled her dress over her head. "Just think, we've almost caught up with them. It won't be long now," she said.

"I wonder how my grandfather knew where they are," Sallie said.

"Yo' grandfather know everything, Miss Sallie," Liza told her. "He got eyes in de back of his haid."

The four girls laughed, and hurriedly finished dressing.

"This is getting exciting," Polly squealed. She turned her back for Liza to button her dress. "Let's hurry."

"Bring your bags," Mandie told them. "Joe said we had to go." She snatched Snowball from the bed, grabbed her bag and rushed out of the room. The others followed.

Mandie led the way as the girls raced down the stairs. Then suddenly there was a scream and Polly tumbled down on top of the others. Mandie, Sallie, and Liza managed to catch themselves, but Polly fell several steps before she could stop.

The pain showed on her face. "Oh, I must've broken something!" she wailed, rubbing her ankle.

Dr. Woodard rushed to the stairway and examined the girl's foot.

He shook his head. "It looks like you've got a nasty sprain in that ankle," he said.

"Oh, no!" Polly moaned.

The doctor picked her up, carried her down the steps, past the anxious faces below, and set her on a chair by Morning Star.

"Sprained ankle," he said to John. "Let me get my bag."

The doctor quickly bathed Polly's foot in a strong-smelling liniment. As he began to bandage her ankle, the girl winced with pain.

"You won't be able to walk on that for a few days," he told her.

"Of all the luck! What will I do?" Polly asked.

Morning Star patted her hand and said, "I take home."

"Home? But I don't want to go home. I want to see those bandits when we catch them!" Polly protested.

"I'm afraid you'll have to go home, or else stay here a few days 'till it heals," the doctor told her. "It will be a miserable trip back over the mountain."

"I am sorry, Polly," Sallie told her. "My grandmother will help you to get home."

"But I don't want to go home," Polly argued. She turned to Uncle John and asked, "Can't I go on with y'all?"

"Polly, I'm sorry but I don't think that would be a good idea. Your ankle will be painful for a few days, and we may be going into a rough part of the woods," he answered. "Morning Star will be going back to my house and you can go with her. I'll send Liza back with you, if you like."

When Liza heard this, her mouth dropped open. Here they were, getting near the bandits, and now she would have to give up the excitement to go home with Miss Sweet Thing. Like Miss Amanda said, why did they ever bring her in the first place?

After a quick breakfast, Mandie and Liza talked out in the yard.

"I jest don't like dat girl," Liza grumbled, throwing her blanket over the pony. "And now here she breaks up my tea party."

Mandie grinned at her friend. "I'm glad she has to go home. You'll be doing me a favor, getting her out of my way," she said.

Liza tossed her head and laughed. "Yeh, I guess you be right, Missy. I'll take dat Miss Sweet Thing right back home so she can't chase yo' Mister Joe no mo'. But she oughta not acome in the first place. She ain't nothin' but trouble."

Mandie avoided Polly until the Indians were ready to leave. Then she waved good-bye as Polly rode off with Morning Star, Liza, and the two braves. She stared after them for a long time, relieved to see Polly go. She knew she was jealous and shouldn't be happy over her friend's misfortune, but she kept telling herself it was better this way. After all, Polly had her own accident. Mandie had nothing to do with it.

Some time later, loaded with food and good wishes from the Woodards, the group, led by Uncle Wirt and Uncle John, once again continued their journey. Joe stayed close to Mandie, with Snowball on her shoulder, and Sallie and Dimar rode right behind them. Tsa'ni brought up the rear as usual. *There is something wrong with that boy,* Mandie thought. *He always stays far behind the rest of us. He doesn't talk much and what he does say is argumentative. Why did he even come along?*

Uncle Wirt took a shortcut he knew—up mountainsides, down inclines, across rivers, and through thick underbrush. Mandie began to wonder if they'd ever get there. Suddenly an Indian on horseback appeared out of nowhere and waited on the trail ahead of them.

Mandie squinted in the bright sunshine. Instantly, a big smile spread across her face. Digging her heels into the sides of her pony, she raced around the men ahead of her. She ignored their yells to slow down. Nothing could stop her. Catching up with the Indian rider, she got close enough to grab one of his wrinkled old hands.

"Uncle Ned! Uncle Ned!" she cried. "What are you doing out here? We left you in bed."

The old man smiled at her and said, "Gold bad luck. Come see gold not make bad luck for Jim Shaw's Papoose. I promise him."

Just then Sallie rode up, looking very concerned. The other men and boys gathered around too, demanding to know why the old Indian had left his sickbed and come riding through the mountains like this.

"No more sick," Uncle Ned insisted. "Go find bad men." He patted his bow and arrows slung over his shoulder, and slipped down from his horse. "But now, time to eat," he said, finding a place to sit by the cool, tinkling stream.

Mandie sat down by him with her food, while Snowball curled up in the grass at her feet. "I've been thinking about what you told me, Uncle Ned—about tithing," Mandie told him. "God must be giving us blessings in advance. So much has happened. Tsa'ni was not killed when he fell off the railroad tracks. And you didn't die when the baggage car crashed. We have a lot to be thankful for already. Can there possibly be more?"

"Big God love Papoose," the old man said. "She ask. He answer."

"Yes, I'm thankful for all the prayers He has answered," Mandie said. "And I pray that this chase will soon be over. We have to get the gold back so we can make our tithe."

Mandie sat staring at the clear, sparkling stream as Joe came up to join them. "Did Polly get home all right, Uncle Ned?" he asked.

"Yes, foot big," the old Indian answered, holding up his hands to illustrate. "Sore."

"I imagine it had swelled pretty badly by the time she got home," said Joe. "Too bad she got hurt and couldn't go the rest of the way with us."

Mandie fought the jealousy that rose inside of her. "I don't think Polly should have come in the first place," she said. "She's not used to this kind of life. She has been brought up in town as a lady. She can't take the rough ordeals we get into sometimes."

"Oh, give her a chance," Joe argued. "She has to learn."

"Well, this was too long a trip for her to learn on. Let her learn something somewhere else," Mandie retorted.

"Mandie!" Joe exclaimed. "You ought to be ashamed of yourself talking about your friend like that."

"She's no friend of mine!" Mandie shot back.

"Mandie!" scolded Joe.

Uncle Ned smiled, looked at the two of them, and said, "Papoose got jealous streak for Joe."

Mandie's face turned red as Joe whirled to look at her. Grinning, he said, "Is that so, Mandie? Then you must think more of me than I thought you did."

Mandie jumped up and headed toward her pony. "It's time to go," she called back, picking up Snowball on her way.

Joe ran to catch up with her. Putting his hands on her shoulders, he turned her around to face him.

"Mandie, you don't have to be jealous of Polly," he said. "She's just a friend, that's all."

Mandie shook free from his grasp. "Oh, yeh," she replied sarcastically. She mounted her pony.

As the others got ready to move, Sallie rode up beside Mandie. Having witnessed the scene between Joe and Mandie, she tried to relieve the tension. "I would like to ride beside you, Mandie, so we can talk," she said.

"Of course, Sallie. Come on."

Riding off behind the men, the two girls talked back and forth about nothing in particular, but carefully avoided the topic of Joe. Finally Mandie decided to tell Sallie about the school in Nashville. She hadn't said a word about it to anyone else. She was hoping that somehow she wouldn't have to go.

"Sallie, do you know what my mother is planning?" she asked. "She is planning to send me away to school—far away from home."

"Oh, Mandie!" Sallie cried. "You will have to leave all your friends and your nice home?"

"Right. Mrs. Woodard gave me some papers for Mother," Mandie explained. "Mother had asked her to find out about a place called Miss Tatum's Finishing School, way out in Nashville."

"Do you have to go?" the Indian girl asked.

Mandie brushed a branch out of her way. "I don't know," she replied. "I told Uncle John I didn't want to. He said we'd talk about it with Mother when we got home. I don't want to leave all my friends and family to live at some school where I don't know anyone. That name sounds silly anyway. Imagine going to a 'finishing' school. Everyone would laugh at me."

"I would not laugh at you. I would feel sorry for you," Sallie told her. "Why can you not go to school in Franklin where you live now?"

"That's what I asked Uncle John, but he said they didn't teach some things my mother wants me to learn. I can't imagine what things they are, but I know I'd rather go to school at home where my friends are," Mandie said.

"I have heard that some of the girls enjoy going to these schools away off," Sallie told her. "They make new friends."

"I don't want to leave my mother and Uncle John and Liza and Aunt Lou and everybody. I'd even have to leave Uncle Ned. He couldn't come to a girls' school to watch over me," Mandie said.

"You do not know my grandfather," Sallie laughed. "He promised to watch over you, and nothing will keep him from doing that."

"It would be a hardship on him. He'd have to find a place to stay in Nashville. He couldn't very well stay at the school, and it'd be too far away for him to go back and forth," Mandie replied. She looked at her friend pleadingly. "Please hope and pray that I won't have to go."

"I will," Sallie promised. "Now I understand why you have been so upset since we got to Doctor Woodard's house."

"Upset? You mean you could tell it?" Mandie asked.

"Yes, you have not been as cheerful as usual," Sallie answered. "I believe you hurt Joe's feelings back there, but I understand now."

Mandie's eyes widened. "Hurt *Joe's* feelings? *He* got mad at *me*!" she said defensively.

"Did he? I think *you* caused the problem by criticizing your friend, Polly," Sallie told her bluntly. "Of course, it's none of my business, but I hate to see my friends angry with each other."

"You think I caused it?" Mandie asked, trying to remember exactly what she and Joe had said.

"Yes," Sallie replied. "I heard my grandfather say you were jealous, and I agree with him. Think about it, Mandie. You and Joe have been close friends all your lives. Suddenly Polly meets Joe and decides she likes him, too. That is enough to make anyone jealous."

Mandie frowned in bewilderment. "Then, what should I have said or done?" she asked.

"Just ignore Polly's attitude toward Joe," Sallie advised. "She will become disenchanted sooner or later. I think she is only flitting about. She is not serious about anyone or anything. That is just her personality. Some people are like that."

Mandie knew her friend was right. "Thanks for your advice, Sallie," she said. "I guess I have been mean, and I'm really sorry. I'll have to do something about it."

At the next rest stop, when they dismounted, Mandie walked over to Joe, smiled apologetically, and reached for his hand. "Joe, could we take a little walk?" she asked.

Joe was happy to see his friend smile. "Sure, Mandie," he replied with a big grin. "Let's walk down the stream a little ways."

They strolled silently for several minutes, then stopped to watch the tiny cricket frogs hopping along the edge of the stream.

As they stood close together, Mandie faced Joe and swallowed with difficulty. "Joe, please forgive me for acting like I did about Polly," she said. "I'm really sorry. I won't do it again."

Joe turned to face her, and smiled. "It's all forgiven, Mandie. I understand," he told her. "I've been riding next to your Uncle John. He told me that you were upset because they were thinking about sending you away to school. I don't blame you. I'd be upset, too. In fact, *I'd* just plain rebel."

"Oh, Joe, it would be awful to leave everyone and go away by myself to some strange place with strange people," she told him, petting Snowball on her shoulder. "I just couldn't stand it."

"I'm sorry, Mandie. If I can do anything to help you out, I will," Joe promised. "I don't want you to go away either. I'd hardly ever get to see you."

"I know. I'd probably only get to come home for holidays, and there aren't many of them," Mandie said. Tears glistened in her blue eyes. "I just don't know what to do."

Joe pulled the bandana from around his neck and wiped away her tears.

"Don't cry, Mandie. We'll think up some way to get out of it," he said. "Maybe when your mother sees how you feel, she won't make you go."

"Maybe," Mandie said. "But she really wants me to learn how to be a proper lady."

"A proper lady?" Joe laughed. "That's funny. I thought you were a proper lady already."

Mandie giggled. "You know what she means. She wants me to learn how to put on the social airs."

"I'm not so sure I want my future wife to learn all that nonsense," Joe told her. "You might get so you think you're better than I am."

Mandie jerked his hand. "Don't ever say that! That will never happen! You know that!"

"Let's hope it doesn't!" Joe said.

Rejoining the rest of the group, Joe and Mandie continued on their gold-recovery mission. But, somehow, they had to find a way for Mandie to get out of going to Miss Tatum's Finishing School.

CHAPTER TWELVE

THE CREATURES IN THE WOODS

As the group got a glimpse of the wealthy Mr. Vanderbilt's mansion in the distance, Uncle Ned held his hand up signaling them to halt.

"Must be quiet. Go slow now," he told them. "Into woods." He pointed to a faint trail leading off to the left from the main road.

They followed him into the dark woods. The sun sank lower in the sky, and thick trees blocked out most of the remaining daylight.

The old Indian stopped in the thick underbrush and dismounted. "Leave horses here," he said. "Bring rope, bow, arrows."

"Joe, we must be awfully close now," Mandie whispered excitedly.

"Yes, and you stay back," he whispered, slinging his rifle over his shoulder. "I'll go ahead with the men."

Mandie took Snowball in her arms as she and Joe joined the group around Uncle Ned. Dimar stood ready with one hand on his bow and arrows and the other on his rifle. Tsa'ni trailed along behind.

Uncle John spoke in a loud whisper. "We will move forward slowly," he explained. "And when we spot the cabin, you young people stay back out of sight."

"I would like to go with you," Dimar volunteered.

"We'll probably need you boys later, but let us men handle things first," Uncle John answered. "We'll let you know what we're going to do."

They crept quietly through the woods until they came within sight of an old rickety cabin. Uncle Wirt pointed to the woodpile nearby. Running over to it, he held up one of the long cloaks the bandits had worn. It was just as Uncle Wirt's son, Jessan, had said.

There were three horses tied behind the hut, and an old wagon stood in front. The strong odor of fish cooking filled the air, and a faint sound of voices came from inside the hut. There were no windows in the hut—only one door, and it was standing open.

Uncle Ned slipped behind a tree on one side of the cabin, and Uncle Wirt moved into position on the other side. Uncle John hid behind a tree between the other two. The young people huddled together where they were, waiting breathlessly.

Suddenly Snowball jumped down from Mandie's shoulder and darted for the door of the hut. Mandie caught her breath and froze. When the kitten stepped into the clearing around the cabin, they all watched and waited anxiously.

Snowball walked straight through the doorway of the cabin. Immediately, there was a big commotion inside. The cat meowed loudly. "Hey, come hyar, you cat!" a gruff voice hollered.

Snowball ran out the door with a big, burly man close behind. He stooped and grabbed the kitten. Snowball started biting and scratching. The man shook him violently.

"You dumb cat! Bite, will you? I'll kill you for that!" he yelled.

The kitten managed to get loose, but instead of returning to Mandie, he ran in circles around the clearing. The man grabbed an axe from the woodpile and chased the cat furiously.

Mandie could stand it no more. She had to save her kitten. Breaking quickly through the underbrush before anyone could stop her, she ran into the clearing, intent on rescuing Snowball.

When the bandit saw her, he whirled and started in her direction. "How did you git hyar?" he bellowed. "Hey, you're that gal on the train with that cat, ain't you?" he said as he got closer.

Mandie began to chase Snowball, and the man chased her. Then, all of a sudden, a sharp arrow whizzed across the clearing and grazed the bandit's leg. He screamed and fell to the ground, clasping his bleeding leg.

A second man edged out of the hut to see what was going on. Uncle Ned and Uncle John rushed forward and knocked him down. With Uncle Wirt's help they tied him and the wounded man to a tree away from the clearing.

The third man, still inside the hut, called out. "What's goin' on out there?" There was no answer. He came to the doorway. But when he saw the others in the yard, he slammed and barred the door.

Mandie hurried with Snowball to the shelter of the trees. "Snowball, why do you always have to cause trouble?" she scolded.

Uncle John summoned the boys. "All right, come on if you want to help," he said.

The boys followed quickly.

"How are we going to get that man out of the cabin?" Joe asked.

"We can shoot him out," Uncle John suggested. "The cabin has enough holes in it to shoot through. Or we can just wait for him to come out. He has to, sooner or later," he said as the two old Indians joined them.

"Why do we not burn him out?" Tsa'ni asked.

"Burn him out? Suppose the gold is in that cabin and it burns up," Dimar protested.

"Gold wouldn't burn up," Uncle John informed him.

"Fire dangerous!" Uncle Wirt added.

"I agree," said Uncle John. "He doesn't really have a chance. We're all armed. The odds are in our favor. Everyone get your weapons ready. I think we can get him to surrender."

As soon as the bows and arrows and rifles were aimed and ready, Uncle John called to the man inside. "Come out!" he said. "We've got you completely surrounded, and we are armed."

There was no answer. Everyone waited silently, their weapons pointed at the only door of the old shack.

Mandie and Sallie remained at a distance, watching and biting their fingernails, afraid someone would get hurt.

Slowly, the door to the cabin opened, and the last bandit, seeing all their weapons, hurried out into the yard.

"Don't shoot! I give up!" he called as the men and boys advanced.

Quickly, Uncle Ned threw his rope around the bandit, and Uncle Wirt helped tie him up. After leaving him with the other two, Uncle Ned and Uncle Wirt joined the others.

"All right, let's go find the gold," Joe said, leading the way into the cabin.

The girls started to come forward and follow, but Uncle Ned waved them back.

"Stay!" he called to them, as he, too, entered the hut.

Mandie took the rope she was carrying and let one end dangle so that Snowball could play with it. Worry clouded her face. "What if they don't find the gold in there, Sallie?" she asked. "Those men might've spent it."

Sallie laughed. "I do not think they could spend that much gold so soon."

Snowball scratched around at Sallie's feet, throwing dirt everywhere.

The Indian girl looked down. "Why does Snowball keep scratching in the dirt?"

"I don't know," Mandie answered. "Snowball, please be still."

Then she saw what the kitten was playing with. It looked like a string, but when she stooped to pick it up, it wouldn't come all the way out. Part of it was buried under the ground. The more Mandie pulled at it, the more excited she became.

"Sallie, look!" she cried. "This string is attached to something underground!"

Sallie knelt beside her. "Do you think it could be one of the drawstrings on the bags of gold?" she asked.

"Oh, I hope so," Mandie replied as both girls started digging with their hands.

They were right. Within minutes they had uncovered one of the bags of gold. And from the looks of the tangled web of strings, it appeared that the other bags were there, too.

Mandie picked up Snowball and the bag of gold. "Let's get Uncle Ned!" she exclaimed, heading for the cabin. Sallie stayed right behind her.

As they got to the doorway, Mandie shouted. "Uncle Ned, we've found it!" They all stopped their searching and gathered around her. "It's buried out there where we've been standing all this time," she said, laughing.

With everyone helping it didn't take long to uncover the rest of the gold. After loading it into the old wagon in front of the cabin, they hitched up two of the bandits' horses. Then they brought the bandits back into the clearing and made them get into the wagon.

Uncle John looked at them with great satisfaction. "We're taking you into town and turning you over to the authorities," he said.

"Mister, please don't do that," one of them begged. "You've got yer gold back. Jest let us go."

Uncle John climbed in beside them. "How did you happen to know about the gold anyway?" he asked.

"Well, it's sorta like this. We got some friends you'ins knows. Rennie Lou and Snuff. They still in that thar jail but we'ins got out. They was the ones what told us about the gold," one of the bandits replied.

"Then we just hung around 'til we found out what you was gonna do with it. I acted like an ol' drunken bum and laid in that thar alley behind the bank in Bryson City while you'ins were loadin' it up," he said proudly. "I heard the whole plan."

"Oh, hesh up!" yelled one of the other bandits.

"Rennie Lou and Snuff," Uncle John repeated. "The man and woman who kidnapped Mandie, Joe, and Sallie in the mountains and then tried to burn down your barn, Uncle Ned. Remember, we took them into town and turned them over to the law."

"Bad people," Uncle Ned said. "These bad people, too."

"Take to jail," Uncle Wirt told him.

So that's what they did. On the way into town, the young people rode their ponies behind the men, while Uncle Ned drove the wagon full of gold and bandits.

When they turned the bandits over to the jailor, he said he would summon the local doctor for the wounded man.

Then Uncle Ned headed the wagon in the direction of the huge bank in downtown Asheville.

Uncle John knew the banker, and it didn't take long to unload the gold and place it in the bank's vault. It would be safe there until they could start building the hospital for the Cherokees.

Since it was getting late and they had missed their hotel stay, thanks to the bandits, Uncle John checked them into the hotel in Asheville for the night. Early next morning they began the trip back to Franklin. Elizabeth and Morning Star would be waiting for them.

It was exciting to stay in the hotel, but Mandie was anxious to get home and tell her mother all the wonderful news. Yet on the other hand, she dreaded any further discussion of the school in Nashville.

CHAPTER THIRTEEN

GETTING THINGS SETTLED

When the tired travelers finally reached Franklin, they found Elizabeth and Morning Star waiting for them in the parlor. "Oh, John, I'm so glad you're home," Elizabeth said, greeting her husband with a hug.

John kissed her. "We're all dirty, tired, and hungry," he replied, "but very happy to be here."

Elizabeth looked over the entire group. "You young people had better get cleaned up," she said. "Then go out in the kitchen and get a bite to eat. But after that, into bed, every one of you. You all need a nap—and no arguing."

There was no protest. Mandie's eyes sparkled. "Oh, Mother! Isn't it wonderful?" she bubbled. "The gold is safe. We finally found it. The bandits are in jail, and the gold is in the bank at Asheville!"

"I'm glad, dear." Elizabeth smiled. "We'll discuss your trip more after a while. Now go along with the others." She waved Mandie on through the doorway to clean up.

Jenny and Liza weren't around at the moment, but Aunt Lou waited for the youngsters in the kitchen. The old woman smiled and put her arms around Mandie. "My chile!" she said. "I knowed de good Lawd gonna send you back safe!"

"Aunt Lou, we found the bandits and the gold," Mandie said excitedly.

"I knowed you would." The old woman grinned. "Now, y'all jest get your food waitin' there on the stove and then git on upstairs to rest. I'se got to take some of this out to Mister John, and Mister Ned, and Mister Wirt and Miz Lizbeth."

The hungry young people gathered around the cookstove and began filling their plates, while Aunt Lou piled a large tray full of food for the adults.

Mandie and her friends could hardly hold their heads up as they ate at the kitchen table. They were too tired to talk—almost too tired to eat. They might have fallen asleep at the table had it not been for Aunt Lou's bustling in and out to wait on the adults. Aunt Lou finally sent them to bed, and they readily obeyed.

After that much-needed nap, as soon as Mandie could get away from the others, she hurried over to Polly's house. She had to make things right with her friend.

Polly sat on her front porch with her foot propped up on a stool. "Hello, Mandie," Polly greeted her. "Aunt Lou told our cook that y'all had got home. Do sit down and tell me what happened."

Mandie related the details of their trip to her friend and then fell silent.

"There's something you aren't telling me, Mandie," Polly said.

"Yes, there is," Mandie replied, twisting around in her chair. Her heart pounded as she tried to find the right words. "I don't know how to explain it, but I've had some bad feelings toward you, and I want to ask your forgiveness for being rude."

"Bad feelings toward me? When?" Polly asked in surprise. "And how can I forgive something that I don't even know about?"

"I suppose—I got a little jealous of, uh, of you and Joe," Mandie faltered.

"Me and Joe? That's funny." Polly laughed.

"And then when you hurt your foot, I was glad you had to go home," Mandie confessed. "Will you forgive me?"

Polly looked as though she couldn't believe it. "You were glad I had to go home? But then, why did you ask me to go along in the first place?" she asked.

"Because you're my friend," Mandie told her. "It probably doesn't make sense to you, but will you please forgive me?"

"Sure, Mandie," she said. "I know I talked like I was brave, but I have to confess I was getting tired of all that running around all over the mountain. And I sure didn't want to come face to face with those bandits. So you see, I was glad to come home, but I didn't want anyone to know it."

Mandie giggled. "Oh, Polly, I'm sorry," she said. "I am so glad for your friendship, and I wouldn't want to do anything to spoil it."

Polly changed the subject. "Guess what? My mother is sending me away to school," she told Mandie.

"No!" Mandie couldn't believe it. "Where?"

"All the way to Nashville," Polly replied.

"Not Miss Tatum's Finishing School for Young Ladies?" Mandie gasped.

"How did you know?" Polly asked.

"Because my mother has the same idea, but Uncle John said we'd talk it over," Mandie told her.

"You don't want to go?"

"No, I don't," Mandie said. "Don't tell me *you* really want to go."

"Oh, yes," Polly assured her. "I think that would be great fun to live at a school that far away from home."

"Well, I don't," Mandie stated flatly. "And I hope I can talk my mother out of it. I don't want to go so far away and not be able to see my friends and my family."

"My mother doesn't know that I know it, but she had other motives. You see, if I go away to school, she'll be free to travel all she wants to," Polly said. "I'll be more or less on my own, and that suits me fine. I wish you'd go, too, Mandie. We could have lots of fun together way out there away from everybody."

"Sorry, Polly, but I don't want to go. I may have to, but I'm not going without a fight," Mandie told her.

When Mandie got home, she found Uncle Ned alone on the front porch, and sat down beside him. Another matter still troubled her.

"Uncle Ned, I've been trying to figure out how we can give ten percent of the gold to the Lord," she said, leaning back on her hands.

"Cherokees make Papoose boss of gold," he said. "Papoose give tithe."

"But I mean, what can we actually do with the ten percent? Should we just give it to your church at Bird-town, or should we do something else with it?"

The old Indian thought for a moment, and then a big grin came over his wrinkled face. "Church no have music box," he told her.

Mandie smiled broadly. "Then that's what we'll do. We'll buy the biggest, most expensive organ we can find to put in your church," she said excitedly. "Do you think the other Cherokees will agree?"

"Cherokees give gold to Papoose," Uncle Ned told her.

"Yes, but I have to use it for the good of the Cherokees," she replied. "It really belongs to them. I'm only going to spend it for their good."

"Get music box for church," the old man said, nodding his head. "That be tithe. Then watch window open and Big God throw blessings out to people."

"We have already received many blessings," Mandie said gratefully.

"More to come," Uncle Ned assured her.

Mandie leaned forward and lowered her voice. "Uncle Ned, did you know that my mother is planning to send me all the way to Nashville to a finishing school?"

"No!" he exclaimed.

"Yes, and I will have to leave all my friends and family, and go to this strange school where there are all strange people and I won't know anyone," she complained. "And worst of all, you can't go with me, or even come to visit. What will I do, Uncle Ned?"

"Not good," her old friend muttered. "Must not send Papoose so far away."

Mandie stood up. "I'm going to talk to my mother and Uncle John about it right now. I'll let you know what happens."

Mandie found her mother and Uncle John in the small sitting room adjoining their bedroom. Entering, she sat down on a footstool near her uncle.

"Uncle John, have you talked to Mother about the school yet?" she asked, holding her breath. She feared his answer.

"That's what we've just been talking about," he replied.

"Well, what did you decide?" Mandie asked.

"That you won't be going to Nashville to school," Elizabeth answered. "However—"

"—That's good news," Mandie interrupted. "I'm so glad I don't have to leave my friends and go all the way to that strange town."

"Amanda, wait until I've finished," her mother reprimanded. "You won't be going to Nashville, because we've decided to send you to the school I attended in Asheville. It will be much closer. Also, your grandmother lives in Asheville. Remember?"

Mandie took several deep breaths to steady her voice. "But, Mother," she protested, "why do I have to go anywhere out of town? Why can't I go to school right here in Franklin?"

"The school here in Franklin doesn't teach everything you need to learn, and their standards aren't as high," Elizabeth explained. "You must be prepared for society."

"Once you get settled in and make some new friends, you'll like Asheville, dear," Uncle John tried to comfort her. "It's not very far away, and you can come home whenever you like—on weekends and holidays."

"Oh, phooey!" Mandie said in a defeated voice. "I want to live at home all the time, with you and Mother."

"But, Amanda, all girls have to be educated," her mother said. "Just be thankful that we can afford a private school."

Mandie didn't answer.

Uncle John made an attempt to smooth things over. "Let's try it for a little while, and if you don't like it, we'll bring you home. But I really think you'll make new friends there. And you'll be able to get better acquainted with your grandmother. You know, you've only seen her once."

Mandie remembered when she met the heavyset woman in the expensive clothes. Her grandmother had not been very friendly. Mandie wondered if she could ever break through that cold wall between them.

She stood up. "I guess I have to go if you say so," she said, managing a reluctant smile. "But at least I don't have to go to Nashville."

Elizabeth looked at John as Mandie left the room. "She doesn't realize how much we'd like to have her stay home where we can be with her every day, but there are things you have to sacrifice sometimes," she told him.

"I really meant that, Elizabeth, when I told her we'd bring her home if she doesn't like the school," John reminded her.

"Yes, I agree," Elizabeth replied.

Mandie rushed back downstairs to Uncle Ned on the front porch. "Uncle Ned, I don't have to go to Nashville to school after all," she told him, excitedly.

"Papoose stay home?" he asked, smiling.

"No, not exactly," she answered. "I have to go to a school in Asheville where my mother went."

"But that not far," the old man assured her. "I go see Papoose in Asheville."

"Will you, Uncle Ned?" she asked eagerly. "I won't know anyone there and it'll be awfully lonesome."

"I promise Jim Shaw I watch over Papoose. Keep promise," the old Indian told her.

Mandie looked at him suddenly, surprise dawning on her face. "You know what? We just planned the tithe, and I've already got a blessing. I don't have to go all the way to Nashville to school," she said excitedly.

"Blessing number one," Uncle Ned agreed. "More to come. We thank Big God."

"Oh, yes, Uncle Ned," she said, reaching to take his old hand in hers. The two of them looked up toward the morning sun.

"Thank you, God. Oh, thank you," she whispered.

"Thank you, Big God," the old man echoed, quickly wiping a tear from his eye.

Mandie knew God's blessings were beginning to shower down upon her.